Colour me in

Nicola Sellars

Copyright © 2014 Nicola Sellars

All rights reserved.

No part of this publication may be reproduced or transmitted in any form or by any means, electronic or mechanical, including photocopying, recording or any information and retrieval storage system, without permission from the author.

ISBN:1495232085

ISBN-13:978 - 1495232084

Acknowledgements

A huge thanks to all the friends in Italy and England who have helped me in the writing of this book.

My heartfelt thanks go to Mario Marcuz, Donato Cardigliano and Alessandra Cecchi for their stories about La Pantera. To Claire Flower and Sarah Lane, for their student stories and anecdotes. To Jackie Leeder, Cara Cacciatore, Julia Gibson, Louise Lovell, Daniela Mennichelli and Paola Simonetti for their friendship, and support during the period that inspired this book.

To the friends who patiently read it and made their comments: Nicky Gravestock, Nicola Padden, Tracey Gurr, Jenny Simmons, Mirella Pavesi, Federica Sano, Pauline Pollard, Federica Grandi, Tim Robinson, Jay Blackwood, Kate Thomson, and Melanie Lamus.

Special thanks to Leela Grant and Sally Davies who carefully proofread the manuscript at different times and made it readable, and to Claire Williamson whose final edit was the essential last piece of the puzzle. Thank you all. I could not have done this without your help, support and encouragement.

Last but absolutely not least
Thank you so much to Miche Watkins for the wonderful cover painting. For more of her wonderful art
www.michewatkins.com

Colour me

Colour my walking
with earth and sand
colours, to ground me,
to hold me down,
so I don't float away.

Colour my breathing
with strong flames,
orange and red,
to fire me up, so I have
the energy to transform.

Colour my sleeping
with hues of lavender,
to softly waft me
to a land, where
I can be at peace.

Colour my awakening
with blues of the sky
and turquoise of the sea,
so I can be washed
clean, in my renewal.

Colour my knowing
with honey and lime
so the time to taste
this bitter, sweet life
does not pass me by.

Nicola Sellars

Chapter 1

The different shades of blue and the direction of the brushstrokes seem to give it movement. I think it looks quite realistic. This has been my dream for so long . . . to paint the sea.

When I stand back I can see that it's rolling across the dining room wall and crashing in waves against the frame of the kitchen door, it really is. I've painted the sea. I can hardly believe it. I find myself doing a little skip in the middle of the floor.

I could paint some foam to strengthen the sense of waves breaking. I'll do different shades of white, bright white for the crest and darker for the shadows.

My mother-in-law's little ginger cat has curled herself up in the tiny patch of shade at the bottom of the palm tree in the courtyard. Even she can't cope with the mid-morning heat.

The blinds are still open and sun is pouring through the kitchen into the dining room in a big rectangle stretching across the floor.

I catch sight of a scarecrow creature in the big hall mirror, she has short, spiky, red hair, and streaks of paint down her arms. Her tee-shirt is layered with old paint and her shorts with various shades of blue. Her cheeks are round and puffy; the bloated look hasn't yet gone. I'd rather look at the wall. Now for the foam.

I'd like to explain why I'm doing this but it won't be easy. I think I'll have to go back a long way.

***

It was late summer 1989, a few weeks before the start of my exchange year at Bologna University in Italy.

As we pulled out of Naples the sides of the train seemed to be bulging out. 'Acqua, Panini. Acqua, panini,' called the men carrying baskets brimming with bottles of water and ham rolls wrapped in cling film, as they stepped over the bags and bodies lining the corridor.

Nicola Sellars

I constantly had to flatten myself against the side of the train to let someone go by. Sweat trickled down my chest and back. What a great way to travel. I was pinned in place by a bag on my feet and the right arm of a large round man wearing what had probably started out as a white tee-shirt, now clinging to every curve of his sweat covered torso. Slowly managing to turn away from him, I came face to face with a broad grin.

'Train's late as usual,' he commented cheerfully, as if comforted by this fact. Our noses were almost touching; I managed to move my head a little away from his. To my untrained ear, his accent sounded the same as my friend's grandparents' so I thought he was probably from the same part of Calabria. 'Hopefully we'll make up the time later, usually it goes a bit faster once we get past Rome,' he grinned. 'Do you do this trip often?'

'No,' I replied, trying not to giggle at the corny line. 'This is the first time. I've just been to visit a friend who's staying with her grandparents near Crotone.'

'Ah, you're not Italian.' It only takes a few words before I'm found out. 'Now, let me guess.' He was about my age; early twenties, short, medium build, his ordinariness rendered almost beautiful by long thick curly eyelashes. 'German?' I shook my head. His next guess was American, and then we came to English. 'Ah, yes,' he said, 'of course. My English isn't much good, we did some at school but I never really got the hang of it. I find French much easier.'

'And you?' I asked, wanting to know if my guess at his accent was right. 'Are you from Calabria?'

'Hey, yes.' He raised his eyebrows and grinned. 'An English girl who can recognise Italian accents.'

'Well, only that one because I've been surrounded by it for the last two weeks.' To my embarrassment I could feel myself blushing. 'I study languages, well, just French and Italian.' The blushing made my face feel as if it were burning as beads of sweat formed on my forehead and

Colour me in

trickled down over my nose and into my eyes. I couldn't reach for a tissue and had no sleeves to wipe them away. I bent down and pulled the bottom of my cotton top up far enough up to wipe my face, without, I hoped, exposing too much flesh.

'I should study English, it's so useful. Do you teach it?' I finished wiping my face and dropped my sweaty top back down again. He was watching me carefully.

'Well, I hope to. I'm starting a year at Bologna University in October, studying Italian. I need to get a few hours teaching to help pay the rent.'

'So you live in Bologna.' The broad grin lit up his face. 'I live in Bologna.'

'Ah,' I replied.

***

Somewhere there is green paint. I'll look out all the odd tins lying around the house and see if I can get anywhere near it. I know there are more tins of blue somewhere because Assunta, my mother-in-law, let Beppe paint his bedroom blue. There should also be some of the yellow that Alberto used on the gate. There is plenty of white and there are the tubes of acrylic paint I bought a few months ago to do the picture for Michela. Unless Assunta threw them away, they're probably still up in Michela's room.

There's a little cove nearby where we taught the children to swim. The sea is deep turquoise and seems to go down forever. How wonderful to be there right now, standing on the bottom of the sea unable to hear or see anything of the world above me. Wrapped in iridescent peace. I wish I were able to capture it.

***

My neck ached from bending backwards to stare at the beautiful arched ceilings of the porticos above me, decorated with intricate patterns and fulsome cherubs.

'Look out, Lori! Scusi, signora.' Jenny grabbed my sleeve and pulled me along the pavement. 'Look where you're going, can't you?' she said crossly. 'You nearly knocked that poor woman over.' I turned and saw the woman in question walk off in a flurry of gold jewellery. Jenny went on, 'You go around with your head in the clouds as it is, but you're even worse here!'

'What am I supposed to do if they decorate the porticos with beautiful paintings that I have to look at?'

'Just remember that you are in a street full of people.' She linked her arm through mine, in an attempt to keep me under control.

The Bologna University buildings were astonishingly beautiful; many of them built in the same ancient red brick as the rest of the medieval city centre.

'This is the oldest university in Europe.' Jenny had been doing her research. 'They say it dates back to 1088!'

'As long as that!'

'Yep, Dante studied here.'

I felt awed by the giant wooden doors leading into the university faculties in Via Zamboni, one of the main university streets. We actually had to walk through one into our faculty. I had to keep pinching myself. I had finally succeeded in coming away to study in a beautiful Italian city. I had a strong desire to paint it but was sure that I could never do it justice.

Piazza Verdi, the square at the centre of the university, was covered in posters of all sizes and colours advertising meetings, concerts, films, discussions, parties, everything you could think of, pasted onto billboards and walls. Even the magnificent pillars had posters wrapped around them; everywhere was alive with politics and culture.

'A seat of learning,' said Jenny, 'that's what it feels like. The posters show a layer of current culture on top, but you can feel the learning underneath.' I wasn't sure that was what I could feel.

Being here, surrounded by all this vibrancy and beauty felt like ample compensation for bowing to my father's

Colour me in

wishes and giving up my dream of studying art. He had wanted me to study law, but we had reached a compromise and I had followed Jenny into languages. We had chosen the same university to study French and Italian. It was a four-year course, with the third year abroad. We had both changed from French to Italian as a main subject at the end of the first year, so that we could do our year abroad in Italy.

Jenny and I had been close friends since the first year in secondary school, supporting each other through the usual insecurities of adolescence: parental rows, disappointment and embarrassment; while discovering art, music, clothes, and make-up.

She was the friend I'd talk to when the pressure of my father's constant demands to study harder and do better in exams, got too much. Jenny was clever and confident, while I was supposedly artistic and scatter brained.

***

I've found yellow gloss, green emulsion and several shades of blue plus the tubes of acrylic.

By mixing the blue with a little yellow gloss I'm getting a pretty good turquoise. The wall nearest the kitchen is crying out for a deep turquoise sea I'll use a narrow brush there and add some different shades of turquoise. You can create amazing textures by using gloss and emulsion paint together, gloss on emulsion, emulsion on gloss, varying the thickness to create different effects.

Whatever I do though the memories keep returning, conjured by the brush strokes, as if they want to spread themselves before me on the wall. I want to stay with the early university memories, but other more recent ones are crowding in.

***

I can see and smell the bright cleanness of the gynaecologist's office. 'You don't mean that 'M' word, right?' I giggled nervously. I had a slight pain, which could possibly be to do with my menstrual cycle and he was harping on about HRT. I'm 37 not ready to face middle age let alone the menopause.

'Was there anything else?'

'Ah, yes . . . could you examine my breasts please? I think the last time was when I came to see you about three years ago. I'm not very good at it myself.'

'Of course.' He pointed towards a flower-patterned screen. I went behind it and took off my jacket. I pulled my sweater over my head, then my T-shirt. My fingers felt thick as I fumbled to pull out the hooks of my bra. I slipped it off and then walked self-consciously round the screen to the narrow examination bed and lay down.

In Italy medicine is much more divided up than it is in Britain, general practitioners refer patients to the relevant specialist and gynaecologists examine breasts as well as dealing with reproduction and contraception.

The gynaecologist followed me, waited until I was settled and then rolled my left breast under the palm of his hand. His touch was cold; I felt a shiver ripple across my shoulders.

'Left is fine.' His tone was cheery but business-like. He moved over to the right, rolled his hand and then stopped. I breathed in and stayed still, holding my breath. He looked down at me. I held my breath.

'There's a lump.' His face was suddenly softer. I didn't want that face. I wanted the professional one.

'There, can you feel it?' I could: hard and heavy.

'You will need to have a mammogram to check that out.' I lay absolutely motionless still unable to breath out.

'It's probably just a cyst; it's mobile you see. If it were anything serious it would be fixed and wouldn't move.'

I clung on to those words. I clung hard to them. I clung to them while I got dressed, even thicker fingers fumbling with my bra hooks. I clung on to them while I made an appointment for a mammogram. I clung on to them while I

Colour me in

told Alberto.

'We don't need to tell the children, I am sure it's just a cyst.'

I told Jenny and Simona I was sure it was just a cyst.

I got busy. I got a loan from the bank and bought the new computer I needed so I could do more translation from home. I ordered a new mattress for our bed as we'd had the same lumpy one since we were married. I persuaded Alberto to paint the bedroom walls to cover the depressing grey we had inherited from the previous occupants. I didn't ask myself at the time why I was bringing my work home and making it a more comfortable place.

***

I go to the little downstairs bathroom to get some toilet roll. I blow my nose, dry my eyes and go back to the dining room. I've got to get this done, brighten this room in one day.

The shade of turquoise I've created is not bad but for more contrast I'm going to mix light blue and green emulsion and see if I can create a creamier, paler version as well. Then I want to paint some areas of the wall with strokes of the paler turquoise emulsion and streak the darker gloss on top of that. I've really no idea what it will look like but today I'm free to experiment.

***

'Dubbio,' said the little moustached man in the white coat. In English that would be 'Doubtful' or 'Suspicious.'

The lump, which I had felt hanging heavy in my breast ever since the visit to the gynaecologist, was 'Suspicious.' I hadn't expected that. I'd almost succeeded in convincing myself that it was just a cyst, as the gynaecologist had suggested.

After the mammogram, I was called into a tiny examining room. Once again I had to strip to the waist. I removed my jumper, tee-shirt and bra behind the curtain at the end of the room. I remember thinking that it was about time I treated myself to some new bras. Then the little moustached man in the white coat indicated that I should get up on the examination table against the wall. He rubbed gel onto my right breast and, picking up some instrument, ran it over the gelled area, all the while looking at a computer screen. I couldn't see the screen but his face looked very serious as he handed me white tissue to wipe the gel off.

He was speaking, telling me that I had to enter into a cycle of further tests. Why couldn't he smile? People in white coats look scary enough but it's better when they smile.

As he talked, I found myself entering a kind of plastic bubble. I could hear him offering me the alternative of going back to my gynaecologist at Ospedale St. Orsola, or going to see the surgeon here at Ospedale Maggiore. The word 'surgeon' jarred my ears. I was tucked well inside my bubble by then, muffled from the world outside. I could hear and see perfectly well but I couldn't feel much and everything seemed distant. I managed to ask if doing the treatment here would be quicker. He looked at me kindly and said, 'If you'd like to come with me to the office, I could call the surgeon now. She does a clinic everyday maybe she could see you tomorrow.' That word 'surgeon', again. He looked me straight in the eyes. 'This has to be dealt with quickly.' I didn't want to hear this. I recognised, through my bubble, that he was being kind and doing his job efficiently but I didn't like his choice of words. There was a tight knot in the pit of my stomach.

I followed him out into the corridor and along to the office. It was in a new part of the building, quite light and freshly painted. We passed my friend Gina waiting for me on one of the chairs along the corridor.

'I won't be a minute,' I told her. I wondered if my knees were going to give way. The knot in my stomach got tighter and spread upwards.

Colour me in

A secretary sat behind the desk. Two nurses stood near her, crowding out the small office. The kindly, efficient little moustached man in the white coat picked up one of the phones. After a few minutes he informed me that I could go to Dottoressa Calchi's clinic tomorrow morning at 8.30 sharp. Walking back down the corridor tears blurred my bubble. When Gina saw me she rose to her feet, her face full of concern, and wrapped her arms around me holding me for a minute before we could walk out of the hospital and into the world.

***

Assunta's big black dresser is oppressive. The top section with the plates on the shelves is okay, the colours of the plates break its darkness, but the lower part is solid black. I'd love to paint a big strong hot sun on it. Do I dare though?

***

Gina handed me a large glass of red wine. Holding the glass in my hand and watching the light reflected in the wine felt reassuring and normal. I clutched the glass tightly trying to hold on to the everyday world now slipping away from me. I felt muffled by my bubble as if living in a parallel reality. The world went on turning but at a distance, my relationship to it now tenuous. There was tightness in my stomach, which has never gone away.

We had decided to have lunch in a café near the hospital. 'It may just be a cyst though,' said Gina. 'They are saying you need further tests, right?'

I nodded, 'Yes, he didn't say which tests but he looked very worried.' I took a sip of my wine. 'This feels serious.'

Gina leant over the table and touched my hand. Thank goodness she had come with me. I hadn't realised how much I would need someone. Gina was a good friend; her daughter was Michela's age. We had known each other since before we were both pregnant. We had gone through pregnancy, babies, infants, first steps, first words, first school, together.

'Lori, you have friends you can count on you know that.'

I squeezed her hand. I knew I could count on her and Jenny was back in Bologna. She and her partner, Carlo, had studied in Rome, Paris and Germany before going to work in Brussels for the last ten years. Jenny was an interpreter and Carlo a translator. Carlo's homesickness had brought them back to Bologna and Jenny said it was more relaxed after Brussels. I hoped they would decide that Bologna was their permanent home. Simona and Francesca, great friends since university days, were both still living in Bologna. I knew I had support.

I drank the wine and tucked into a plate of pasta - funny how my appetite had not been affected. I had a sense of having to store up my strength for whatever lay ahead.

'I'll tell Alberto it may be . . . it may be a . . . problem, but I can't tell the kids until I know for sure. I don't want to scare them needlessly. Before I tell them I want to know how bad it is what my chances are of . . . .' I felt shaky. Gina, though, had no problem with saying the real words.

'Lori if it is breast cancer you will get through this. You said the lump is not very big. Nowadays few women die of it, especially if it's caught early enough. I'm sure you'll be able to tell the kids that you'll be all right.' She was trying.

'Well, maybe it will be just a case of cutting it out and that's that, hey, a simple operation. It may not be that bad.' I was trying, too.

I remembered a friend in England who had undergone chemotherapy, which had made her very ill. I, however, was only going to have a lump removed so surely I would not need it. 'I can handle surgery,' I said slowly. 'I can cope with being weak for a while and having a smaller, scarred breast, just as long as I don't have to have chemotherapy.'

***

To paint a really shining sun on this dark dresser will take several layers. I haven't got much yellow paint left. I feel

Colour me in

panicky at the thought, as I've become really attached to the idea of painting a sun. It'll take something stronger than just yellow to cover the black dresser, so, maybe I could add red from my acrylic gouache paints to some of the yellow paint. There's an idea! It shouldn't take much red to make orange. I could create a few different shades of orange to make a really vibrant sun that could obliterate the black of the dresser beneath it.

Leo has been popping into my head a lot lately. The day I first met him was one of those special days that is etched on my memory forever.

Chapter 2

'Hey, Jen, can we go to the shop where I saw that green top the other day? I think it's down this street.' After six weeks in Bologna we were settling in well, but it still felt new and exciting. I dived down a narrow stone-paved street full of little shops with beautifully arranged windows. Jenny followed me and then stopped.

'What's that sound?'

I stopped too and listened. It sounded like the beating of a drum. Gradually we could make out the hum of voices, growing louder.

As we listened, the hum turned into shouting, then violins and trumpets joined the drum. Drawn to the sounds, we hurried to the end of the street as it opened out onto via Independenza, the main road through the city centre.

A colourful river of bodies flowed past us, as wide as the road. Among them was a street band surrounded by people dancing to the music. The group following them was chanting. We strained to try and make out what they were saying. Our feet moved forward and we were swept into the crowd.

'Hey Jen, it's started already, the demo Simona told us about.' That must-have green top was pushed out of my mind by the colours and sounds of the demonstration. There was a long banner stretching right across the road, held up by at least six people chanting, 'Economia Sommersa – Contro le privatizzazioni!' (Economy Subjugated – Against Privatisation).

'It's the Economics faculty,' I said.

'Hey,' said Jenny. 'Isn't that Francesca, Simona's flatmate?'

'Oh yes, so it is.' Holding one end of the long banner was a short, slim woman with long, dark, straight hair tied back off her face. The banner pole was much taller than she was. I admired the steady way she carried it.

'These must be the economics students who have

Colour me in

occupied the library,' I told Jenny.

I ran over to Francesca. 'Lorraine, I'm so glad you came.' She kissed me on one cheek but while leaning in for the second one she nearly brained me with the banner, so I ducked out of the way and made do with being lopsided. In just a few weeks I had got used to kissing people on both cheeks.

Jenny came up and said laughingly, 'We'll kiss later, Francesca. I don't want you to tip over!' Francesca laughed and the pole wobbled. I held my hands out towards her, but she was ok.

'Simona's around somewhere,' she said. 'You'll be able to kiss her.'

As she spoke I caught sight of Simona's thick, black, wavy hair bobbing up and down as she chatted to someone in front of us. I ducked round the banner and went up to join her.

We met Simona on one of our first days at the university. She came to our rescue as we hunted for the Italian literature class we were supposed to attend. She led us into a packed lecture hall where we could hardly see the lecturer, let alone hear him. She then went off to her own psychology lecture but we arranged to meet for lunch in the canteen afterwards. Simona explained that a lot of students were angry about packed lectures, unavailability of lecturers for tutorials and seminars and the general lack of facilities. She told us that a number of economics students had occupied their library over these issues. Later that day we met Francesca her flatmate, who studied economics, and she took us to a meeting in the occupied library.

Jenny and I had been to a few meetings against the poll tax and had become involved in a campaign against a vociferously right-wing professor at our university, but an occupation was a totally new experience for us. As we walked in under a huge banner saying "Facoltà Occupato" we were immediately surrounded by walls covered in a colourful blend of posters advertising meetings; plus poems and cartoons lampooning lecturers, university bigwigs and government ministers. The room was filled with a haze of cigarette smoke and chatter as groups of students sat around talking, laughing and writing leaflets. I had a sense of being subversive, of being involved in some kind of rebellious underworld, which was deliciously exciting. I had the same feeling as we marched along in the demonstration, thinking, "my father would have a blue fit if he could see me now!"

Simona was walking with another student who she introduced to us as Sandro. He tried to shake hands but was clutching a large pile of leaflets so just grinned. I thought he looked fun; he had a round face and blond hair sticking out at various angles, haphazard rather than cool. I immediately warmed to him.

'What do you study?' I asked him.

'Law.'

'Ah.' I wasn't sure how to reply to that. 'Is it interesting?'

Sandro laughed, 'Sometimes, but it's pretty heavy.'

'It's unusual to see a law student on a demo. At home they tend to toe the line, though not all of them;' I added hastily.

'Oh a lot of them are like that here too,' said Sandro. 'But there are quite a few of us here today. We could do with an occupation ourselves but the law faculty is very divided. The CP is big . . ..'

'The who?'

'Cattolici Popolari, a right-wing Catholic organisation. It's racist, against abortion, against freedom of education, very elitist.'

'Oh, nice people.'

'Yes, they are lovely, but we have even worse. There is a student fascist organisation too. Last year there was a fight between left-wing students and fascists.'

All this made the young conservatives at our university

Colour me in

sound positively cuddly. I concentrated on Sandro's words as I walked, my eyes on him as he spoke, making it easier to understand. I was pleased that my Italian was progressing, but among the noise and the marching I needed to concentrate hard. I didn't notice the tall student crossing my path until I tripped over his foot and bumped into a metal object that turned out to be the megaphone he was chanting into. I stepped back and looked up into deep, dark eyes. He was leading the chanting for that section of the march. He flashed me a look but didn't stop his chanting. I stuttered my apologies.

Sandro laughed as he supported my arm and guided me along, calling out a greeting to the student with the megaphone, whose name I didn't catch.

Later that evening, tired and marched out, a large group of us squeezed onto benches at several tables in Lo Nagro, a favourite bar with students. It was in an old stone building with a flagstone floor and stone walls covered with peeling white paint. The place was packed with marchers, sitting on benches at long wooden tables, chattering enthusiastically.

Sandro, Simona and I went up to the bar where we had to wait to be served. Getting drinks successfully back to tables was no mean feat; you had to squeeze around benches holding the drinks up high trying not to spill them onto people's heads.

Finally we reached our table, hands full of sangria jugs and bottles of beer. I was wedged between Simona and Sandro. Jenny was opposite, next to Francesca. Someone had ordered crostini: slices of bread lightly toasted in the oven and covered with various toppings, including tomatoes, cheese, pesto sauce and olives. Suddenly realising how hungry I was, I tucked in gratefully.

The November day had given way to a cold dark evening, but in here it was bright and warm. The chatter and smiles seemed to be raising the temperature.

While listening carefully to what Francesca was saying

about the demonstration, I broke my concentration for a second to look up towards the door. There he was, standing in the entrance: the student I had bumped into with the megaphone. My stomach turned a somersault. He held his head high and scanned the room, taking everything in. He was tall and slim with a goatee beard and dark tousled hair. His long, black overcoat hung around him like a cloak. He stepped into the bar, two other male students right behind him. They greeted person after person with a nod, a handshake, a slap on the back; rather like the arrival of royalty.

'Ciao. It went well, didn't it?'

'Oi, Leo, do you want a beer?' someone being served at the bar called out to him.

Leo. What a great name.

'Yeah, Mario, thanks,' came the reply. I could no longer focus on the discussion at our table. Leo walked through the bar, squeezing between the tables and stopping to talk to people, laughing and joking.

Simona's words penetrated my haze.

'We're going back to ours to eat in a while. We'll make a big pot of spaghetti. Do you two want to come?'

'Thanks Simona, great idea!' said Jenny enthusiastically. I wasn't so sure. Simona and Francesca lived in a student flat and Sandro lived with five other students just round the corner from them. An intense discussion ensued about what food they had between them, who had the sauce and who had the pasta. I didn't want to leave.

Then Leo was standing opposite me. I glanced up and met his eyes. I could feel myself going red. I bent my head and stared at the scratch marks on the table.

'Hey, Sandro,' he said. Oh wow, they know each other. Of course they know each other.

'It went well. How many, do you reckon?'

'500, maybe.'

'Not bad for such short notice, huh?'

Colour me in

'No, not bad,' agreed Sandro. 'Is the meeting on Monday?'

'Yeah, I think it's in one of the lecture halls which is good, bigger than the space available in the library,' replied Leo.

I felt his eyes wander over me and forced myself to raise my head. Is my fringe sticking up? I bet my cheeks are glowing like a little girl's.

'Have we met before?' His smile transformed his face making it more human, cheeky almost.

'Yes, I . . ..' I mumbled. He peered down at me. I willed myself to speak, my mouth felt very dry. 'I . . . I bumped into you on the demo you had the megaphone. I'm sorry.'

'Oh, right.' Maybe there was recognition. 'Don't worry, lots of people bump into each other on demos. Are you English?' I nodded.

'Really? That's great because I'm looking for someone to give me extra English lessons. I'm going to London next year with Erasmus. You here with Erasmus?' He named an exchange programme many students use to study abroad.

'No, I'm here for a year as part of my Italian degree.'

'A year! That's great. Right then, let's do it, let's arrange lessons!' Then, almost as an afterthought he added; 'If that's okay with you?' At that point someone else caught his attention and he wandered off. To my delight his name came up in the list of those expected for dinner at Simona's. That decided me, spaghetti for dinner it was.

We bought bottles of cheap red wine at the bar before walking round to Simona and Francesca's place. Their kitchen was lovely and big, apparently often home to communal dinners. I had butterflies in my stomach.

'Lori, what are you doing?' Jenny protested as I splashed her with red wine, my hands were shaking so much. Why was I so nervous? What if Leo didn't come? Worse, what if he came with a girlfriend?

The pasta was ready, we were all about to sit round the

table, I was feeling panicky, when finally the doorbell rang and in he walked with Sandro and Mario, carrying loaves of bread, bottles of beer and more wine.

We all settled round the table, which had been lengthened by the addition of a desk. I was both amazed and embarrassed when Leo sat beside me and started asking questions about London. After a stuttering start, I managed to reply to them. I couldn't believe my luck. I felt tingling down my left arm, as every now and then it brushed against his right.

Everyone was chatting excitedly about the demonstration and making plans for the next step. A lot of good-natured teasing went on; Sandro often teased Leo. At around midnight, a few people got up and started taking orders for doughnuts. Doughnuts at midnight! Apparently a nearby bakery was open all night. So there I was, sitting in a crowded kitchen in Bologna next to a gorgeous student leader, eating doughnuts at half past midnight. It's hard to believe even now.

***

The cat has come in. She has run out of shade in the backyard. I've left a shallow tray of blue paint on the floor and she's sniffing round it. Wouldn't it be fun if she trod in it and then walked over the pale, tiled floor? I could dip my fingers in it; trail smudgy lines along the doorframes. I could walk around the house with many-coloured fingers, red, yellow, green, trailing my coloured trails, bringing colour to even the darkest corners.

Chapter 3

She barely said hello, didn't even shake my extended hand. We met in the corridor and stood, there was no invitation into an office or to sit down anywhere. She was wearing a leather biker's jacket and had a helmet tucked under her left arm: the modern mobile surgeon in flight, on her way to an important meeting clearly far more important than telling me whether or not I had cancer.

'Oh yes, it's malignant.' She spoke in a "Well we all knew that, didn't we?" tone. The dark brown tiled floor seemed to come up to meet me. I held onto Francesca's arm. I should have understood, from the little hints and scraps of information she had thrown me over the last few days, that my lump was cancer. I should have known better than to hold out any hope. But I hadn't known better.

When I'd seen her the week before, she had described the lump as "suspicious", but had not made it clear that it was cancer. Presumably she had felt unable to say until the biopsy results had come that day. I had had to read between the lines and try to guess what she was telling me. Now, her impatient tone and manner suggested that I should have known and that I was wasting her time, standing in a draughty corridor on the tenth floor of Ospedale Maggiore while she really wanted to go and catch her train and attend her important meeting. She started walking away from me down the corridor.

I wanted to call her back and say, 'Don't leave me! What happens now?' But I couldn't. The world was colourless.

She stopped walking and turned back towards me. 'The pre-op x-ray shows you have two small lumps on your lungs.' The knot in my stomach tightened but the rest of me felt like soft jelly. I clung to Francesca's arm. I don't know how my knees held up.

She began to walk away again, towards the big double doors at the end of the corridor. I must have followed, ambling blindly after her with tears in my eyes, "That's it, cancer. I've got cancer." She carried on talking about the lumps in my lungs. My bubble settled around me.

I had been glad when I'd met Dottoressa Calchi a few days before to see that she was probably not much older than me, a little shorter with slightly greying blonde hair. I had assumed that she would be more sympathetic and understanding than a male surgeon.

She stopped her march away from me for just a minute as we came to an easel with a large pad of paper on it, the type used in conferences. She proceeded to draw a picture of what she said were my lungs with two lumps in them. She explained that, as the lumps were tiny, keyhole surgery could be used to remove them. She seemed quite excited about this part. The words "lumps, lungs, keyhole surgery" pierced my bubble.

Then she was gone. The heavy plastic double doors swished against each other as her voice came floating back, 'see you in the operating theatre on Monday.'

No colour anywhere. Cancer in my breast, my lungs, where else? Standing in the corridor in tears, the faces of Michela and Beppe rose up in front of me. Their mother has cancer. Francesca's arms crept around me. I mumbled something about going to the loo. She took my hand. I leant against the basin, head down; more tears, I wanted to flow with them out of my body and down the plughole.

I shuffled out of the loo and into an office where the anaesthetist was waiting to see me. There was a doctor with him who I'd met the other day. 'How are you today?' He asked in English, seizing an opportunity to practise the language.

'Not too good, I've just been told that I've got cancer.' Silence. I think he told me that they'd do something about it; I'm not sure what he said.

I went back to the loo for another cry after the anaesthetist and then went home to tell Alberto and the kids. How was Beppe, still my baby at six years old, going

Colour me in

to take it? It would probably be even tougher for Michela, who was a fairly grown up thirteen. She was going to be acutely aware of everything that was going on. I had not told them anything so far, not wanting to scare them needlessly, trying to convince myself that everything was okay. I'd been running too close to Alberto's method of avoiding the truth until it slaps you in the face.

***

My sun, a ball of orange and yellow fire radiating heat, hope and light, is nearly finished; a dynamic fireball sun, to warm you to your very soul. Although it needs some more layers in places it does look hot somehow. I can imagine it spinning off the dresser and whirling around the room with its own force, warming everything it shines on.

My hands are really sticky again. I now have red, yellow and orange streaks all down my shirt and shorts, much better than just blue. I need to clean my hands and then I think my turquoise emulsion may be dry enough to paint some gloss streaks across it. It doesn't matter if it's not totally dry; I think I'll get a more interesting effect if it's still a bit damp.

***

Curled up in my single bed in the room I shared with Jenny, I relived every word Leo had said to me and laughed at every joke all over again. A voice whispered in my head, telling me that he was too good to be true, that someone gorgeous like Leo couldn't possibly like me and that his only interest in me was to help him with his English. After a struggle I finally hushed it and fell asleep.

I awoke with a niggling headache, dark and light thoughts still jostling for position in my head. Jenny's bed was empty. I sat up and slowly swung my legs over the side of the bed. Standing up carefully I pulled a big woolly jumper over my pyjamas. Jenny was moving gingerly around in our narrow corridor of a kitchen making a cup of tea.

Maria and Gabriella, our flatmates, had gone to their respective parents' for the weekend, to Pescara, a seaside town on the east coast, in a region called Abruzzo.

We decided to make scrambled eggs on toast. Just the thing for those Sundays after a night out when you could make breakfast last all afternoon and talk about what happened the night before. I made toast on a griddle on top of the cooker, while Jenny scrambled the eggs. We sat down to eat at the little table we had pushed against the wall so that it was just possible to squeeze past it if you breathed in hard.

'Fancy him sitting next to me.' Nursing my cup of tea and my headache I relive the previous evening yet again. 'It was so lovely talking to him. He's clear about what he wants. We have so much in common; we care about the same things and he's a good listener. He asked me lots about myself about university, about the poll tax and the Anti-Nazi League. He really wanted to know, he really listened, about personal things too . . ..'

'Lori, I don't want to put a dampener on how you're feeling but he is one hell of a smooth-talker.'

'D'you think so? He seemed really genuine to me, I've never met anyone like him before.'

'Of course you haven't.'

'Stop being sarcastic. Don't you think he's gorgeous?'

'He's not bad.'

'Not only is he gorgeous,' I went on, trying to ignore her cynicism, 'he's clever, political, funny and sweet and . . ..'

She shook her head. 'Sweet? No, not really.'

'Oh but he is. He's lovely and he really listened to me. He didn't just talk about himself.'

'Of course he didn't he hasn't got into your knickers yet.'

'Oh, so cynical for one so young.'

Jenny raised her eyebrows at me, as if to ask, 'Are you sure I'm wrong?' Of course I wasn't sure, but I was trying to push that niggling voice to the back of my mind.

Colour me in

'Hope he calls soon, though.'

'You left it that he would call?'

'Yes, he wants English lessons.'

'Oh that old chestnut, if I had a thousand lira for every time a bloke has said that to me.'

'Oh Jen stop it. I don't know what's going to happen but I really like him. No-one that gorgeous and that interesting has ever paid me any attention before.' I paused as the truth of my own words struck me. 'He seemed to like me.' I looked straight at Jenny. 'Do you think he was just stringing me along?'

'No . . . no Lori I'm sorry; I didn't mean it to sound like that. Just don't get your hopes up too much. He seems like a bit of a smooth operator that's all.'

'Maybe he's out of my league.'

'Lori, no one is too good for you. You may be too good for him.'

'Well, I'll just have to see if he rings.'

'I think I heard him telling Francesca that he would be in the meeting tomorrow afternoon,' said Jenny.

A happy bubbly feeling started to rise in my stomach. 'Of course, I remember them talking about it, to discuss the demo and how to take the campaign further.'

'Yes that's the one, four o'clock I think.' 'Oh well done Jen, I had forgotten. I want to go anyway.' 'Me too, the whole thing about privatising education is horrendous. I want to see what happens next. Francesca was saying that students in economics really want the occupation to extend to other faculties.'

'Yeah, Leo was saying that it will have to. Apparently the government wants to bring in a reform allowing big business to fund certain faculties and have a say in how they are run and what the students study.'

'Yes it's all very worrying. I can imagine they would love to do that at home.'

'Don't they already?' I asked, 'I'm sure big business is

involved in a number of British universities.'

'Could be. Wouldn't be surprised,' replied Jenny, grinning. 'So we're going along tomorrow for purely political reasons?'

'Absolutely,' I replied. 'Hey, Jen.'

'Yes.'

'Please don't say anything to Simona or Francesca or anyone else about Leo. I don't want to look foolish. He's probably got loads of women after him. He's almost certain to have a girlfriend.'

'Lori, the way you've been behaving, they'll guess in seconds!'

'No, they won't. I can be cool you know.' I got up, wandered into our room and went over to the wardrobe. 'Now, what am I going to wear to the meeting tomorrow?'

***

Alberto was in the kitchen. He saw it in my face and stood up. I walked towards him and he came forward a little awkwardly to give me a hug. We stood still for a moment. When I drew back from him he had gone white.

Luckily the children were in the other room watching TV. I had called out 'ciao' to them as I came in and had barely got a 'ciao' in reply. I sat down at the table and put my head in my hands. Alberto pulled a chair up beside mine and wrapped his arms round me. I leant into him gratefully. When I looked up at him I saw tears in his eyes.

'How do I tell them?' I whispered.

Alberto looked helpless.

I told him what the doctor had said and he was angry at the way she had told me and left me in the corridor. 'But that's awful! She didn't explain it to you properly and she left you standing there on your own.'

'Well, luckily Francesca was there.' Looking back, it seemed worse than it had at the time. I'd felt so overwhelmed that I had hardly had the strength to feel indignant, let alone angry.

Colour me in

'Oh, I wish I'd been there with you.' He stood up. 'Right, next time you see her; I'm coming with you. She treated you really badly. That's not happening again.'

It was a relief to hear him talking like that.

'Can we tell the children together?' I asked.

'Of course Lori, we're in this together. We'll talk tonight after they're in bed and work out the best way to tell them.' I wasn't sure that there was a best way but nodded happy for him to make a decision.

Alberto set about cooking some pasta for tea, so I went into the living room to join the children. Beppe, with his dark, curly hair and long eyelashes looked very like his father, whereas Michela's hair, though predominantly dark, did have natural red highlights in it, a reflection of my red hair. At that moment I just wanted to be with them, to listen to them, smell them and drink in their energy. I tried to give Beppe a hug while he was watching TV but he wriggled me off, looking impatient. Michela put a CD on loudly and started to dance.

'Switch the TV off, Michela, if you want music on. We can't have both.' She went over to the television.

'No!' shouted Beppe, 'I'm watching it.'

Michela turned to me. 'Mamma I want to listen to music. He has been watching TV all afternoon. I want to dance. It's my turn.' She sounded determined.

'I want to watch TV.' Beppe hurled himself at Michela's legs, trying to pull her away from the TV. 'You go and listen to music in your room.'

Michela yelled, 'Mamma get him off me! Get him off me!' Then she started hitting him and he started yelling.

'Just stop it, both of you!' They didn't hear me above their yelling, the sound of the TV and the blaring music. I sat on the sofa with my head in my hands. Energy seemed to be draining out of me already. Alberto came rushing into the room, a look of fury on his face. At that point, Beppe whacked Michela across the legs and she grabbed him by the hair and started pulling. He screamed.

'Stop it you two, at once!' shouted Alberto. 'How dare you make so much noise, look what you are doing to your mother! She's got cancer. She needs quiet, not this chaos.'

Michela let go of Beppe's hair and stood up, her eyes round with shock. Beppe, still on the floor looked up not sure what had been said. Silence. Alberto was shaking. He slowly sat down in an armchair. He looked at me apologetically, so much for planning the best way to tell them.

'Is it true?' Michela found her voice. 'Mamma, is it true?'

'Is what true?' Beppe demanded to know. 'What did Papà say?' His voice turned into a wail of frustration. I licked my lips. My mouth felt very dry. I took a deep breath and looked at Alberto to indicate that I would reply.

'I've been to the hospital,' I began. 'They have found a lump in my breast.'

Beppe still looked confused.

'Cancer?' whispered Michela. I nodded. Beppe, still looking confused, climbed onto my lap. Tears started trickling down Michela's face. Alberto got up and put his arms round her and they sat down on the armchair together.

'Everything will be fine,' said Alberto. 'The doctors are going to take the lump out and then Mamma will be okay.'

'What is cancer?' asked Beppe.

'It's a disease . . ..' began Alberto.

'Cancer kills you,' replied Michela. Alberto shot me a helpless look.

'Hey now, it's not so bad. I have a fairly small lump in my breast. It is cancer but it's not very advanced. It would be a very long time before it hurt me, but it will never hurt me because I'm going to have an operation in a few weeks to take it out.'

'Will you be all right then?' asked Beppe.

'Yes, darling, I'm sure I will.'

Colour me in

'So cancer doesn't kill you?' he wanted to know.

'Not always, and almost certainly not in my case, it's a fairly small lump.' "Medium sized," the doctor had said, but I was choosing words for minimum impact.

'So there's absolutely no chance of you dying?' Michela wanted to know.

I remembered the lumps on my lungs, "tiny"; the doctor had said they were.

'Almost no chance.'

'But still some chance? Oh Mamma!' Michela started crying again.

'Darling, the doctors will know more after the operation. Once the lump is out, everything should be fine, but they can't say at this stage.'

Michela wanted absolute reassurance; I wished I could give it to her.

***

The sun drying on the dresser is looking good. The cat is curled up next to it, contentedly, as if it were warming her.

I have spread the gloss on as thinly as I could over the damp emulsion, and I think it looks watery. It almost looks as if you could dip into it and come out refreshed. Fanciful I know, but I'm actually quite pleased with my turquoise patch of sea.

Chapter 4

On the face of it, the morning was normal. One of those ducking and diving mornings where everyone is shuffling from bedroom to bathroom to kitchen, trying to do washing, dressing, breakfasting as quickly as possible, among the hunt for socks, toothpaste and marmalade, hampered by sleep. Beppe was wandering around in his underpants shivering, unable to find his trousers, and Michela was grumpy because her favourite school shirt wasn't clean.

I had wanted to slip out before the children were up but Alberto had insisted that they would all take me to the hospital and then he would drive them to school. I had to be at hospital by 7.30 and they started school at 8.00, so it worked out okay time-wise. I found Beppe's trousers and he let me help him into them, followed by tee-shirt and jumper. It was a long time since I had helped him dress. I didn't want to let him go. When he moved away to pick up his socks and pull them on, I found myself wondering when I would hold him again, but told myself to get a grip as I would see him that evening.

Michela, making do with another shirt, dunked biscuits into milky coffee at the kitchen table. 'So, Mamma, you will be home on Wednesday. Is Papà picking you up?'

'No, I'll be let out of hospital in the morning. He can't take too much time off work.'

'You'll probably be quite weak, won't you, so you'll need someone to collect you? Maybe I could come from school with Elisa and ask Gina to pick you up.'

My friend Gina was collecting the children from school the day I left hospital. Alberto couldn't take any time off that day as he wanted to take the next couple of days off, tagged on to the weekend, so he would be around for my first few days at home.

'Don't worry,' I took her hand. 'Jenny will collect me and I'll be home before you get back from school.'

Colour me in

'We are coming in to see you today, aren't we? After school.'

'If you really want to but I'll be very woozy and not very good company, so I'll understand if you'd rather not. You could go home with Gina and Elisa for the afternoon instead.'

'No. Mamma, I want to come and visit you this afternoon.' Alberto walked into the kitchen. 'Papà, you promised you'd pick us up from school and take us to visit Mamma today. You promised, Papà.' Her voice started getting high again. I touched her hand.

'Of course you can come, darling. I just wondered if you'd rather . . ..' I saw the look on her face. This was hard on her. One of her best friend's grandmothers had recently died of breast cancer. Fortunately though, most of the stories we had heard were of survival.

It was amazing how many stories I had been told since being diagnosed, of women who had survived breast cancer and were living active lives now. Those stories really helped. I wished they were the only stories my children had to hear.

***

Yesterday's meeting had led to a lively picket outside the vice chancellor's office, an argument with some University bureaucrats and a tussle with the police. Everyone had started to leave and I didn't know when I would see Leo again. I finally got close to him. I had to seize my moment.

'Um, well, I know you're very busy, but maybe you'd like that English lesson sometime.' As the words left my mouth, I wanted to pull them back feeling that I must look really pathetic worrying a student leader with such mundane things. Leo just smiled.

'Yes, absolutely.' He thought for a moment. 'How about tomorrow afternoon? I should be free around three o'clock. Is that okay, or do you have a lecture?'

'No, um, nothing, no, that's fine, great.' As I replied, I realised that I had no idea how to teach English to an adult.

Nicola Sellars

I'd only taught a few lessons to a friend's children. I could hardly teach Leo nursery rhymes! I tried to calm down, telling myself I'd cope, as his English was quite good. He just needs conversation. Speak slowly and you'll be okay. The butterflies stayed with me until he arrived the next day in fact they didn't go away, even then.

***

I didn't want to be in hospital, the metallic cleanliness, green and cream walls, beds without curtains to pull round them, there was no hiding place or privacy.

There were six in the ward; four of us to have lumps removed from our breasts, one for a hernia operation and Claudia who had a stomach ulcer. She'd been in hospital for a few weeks.

Marta in the bed opposite me was in her early forties and had three children. One day her youngest had stuck her hand down her mother's blouse and found the lump, which was now about four cm in diameter. She didn't know whether or not it was malignant. She would know after the operation.

We were all chatting nervously trying to find some comfort in kindred spirit. Strangely this seemed easier once we were all in our nightclothes, vulnerable and helpless together.

I remember curling up inside my bubble, woozy from the pre-med, waiting to go into the operating theatre. Only barely aware of the indignity of lying on a trolley in the corridor, my hospital gown flapping in the breeze caused by the opening of the double doors to the operating theatre every time someone went through them.

When I came round my face was wet with tears. With a sad and gentle smile, the mother of Claudia in the bed on my right gave me some rescue remedy. The taste of alcohol lingered on my tongue. The cancer has gone and I am okay.

The ward doors swished open. I looked up hopefully. It was a young couple visiting the woman on my left. The

Colour me in

woman diagonally opposite me to the right, who had had the hernia operation, had her sister with her. She had come in with her that morning and was to stay all that first night, sitting quietly by her sister's bedside.

The man sitting with Marta opposite must have been her husband. She waved at me.

'How you feeling?'

'Okay. I seem to have stopped crying.' She nodded.

'Me too, I cried buckets when I came round.'

'Well it's out now,' I said.

'Let's hope that's it,' she added. She nodded at the man sitting on the chair beside her bed. 'This is Luigi. He's going to bring the children in later.' I smiled at him. He was holding her hand.

We weren't supposed to have mobile phones on in the ward. I had switched the ring tone off on mine but kept the phone on, in case there were messages. I leant over to my bedside locker where I had put the phone in the drawer. There was a message from Alberto.

"I hope it all went okay. Will see you this afternoon, with the children." At least he was coming in, but some hand-holding right now would have been nice.

The doors swished and in bustled Jenny. She rushed over to my bed and gave me a big hug. As she straightened up, I saw my mother's pale face peering down at me. She bent down to give me a kiss. She looked unsteady, and Jenny helped her to sit down. She took hold of my hand.

'Didn't Dad come?'

'Yes he did, he's just gone to the loo. He'll be here in a minute.' She squeezed my hand.

'I wanted to be here sooner but our plane was delayed.'

'It's okay, Mum, you are here now.' Jenny returned from chair hunting and placed one next to my mother's. She then came and sat down at the other side of the bed.

'You don't look too bad, considering,' she grinned. 'A bit pale but that's to be expected.'

'I felt shaky when I came round, but Claudia's mother gave me some rescue remedy.'

'Here, dear, I've got some.' My mother let go of my hand and rummaged in her handbag. She handed me the little bottle. 'You hang on to it. You can take it whenever you feel wobbly.'

I was quite astonished that my mother had even heard of rescue remedy. Like my father she'd always seemed to have unwavering faith in doctors and 'proper medicine.' I would never have expected her to have time for any kind of complementary remedies, but I was glad to see that I was wrong.

'Have some more now,' she said. 'It will help.'

'Thanks, Mum.' I squeezed a few drops onto my tongue.

I looked at the empty chair. 'Is Dad okay, do you think?'

'Oh, he'll be here in a minute.' Irritation crept into my mother's voice. Jenny mouthed something I couldn't quite make out.

'Thanks Jen, for going to the airport.'

'And for waiting,' added my mother. 'Our plane was over an hour late.'

'No problem,' smiled Jenny, 'I had a good book.'

The doors swished again. A frail, elderly man shuffled through them. I hardly recognised my father, it was a long time since we'd seen each other. He hated flying, so I generally only saw him when I went to England. His old dominant force seemed to have melted away with the weight he had lost.

He looked around the whole ward before he saw me, and then walked slowly over to us. He stood awkwardly by the bed until my mother practically pulled him down onto the chair beside her. After what seemed like an age, he managed to look at me. 'How are you? Bearing up?' I had to smile at this familiar phrase.

'Yes thanks Dad, I guess I am.' Out of the corner of my eye I saw my mother wince.

Colour me in

***

I can still see the shine in Leo's eyes and the smile playing around his lips as he teased me. He made up English words, swearing that his teacher had taught him them at school. Then he'd make up Italian ones and try to pass them off to me as real. When we were alone being cool didn't matter he was just Leo.

He talked about his father who had died when he was twelve. 'He worked in the factory all his life.' He had been a metal worker in a factory in Modena where they lived, just half an hour by car or train from Bologna. 'He would have been so proud of me getting to University.'

'What would he have thought of your politics?'

'I think he would have been proud that I was active. He may have preferred me to be in the Communist Party like him, but I'm not entirely sure. He joined them when he was just a lad, in the fifties, when they though the revolution was around the corner. He was never happy with the bureaucratic reformism that ruled the party from the top down. He was a visionary, not someone who always followed orders. He wasn't afraid to question them and think for himself.'

'He'd have been proud of you Leo. You've got that from him.'

The smile I received lit up the room. I just sat and stared at his warm mouth. I suddenly felt nervous and awkward what to say next? "Concentrate Lori this is an English lesson. Stop staring at him and teach him something!"

I asked Leo to tell me in English about the exam he was studying for. I bent over my notebook to jot something down. When I looked up, he was looking straight at me. Oh goodness, I was staring at his mouth again. I looked up, our eyes met and my stomach turned over. I opened my mouth to speak and then saw his face coming towards me. My gaze shifted down to his mouth as our lips met. 'Oh my God, how did that happen?' I closed my eyes and felt his warm, soft lips on mine. A shiver went right across my shoulders and down my back.

At the end of the kiss Leo pulled away, looking down at me. I smiled up at him but he looked dazed. He turned away and then back again, as if he wanted to say something but wasn't sure. A question hung over us. Then there was a knock on the door, it opened and Jenny hurried in.

'Excuse me, Lori. Oh hi, Leo! Sorry, I left my notebook I need it for this afternoon's lecture.' She smiled apologetically as she picked up the notebook from her desk. 'I'd forget my head if it were loose,' she added quickly in English and closed the door behind her. We were alone again, an embarrassed tension hanging in the air.

After what felt like ages, I said, 'Did you hear what Jenny said to me in English?' He shook his head. 'I'd forget my head if it were loose.' I began to teach him what it meant. We spent the rest of the time studying English. When the lesson ended, he hugged me quickly and left.

I sat down on my bed, utterly confused. That kiss had been amazing, for me at least. He must have changed his mind and realised that he didn't really fancy me, it was just a mistake. I could feel tears in my eyes. How was I going to survive until the lesson next Tuesday?

***

Stretching up to paint the top of the wall feels as though it must be good for my right arm. It doesn't hurt so much now, and the swelling seems to have gone down completely. The doctors told us to keep doing the exercises to keep our arms working after the lymph nodes have been removed and to stop excessive swelling. I don't do them often enough but all the painting I have been doing lately must be doing it good.

***

I held on to Beppe who clambered on to the bed beside me. It was great feeling his warm body next to mine. I savoured the cuddles he usually ducked away from and didn't want to

Colour me in

let him go. Finally he wriggled out of my grasp.

Michela leant over to give me a kiss. 'Are you okay, Mamma? Have they taken the cancer out?'

'Yes, they have.'

I decided not to remind her about the lumps on my lungs.

Alberto was carrying a big box of chocolates. I couldn't face them but he and the children ate them. A little boy was watching us, clutching some toy cars. I offered him a chocolate. He turned out to be Marta's son and was about Beppe's age. After a little while, they started rolling the cars to each other under Marta's bed.

Alberto watched them intently and I had the feeling that he would rather be playing with them than sitting awkwardly next to me. I took hold of his hand, he squeezed it and smiled but there was a distant look in his eyes. After a while he cleared his throat. 'I contacted the bank's head office and reminded them about my application for a transfer to a branch in Calabria. Turns out I know a bloke who works there. You know I've had the application in for a few years now, but I thought this would be a good time to try and speed them up and find out if there were any chance of my being transferred down to Calabria soon. He said he'd look into it.'

I felt my body grow rigid under the covers.

'Can I have some water, please?' My mouth felt dry. Alberto picked up the plastic cup of water from the locker beside the bed. I swallowed it down.

We went to Alberto's village every summer and sometimes at Christmas or Easter. It was a lovely place for a holiday close to the sea. I know he used to dream of going back there to live but had not mentioned it for so long that I'd assumed he'd dropped the idea.

'What do you mean?'

'Well, maybe he can speed it up, you know, so we could go this year . . .. I said I would take a post anywhere in

Calabria but would prefer Crotone.'

'Why now?' I could feel the tension in my voice. Alberto let go of my hand and began rubbing his together as if he were about to do something.

'Well, because you're ill.'

'I don't think I could cope with a move right now.'

'It won't happen that quickly. It still may not happen for years but, if it could, it would be a perfect place for you to convalesce and get better.'

A sick feeling crept into the pit of my stomach and my bubble thickened around me.

***

I've found a small tin of black paint, I've taken the lid off and I'm sitting on the floor staring at it. It seems weird after all the work I've done this morning but I have such an urge to mix it up with the blue to create a dark angry sea. If I smear it onto the still damp paint on the wall I could make it a scary night sea. A sea you don't know or understand, where anything could happen. How am I going to stop myself from doing that? I take deep breaths to stop the panic from rising.

Maybe though, maybe dark is not angry, dark can mean deep and peaceful away from surface hassle and pain. I could perhaps paint a cave, a secret cave beyond the waves, where I can hide.

***

Leo cancelled our second lesson and I didn't see him for what felt like a very long time. But then one evening when I was alone in the flat, struggling to write an essay and trying not to think about him, the doorbell rang. Thinking it was probably one of the girls who had forgotten their key, I went to answer it. I couldn't believe my eyes; Leo was standing in the doorway. He was somehow managing to look cool and awkward at the same time. I think I must have stood with my mouth open for ages. Eventually I found my voice and asked him in. I led him into the kitchen

Colour me in

and offered him coffee. I was glad when he accepted as I had something to do with my hands and didn't have to look at him. No one else was in, neither of us spoke and I felt the silence between us. I put the coffee in the little coffee maker trying not to spill any and then placed it on the cooker and lit the gas under it. As I was reaching up into the cupboard for cups Leo spoke at last.

'So, how's my English teacher?'

'I'm ok.' I took the cups down and put them on the table trying not to shake. 'I . . . I'm not sure whether I am still your English teacher . . . you cancelled the last lesson without making another appointment.' I didn't want to sound churlish or school teacherish, but on reflection I think I probably managed a bit of both.

'Sorry Lorraine.' I loved the way he pronounced my name, heavy on the first syllable. 'Things have been crazy lately. I had an essay to do and as I had to go to Modena to see my mum, I stayed there to finish it because here it's impossible to work. My phone rings all the time and people keep coming round. There's such a lot to organise. You know what I mean?' I nodded, not sure that I did. The coffee maker was bubbling so I switched it off and poured out the coffee. I let Leo put in his own sugar.

'When did you get back?'

'A couple of days ago.' Leo knocked his coffee back in two swift gulps and I found myself watching him intently. I had to pull myself back to the conversation.

'Right, and now you want an English lesson?'

'Can we do one now?' As I hesitated he added, 'but if you're busy . . ..'

I got up and wandered into my room with vague notions of picking up the exercise book I'd made notes in during the previous lesson. He followed me and saw the notes and books on my desk.

'Oh, you're writing an essay. Look, we can do it another time.'

I couldn't let him leave. 'No, it's fine. I can finish the essay tomorrow it's not urgent,' I lied. 'Let's do a lesson now.'

I sat at the desk and motioned for him to pull the other chair over. He didn't. Instead he leant down over me and stroked my face. 'Oh my god,' flashed across my mind. I was not expecting this. I froze afraid he would pull back, not sure whether to react, afraid of repelling him. He crouched down in front of my chair, looking at me earnestly, straight in the eyes. I bent down slowly, my face leaning towards him. He lifted his up to meet mine and we kissed again. It was just as wonderful as the first kiss.

'This feels right,' I told myself. 'There is nothing wrong here, this feels right.'

The kiss was over and he stood up. I held my breath, praying that the awkward feeling would not descend on us again. 'Speak,' I told myself. 'Say something intelligent.'

'I heard the radio program about the Ruberti reform,' I said.

'Hey, what did you think? It went well, didn't it?' He smiled.

'It was a good discussion. I think a lot of people will be much clearer now about the issues,' I said.

'Great, that's what we want.' He chuckled, 'Giacomo from economics was good, wasn't he?' Leo stood with his hands on his hips mimicking the Neapolitan accent. 'Economics students have led the way, now it's time for everybody else to follow.'

I laughed gratefully, dispelling my nervousness a little.

'I hope they do follow,' I said.

'They have to,' he said firmly, pulling the other chair over to the desk and sitting down. 'How can we let businesses dictate what we study? You know that if the government has its way, faculties like Political Science, Economics, Italian and Humanities will all be starved of funds because businesses see them as less important. They are not going

Colour me in

to produce the engineers and scientists they want to make them money.'

'I'm sure they want to do that in British Universities too, our Vice Chancellor is friends with Margaret Thatcher. I'm sure they'd love to do that.'

Leo nodded. 'I'm sure they would. Has anything like this happened in any of your universities?' He looked straight into my eyes. 'You and Jenny haven't come across politics just here in Italy have you? You both seem to be quite political. Where does that come from? Your family?'

I laughed. 'My father is conservative through and through and my mother has always voted like him. I guess at some point I began to question their views. Probably during the miners' strike.'

'That was a few years ago, wasn't it?'

'Yeah, it ended a little over four and a half years ago. My uncle Ben, mum's younger brother, supported the miners. I remember him coming over to our house. He had a huge row with my father.' I smiled happily at the memory. 'It was brilliant, hearing someone who was not afraid to tell my father he was wrong. Listening to Uncle Ben, I found myself agreeing with a lot of what he said: that the miners had a right to a livelihood and that what Margaret Thatcher wanted to do would destroy communities and cause misery to so many people.'

Leo smiled and continued gazing at me. I chattered on nervously; 'We also had a dispute at university against a very right-wing lecturer who wrote nasty articles in the Sun newspaper using the name of our university in his by-line. That was really what made Jenny and me feel we wanted to do . . ..''

Leo leant towards me. I started to lean too, and my eyes went to his lips. It was awkward as we were both sitting on hard chairs. I started to giggle as our noses clashed and I nearly fell off my chair.

We stood up and he slipped his arms around my neck

and our lips touched. Leo held me very firmly as though he didn't want to let me go. Then he stepped back for a second and looked me straight in the eyes. He stepped towards me again and stroked my hair, his hands drifted down the sides of my face, down my neck and to my shoulders, which shivered with excitement. I ran my hands down his back, tracing the curve of his spine, an excited voice inside hardly daring to whisper, 'This is really happening.'

We kissed again, this time harder and longer, hands started creeping under clothes and I began to tingle all over. As I came up for air, I felt the need to say something.

'Well, so much for the English lesson,' I laughed.

He laughed too. 'We can talk English if you like.'

'If you want to,' I said in English and moved in for another kiss. As it ended, he began to unbutton my cardigan. I tried to pull his jumper over his head. We laughed as he got caught in it. I collapsed in giggles as he struggled to pull off my tight jeans.

I was grateful that I had a key to our bedroom door because the last thing I wanted was Jenny coming in right now. Leo helped me pull off my T-shirt. It felt so sexy until I remembered that I was wearing my greying M&S sensible bra. I made a mental note to wear my lacy one next time, praying that there would be a next time. Strangely though, as the layers peeled off, I felt less awkward. I ran my hands over his chest and his skin felt soft.

There was that fantastic feeling of skin on skin as we held each other close, just pulling back slightly for another kiss. The voice in my head whispered, 'I am with gorgeous, cool Leo and he wants to be with me.' He held me by the waist and propelled me onto the bed. I loved the way he held me. Every place he touched tingled. I think he was happy, too, because he had a lovely smile on his face and I know I must have had a big grin stretched across mine.

***

Colour me in

I'd love to be locked forever in the memory of that first time with Leo. It felt magical then and I need magic. I wish magic were not such a transient thing. I wish it were something you could hold on to forever. I want to take these magical memories with me into my cave and paint them on its walls and keep them there, away from the turbulent world, so that nothing can take them from me.

Chapter 5

The book felt heavy in my hand but I carried on reading having given up trying to sleep. A distant clock chimed three in the morning. The woman in the bed on Marta's right was groaning and suddenly let out a blood-curdling yell. I felt my whole body jerk with alarm. There was rustling in the nearby beds as the others woke up. A nurse came scuttling in to see her and, after a few minutes, calmed her down. She never talked. I think she had learning difficulties. I wondered how much she understood of what was happening to her. I wished I could yell like that.

In the morning I found that my legs had given up working. I couldn't stand up. I tried but I went straight down again. Luckily the nurses making my bed caught me as I fell. They sat me up in bed and said that eventually I would get my equilibrium back. I watched with envy as the others got up and walked to the bathroom, sponge bags in hand. How nice to pee by yourself in a proper loo, have a wash and brush your teeth.

Later, when I finally did manage to stand up, I was amazed at how proud of myself I felt. Just one day of relative immobility and I was so happy to be able to walk out of the ward all by myself, carrying the bag and tubes draining the liquid off my breast.

Grazia in the bed on my left was a small, slight woman in her late sixties. She had been told that her lump was probably benign but had not had a biopsy, so she would know in a few days when the report on her lump came back from the lab. Considered to be in less need of attention than the others the two of us were moved to another ward, further from the nurses' station, to make room for more urgent cases. My breast wasn't draining very well but it wasn't deemed a big problem.

Late in the afternoon, at Grazia's request, a priest came to see us and said a prayer. I felt very strange. I had been to a few Catholic Church services over the years, as Alberto's

Colour me in

mother was a devout Catholic, but it still felt odd. I was hoping to find it comforting but I didn't. It seemed incongruous, with my head bent in a hospital bed listening to him praying. I wanted to jump up and say, 'I'm not dead yet.' I need something strong and full of hope, not sad mumbling.

***

The City was covered in beautiful Christmas lights. Jenny and I couldn't get over how tasteful they were compared to the tacky brightly coloured efforts we were used to at home. Rows of white lights forming arches and swirls were strung across the main streets. All the way down Via Independenza, from the station to the centre and all along via Ugo Bassi and Via Rizzoli.

Bologna boasts two medieval towers built by the Asinelli and Garisenda families in the Middle Ages to show how wealthy and important they were. The shorter Garisenda tower leans towards its neighbour and has apparently been sinking slowly for centuries. They stand majestically at the top of via Rizzoli in the centre of the city, beautiful and grand. Now they were covered in strings of tiny white lights running down from the top to the bottom. It was breathtakingly beautiful.

Ever since the first time I saw them, I have loved the Bologna Christmas lights. Even in sad times they have always lifted my spirits.

One day, shortly after the lights went up, Jenny and I were in Piccolo Bar with Francesca and a few other economics students when Sandro rushed in followed by three or four others all shouting excitedly. To my delight Leo was with them, bringing up the rear.

'Have you heard the radio?'

'Why, what has happened?'

'Palermo have occupied!' panted Sandro.

'What?' Francesca jumped up and hugged him. 'Really? Are you sure?'

'Yes, the Department of Humanities and Philosophy, thousands of them, over the Ruberti reform. Finally it's happening.' Leo beat Sandro to a reply, unable to keep the excitement from his voice.

'Do you think it will spread to other universities?' I asked.

'Hope so,' replied Sandro. 'It looks like it will spread to other departments in Palermo. They seem very organised.'

Someone turned the radio on behind the bar. A popular independent station was on with a phone interview from the Humanities Department in Palermo. We huddled around it. Leo sat close to me. I wanted to hold his hand but didn't quite dare.

The rest of that day was spent writing leaflets, telling everyone the news, and talking about how to build up the campaign here in Bologna. That night we held a party in Sandro's flat. To my delight, as we were leaving, Leo whispered in my ear inviting me back to his place as his room-mate was away. He made no mention of going back to Modena for the weekend.

I chattered all the way home like an excited child, hardly believing my good luck, praying that this time we were going to spend the whole night together. When we stood in his bedroom and finally kissed, my lips tingled and shivers ran all over my body. Pulling each other's clothes off and giggling as they got stuck, I don't think I had ever felt so happy. And after sex I curled up beside Leo, my head on his chest and prayed that I would never have to move from there.

Leo and I got up late and went out for breakfast in the bar on the corner near his flat. We then wandered into the centre of town, mingling with the Saturday shopping crowd. In piazza Maggiore, a guy dressed from head to toe in leather was playing music through massive speakers and playing along on the guitar. Crowds of people gathered around to listen.

Colour me in

I felt full of colour and sparkle like the shop windows. There were stalls everywhere selling Christmas decorations and others with every kind of nut brittle, sticky toffee and chocolate-coated honeycomb. An elderly man with a small grate was roasting chestnuts, which he would scoop up for you into a little paper bag. Leo bought some and we munched them as we walked all the way up via Independenza to Montagnola, the big market near the station.

The air was damp and heavy but pierced with warmth from the chestnut grates and the bright lights of the decorations and stalls. Everyone was wrapped up warm in big coats and scarves. Leo wore a big black overcoat and a woolly hat pulled down over his ears. It had very fine grey and black stripes and he still looked incredibly cool. I didn't have one and my ears were cold in spite of my thick shoulder-length hair. I put my hands over them as we walked. When we got to the market I admired a bright green woolly hat hanging up on one of the stalls. I had decided, though, that any spare cash I had was for Christmas presents. I was not looking forward to going back to England for Christmas but Jenny and I had booked our flight ages before, at the behest of our families, and there was no getting out of it.

As we meandered among the stalls, I caught sight of Simona coming towards us through the crowd. I looked at Leo. Did he want us to be seen together? We weren't holding hands, although I really wanted to. When Simona appeared with Francesca and Sandro they greeted us warmly. Sandro suggested going for a drink and something to eat in the bar at the corner of the market. As we were heading for it, Leo disappeared, mumbling something to Sandro. He reappeared a few minutes later and we lunched on sandwiches and bottles of beer.

The boys decided to go and visit a friend that afternoon and the girls invited me back to theirs for cake, an irresistible invitation. We left the café together, girls going in one direction, boys in another and I had no chance to say anything to Leo. Just as I was about to turn and follow Simona along the street, he came up and pushed a paper bag into my hand. He smiled and then turned to run and catch up with Sandro. I opened the bag and there was the bright green woolly hat. I was walking on air as I followed the girls along the road to their flat.

***

The kitchen in the flat Simona and Francesca shared with four other girls was different from the usual cramped student flats. It will always be etched on my memory as the place where we had dinner after the demonstration when Leo sat beside me.

At one end was a big open fire with a large red and black poster of Che Guevara on the wall above it. There was a big basket of logs by the fire standing on an old woven rag rug. In front of it was a huge sofa and two very worn leather armchairs draped with colourful crocheted blankets. Against the wall opposite the fire was a large dresser. There were plates arranged on its shelves, interspersed with books and piles of notebooks, with rows of mugs hanging on the hooks along the front of the top shelf. I loved the country farmhouse-meets-urban student feel.

'Oh great, the fire is still alight,' said Simona. 'The girls must have added more logs before they went out.' She threw a couple more logs on the fire and we all settled ourselves on the sofa and armchairs with mugs of hot chocolate and slices of Francesca's sponge cake. The smell of wood burning and the crackle of the flames filled the room.

I was gazing into the fire, lost in happy daydreams, when Simona asked.

'How come you were at the market with Leo?'

I couldn't stop the big grin from spreading across my face.

'Well, well, so it wasn't an accidental meeting?'

I shook my head.

'You and Leo?' Francesca sounded amazed.

I nodded.

'Oh my God, really?'

Simona sounded amazed too. I was taken aback.

'So is this serious?' asked Francesca.

'Well I think so, it's early days yet but I really like him.'

'Oooh, how exciting,' said Francesca. 'He must have split up from Cassandra.'

'Who?' I had been cuddling my chocolate mug. My hands shook as I put it on the coffee table.

'His girlfriend, well, ex-girlfriend.' Francesca seemed embarrassed.

'Come to think of it, I haven't seen them together for ages, so they must have split up,' added Simona hastily.

'Girlfriend?' My grin faded. I clutched my knees.

'He wouldn't do that.' Francesca always seemed to see the good in people. 'He wouldn't two-time anybody he's not like that.' My mind was racing. He walked all round the market with me today. Surely he wouldn't have done that if he'd had a girlfriend. But then he didn't hold my hand.

'Honestly, Lori, don't worry, really. She hasn't been around for ages they must have split up.' Francesca was probably feeling guilty for letting the cat out of the bag. I usually admired her honesty but at that moment I would rather not have known. Something cold crept into my stomach.

'Does she study here?' I asked.

'No, she studies in Milan. She's from Modena, like Leo,' replied Simona.

'Childhood sweethearts,' added Francesca.

'Really.' I took a deep breath. 'So, he could have one girl in Milan or Modena and another in Bologna.'

'No, Lori, I'm sure he hasn't.' Francesca was really trying now.

'Honestly, forget about her,' added Simona. 'It was a long time ago. Tell us how it started between you two. Was it a cold autumn afternoon among the English verbs?'

'Well, um, yes,' I managed a chuckle. 'It was just like that.' I blushed and tried to focus on the good memories to warm up the chill in my stomach.

***

Magic never lasts long does it? Poof! It disappears into thin air. Or it can slowly change colour from magic to something duller, so gradually that you don't notice. One day you wake up and the magic has gone.

This is why I have to create my own magic. This oppressive dining room is being turned into a seascape. I must paint birds, free-flying, colourful birds. I could paint an area of rock with birds perched on it, maybe like big seagulls but more colourful. Magic seagulls.

***

'Look what I've done for you. Aren't you lucky?' Dottoressa Calchi stuck the syringe into my scar. Surprisingly it didn't hurt. She drew it out again full of blood and emptied it into a stainless steel dish. She then stuck the needle in for more. I was in outpatients a few days after my release from hospital. Large blood clots had formed in my breast. As they gradually dissolved, the liquid had to be syringed out. The doctor was fond of cracking jokes about how she had created this big breast for me when I had been worried about what shape my right breast would become.

Before the operation I had never managed to have a serious discussion with her about what my breast would look like afterwards. She was not prepared to talk about it seriously, always joking as if I were a fool to worry about such a vain thing as aesthetics. Now it was sore and huge and swollen and she was having fun with it. I had to lie on a trolley every other day for three weeks, having my breast syringed out, listening to her inane jokes.

Colour me in

One day, as I lay on the narrow treatment bed, Dottoressa Calchi said, 'You have had this lump for two years.' I wasn't sure of the significance of this piece of information. 'What happened to you two years ago? Did someone close to you die? Quite often the death of a child seems to cause it.'

I felt a sickness in my stomach as it dawned on me. Almost exactly two years before both my friend Janine, who had had cancer, and my grandmother had died within a day of each other. I had called my mother to say that Janine had died, but before I could say a word she had said, 'Your grandmother's in a coma.' I couldn't believe it. The following week I had flown over to England for two funerals, my grandmother on Thursday and Janine on Friday. Tears welled up as I lay draining on the hospital trolley. I didn't know what to think.

A few days later, back on the trolley Dottoressa Calchi suddenly said, 'Did I tell you that you would have to have chemotherapy?' Once again she had me speechless. No one had warned me.

I tried to sit up and gasped for breath as I did so. Luckily the nurse realised that I was having difficulty breathing and helped me up. My words to Gina echoed round my brain, 'I can take anything but chemo.' Gradually my breathing became even. I licked my dry lips and found my voice.

'Why?'

'In your kind of case it is standard prevention.'

'Prevention!' I had only ever heard of chemotherapy for zapping existing tumours.

'But my lump has been removed.'

'Yes, but cancer cells may have travelled into your lymph nodes and from them into the rest of your body.'

'But you told me last week that my lymph nodes were clear.'

'Oh, right, that's true, but the cells can travel via the blood. To be sure, we have to give you chemotherapy.' I could find no words.

The doctor said I would soon have a meeting with the head of Oncology at Bell Aria hospital and he would explain more clearly why I had to have chemotherapy. 'He'll tell you all about it and we'll talk about maybe sending you to Milan for tests on the lumps on your lungs.'

I had to grip the rail along the side of the bed to stop myself from floating up and hitting the ceiling, to then come crashing down into the dark cavernous pit below the bed.

I had thought it was coming to the end. The swelling in my breast was finally going down and my lymph nodes were clear. I had thought that this meant the cancer would not spread, but apparently it could spread through my blood, and there were the lumps on my lungs to worry about. I can't tell the children they have been through enough. How are they going to cope with me losing my hair, going bald?

Where is my bubble when I desperately need it?

***

It was probably the hardest goodbye I had ever had to say. At the bus stop I held Leo's hand tightly as we waited for the airport bus. It seemed to arrive so suddenly that we only managed a quick peck instead of a proper goodbye kiss. I felt bereft. Jenny shoved me onto the bus with my heavy rucksack and carrier bag full of bottles of wine.

Why was it that when I was finally happy it had to stop? I hoped and prayed this was a temporary separation. The spectre of Cassandra haunted me, however hard I tried to forget about her. The thought of him being with another woman all through the Christmas holidays was driving me mad. Maybe when I got back he'd confess and tell me that our relationship had to come to an end. I had thought about asking him, but when things were good I didn't want to spoil it, and when he was tense and distant, I concentrated on getting the warmth back and was afraid of saying anything that could widen the gap between us.

Colour me in

We were to be away for three weeks, the whole length of the holidays. This was largely because the later in January we returned, the cheaper the flights would be. I had no idea how I was going to survive for so long.

Chapter 6

A pale green May day was turning gently into evening. I put the supermarket carrier bags on the table and started pulling out packets of pasta, mozzarella and tomato sauce, thinking about what to make for dinner.

Alberto and the children had gone to the park and were due home in a few minutes. I was recovering well from the operation but there was no lift in our building and I had just walked up five flights of stairs with two large carrier bags. I poured myself a drink of water and sat on the kitchen balcony, enjoying a moment's stillness.

The phone rang. I got up slowly and went to answer it. The impersonal voice on the other end echoed as though it were in a bare corridor.

'Signora Browning?' Married women kept their surnames in Italy.

'Yes, that's me.'

'This is Ospedale Bell Aria. You are due to come for chemotherapy on Thursday.'

'This Thursday?' My heart was thumping. Today was Tuesday how could I start chemotherapy in less than two days time? I sat on one of the chairs at the kitchen table.

'What time?' I felt my bubble creep round me.

'7.30 a.m. and don't eat breakfast. You must have an empty stomach as you have to have blood tests.'

'Um, okay.'

I put the phone down. That was it. I was about to start chemotherapy. My bubble was back with me and was turning dark grey.

***

I love the view of San Luca; the beautiful cathedral perched on its hilltop just outside Bologna. You can see the porticos running all the way up the hill to the cathedral.

Every year on the first Sunday in July, a procession carries the icon of the Madonna and child down from the church into the city. The tradition began back in 1433,

Colour me in

when it had rained since April, threatening to ruin the crops in the fields. The procession took the Madonna into the city and, as they reached the city gate at 'Porta Saragozza,' the sun came out. Now she stays in the city for one week every year to ensure plenty of sunshine during the summer months. For nearly two hundred years she was carried up over the grass and mud. Finally enough money was raised for a proper pathway and nearly four kilometres of porticos were built connecting San Luca to the city. In the bus from the airport my eyes focused joyfully on the sight. Home at last!

It was Monday 15th January, half way through the month already. The time away had dragged so slowly. New Year's Eve had been really hard, seeing in 1990, entering a new decade knowing that the only person whose lips I wanted to kiss was hundreds of miles away. Was Leo feeling as miserable as I was, or was he enjoying himself? Whose lips was he kissing?

We came to our stop and I scrambled off the bus as quickly as I could. My huge rucksack became miraculously light as I tore up the road towards our flat.

'For God's sake, Lori, slow down,' puffed a breathless Jenny behind me. 'A few seconds isn't going to make any difference.'

The flat was empty and had a strangely abandoned feel to it. Dishes were piled high in the sink and the place was distinctly dusty and untidy. This was unusual as Maria and Gabriella were usually very house-proud. I studied the notice board and telephone table for messages. Nothing.

'He hasn't called.'

'Of course not, why would he call before you got back?'

'I think he thought I was coming back a few days ago.'

I continued hunting through the messages on the notice board above the telephone table in the hallway. 'There's nothing from the girls either to say where they are, no messages from anyone. I'd have thought Francesca would have called.'

'Lori, calm down. Let's make a cup of tea.' Jenny walked into the kitchen. 'Relax for five minutes then we can phone Simona and Francesca and you can call Leo.'

I stood in the hall looking at the phone. I couldn't sit down and relax. I looked at the clock. Seven thirty, a good time. They would be back from lectures by now and would not yet have gone out for the evening. I picked up the phone and dialled. It rang, no reply. 'Simona and Francesca are out,' I called to Jenny and put the phone down. I took a deep breath and picked up the receiver again. This time I dialled Leo's number, again no reply. I tried Sandro's, no-one. I sat down at the kitchen table and picked up the mug of tea Jenny had just placed there.

'I haven't found anyone in at Simona's, Sandro's or Leo's.'

'Really? No-one at all? That's quite a lot of people all to be out at once, especially at this time.' Said Jenny. Italians could usually be found at home at meal times, even students. Six people lived at Francesca's, five at Leo's and six at Sandro's. Where were they all? 'Well, we'll find out soon enough,' she added cheerfully. 'Someone will ring. What do you fancy eating, pasta with tinned tomatoes or pasta with tinned tomatoes?' I shrugged. 'Unless you want to run out to the shop down the road which is closing about now.'

'I'm not really hungry. Let's just go out.' My stomach felt nervous and knotted.

'Lori, I'm not going out on an empty stomach, roaming the streets looking for Leo. Let's eat first and then go out. In the meantime someone will probably ring.'

Reluctantly I realised she was right and I didn't really want to go out on my own.

'We can try the occupied library,' I said, 'and then Piccolo bar, Lo Nagro . . ..'

I ticked off possibilities on my fingers.

Colour me in

After dinner we set off, economics library first. To my surprise there were very few people there and no-one we knew. I remembered Giacomo, the tall Neapolitan, declaring that Economics would be occupied until the Government saw the error of its ways and wondered if he were right.

'Where are they? Where is Francesca?'

'We probably should have asked the people in the occupation,' said Jenny. 'Never mind, we'll find them. Now where?'

'Piccolo bar, as it's near.'

As we crossed Piazza Verdi to Piccolo bar I saw that the tables outside were in use. It was incredibly mild for January. Even at that hour, most people were in light jackets or jumpers. I was hot in my big overcoat. I felt hopeful that someone we knew would be in there, but no. Just as we turned to leave, I heard a voice say, 'Hey, English teacher!'

I turned and recognised one of Leo's flatmates. He had asked me shortly before Christmas if I would give him English lessons.

'Oh hi, how are you?' I couldn't remember his name.

'Fine, when are you going to start teaching me?' he grinned.

'Whenever you want, I've only just got back from England today, if you call tomorrow we can sort something out.'

'Fine, I'll call you tomorrow. I've got your number, haven't I?'

I nodded. 'Yes, I think so. Do you by any chance know where Leo is?'

'He's in the occupation, of course, where he's been every hour of the last few days. Oh, but you've only just got back. You've missed a lot of the fun.'

'We've just been to the occupation and there's no one there,' said Jenny, confused.

My mind was racing.

'You don't mean . . ..'

'Political Science is occupied.'

***

'You are coming with me, aren't you?' Alberto carried on drying the plate he held in the tea towel. 'Your boss has promised you can have time off.' He slowly put the plate down, stood still for a moment, then picked up another one and began to dry it. I sat down. He had promised that we were in this together.

'I don't know.' He said at last, 'I have a very important presentation on Thursday. The team is coming down from Milan. We've been preparing it for months.' His voice seemed to shake slightly. He put the plate down and turned towards me, his face white. I felt helpless. I wanted to demand his support but he seemed so vulnerable.

The phone rang. It was Francesca calling to see how I was. She sounded a little shocked when I said I was starting chemotherapy on Thursday.

'I know it's a cure,' she said, 'to prevent the cancer from coming back, but ironically it makes it seem all the more real somehow.' I nodded, even though she couldn't see me. I couldn't speak.

'Jen and I wondered if you were free for coffee tomorrow morning. We've both got some time, maybe you fancy meeting us in town?' I nodded again. 'Lori?'

'Yes . . . that would be fine, great idea.'

'Alberto's going with you to chemotherapy, is he?' Alberto was watching me carefully, his face still pale.

'There is a problem,' I said. 'It just happens that this Thursday he has a really important presentation that he's been preparing for months.' Alberto sat down and put his head in his hands.

'Well, maybe I could come . . ..' I could almost hear Francesca working it out on the other end of the phone. 'I'm teaching a class that morning but maybe I could get my colleague to cover it.'

'Oh Francesca, that would be great!' Some of the tension flowed out of me in a big sigh as I spoke.

'I'll talk to Jenny because I have a feeling she has some time off over the next few days. She's interpreting at a conference over the weekend but I think she's around til then. We can discuss it tomorrow over coffee. Don't you worry, one of us will come with you.' Francesca always managed to sound reassuring. 'Listen, Lori, I must go now. How does Luigi's at eleven sound?'

'Fine.'

'Right then, see you tomorrow and don't worry darling either Jen or I will be there to hold your hand on Thursday. Sending you a phone hug, big kiss. Ciao.'

***

Not bad for a few hours work. The yellow sun streaks on the turquoise water are a nice touch.

Right now I'm going to paint a rock and put some birds on it. I'll mix some of the black with white for different tones of grey and maybe add some yellow for a warmer look in places and perhaps a little mossy green on top. I'll paint some birds flying, too, but I'll need to paint a sky first.

***

As I started down via Petroni, Leo's flatmate's voice echoed in my ears, calling out something about teaching him English in the occupation.

The Political Science Department was in Strada Maggiore, a couple of streets away from Via Zamboni, so we needed at least five minutes to get there. Jenny had to run to catch up with me.

'Do you think any of the other faculties are in occupation?' she asked.

'We came past the Humanities Department. Did you notice anything?'

'I think I saw a big poster in the window but I didn't really look at it. We were rushing, remember, as we are now,' she added pointedly.

'We'll soon find out,' I said, 'Leo will know. Simona was saying before Christmas that there was a very strong feeling in favour of occupying Humanities. After all, they were the first to occupy in Palermo. I wonder how many other universities are occupied. Hey, how brilliant!'

As we rushed down Strada Maggiore towards the Political Science faculty, we saw a group of students gathered on the pavement outside.

The entrance to the faculty was a huge stone arch doorway with an enormous wooden arched door inside it. The door contained two smaller doors, which were open. Across the stone archway a red banner was hung with the word *Okkupata* (Occupied, spelt with Ks instead of Cs) written in big black uneven letters. The arch gave way to a vast stone courtyard. To the right and left of the doorway were rows of bicycles.

We walked through an open metal gate and into a square courtyard from which a large stone staircase swept up to the right with statues at the bottom of it. There were doors off the courtyard into offices and smaller halls. Students were crowded into every space and every conceivable bit of wall or notice board was covered in posters and banners.

My eye was caught by a bank of sheets of A4 paper stuck together with the heading *FACOLTA' OCCUPATE* (Departments occupied). Below it was written *Rome*, with a long list of departments, 'Hey, Jen, look at this!' I translated as I read them out: 'Psychology, Humanities, Political Science, Architecture and Engineering. Oh wow, even Engineering have occupied at Rome. I did a quick count, looks like about 16 departments at Rome. Can you believe it?' Under Palermo was the same long list of faculties.

'They are occupying all over!' Jenny's voice was incredulous as she read them out, 'Perugia, Torino, Firenze, all the main universities, Milano, Cagliari, Trento, Bari, Lecce. They've occupied from the top to the bottom of

Colour me in

Italy.' We hugged and jumped up and down in our excitement.

'How fantastic!'

I was desperate to find Leo. He would be so happy. I couldn't wait to share all this with him.

'Now, where will Leo be do you think?'

'In the centre of it all no doubt,' replied Jenny.

'And where is that?' She laughed, holding her arms out, as if to say "everywhere". The whole of the courtyard in the centre of the Political Science Faculty was full of students talking, writing banners, chatting, sitting on the ground and all the way up the stairs. No sign of Leo. The main courtyard led into a second one, also full of students sitting talking, some with notepads writing, a few waving their arms about in earnest discussion. Leo wasn't there. We went back into the main courtyard where an archway on one side led out into an enormous garden.

'I didn't know this was here!' I gasped.

'I came here one lunchtime with Simona, we ate our sandwiches sitting on the grass, the first or second week we were here,' said Jenny.

'How lovely.'

Due to the mild evening, the garden was full of students sitting in circles on rugs and sleeping bags, talking excitedly or passing round joints. As we stood at the entrance to the garden, I felt a hand on my shoulder. 'Hurray the poster girl is here!' It was Sandro's voice. I turned round and gave him a big hug and kiss on both cheeks. Jenny followed suit. I had gained a reputation for being good at writing posters.

'We've been busy while you were in England.' He was grinning broadly.

'This is incredible! Sandro, you must tell us all about it.' Jenny linked her arm through his. He linked his other arm through mine.

'Poster girl, you are coming with me we need your help.' Then turning to Jenny, 'Would you like to walk with me and some other law students over to my department to give out leaflets?'

'Is the Law Department occupied too?' she asked.

'Not yet, we have a public meeting the day after tomorrow. That's what the leaflets are for. Tonight we are going to leaflet around via Zamboni, the other occupations and the bars, and then tomorrow morning we will leaflet outside the Law Department as the students come in.'

He moved to walk forward then turned to us again and said, 'Girls, have you heard about our name?' We shook our heads.

'This great student movement of ours is called 'La Pantera' (The Panther).'

'An impressive name,' said Jenny. 'Why?'

'A panther escaped from Rome zoo recently and has been roaming around the regions of Lazio and Umbria and none of the forest rangers or carabinieri have been able to catch it.' He chuckled. 'They have been called out to sightings and there are traces of it but no panther. It has just disappeared. Always one step ahead of the authorities, that's us.'

'And this movement has been named after the panther?'

'Well, a couple of publicists came up with the slogan, 'La Pantera siamo noi!'" (We are the Panther). Sandro started walking in an exaggerated panther prowl.

'Hey, Jenny, Lori!' Simona appeared. She hugged and kissed us both while jumping up and down, 'Isn't this great? You must come and visit the Humanities occupation.'

'Is Humanities occupied too?' asked Jenny.

'Oh yes, of course we are, we were the first, as always!'

I started jumping up and down shouting, 'We are occupied, we are occupied!'

'Francesca and I tried to call you in England the other night,' said Simona. 'I think it was Jenny's number but we got no reply.'

'Oh. What a shame you missed us.'

Colour me in

'Come on girls, we have posters to write, leaflets to give out, no time for chit chat.' Sandro looped his arm through mine again and led me back towards the entrance to the department. I turned my head to check that Simona and Jenny were following. They were deep in conversation. Just before we reached the main entrance, Sandro turned down a corridor to the right and into a classroom where students seated at long white tables were writing out posters. Leaning against the wall at the back, deep in conversation with a tall lanky student in a leather jacket, was Leo, my heart skipped.

'Hey, Leo,' Sandro called out. 'Look who I've found!' Without waiting for a reply he led me to a table and pulled paper and pens in front of me. I didn't want to sit down. I wanted to throw myself into Leo's arms. I stood by the table as Sandro found me a poster to copy.

Leo looked around for a second and then saw me. He smiled. My heart skipped again. I smiled back and just stood fixed, grinning. He said something to the guy with him then slowly moved down the room. He walked around the table until finally he came to my side. 'We need you,' he said, 'someone has got to write decent posters round here!' He threw that remark at Sandro.

'Are you insulting my poster writing? The cheek!'

Leo kissed me on both cheeks in the normal greeting. I guessed he didn't want to make a big show. He then slipped his arm round my shoulders just for a second and whispered in my ear, 'Good to see you.' Then he sat down beside me.

'Leo, you can talk to her but don't distract her from her purpose, just help her.' Sandro made sure we had plenty of paper and markers to write with.

'He's worse than my mother, the way he fusses,' laughed Leo. Sandro picked up a pile of leaflets from the table near the door and headed out towards the entrance. Jenny and Simona were right behind him and a trail of students armed with leaflets followed them out of the room.

I looked at the pens on the table and then turned to look at Leo. I wanted to hold him, to kiss those lips, to feel his skin on mine. A little shiver ran across my shoulders. 'Well, you did it,' I grinned, looking around, 'You're in occupation.' Leo smiled.

'It was easy. Have you seen how it has spread all over the country?'

'Yes, I was reading the huge list on the wall near the main door. Isn't it wonderful?'

'It's great but there's so much to do, we want as many faculties as possible to occupy. Next week we'll have a big public meeting to discuss the way forward. I think we should occupy the Vice Chancellor's office. That'll teach him; the nerve centre of the university.' He laughed, 'You know our Vice Chancellor is a leading mason in this country?'

'No, I didn't.'

'Well he is and he wants his mason friends in big business to run the universities, a cosy club of money-makers. Well, we are here to make sure they don't!'

'Absolutely.' I grinned and began my poster writing. Leo picked up a pen and we worked together in silence for a moment. Then he described the events leading up to the occupation of the Political Science Department, his eyes sparkling with excitement. I could not stop staring into them.

After a while, a group of students came in with boxes of pizza and bottles of beer, handing out slices to any one who wanted them in return for a small contribution. I was hungry as I had eaten very little of the pasta Jenny had forced on me earlier. I gave some money and munched my way through a hot slice of Margherita.

As the evening passed, things gradually quietened down. Some students drifted home and others grabbed sleeping bags and went upstairs to the lecture halls to sleep.

Colour me in

The flatmate of Leo's I had met earlier at Piccolo bar appeared and invited us to join him and some friends for a smoke in the garden. Just as we were moving out there, Sandro and Simona appeared and came to join us.

'How did the leafleting go?' asked Leo.

'Pretty well,' replied Sandro. 'We went round all the bars. We'll do the faculty in the morning but it's best to do bars in the evening. People are sitting around and willing to talk.'

'We had some good discussions,' said Simona.

'Is Jenny not with you?' I asked.

'She's gone home, said she was tired,' replied Simona.

We reached the garden and sat down with Leo's flatmate and his friends in a circle under the stars. Leo ran off and came back with a sleeping bag that he then put over our knees. Someone handed a spare blanket to Simona and Sandro. Thus, cosily tucked up, we continued our discussion.

'We had some arguments as well,' said Sandro. 'When we started out there was a group of Popular Catholics hanging around outside the faculty. They were angry and said we were the threat to our education, not the government and university authorities.'

'They always say that,' said Leo.

I gazed up at the stars, feeling the warmth of Leo's body next to mine. I longed to hold his hand but somehow felt that I shouldn't. After a while Sandro and Simona said they were off to sleep in the Humanities occupation. I whispered in Leo's ear, 'Are you sleeping here tonight?'

'Oh yes,' he nodded. 'As many people as possible must stay and protect the occupation.'

'You want company?'

He seemed to hesitate for a second.

'Yes, I would love it.' The stars were so beautiful.

'Right, well I'd better go home and get my sleeping bag.' I started slowly to my feet thinking, 'If I don't go now, I am never going to want to move.'

'Just a sec, Lori.' Leo pulled me back down. 'Stefano, one of my flatmates, has gone home tonight because he hasn't slept at all for two nights, he's been downstairs protecting the occupation every night and is shattered. He's left his sleeping bag around here somewhere, I'll find it, as long as no one else has crawled into it, you can use it. It's like mine,' he grinned, 'with a zip all round.'

'That you can zip together, you mean?' I was grinning too. He nodded.

Chapter 7

As Jenny and I walked into the hospital I felt nervous, as if I were going for an interview. I had to queue to have my blood taken; they took three tubes. After that I had to see my assigned doctor, Dr Mori. He had long, dark hair tied back in a ponytail and seemed quite pleasant. He examined me, said he thought my scar was healing well but suggested I rub almond oil in to soften it, as it was very tight and was causing my breast to bend over in the middle. He asked me a few questions and then I was free to go. By this time I was starving so Jenny and I went to the hospital café for breakfast. We each ordered a cappuccino and pastry.

Jenny took my hand, 'You okay?'

I wanted to grin and say something light but I felt sad, and worried about Alberto.

'I know he had to do a presentation and it's important, but surely someone else could have given it, or at a pinch they could have delayed it for a few days. I mean, husbands go to chemotherapy with their wives, don't they? Look at all the couples here today, that's what they do.' I couldn't help feeling that Alberto did not want to be with me right then.

'Oh well, he can come next time. You're having eight cycles, aren't you? There's plenty of time for him to do the dutiful hubby bit.' She looked at me and grinned in an attempt to cheer me up. 'Hey, I wouldn't have missed it for the world!'

'Of course not,' I grinned back.

'Seriously though, Lori, we've not had much time together since Carlo and I came back to Bologna. At least today we've got time to catch up.'

As it turned out, we had plenty of time to chat; it was afternoon before they called me for chemotherapy.

When I heard my name, I tried to stand and found my knees unwilling to bear my weight. I put my hand out to grab Jenny's arm and, with her help, managed to follow the nurse into a small ward with just three beds in it. The nurse told me to get onto the bed by the window. Jenny sat on the chair beside me. The elderly woman on the bed next to me looked very frail. A woman probably about my age sat on a chair beside her, holding her hand. She smiled as we came in. A younger woman reading a magazine occupied the other bed. No-one was with her. She seemed to have a robust, determined air about her. Brave, I thought enviously.

The nurse came towards me with the drip. My fear of needles gripped me and I felt shaky. Jenny offered me her hand. As the needle went in, it stung. I squeezed Jenny's hand hard. Maybe I was somehow trying to pass on some of the pain and fear. I squeezed so hard that she yelped and pulled her hand away. I hadn't realised that she was wearing two rings. She showed me the marks; I had dug them deep into the flesh of her fingers. Poor Jenny, in that moment I think she felt more pain than I did. The nurse then hooked up a bottle of clear liquid and connected it to my drip. I found myself thinking, 'This is it, I'm having chemotherapy.' A tear trickled down my nose.

***

I now understand why this shade of green paint makes me feel sick. I've been constantly mixing it with blue to make turquoise, as I can't stand to look at it. Now these memories have brought it back to me. It's the green of the nurses' uniforms in Ospedale Bell'Aria where I went for chemotherapy. This colour takes me back there, to the drips and the little tubes of blood.

I will carry on mixing it, making different shades, different greens to obliterate it into something else.

***

A bright orange shirt caught my eye swaying in the breeze above a market stall covered in bright coloured dresses and tops. As I shuffled slowly around Montagnola Market I found its colours and sounds strangely comforting. The familiarity and brightness lifted my spirits and made me feel

Colour me in

that everyday life goes on, even though I didn't feel part of it any more. I drifted between the rows of stalls, one selling jeans, another handbags. I mustn't forget why I came: I needed to get myself a pair of comfy sandals for the summer and a couple of tee-shirts for Beppe.

Then I saw the scarves, hanging like an exotic curtain over their stall, speaking of foreign lands, - of Africa, India, Egypt, - beautiful and alluring. I stood mesmerised. Scarves, a voice whispered, you could wear scarves! The doctor had told me my hair would start falling out two or three weeks after the first chemo, so any day now. Alberto had taken me to buy a wig the previous weekend. We had ended up buying one a similar length to my own hair but paler than my bright red. I had fancied a brighter one but Alberto thought it was too much. I had ended up agreeing with him, much better just to blend in and not look different.

But to look exotic like these scarves! I fingered a batik scarf in blue, orange and green as it waved gently in the breeze, an African Queen!

'Can I help you?' The man behind the stall smiled and pulled the scarf down for me.

I put it against my face. He held up a small mirror for me to see myself. I slipped it onto my head for a moment. It suddenly seemed too bright. Although I wanted colour, its dazzling brightness made me look incredibly pale. As I slipped it off my head, I noticed hairs coming off with it. I touched my head and loose hairs stuck to my fingers. "It has started!" All I could do was stare at the scarf in my hand. Then I shook it to get my hair off.

The stall-holder asked if I needed help. I don't know if he understood what was happening. I handed him the scarf and was about to thank him and go, better to stick to the wig, I would never have the courage to wear such a scarf anyway.

Then I saw it . . . lying on the top of a pile, pale duck egg blue with embroidered patterns, sequins and a long fringe all the way round. I felt a thrill of excitement as I found myself nodding towards it.

'May I look at that one, please?' As he handed it to me it started to unfold and I saw that it was a triangular shape.

'Try it on.' He held up the mirror again. The transformation was amazing; the scarf fringe framed my face and transformed me from pale housewife to exotic Cleopatra. I smiled at the person in the mirror. Maybe this is what happens when you step into another world, it's not all bad, there is magic there to ease you through.

***

The waiters arrived with the pasta. I lifted my fork to eat my *Tortelloni con panna e funghi* and there, on the top of the pasta with the cream and mushrooms, was a little pile of red hair. 'Mamma.' Michela leant over and swept some loose hairs from my shoulders.

'Gosh that happened quickly.' I scooped the hair from my plate.

'I'll order you some more.' Sara started to lift her arm.

'No, Sara, there's no point. It will keep falling out. At least it's clean!' I laughed. 'I washed it this morning.'

Alberto looked uncomfortable. We were having Sunday lunch in Da Vito's, a traditional trattoria just round the corner from our flat, with Sara, Alberto's older sister, her husband Dario and their two children, Roberta and Luca. Some more hair fell onto my plate.

'Sorry,' I said. I moved my head and created a mist of hair again. It was raining hair!

'I should have worn my wig. I didn't realise it was going to happen quite so quickly. Some fell out yesterday but then it seemed to slow down, though there was some on my pillow this morning.' They were all staring at me again. 'I'm so sorry.'

'Lori, do stop apologising.' Sara leant over the table and touched my arm.

'It's funny, Mamma,' said Beppe. 'A clump of hair falls

Colour me in

out and you say "Sorry" as if it's your fault!'

'You are taking this very well.' Dario smiled at me across the table.

'Oh thank you, Dario. I'm just sorry it had to happen here in front of you all.' I looked nervously around the restaurant, half expecting to find everyone staring at me.

'You didn't plan it,' said Sara. 'Come on, Lori, do you want to go away and watch your hair fall out all by yourself? How sad would that be?' We laughed.

'Yes, but here in front of all these people?' I felt very shaky.

'No-one is looking,' Sara smiled, 'Honestly, don't worry.'

Alberto had put his head down and was concentrating on his pasta. I got up. 'Listen, I'm just going to pop home and get my wig. See you all in a minute.'

I left the restaurant and walked round the corner and across the road to our building. I blinked back the tears. 'No Lori, you are not going to cry over this. You knew your hair was going to . . ..' It didn't work. I could hardly see the stairs as I walked up them, holding firmly on to the banister.

Once in the flat, I went into our bedroom. The wig was on a shelf in the wardrobe, still in its plastic bag; I had no desire to take it out. 'I still have some hair,' I reasoned. 'I don't need it yet.' I opened my dressing table drawer and there on the top lay my beautiful new scarf. I sat in front of the mirror and placed the triangle on my head. I took the two side corners round the back of my neck, crossed them over and twisted them as I brought them round to the front. Then I intertwined them around my head. I suddenly felt nervous. Could I do this? Could I walk into a restaurant wearing such a noticeable scarf? Alberto would hate me drawing attention to myself.

I felt very nervous but the scarf looked good. I took a deep breath. I have to get used to this, I thought. In the height of summer it will be too hot for a wig and sometimes

I will have to wear a scarf. I could do with some big hoop earrings; if I'm going to do the gypsy look then I may as well go the whole hog.

***

The rocks have come out as grey and black blobs. I hadn't realised that rocks were such hard things to paint. I can't seem to get their cragginess. You know that old world worn look rocks have, mine just look fairly bland and characterless. I'm going to have to put more black lines in, deepen their cracks and make them really craggy.

***

'They've got guns!' Jenny's voice, little more than a whisper, was shaking. I took hold of her hand. Somehow it felt comforting as we came face to face with rows of grim, tight-lipped carabinieri, blocking our entrance to the church in their big black overcoats and large peaked caps. High up, in front of their chests, they were each holding a rifle.

I heard Jenny breathe in sharply as some of the students immediately ahead of us tried to rush through the cordon of carabinieri. I could hardly believe my eyes as I saw some of the carabinieri respond by lifting their rifles and bringing them down on the heads of the students trying to push against them. They were all using rifles to beat the students back. I heard a blood-curdling scream, followed by shouts of anger.

It felt as though a whirlwind had hit our part of the march as some people surged forward, joining the push against the carabinieri, and at the same time others pulled back to get out of the way of those deadly rifles.

We were outside S. Lucia, a magnificent church, now deconsecrated and used for meetings and functions. Here the Vice Chancellor and Minister of Education were holding a meeting. We had marched from piazza Verdi that morning to protest against the Ruberti reform. As we had set off to march to the Two Towers then down via Castiglione to the church, Sandro had said he reckoned that

Colour me in

there were about three thousand of us. We had been walking quite near the front, behind a large banner saying '900 idée contro il IX centenario' (900 hundred ideas against the 9th centenary). This referred to the celebrations the university was currently holding to mark nine hundred years since the university was opened.

Gradually things quietened down. I saw Sandro and Leo moving around among the people in the front, trying to calm them down and check who was injured. A young man supported between two people passed close by us, blood pouring from his neck. Francesca came into view struggling to help a young woman with a badly bruised forehead down the steps.

'That bastard over there struck her head with his rifle butt.' Francesca's voice was squeaky with anger as she nodded in the direction of the carabiniere standing almost directly behind us. We rushed over to help and between us we took her down the steps to the street and into a nearby coffee bar where the injured were being given glasses of water by the barman. Francesca stayed with her while Jenny and I returned to the demo.

The air felt tight with tension. We had marched in peace to protest against the Vice Chancellor's plan to hand over chunks of the university to private companies and we had been met with carabinieri carrying rifles. They had been ordered to use them to defeat us. I looked around at the faces of the students around me, jaws clenched, eyes alert but full of fear. I caught sight of Simona holding Sandro's hand a little way away. The stiff figures of the carabinieri were holding their rifles up across their bodies, ready for use. We all stood still, hardly daring to breathe.

Then Jenny squeezed my hand. 'Listen.' A solitary voice rose from the centre of the students.

'C'ha la mamma maiala' (his mother is a pig) and then a few more voices replied:

'E il padre, becco' (and his father is a billy goat).

The first student repeated his line, 'His mother is a pig.'
And we all replied, 'And his father is a billy goat.'
He repeated the line again, 'His mother is a pig.'
We all replied again, 'And his father is a billy goat.'

I found myself breathing more easily as we continued the chant. Gradually the tension began to ease. Slowly people started moving around again, giving out leaflets as they chanted. The carabinieri stood firm, but obviously hadn't been ordered to beat us for insulting the birth of the Vice Chancellor. We chanted for at least half an hour and then turned away and marched back to piazza Verdi.

***

The taxi drove past the two tall palm trees I remembered from the first time I came this way. I hoped Alberto wouldn't be too long. He was going to take the children to school and then come and join me at the hospital.

We pulled into the hospital grounds at around twenty past seven. I was near the front of the queue for blood-taking. I recognised a few faces, people who were probably doing a similar cycle to me with three weeks between treatments.

The doctor I saw this time was not the one I was supposed to see regularly. He told me that my hair would grow back pretty much the same as it was before. I felt this was strange because my assigned doctor had told me it could grow back any colour or thickness and had said it was all pretty much a lottery. I was beginning to realise that the chances of two doctors giving you the same information was as remote as winning the lottery.

I wished Alberto would come. I wanted someone with me so I could talk through and laugh about all these doubts and contradictions.

After seeing the doctor, in spite of my hunger, I decided to wait for Alberto before going to get breakfast. I looked at my watch, strange, I would have expected him at least half an hour ago. He had to drop off Michela at middle

Colour me in

school and Beppe at the primary school next to it, both by eight; it should take only about fifteen minutes from there. I tried calling his mobile and got no answer. I called home but he wasn't there. I left a message and sent him a text.

A few minutes later I called Jenny. I was worried about Alberto and didn't want to be alone for much longer. I really wanted a hand to hold, especially later when the needle went in. I sat on a seat in the corridor and waited, wishing I had brought something to read. Jenny said she would try and track Alberto down and let me know.

While I sat waiting, I spotted a woman I used to teach English to privately. She came out of an examining room a little further down on the other side of the corridor. She was with a very gaunt-looking bald man, whom I recognised, with shock, as her husband. Last time I'd seen him he had been round and robust, a lovely man, always very cheerful and chatty. Quite often I had turned up at their flat to teach her and she hadn't been there. She'd been delayed at work or had occasionally forgotten the lesson. He had always been very apologetic, offering me coffee and chat until she came home. I wanted to run after them and introduce myself but hesitated and they disappeared into another room.

Nearly an hour passed and I was getting worried and very hungry. I was just about to go and get breakfast when Jenny appeared. She had to stand in the corridor in front of me as all the chairs were taken. There were never enough chairs for everybody; often people waiting for chemo had to stand. She crouched down in front of me and took my hands.

'I found Alberto,' she said.

'Is he okay? Are the children all right? What happened?'

'He's fine. He's gone home.'

'What? Why can't he come here? What has happened? Are the children all right?'

'The children are fine. He took them to school on time,

no problem.' She pushed her hair back with her hand as if waiting to tell me something. It was unusual for Jenny to have difficulty speaking.

'Lori, I went to the school. I popped into the primary school, Beppe was there and he said Michela was at school too. It's okay, I said nothing to worry him,' she added. 'Then I called at yours, no sign of him, I couldn't track him down anywhere so I decided to come straight here to be with you. I thought that maybe he would have turned up by now.' She took a deep breath. 'Lori, I found him sitting on the hospital steps, the steps to this building.'

I had to take this in. 'He was sitting on the steps!'

'Yes, he drove here, parked the car in the car park, walked to this building, then sat down on the steps. When I saw him, he had his head in his hands. I almost walked past him before I realised who it was. I think he'd been crying.'

'Crying! Oh, goodness!'

'He was, of course, incredibly embarrassed to see me and quite surprised to learn how long he'd been sitting there. He had been there for over an hour and a half! Can you believe it? Totally unable to get up and come in.'

'He could have called me and told me. I could have gone out to him.'

'He couldn't have coped with that. He was more upset about being upset than anything else, if you see what I mean.' I nodded. I knew Alberto's pride. 'He kept saying, "I don't like hospitals." Then he said, "I tried to go in but I can't." He said that he felt a failure and that he had let you down.'

I sighed. 'I wish he could have told me he felt like this. I sensed he was reluctant to come but I didn't know how hard it would be for him.'

'I don't suppose he did. I think he shocked himself.'

I hadn't realised how much Alberto had been struggling with all this. I wanted him to be with me, to share this with me, to act as he had said he would when I first told him about the doctor's diagnosis, but he couldn't because he was suffering himself.

'I think maybe sometimes it's harder to support someone with cancer than to go through it yourself.'

'No, Lori, really, I doubt it, you've got the hardest job.'

***

Alberto was home when Jenny drove me back from chemo. He had collected the children, cleaned the flat and made dinner. He hugged me but seemed unable to say anything.

'It's okay.' I said, when we had a chance to talk. We were standing in the kitchen; the children were in the living room watching TV. 'Jenny can come to chemo with me again next time. I think my mother is coming over to stay for the one after that, so I'll be all right.'

'I should be there for you. I should be able to do something to make this better for you.'

'You can't take it away, Alberto.'

'I wish I could make it easier.'

'Being here when I get home with dinner ready makes it a lot easier.'

'Does it? It's not much though, is it?'

'Yes it is. These are the things that count, and being with the children, reassuring them that I'll be okay, making things as normal and safe as possible for them. These things are great.' I wanted to walk over to him and take his hands, but he held himself stiffly almost leaning away from me.

'I can make a better life for us,' he said quietly. 'Maybe I'll hear about the transfer soon. Now wouldn't that be perfect? If we could all go down and live in Calabria, in Zio Donato's old house. It's a great house with a long balcony. You can see the sea from it.'

'Alberto, are you seriously considering uprooting us all down to Calabria, right now when I'm going through chemotherapy?'

'Lori, don't you see? It would be good for you, all that fresh air and peace and quiet to recover in, away from the smog and humidity of Bologna.'

'I do love the fresh sea air, but living there would be so different from being on holiday. We live in a lively, vibrant city. The children are happily settled here. They like their schools and have lots of friends. Just the other day three of Beppe's friends came round, they played so happily together, and he's doing really well at school - don't you think that's important?'

'Of course I do, but the village school has a good reputation. You know he has friends down there too that he plays with during the summer.'

'Michela would find it hard . . ..'

'She would adapt.'

It felt like a game of ping-pong. I sat down at the kitchen table. 'I just want to stay here at the moment and get through this as quietly and calmly as possible.'

Alberto looked thoughtful. Eventually his face softened and he sat down opposite me.

'I understand that, Lori, of course I do. The transfer probably won't come through anyway.' He looked down at the table as he spoke. 'It's just that I've spoken to a mate of mine in head office and he said he'd see what he could do.' I looked at him; he was clearly very serious about this. I was not prepared for his next line, though.

'Lori, if it comes up, I want to take it.'

***

This is thirsty work. I'll get a glass of water from the kitchen and I could do with something to eat. In my eagerness to start painting as soon as the family left, I forgot to eat this morning. They went straight out to have breakfast in the local café, something the children still regard as a treat.

Chapter 8

I love the way the smell of freshly ground coffee mixes in with the aroma of pastries in Italian cafés, creating a wonderful atmosphere, strong and yet sweet.

My nearest bar with its run-down art deco style - brass edging around the top of the marble-topped bar, shelves behind crammed with every kind of liquor bottle - was a favourite refuge of mine. There was a counter at one end where you could buy a huge variety of freshly ground coffee. In front of it were stands full of sweets and chocolates, which I never managed to walk past. This was the place where I sought solace and comfort when I needed them.

Prior to the cancer, I would usually drop in on the way to the language school for a cappuccino and pastry. I had stopped teaching there for the moment but still did a few private lessons and some translating at home. Coming out to the bar for my breakfast was an important ritual for me, a continuation of normality.

The bar was owned and run by a brother and two sisters and the son of one of the sisters. The last time I'd gone back to England for a visit, Enzo, the son, had joked about sending me my morning cappuccino via the internet.

The morning after finding out that I definitely had cancer I went in there for breakfast. Sometimes it was hard to stay alone in the mornings and going into that sweet, warm, coffee-filled atmosphere with its cheerful chitchat lifted my spirits. I had almost burst into tears as I'd told Lili and Enzo my news. They had been very kind and concerned but had then regaled me with tales of Lili's uncle who currently had bladder cancer and another relative who had recently had breast cancer. Everyone had a story.

Enzo, was standing behind the bar with his Aunty Lili as I walked in and they smiled warmly. 'You look nice,' said Lili. I was wearing my new wig rather self-consciously. It was itchy especially when the weather was warm.

'Does it look okay?'

'Yes, it looks fine. It really suits you.'

'Thanks, Lili.'

'The usual?' She asked, referring to the cappuccino and pastry I always had.

'Yes please.'

A group of women were standing at the far end of the bar chatting. I recognised Marita who ran the newsagents down the road. I sometimes went in there with the children to buy magazines and the latest stickers for Beppe. We'd just say hello and chat a little, never more than that. That morning she called across the café to me.

'Your hair looks different. Have you just had it done?' I was stuck for a moment.

'Um yes, kind of.' I managed a smile.

As I left the café I was certain that Lili would tell Marita why my hair looked different. I was glad; I hadn't wanted to tell her myself in front of a café full of people.

The next time I went into the newsagents, Marita was really sweet. 'I'm sorry to hear about what has happened to you,' she said. We talked about it for a while. She, too, had her stories, but she was also a good listener. The next time we met in the café she insisted on buying my cappuccino and pastry for me. Lidia who worked with Marita also turned out to be sympathetic and easy to talk to. She told me that she lived with her elderly mother and I realised that I had often seen her wandering around the area, always keen to stop and chat. Whenever my own four walls got too much for me, I knew that I could pop out to the café or newsagents for a chat and a cheer up.

***

Shivering, I hurried across piazza Verdi. February was much colder than January had been and it had rained all night. I looked down to step over a puddle, and when I looked up I saw a male student rushing towards me, head down with a pile of files under his arm. I couldn't get out of his way in

Colour me in

time and we collided. 'Ow!' He trod on my right foot.

'Oh no! Sorry, I'm so sorry. Oh hello. It's you, the English girl. We met on the train, remember?' A big grin swept across his round face. He seemed to know me. Gradually the penny dropped, it was the guy I had been next to on the train coming back from Calabria last August.

'Yes, of course.'

'I'm so sorry, did I hurt you? Oh your foot, oh I'm sorry, here, let me take you to the hospital.' He looked down towards my foot as I leant slightly to the left, trying not to put weight on it.

'I can take you to hospital.' He seemed flustered and genuinely concerned.

'It's okay, just bruises it will heal.'

'Are you sure?' A worried frown appeared across his forehead.

'Honestly, it's fine.' I tried to hobble away but pain shot across my foot. It showed on my face.

'Oh, goodness, I'm so sorry.' He took hold of my right arm to support me. 'I'm too heavy, your foot took my weight.' I couldn't speak. The pain made me breathless.

'Listen, um, let me buy you a coffee.' I looked doubtful. 'I've got to say sorry somehow,' he went on. 'You need to sit down and take the weight off your foot.' We were standing right outside Piccolo bar. Sitting down would be good. He helped me to a table just inside the door. 'Coffee?'

'Cappuccino, please.' He went up to the counter. My foot was very painful. I wondered what I had done to deserve this.

When he came back from the bar, he seemed quite cheerful.

'Well, how's life treating you in Bologna?'

'Fine. It's lovely here.'

'Your studies going okay?' he asked. 'Is it Italian you are studying?'

'I'm studying Italian with literature,' I replied. 'I'm really enjoying the course. Some of the books we are studying are great, although . . ..' I paused. He looked at me enquiringly. 'I haven't studied since we got back after Christmas.'

'Ahh . . ..' Then he added, 'the occupation in your department, I assume you're in Humanities and Italian studies.'

'Yes, I am.'

'How do you feel about it? Is it a nuisance, stopping you from studying?' He asked a little tentatively.

'Oh no!' I replied, 'I'm glad they have occupied. I agree with it. I'm involved.'

His eyebrows rose slightly. 'Right,' he said. 'Well, they have got a point.'

'Do you agree with them?' I asked.

'Well, I don't think having companies dictating what we study would necessarily be a good thing, but if done correctly maybe it could be okay, if the money were given to improve courses.'

'But they would be putting money into the courses they wanted, engineering courses, science courses, things they need for industry. All other departments would be starved of funds.'

'Do you think so? Obviously serving industry is no bad thing if it creates jobs.'

'That's true,' I said. 'But do you think the sole purpose of universities is to serve industry? Don't you think we have a right to education for the sake of learning?'

'I guess so. Don't get me wrong I do believe education is a very good thing in general but the economy needs certain things. At times students have to be steered towards studying what society needs.'

'What do you study?'

'Economics.'

'Ah.'

'Don't say it like that. We're not all boring accountant types.'

Colour me in

'Oh I know,' I laughed, 'one of my best friends studies economics, Francesca. She was one of the leaders of the occupation in your department library before Christmas. Did you not agree with that?'

He swallowed, 'Well, actually yes, I did agree with the reasons. We've been having a lot of problems with the shortage of books and materials we need and absent professors. A friend of mine worked really hard to prepare for an aural exam but the professor who was to examine him didn't turn up. The exam was cancelled. My friend had been due to go home straight afterwards because his mother was ill and instead he had to wait several days to do the exam. It often seems that students are very low on the university's list of priorities.'

'That's awful. Was his mother all right when he got home?'

'No, she was very ill, but I think she's well now.'

'How can a student have a right to an education when professors care so little about our time? I think problems of access to books and lecturers would be worse in the faculties that the university authorities considered to be less important,' I said.

'Why do you care so much? This isn't your country. You're going back to England soon, I presume?'

'Education is important everywhere, and anyway there are similar problems there. I remember a friend of mine who studies sociology telling me about an argument she had with the head of her department who believes that students should study what society needs them to study, not what they want to study.'

'I agree with you that education is important, I really do.' He sounded more conciliatory at this point. 'My parents never had the chance to study beyond primary school. We've been lucky to have the chance to get to university, really lucky, and I'm grateful, otherwise I would have to run a pizzeria like my father.' He paused, and then continued,

'He's lucky to have a job, though. There's so much unemployment in Calabria. I think that whatever is necessary to get money to the universities and give more people the chance to study and get a good job, is good.'

I nodded. 'But we can't let governments and business decide what we study and invest money in universities just to make money. That's not what universities should be about, surely?'

'No, you're right, they shouldn't,' he smiled. 'I am glad I bumped into you . . . oh sorry, I didn't mean . . . How's your foot?'

'Oh, it's not so bad now.'

'So,' he went on, 'given that we both agree that study is important, what were you studying here, before you got involved in the occupation?'

'Well, we've read quite a few books. Some Italian literature is just wonderful, you have some great writers.' He nodded, smiling. 'We've just read *Se una notte d'inverno un viaggiatore (If on a winter's night a traveller)* by Calvino. I really loved it, I had to read it in English as well, to be sure of understanding it, such an amazingly original book have you read it?' Alberto shook his head. 'You must, it's lots of different stories, in a way, it's really about writing, he's playing really with the idea of why we read novels, I think . . . anyway I could lend you my copy in Italian. I'm going to read more by him, maybe the trilogy beginning with *Il Visconte Dimezzato (The Cloven Viscount)*. My friend Simona has read it and says it's amazing. Next term we are going to read Dante, that should be an interesting experience. I have to do an exam on him.' I stopped, surprised at my enthusiastic outburst. He was looking at me, vaguely amused. 'How much longer have you got to study?' I asked.

'Well, ideally I would like to graduate next year, by the summer I hope, but I'm not sure I'll manage it. I have four more exams to do. I'm trying to do them by this summer and then it will take about a year to do the thesis.'

'Well, good luck with that. Are you planning to stay in Bologna to look for a job or do you want to go back home?'

'My mother wants me to go home but there are so few jobs. I've explained to her that I will almost certainly need to get a job around here for a few years before going back down there to live.'

'Seems reasonable.'

'Yes, it is necessary.'

'Does she accept that? It would be good for you to have the experience of living and working in Bologna? It's such a lovely city with such a lot going on.'

'It is, but my mother won't accept that as a good reason not to return home.' He chuckled, 'She has always planned for me to go home, get a good job and marry Maria Teresa, one of the girls from the village. She's got it all worked out.' He suddenly looked embarrassed at having told me that. The phrase 'mother's boy' came to mind.

I finished my cappuccino and then wriggled my foot. It didn't feel too bad. 'Well, thanks for the coffee, I must be getting on.' I started to get up slowly.

'How's your foot?'

'It's much better thanks, hardly hurts at all.'

'I'm so sorry,' he said, 'that I trod on your foot.'

'That's okay, no real harm done.'

'But,' he added, 'I'm not sorry that we met again. I'm very glad to see you.'

'Yes, it was nice to see you.' Did I mean that?

He pulled a notebook out of his pocket, 'Listen, could we swap numbers? I've recently found out that I have to do an exam in English so I'll need a few lessons.'

'Fine, and you should come along to one of the debates. Tomorrow night there's one in Humanities called: "Whose education, theirs or ours?" I'm sure you'll find it interesting.'

'Maybe I will,' he grinned. 'You'll be there, will you?' I

nodded. 'Let's swap numbers anyway, just in case we don't get a chance to talk.'

He handed me his notebook and I scribbled my number. He wrote his on another sheet and tore it out of the notebook and handed it to me. He looked at what I'd written.

'How do you say your name?'

'Lorraine.' I pronounced it slowly.

'Lorraine,' he repeated, as if savouring the word, but it did not sound as good as the way Leo said it.

'By the way, what's yours?'

'Oh sorry, didn't I write it?' He took back the piece of paper, saying as he wrote,

'My name's Alberto.'

***

I'm having a picnic lunch. I've spread a tablecloth on the floor in front of my sea with my lovely orange sun shining down on me from the dresser.

It's the fennel season. I have fresh fennel, some salad, crusty white bread, Parma ham and local cheese. It's a shame the children aren't here they love a picnic. The cat is happy, though. I've just given her some pieces of ham and she's sniffing around in the hope of finding more, delighted that there's food at ground level for a change.

My rocks are looking better; I have to leave them now, at least for the moment. I think the sky will be my first task after lunch, then I'll paint the birds, some on the rocks and some flying in the sky.

Chapter 9

Alberto walked into the flat with a huge grin on his face, like a schoolboy with a new toy. In his right hand he held a bottle of Prosecco.

'Congratulate me,' he said. 'I've got the transfer.'

I was hanging out washing on the balcony. My bubble thickened around me. Out of the corner of my eye I saw Alberto put the bottle on the table. I felt myself stiffen as he came out and put his arms around my waist from behind. I stepped sideways out of his embrace. 'We've done it!' He sounded ecstatic.

My legs started turning to jelly. My hands gripped the metal rail along the top of the balcony. It took a moment to find my shaking voice. 'Are you really going through with this?'

'I start a week on Monday.'

I couldn't breathe. Alberto frowned. I managed to gasp and breathe in and then slowly my breath returned. I gradually let go of the balcony and wobbled into the kitchen to sit down.

'This is a good thing, Lori.' He sat down opposite me at the kitchen table. 'Come on now, this is what we've been waiting for. It will be great: sea, fresh air, peace, a quiet place for you to recover in.' He avoided my eyes.

'I had no idea it was going to happen now,' I managed to whisper.

'I told you; my colleague said he would look into it for me. It turns out there is a vacancy in Crotone. Although they were reluctant to let me go from here.' Pride coloured his voice. 'It's all been agreed to. There are always plenty of applicants for jobs in Bologna.'

I leant forward in my chair, shoulders slumped, head bent. I put my head on the table. I wanted to close my eyes and sleep. I could hear Alberto breathing as he searched for words.

'I thought this would do you good.' Slowly I lifted my

head and propped it up by putting my hands on my forehead. I spoke with no force in my voice at all.

'Alberto, I have six cycles of chemo still to go. That's four and a half months, followed by a wait of maybe a few months, and then a month of radiotherapy. I may also need an operation to remove the lumps from my lungs. What am I supposed to do? Why didn't you tell them you couldn't go this year, that your wife has cancer? Why didn't you say that?' I wanted to make him understand but felt totally incapable.

'I think I did . . .' he hesitated, 'I hadn't expected the transfer so soon. I thought it would take a few months but my friend in head office managed to push it through.'

'Push it through!' I couldn't believe this. The force returned to my voice. I found some energy and managed to lift my head and look straight at him.

'Push it through, now.' He looked confused. 'And the children,' I went on, 'the school term doesn't end for another three weeks. You know Michela has exams they can't leave now.'

'Listen, Lori, I have to accept this transfer. I've been waiting for so long. It will be good for all of us, you'll see, fresh sea air, so much better for you than the smog here, and open space great for the children and for you to get better, eh?' He looked straight in my eyes, defying me to disagree. 'It will be just what you need. When I get there I'll ask my cousin Franco to look at Zio Donato's place, which, as you know, he left to me, and we can start doing any repairs needed. That way, in a few months we'll have a place of our own. Won't that be great? Then you won't have to stay with my mother for too long. When you feel better it will be easy for you to find teaching work. There are plenty of people who want English lessons. Come on now Lori, you knew this was coming.'

I shook my head. 'No, I didn't.' Down in the pit of my stomach the knot tightened. 'What am I supposed to do

Colour me in

about my treatment? From there I may have to travel to Naples for chemo, or Rome. People even come up here for some treatments. You haven't thought about me at all, or the children.'

'Of course I have, this is for you. It will be good for you. I want you to get better, somewhere quiet, clean, healthy.' His voice began to rise in exasperation.

'Alberto, I can't move.' I stood up. 'I'm going through chemotherapy and I'm weak, Michela has exams to take before the end of term. I need your support to get through all this.'

'You have a lot of support from your friends. You don't need me.'

'How can you say that?'

Alberto stood up and grabbed me by the shoulders. 'This is something I can do for you. I want this . . . to make you feel better'.

I felt sick. 'I've told you I just want peace and calm right now. You're not listening to me.'

He looked straight into my eyes. 'You're not listening to me! I want this to give you the peace and calm you need.' His voice rose to a frustrated crescendo.

'How can moving so far away from my treatment, our friends, the children's schools, our life . . . possibly do that?' My voice rose to match his. I wriggled from his grasp and sat down on the nearest chair. I rested my forehead on the kitchen table. It felt cool against my skin. I closed my eyes and my bubble closed around me.

***

I take my picnic things back into the kitchen. The image of my dark cave comes back to me and I want to crawl into it and forget about the world outside. Apart from my children of course, I'd tell them where it was so they could come and visit me when the tide was out but I would have to swear them to secrecy.

Nicola Sellars

***

The helmet, borrowed from Sandro, wobbled on my head but I didn't care. I had my arms wrapped round Leo's waist and was snuggled up against his warm jacket as the old Vespa chugged up the hill. It was far from glamorous and numerous motorbikes were roaring past us but I felt like singing.

It was late March and the protests had all come to an end. From mid-February onwards students in many universities had been ending their occupations and going back to lectures. The Panther was finally tamed. In Bologna we had held a public meeting a week earlier that had voted to end the occupations. People were tired and exams were looming.

Leo and I had decided that we needed to do something completely different. He'd stayed at mine after a party the night before. We had woken up a little before midday and, as our bleary eyes registered that it was a bright sunny day, Leo had decided to call Sandro to see if we could borrow his Vespa to drive out into the countryside. We were heading for a country restaurant where they served local food, specialising in homemade tortelloni.

It was a lovely warm spring day, perfect for a ride in the hills. As we rose out of Bologna, I turned to one side and looked down at the city sprawled over the valley below us. It was a fabulous sight.

After lunch we walked hand-in-hand through the beautiful countryside park, which covered the hill, among the trees beginning to open their buds and the fresh green grass. Now the occupations were over I hoped we could spend more time alone together. It had been fantastic working together as part of a struggle but we had so rarely been alone. Now here we were, a normal couple out on a Sunday, having a stroll after a good lunch. As we walked, we leant into each other and stopped to kiss every few steps, like lovesick teenagers. It was just heavenly.

Colour me in

'Soon it will be picnic season,' remarked Leo. 'It's great here in the summer.' He pointed to some brick structures next to tables with wooden benches. 'Those are barbecues. You can bring your own grill and food to barbecue. It's a great way to spend a Saturday or Sunday. We'll have to organise one, get a bunch of people together, some meat to grill, make some salad at home, bring plenty to drink and a few guitars.'

'Sounds fantastic,' I squeezed his hand.

***

Fear gripped me. I didn't know what to say to Alberto any more, even though he was still with me, I felt alone. He seemed happy to leave, happy not to go through the rest of my treatment with me. I was exhausted and my head felt fuzzy. Was I so hard to live with?

Alberto had promised Beppe that he would play football with him in the park so after supper they went out. Michela had a friend round and they shut themselves in her bedroom.

I slumped into an armchair and picked up the phone. Tears flowed as I punched the numbers. I called Simona. I had a feeling that Jenny would probably be too critical of Alberto. While I did feel hurt, at the same time I felt a growing sense of guilt that somehow this was really my fault.

'Now!' She said, 'he wants to go now?'

'Well, he didn't know it would come through quite so quickly. But he did ask a colleague in head office to push it through, so he obviously wanted it to happen soon.'

'He has said before, though, that he would like to transfer, hasn't he?' she asked slowly.

'Yes, but he hasn't mentioned it for a long time. I suppose I never really took it seriously. Simona, he's happy, he bought Prosecco to celebrate . . .. To celebrate going away from me!'

'Now, Lori, I'm sure that's not why he's happy.'

'What have I done to make him want to leave me now when I need him with me?'

'Does he understand how much you need him here?'

'I've tried to tell him, surely it's obvious.'

'Do you think he's doing this because he really believes it's best for you?'

'It doesn't feel like it, it feels like he's running away from me, abandoning me.' My voice rose and the tears started again. I checked that the living room door was shut; I didn't want Michela to see me crying.

Simona's voice sounded cautious, 'Listen, Lori, I think Alberto does want to help you but he's not really coping very well with your cancer and the treatment. Subconsciously that may be driving him away, but consciously, I think he wants to do what he believes will help.'

'I'm not so sure, Simona, he knows how I feel about living there. He doesn't listen to me, he doesn't want to hear what I have to say.'

'Have you told him how you really feel about this transfer?'

'Yes, I've told him I can't move now and that I need quiet and calm and to stay here.'

'Have you told him you need him?'

'Yes I have but he says I don't and that I have my friends to support me.' I started choking on a fresh wave of tears.

'Oh honey, I wish I were there to give you a hug.'

'So do I.' I managed to find a tissue in the pocket of my shorts and wipe my eyes.

'Lori, I really don't think Alberto wants to leave you. I think you should make it clear to him that you really need him right now and want him to stay. Maybe he can postpone the transfer.'

'The thing is, Simona, why did he put in for it now? What have I done to make him want to leave me? He must have known I couldn't come with him.'

Colour me in

'It sounds as if he hadn't really thought it through. He didn't know when he would get the transfer. Rightly or wrongly I think this is his way of doing something to help and he wasn't planning to leave you.'

I spoke slowly. 'He did say before that if the transfer came he wanted to take it. He really wants it for himself . . . there is a determination in him to go, regardless of what is happening to me. That hurts.' The knot in my stomach tightened.

***

'Mamma, I scored more goals than Papà!' It was nearly dark when Beppe and Alberto returned from the park. Beppe was very tired so he was happy to wash, get into his pyjamas and fall into bed. He was almost asleep as I kissed him goodnight.

Alberto was getting a bottle of beer out of the fridge as I entered the kitchen. He handed me one. I took it and sat down at the table with my hands round the cool glass while Alberto found the bottle opener. 'You kept him out late,' I commented. Michela's friend had gone home and she was already in bed.

'I figured you needed time to think,' he took the bottle from me, opened it and handed it back, 'or to ring one of your friends to talk it through with.' I took a mouthful of cold beer. It cooled my throat and the cool feeling slowly seemed to spread through my body.

'You're right, I called Simona but that doesn't mean I don't need you. I can't do this alone.'

He sighed, 'Lori, I don't think I'm much good to you here. You have all your friends and I can't even make it to chemo with you. At least what I can do is make a nice comfortable home for us in Calabria, a place where you can rest and relax and regain your strength and become well again.'

'Is that really why you want to go?'

'Of course it is.'

'Do you think it's realistic?'

'What do you mean?'

'Alberto, I'm in the middle of my treatment. I can't interrupt it to go somewhere else. I don't know where I could do it. I don't know how long . . ..' Alberto reached out and touched my hand.

'I get that. I've been thinking about it. Of course you need to finish your treatment here.' I felt a flutter of hope.

'It could take the rest of this year, at least.' Alberto's face seemed to pale.

'Really, that long?'

'Yes, I have another six sessions of chemo - that won't be over for nearly five months. Then there will be a wait I don't know how long; people are waiting several months for radiotherapy at the moment, and then about a month of radiotherapy. Then it depends on what happens to the lumps on my lungs. I may need more surgery but they are going to see what happens during chemo. They may disappear or they may be okay and not cancerous.'

'How will they know?'

'They haven't said exactly, but I think the idea is that if chemo has no effect on them then they are probably not cancerous.'

'It's not fair, is it? I mean, you've never even smoked.' It was a mild evening but I suddenly felt quite shivery and rubbed my hands up and down my arms to warm myself.

'At least I can do it here. If we go to Calabria then I will have to travel for chemo.' Alberto sat, beer bottle in hand, staring at the table. 'You can help me here, if you can stand to be around me right now, I really need your support.' My voice was shaking. Alberto looked up.

'What do you mean, if I can stand to be around you?' I didn't want to cry. I blinked back the tears. 'Lori, of course I can stand to be around you. It's just that this opportunity has come up much more quickly than I thought and I'm not much use to you here.'

Colour me in

'You are, especially for the children, taking Beppe out, giving them a sense of normality.' My voice lowered, 'It's just that you seem so eager to go, desperate almost to get away from me . . ..'

'Stop saying that, Lori, I'm not desperate to get away from you, that's nonsense. I just want to do something to help.'

'Then stay and hold my hand through this.'

'So you want me to turn down the transfer?' he asked. 'I'm going to look a right idiot, I push for it then I turn it down.'

My head felt thick and fuzzy, tears were welling up again and the knot in my stomach tightened. I closed my eyes and saw coloured birds flying across a blue sky towards a very bright light.

The chair scraped as Alberto got up and went out of the room. The front door opened and closed again. The sound of his footsteps going down the stairs echoed and faded as he neared the bottom.

***

The smell of grilled chicken filled the air. The wooden table was covered in plastic plates piled high with grilled sausages, chicken pieces, bread, salad and huge bottles of red wine. Sandro and Marco were playing guitars and several people were singing along. I sat at the end of the table next to Francesca and opposite Jenny, drinking in the atmosphere. Most of the songs were Italian ones that I didn't know, but every now and again someone suggested an old Beatles number or a hit that we knew and Jenny and I joined in the singing.

It was Easter Monday, traditionally a day for picnicking. After the formal Easter Sunday spent with family, Monday was the day to head to the countryside with friends and have a good time. We had taken up Leo's suggestion and come to the park on the hill overlooking Bologna with plenty of food, wine and music.

Francesca had stayed in Bologna for Easter as she had an exam shortly afterwards so she had come along, and Maria our flatmate had come with her boyfriend Filippo. The meat was sizzling, the wine was flowing and the singing was fun. I was feeling really happy and tingling with anticipation as Leo was due to arrive soon. His friend Stefano was picking him up from the station in his car and bringing a couple of other people too. I got up to take a turn on the barbecue. There was something wonderful about the smell of grilled chicken in the open air.

As I turned away from the barbecue to get some air on my face, which felt as if it were glowing like the charcoal, I spotted Stefano's old red Fiat trundling up the hill and felt a shiver of excitement down my spine. As it pulled up, I could see that the car was full. It stopped and a woman got out of the front passenger seat, I recognised her as Stefano's girlfriend. Then, there he was getting out of the back seat. My man. I had to finish turning the chicken over; otherwise I would have run to greet him. Just as Leo got out a woman got out of the seat beside him another friend, I supposed. Then I heard Sandro's voice, 'Ciao, Cassandra, good to see you.' A lead weight dropped into the pit of my stomach.

***

I must have gone to bed soon after Alberto went out. I was exhausted but couldn't sleep. The knot in my stomach seemed to spread through my body until I felt tense all over.

Alberto really wanted to go. He said he wanted to help me but when I asked him to stay it was too much for him. I felt sick, I retched and had to struggle out of bed as quickly as I could. I just made it to the bathroom in time and threw up as soon as I reached the loo. I sat on the floor, hugging the loo, exhausted, and then threw up again. I stayed on the floor for what seemed like a long time, breathing heavily, a

Colour me in

harsh, bitter taste in my mouth. Finally, I struggled to my feet and slowly shuffled into the kitchen to get a drink of water.

I sat at the table for a while before going back to bed. I must have fallen asleep and didn't hear Alberto come in but he was there when I woke up, lying on his back snoring softly and looking strangely peaceful.

I heard the children's voices and eased myself up into a sitting position. I touched Alberto's forehead and he opened his eyes. He almost smiled at first and then a cloud seemed to enter his gaze. We got up and ate breakfast without saying anything to each other, our silence filled by the children's chatter.

***

She was tall and slim with long, black, wavy hair stretching down her back almost to her waist. She had the kind of strong intelligent face I would normally have admired, but right now I wanted to punch it..

'Maybe they have stayed good friends,' Francesca's voice whispered in my ear. I was grateful to her for realising how I felt. I was afraid I'd collapse in tears. I started turning the chicken pieces over again.

'How could he bring her here? What's he playing at?' This was Jenny's angry whisper. 'Hey Lori, now you know he's just a two-timing bastard.'

'Maybe they're just friends now.' I was holding on to Francesca's words.

'He owes you an explanation,' Jenny went on. 'Don't let him get away without telling you everything.' At the words 'get away' my knees felt weak. I didn't want him to get away anywhere. I wanted to keep him. Five minutes ago I had thought he was mine and I was the happiest woman on the planet. Now I was the most miserable.

The chicken was done so we piled it on to two large plates. Francesca and Jenny carried them over to the table where the newcomers were gathering and beginning to sit down. Leo had his back to the barbecue. I had no idea how he was going to react to me. Finally, armed with a plastic cup full of red wine I walked over to the table and sat down opposite Jenny who was on the same side as Leo. I could see him clearly. He smiled, 'Ciao Francesca, Lori, Jenny.' So there I was, sandwiched between my friends in his phrase, just one of the girls. I glanced over at Cassandra sitting next to him; she slid her hand over his on the table. It was not the gesture of an ex-girlfriend.

***

I was rocking, rocking, rocking, in my rocking chair. I don't have to think if I rock. The children had come home from school and then gone to a sports event in the local park with friends and their parents. I rocked. I had kept busy all day, a short translation, then the cleaning, then out to get the shopping. I had forgotten they would be going out and now I had to fill the silence. I hadn't wanted to go to the park. I wanted to be alone, but not with these thoughts. He doesn't love me anymore . . .. He wants to leave me. I'm too difficult for him. I rocked and rocked until I had to stop. I felt as if I had been running.

As I sat there panting, I heard a voice say, 'Maybe it won't be so bad . . ..' I don't know where it came from. I got up to make myself some chamomile tea and as I moved around the kitchen it were as if my brain started working again. If he has to go then the children can join him in three weeks when they finish school. Maybe it will be okay here on my own. I get very tired; maybe it will be good to have time to sleep. The children will love spending the whole summer by the sea with their cousins and friends. Maybe it won't be so bad. I took the chamomile tea back to my rocking chair.

I heard a movement in the room and slowly opened my eyes. I was still clutching my teacup. Alberto stood in front of me holding a bunch of flowers.

'Hi there, had a good sleep?' He leant down, took the

teacup and put the flowers in my hands.

'Oh, thank you!'

'Lori, I'm sorry.' He sat down on the sofa. White lilies, I loved their strong scent. 'I suppose I wasn't thinking about what you really need. I guess I thought that your friends could help you here and that I could do my part by creating a better environment for us to live in.'

'You really want this transfer, don't you?'

'Yes, but only if you do too.'

'Could you stay till I finish my chemo?'

'I asked today if the transfer can be postponed and it can't. Well, they said I could have an extra week if I need it but that's all I'm afraid.'

'What did you tell them?'

'I said I would talk to you and get back to them.'

It was a relief to hear him say that. Just the sense of being consulted made me feel better.

'I'm not sure that I can live in Calabria but I don't want to stop you doing something you really want.' Alberto came over and leant down and kissed me on the forehead.

'I don't want to make you do something you don't want either.'

'Well, as you have the job down there to go to, maybe you should go for now and we can see how it goes. Maybe I can try it after my treatment.'

'Thank you,' Alberto kissed me on the forehead again. 'Listen, Lori, I don't want to leave you but you've got your friends to come to chemo with you and look after you afterwards.'

My stomach knotted up. I wanted to say, "but that's not enough. I love my friends, but I need you." But I couldn't say anything.

'The moment it's over you can come down until you have to do radiotherapy. I'll come up and get the kids and stay for a few days, then maybe we can come up for a weekend. Perhaps I can take a day sometimes and make it a long weekend. I can drive up overnight.'

The knot tightened even more in my stomach and the sick feeling started to come back. He was sounding happy again; earnest, but happy, trying to convince me that everything would be okay. He was being too optimistic. It wouldn't be easy for him to drive for thirteen hours to visit me. I still didn't understand why he had to go right then but I couldn't stop him, if I tried we would just argue again and I couldn't face that.

At the same time though, I had a sense that it would be okay to be alone. In fact, there was a kind of longing to be left alone without having to worry about anyone else. Left alone, I could sleep and sleep and scream at the walls if I had to.

Chapter 10

I stared at my face in the mirror. 'No colour.' I had no hair, no eyebrows and no eyelashes: a pale, colourless blob. Tears trickled down my face. Somehow the creature in the mirror didn't seem to be me and yet I felt her sadness.

It was mid-June, shortly after my third chemo, and it was Beppe's seventh birthday. The children had just finished school and in a few days were going to join their father in Calabria. I was determined that we should have a party and that things should be as normal as possible, so I put on my wig and a cheerful face and prepared party food.

People started arriving at around four o'clock. We had decided that Beppe would open his presents in the flat and then we would all go over to the park with a picnic. Beppe had invited his best friends, Matteo, Roberto and Nina, plus Matteo's little sister, Paola. Gina had come to give me moral support, with her daughter Elisa to keep Michela company.

Cristina, the mother of Matteo and Paola, had been a fantastic help, insisting on making most of the food. She had been so supportive lately taking the children to her place after school, allowing me to sleep in the afternoon. Her husband Luigi and the other dads had said they would join us after work for the picnic and games.

Beppe was opening his presents, tearing off the paper with great enthusiasm, hardly stopping to notice who each present was from. I had to keep reminding him to thank people for their presents. He unwrapped the robot Matteo had brought him then moved swiftly on to a parcel wrapped in green striped paper, which he tore off frantically. I was thinking what a shame to ruin such lovely paper as Beppe tore the last shred off to reveal them lying in their box, under their plastic cover, something I hadn't seen for ages. My heart skipped a beat.

'Wow, face paints!' Michela snatched them from her brother's hand. 'Who wants their face painted?' Paola was the first and Michela did a beautiful job painting flowers all over her face. After that all the children wanted their faces painted, so we set to work. Cristina drew lovely tiger stripes on Beppe, Gina made Roberto into a lion, while Michela turned Matteo into a zebra. I was very proud of the butterfly adorning Nina's face. Then Elisa and Michela did each other's faces, each turning into wonderful colourful creatures.

When they all went over to the park, I stayed to clear up, saying I would only be a few minutes. I closed the door behind them, glad of the peace. I picked up crumpled wrapping paper from the floor and threw it away, tidying up the presents into a pile. The face paints were still on the table; some of them had not been put back in their box. I slotted them each into place and stared at the box in my hand. I found myself walking into my bedroom and sitting in front of the dressing table mirror. I put the box down in front of me and looked at my pale skin surrounded by the now itchy wig. My sad colourless face seemed to quiver in anticipation.

As I approached the group in the park I heard a gasp. Then I saw the faces, suspended between expressions, not sure how to react. I felt an urge to run back to the flat and put my wig back on. Was it possible that what had looked really beautiful in the bedroom now looked weird? Didn't they understand how much I needed colour?

Then Cristina saw me, 'Oh wow, Lorraine, you look amazing!' I wore no wig or scarf so the full effect could be seen. I had painted flowers climbing up from my forehead and over my skull as far as I could reach. I had managed to cover my head pretty well, I thought.

'Oh my God, Mamma!' Michela, bless her heart, had no idea how to react. Luckily, Gina turned to her, smiling. 'Doesn't your mamma look amazing?'

'Well, yes, she does.' Michela agreed.

'Your mamma's got a flowery head,' Matteo giggled at

Colour me in

Beppe, who just laughed and carried on with their game, unconcerned.

Later, as I went to get water from the park café, I caught my reflection in the window. It was as if I were looking at someone else, in fact not even a human being, not quite the exotic bird of prey I would have liked, but much better than my usual colourless self. I felt as if I were watching this painted creature from a distance.

I saw a look of sympathy pass between Nina's parents. I didn't want to be pitied. I had felt sad and I had done something about it. I wanted understanding, not pity, but I couldn't explain that.

After a while Cristina said, 'Has anyone seen Luigi?'

'He said he'd be back in a minute,' said Beppe. 'Michela has gone too.'

'They must have gone to fetch the cake,' whispered Gina so Beppe wouldn't hear. A few minutes later they reappeared, Luigi was carrying a large box and Michela carried little paper plates and serviettes. There was, however, another surprise. Luigi's bald head was covered with some of Michela's best designs.

'Oh my God, Luigi, that's amazing!' exclaimed Cristina. A lump came to my throat. Michela had drawn stars and swirls all over his face and head. I was touched by what they had done. I rushed over to Luigi and gave him a hug, so grateful for his solidarity. I hardly knew him. We'd only met a few times and yet he made me feel so supported and normal. Now everyone was laughing and admiring both our heads, openly relieved that it had become acceptable.

I joined in a game of Frisbee for a while, before the tiredness got me and I had to sit down on the grass. Gina took hold of my hand as I tried to explain.

'You don't realise how much colour hair gives you until it's gone, especially red hair.' I manage a nervous chuckle, 'even eyebrows and eyelashes make a big difference. I had to put the colour back into me.'

'Lori, you look great. You do whatever you need.' Gina squeezed my hand.

'You look fantastic, I envy your courage, instead of hiding your bald head you are displaying it beautifully,' said Cristina.

'Body painting is the norm in lots of cultures,' Nina's father pointed out moving, I hoped, from pity to understanding.

'Do you think the colour improves me?' asked Luigi, grinning broadly. 'Obviously there is little room for improvement,' he added, laughing.

'Absolutely.' His wife gave him a hug and inspected his head more closely.

'Beautiful, darling, utterly gorgeous, well done Michela.'

'So, should I do this more often?' he asked with a twinkle. 'Hey Lori, we should start a head painting sect!'

Tears welled up in my eyes. Cristina handed me a serviette. That was the day I started putting the colour back into my life.

***

Maybe this sky is too pale. I'd love to paint an amazing vivid blue like the one Giotto created for his frescoes. Perhaps I could try my own version of one of his religious scenes, my favourite is the Visitation of the Virgin Mary. There's something amazing about the colours he uses and the expression on the faces of his characters. But of course I couldn't, what am I thinking?

I must get a move on though as I have another wall to cover yet. I've got all these different greens. I could do a wood, fields . . . a poppy field, oh yes, lots of green grasses and poppies. I'd have to capture their fragility, poppies are amazing, they can grow in very dry soil and they have a fragile beauty while being strong. I'd love to try and capture that though I doubt I could do them justice.

But I feel as though I need something wilder than poppies, something wild and luscious like a jungle scene. I

Colour me in

often paint colourful birds and flowers but could I reproduce a jungle scene on this wall?

I don't know what to do. I love the idea of poppies, fragile and yet strong but orchids can be so bright and exotic. I'd love to do some colourful birds like toucans and cockatoos but can I really do them justice?

Beppe has a schoolbook with lovely jungle pictures and exotic birds and flowers. I can try and copy some of them. I would love to paint something that captures the luscious vibrancy of a jungle. Palm trees, rubber trees and orchids in Assunta's dining room!

***

The tears streamed down my cheeks. I was crying so much that I choked on my words.

'So this is why! This is why he spends so much time in Modena - because she's there, too. All the holidays and weekends they both go to Modena to be together and I bet he goes to Milan to see her.'

We were back at the flat, sitting in our room. Luckily, Maria and Filippo had wanted to come back to Bologna early to visit some of his relatives so they had dropped us off at home. Jenny and Francesca, sweet friends, had come back to keep me company.

'She used to come to Bologna a lot more,' said Francesca. 'Maybe he's been putting her off, because of you.'

'Well he didn't put her off today, did he? How could he do that? He knew I'd be there. Even if I two-timed someone, which I would never do, I would never want them to be in the same place at the same time, it's lunacy! How did he know that I wouldn't make a scene, go up to her and say, "Hi Cassandra, he never told me about you and never whispered your name in bed either, so I had no idea of your existence!"' I was struggling for breath as I gasped through the sobs. Francesca and Jenny watched me carefully.

'Does he see me as such a mouse? He flaunts his girlfriend in front of me and I'm supposed to just lie down and die! All along he knew I was falling for him and he knew he was staying with her and he never, ever tried to tell me anything, no hint, never!' I blew my nose. 'Do you know what? I did lie down and die, didn't I? I was a mouse . . . not much of a mouse, I didn't even squeak! I said nothing. I acted like there was nothing between us. I let him get away with it. Why am I such a pushover? I'm so pathetic!'

'Lori, you are not pathetic or a pushover.' Francesca sat down beside me on the bed and put her arm round me.

'Making a scene wouldn't have done any good,' added Francesca.

'It may have given you some satisfaction, though,' said Jenny, giggling at the thought. 'You could have embarrassed the hell out of him and got him in deep water with his girlfriend. Maybe you would have felt better but, on the other hand, maybe you would have felt foolish in the end, like you'd let yourself down too.'

'I feel foolish anyway I've been a complete idiot. I ignored the signs. All those times you told me something must be wrong and I chose to ignore it.' I blew my nose again. 'What an idiot I've been. What a total idiot.'

***

I hugged Beppe so tightly that he could hardly breathe. He wriggled out of my arms.

'Bye, Mamma.' He climbed into the back of the car next to a pile of his toys and books. For some reason, Alberto seemed to want to take practically all the children's things with them. He had arrived the night before and was now preparing to drive straight back down to Calabria.

'Why take so much stuff?' I asked. 'They're going to be outside most of the time, on the beach, cycling around, why do they need so many toys and books? And winter clothes! Alberto, it's summer! You can pick up whatever else they need when you come to collect me after my next chemo.'

Colour me in

Alberto spoke quietly. The sight of my scarved head and black, baggy eyes seemed to make him careful around me. His voice was tight, like an impatient teacher trying not to lose his temper with a pupil. 'I may as well take as much as I can now, so there's less to take later.' I looked at him, the caring, flexible Alberto was not easy to discern in this quiet, tense one.

I didn't want to make a scene so I walked into the flat. I found Michela in the bedroom trying to pull the zip shut on her suitcase.

'Here, let me give you a hand.' The case was busting at the seams. 'You got enough in there?'

'Well, I packed all the summer things you helped me sort out and then Papà told me to take more jumpers and warm things.'

I opened her case and took out two large jumpers. Between the two of us, we then managed to zip it shut.

'Mamma, what is happening?' Michela looked distressed. 'Papà seems to think we are going to live there forever! I don't want to live at Nonna's, no way!'

'Darling you only have to stay with your grandmother for a while, until things are more . . . normal again.' I sighed maybe I was not being very realistic.

'The plan is to move into the house Papà's Uncle Donato left him as soon as it's ready, it's his dream to live there, you know that.'

'Yes, his dream, no one else's. Mamma you can't let us stay down there!'

'Let's see for now. It doesn't have to be permanent. You just go and have a good summer. We can talk when I come down in a few weeks.'

I wrapped my arms round her. The knot in my stomach suggested to me that Alberto and I had not really made a decision together.

'Mamma, can't I stay with you?'

'It would be no fun staying here in the humidity and the

heat. Come on, it's bad enough now; it will be baking in July and August. You'll have much more fun by the sea.'

'I want you to be okay, Mamma and I don't want to leave you.'

'This is best, my darling. You'll be fine there. Zia Rosanna has said you can stay at theirs some of the time with all your cousins.' When she was little, Michela had had a big crush on her cousin Rocco. He was Rosanna's youngest and had been about ten at the time. Michela had followed him everywhere. He was now twenty and for the last couple of summers she had complained that she never saw him. He worked in a bar and when he wasn't working he was always out with his friends. Michela caught my smile and blushed.

'Oh Mamma, I grew out of that years ago. Will Antonella be down too?' Antonella was Alberto's younger sister. I was pleased that she would be staying with her mother too for much of the holidays, she was great with the children and they loved her very much.

'Yes, she will, I think she's planning to be there for most of August.'

'Can I come back when the summer is over and go back to school?' I didn't know what to say. Alberto and I hadn't really worked anything out at all. Poor Michela had said goodbye to her school friends for the summer not knowing when she would see them again.

'We'll talk on the phone tonight, okay? You call me when you get there.'

I found myself missing her already and prayed that I'd be able to make it down to see her and Beppe before my chemo ended at the end of the summer. It would depend on how strong I felt between cycles and as each one seemed to lay me lower than the one before, I wasn't very hopeful.

Alberto came in and picked up Michela's case. 'We'd better get going.' He carried the case out. I looped my arm through Michela's and we walked out of the flat together.

Colour me in

The car was packed up and the boot closed. Beppe was sitting in the back. He rolled his window down and let me give him a last kiss.

'Mamma.'

'Yes, Beppe.'

'I left my face paints for you. They're in my bedroom, on the desk.'

'Oh darling . . ..' I hugged him as best I could through the window. There were tears in my eyes.

I watched Alberto get in the driver's seat. He said he would call when they arrived. I wondered why I felt so distant from him. The night we had agreed that he would accept the transfer, even though my chemo-induced lack of sex drive had meant that we just cuddled together, we had felt closer than we had in a long time and I had hoped that the closeness would last. But now I felt further from him than ever. Maybe the geographical distance had contributed to it. He seemed tense and afraid of something. I didn't know what.

***

The sky is coming along okay. I'm going to extend it all around the four walls. I love the feeling of outdoors it gives. The sea seems to look more natural with a sky above it. I do need to touch it up a little, though. As I look at it closely I can see places where there is some white wall showing through. When I have finished the sky I can start on the jungle.

The cat has gone out, possibly fed up since I cleared my picnic lunch away. It's been nice working with her curled up nearby.

***

The church clock struck three. My skin felt twitchy and tense against the sheets. I felt so uncomfortable in it I could barely lay still, and my legs felt rigid as if there were metal rods in them.

Immediately after chemo I usually felt quite hyper and

buzzy, unable to keep still, as if I were on speed. Then I'd come crashing down into sleep the next day. I had gone through that process; it was now Saturday night, but it was as if the sleeplessness of the first night had returned. I had slept for just an hour, to then wake up rigidly alert. I watched thin shafts of light from the slightly open blinds slanting across the ceiling. I heard a car in the street below. I felt a creeping tightness down the skin of my legs and my arms twitching continuously.

I said out loud, 'I'm sorry body; it's not your fault you feel so bad. I did this to you. I inflicted this tumour on you. I'm so sorry.' I had an increasingly strong feeling that my body and I were separate people and that the cancer was all my fault. I had a huge sense of guilt and couldn't help feeling that I should have avoided this somehow.

The restless tension took over and I had to get up. I wandered into the kitchen and got myself a glass of water.

I sat down at the kitchen table. Just before she left, Michela had been making her friend Daniela a birthday card. Cards are not given as much here as they are in Britain. Michela is currently fascinated by British customs, claiming her half Britishness; so she now makes cards for all her friends' birthdays. Paper, card and paint were still on the table, tidied into piles but not put away.

I picked up one of her paintbrushes and dipped it into my glass of water. The pallet hadn't been washed. I swished the wet brush around in some green paint on the pallet, pulled a sheet of blank paper in front of me and began to paint. It came out in swirls; clean green swirls, too clean, reminding me of the green coats the nurses wore. I shuddered and went for the red. Bright bloody swirls joined the green. Mixed with some bright pink, it became a fluorescent red, the colour of one of my chemo drugs, the one the nurses referred to as 'Crodino' because it was exactly the colour of the popular Italian aperitif. I needed to find other colours.

Colour me in

There was little left of use on the pallet so I began opening tubes of paint and squeezing little worms of colour onto a clean plate. The paper was soon covered. I put it to one side and picked up another sheet and began to cover it with colour. I made some shapes this time, vaguely animal like. Soon that sheet, too, was full, so I picked up another and filled it, this time turning to flowers for inspiration. I filled another and another and then went to the living room and took a ream of paper out from under the printer and began to cover sheet after sheet.

I can't tell you what I was thinking while I painted. My whole body moved with my arm. I was totally involved. It was like a drug; the need for colour and brightness took me over completely.

The sun was up and the birds were singing when I finally came to and looked in wonder at what I saw around me. Every surface in the kitchen was covered with drying A4 sheets of paper, covered in pictures of suns, moons, snakes, flowers, exotic birds and animals. It was as if I were seeing them for the first time, like a drunk coming out of a stupor and seeing the havoc she had wreaked.

I paced around the kitchen, examining my paintings with amazement. I made myself a coffee and took it onto the balcony and stared at the rooftops. A steady hum of traffic was already floating up from the road below. I felt calm, much calmer than I had in ages. I put the coffee cup down and had a good stretch. It felt good. My skin was lying better on my body, the twitching had stopped and the rods in my legs were no longer quite so stiff. I felt a great sense of release.

***

One morning, a week or so after the barbecue, I answered the phone to the man from the train now recast as the man who had squashed my foot.

'Hello, could I speak to Lori, please?' I felt like chuckling at the very careful way he pronounced my name.

'Yes, it's me.'

'Oh hello, it's Alberto. Do you remember, the clumsy idiot who trod on your foot?'

'Yes, I remember.'

'I telephoned before Easter but maybe you didn't get my message.'

It came back to me then. Maria had given me a scrap of paper with 'Alberto called' written on it but I had put it down somewhere and forgotten about it.

'I'm afraid I didn't. Messages tend to go astray in this house,' I lied, trying to sound light and cheery.

'Oh that's okay. It's the same in our house, always chaos when you get students together.' He was trying to sound light and cheery, too. 'Well,' he continued, 'I was wondering if you could give me some lessons I have to do an exam in English.'

'Okay, when is the exam?' I was getting used to students ringing at the last minute expecting you to fill their heads with perfect English in just a few days.

'I haven't booked for it yet. I can do it next September or, if not, the following January. It's quite difficult, you have to read a book about some aspect of politics or economics. I'm not absolutely sure which book I have to do yet but they are hard. I don't even know basic English. There is a written exam where you have to fill in the right grammar in the right spaces and then you have to answer questions on the book in an aural exam.'

'Wow, it sounds tough! Have you ever studied English?'

'No, I only did French at school.'

'My goodness, how ridiculous! Fancy expecting you to do all that?'

'We do have lessons. In fact it's easier to pass the exams if you go to the lessons.'

'I'm sure it is.'

'But the lessons are not enough. I desperately need help. Can you help me?'

Colour me in

'Well, I'll give it a go.'

'How much do you charge for a lesson?'

'For poor students it's 10.000 lira an hour.' That would have been around £3.50 at the time.

'Okay, that's fine.'

'You'll need to get a copy of the book you have to study.'

'I'll get that next week. In the meantime we could start with grammar. I think I need you to go through all the tenses one by one. I get them all muddled up.'

We arranged a lesson for the following day, as he was keen to start.

***

Francesca was chattering as she always does when nervous.

'I can't help wondering whether I really am addicted to chocolate or whether I can have the odd bit or the odd bar even, without craving another one a little while later, or is it inevitable that the odd one will always lead to . . ..'

'Damn!' The nurse looked up. I winced. He hadn't found the vein again.

'I'm sorry.' The young male nurse pulled the needle out of my left arm. This was my fifth chemo.

They always use my left arm. I no longer have any lymph nodes on my right side because they removed them with the lump from my breast. As it turned out, they were clear of any cancer cells, but it was too late, they can't be put back in again. Before having surgery I had asked Dottoressa Calchi if I could have them tested so that they didn't need to be removed if they were clear. I had heard that other surgeons did this. She totally pooh-poohed the idea, 'Oh no, we don't do that.' I didn't know enough to argue with her. So they had been removed pointlessly: It was cheaper and less time-consuming, I suppose, than testing them first.

The young male nurse had another needle ready. He tried to look cheerful. 'Let's try again.' The search for a good vein gets harder as you go along, with chemo every three weeks, the three tubes of blood they take that morning plus the blood tests in between chemos and all the tests prior to the operation. My poor veins, and they had a long way to go yet.

I stared out of the window trying to ignore the needle pricks. I could smell Francesca's perfume as she leant towards me and took my right hand. It was a familiar, reassuring smell. I tried breathing slowly in, slowly out.

'Done it! There we are.' The nurse grinned proudly. The needle was in, ready for more chemo. This time the delights of a drug I had not had before called Taxol, which was to take three hours to get into my system.

***

I'd almost forgotten the birds, the ones for the seascape. I've finished the sky and being so caught up in the idea of painting a jungle, forgot my birds. Painting birds is very frustrating, I really struggle to capture their sense of movement and freedom, but I must keep trying. I'll start by painting two birds on the rocks. I'll do them a bit like seagulls but colourful, a kind of cross between a bird of paradise and a seagull.

***

Alberto didn't have a flair for languages but he was methodical and worked hard. The book we had to study, about changing economic systems, was even quite interesting in places. After the lesson finished we chatted for a few minutes. He told me about his village in Calabria and the characters that populated it. He came from a family of four children where he was the only boy and was clearly doted on by his mother.

He asked me lots of questions about my family and I found it surprisingly easy to tell him about my difficult relationship with my father. He said that he thought my father sounded very like his mother.

'My mother is very traditional. She was born before the Second World War, when we still had a fascist government in this country. Her family were very poor. She had to leave

Colour me in

school when she was only seven years old to help her mother in the house. She had to get up at five o'clock to make the coffee and breakfast for her father and brothers who went to work in the fields. Her brothers would come back at seven thirty and go to school. They had to walk across the fields to get there for eight. She stayed at home to clean the house and prepare lunch for them all after school and work.'

'Wow, that must have been tough, tough for all of them.'

'It was a very hard life, very difficult making a living from the land. My grandfather worked from dawn to dusk.'

'Did he make enough to feed his family just from growing vegetables?'

'Not really, he sold any excess in the market but it was really difficult, then at some point his brother, Umberto, my Great Uncle, got a job on the railway as a ticket collector going up and down to Milan. He had a little plot of land, so my grandfather took over his land and produced enough vegetables for my great uncle's family as well and had a bit extra to sell too. I think his brother gave him some money sometimes, but he didn't have much. Great Uncle Umberto also had vines, and they used to make wine. I remember when I was little helping them pick the grapes in the autumn. I think more went in my mouth than in the basket!' he laughed. 'My grandfather could be fierce; he would beat his sons if they didn't work when he told them to. Any time they were not at school they had to work. My mother will not suffer fools gladly, she believes fervently in God and what she calls traditional values.'

'So does she think a woman's place is in the home?'

'Well, to a certain extent, yes, women have to know how to cook and keep the house nice for the men when they come home, but she's not against women studying and having a career. In fact she and Papà argued when my sister Sara wanted to go to university. It was Mamma who fought for her to go, even though they couldn't afford it. She was always determined that I would go to university. Being a boy, I have to get a good job.' It sounded as though that weighed quite heavily on his shoulders.

'Did Sara go to university?'

'Yes, she did. She graduated two years ago and has now qualified as a teacher.' He sounded really proud of her. 'She's the bright one in the family she finds studying much easier than I do. If she'd been a boy, she'd probably have done engineering or something.'

'Couldn't she have done that?'

'Papà drew the line at that. He had a problem with her going to university in the first place. Even Mamma wanted her to do something acceptable for women, like teaching.'

'My dad wanted me to be a lawyer.'

'Really?'

'Yes, he wanted my brother and I to get 'good jobs', even me, but then I have to marry another lawyer or doctor and have babies who will become lawyers and doctors. Nothing else is really good enough.'

'Not even studying languages?'

'Well, he has accepted it as a compromise; really I think because he realised I wasn't bright enough to become a lawyer. What I really wanted to do was art.'

'And he didn't let you?'

'Oh no! Art is just for self-indulgent hippy types. He wasn't going to allow his daughter to live that kind of life.' Frustration seeped into my voice.

'You wish you could do art?'

'Yes, I do. Oh, I suppose languages are okay and I'm glad I came to Italy.' Although now my heart was broken, I wasn't sure.

After Alberto left, I sat at my desk and put my head in my hands and had a good cry. Why did Leo have to have a girlfriend? If he'd been single things would have been different. I felt very muddled about everything. I wanted to talk to Leo and at the same time I didn't. I quite fancied

Colour me in

going back to England and leaving my broken heart behind, but the thought of going back to my parents, having failed to finish the year and face my father's anger, deterred me from that path. Only three more months to go and I'd be done with this country.

Chapter 11

I couldn't stop giggling. Francesca was standing a few stairs below me. Her anxious expression had melted into laughter.

'Oooh this marble is lovely and cool,' I said between giggles as I eased myself down onto the next stair.

'At this rate we may get to the ice-cream kiosk before it closes tonight,' laughed Francesca. 'We've got about three hours!'

The doctor had very casually warned me that Taxol might attack muscles. Well, it certainly had attacked mine. We live on the fifth floor of a building without a lift and my aching leg muscles had really suffered as I tried to hobble down, so I had opted for the alternative bum-sliding method, with hilarious results.

'Thank goodness I'm well cushioned,' I laughed.

'I wish I had a camera,' Francesca managed through the giggles.

'I'm really glad you haven't got one.'

Eventually, after much puffing, panting and giggling, we reached the bottom and Francesca helped me to my feet. The hobble down the road to the ice-cream kiosk was slow, especially as I tried not to lean on Francesca too heavily, but eventually we got there and I gratefully settled myself at a table under one of the umbrellas by the kiosk.

'It feels as if we have just crossed the jungle and fought a few lions to get here,' laughed Francesca. I was grateful for her good humour.

'Well, what flavours do you fancy?' she asked.

'I'll have mango, lemon and fruits of the forest, please.' You could have three flavours in one cone and I ordered all the most refreshing ones. In cooler climes I usually stuck to coffee and chocolate, but it was too hot for them.

In the days immediately after chemotherapy, a trip to the ice cream kiosk was usually the first outing I could manage and if I got there by Saturday evening, I was happy. Today was Sunday. Everything was taking a little longer now, so I was very glad to be out. Francesca came back with the ice creams. Suddenly a serious shadow crossed her face.

'What is it?'

'I've been so stupid.' She looked really worried. 'We've got you all the way down here without thinking about how on earth we're going to get you back up all those stairs.'

'We'll cross that bridge . . ..' It had occurred to me that it may be a struggle but I had been so keen to get out that I had decided to worry about it later. 'I can go really slowly, one step at a time. I reckon that, well-lubricated by ice cream and maybe a beer or two later, I'll be okay.'

'Mmmm.' Francesca didn't seem convinced. Then she brightened up again. 'Of course, why didn't I think of it? We can always go back to mine.'

'Oh right, you're on the ground floor.'

'Yes, I think it would be best, give your aching muscles a rest. I can pop up to yours and get whatever you need. It would give you a change of scenery.'

'That would be really nice and it means you'll be at home. I've been keeping you away all this time.'

'That's not a problem, Lori, you know it isn't, but from mine you could go out whenever you wanted, instead of worrying about all the stairs. You could stay there until your legs hurt less.'

'Thank you Francesca, I'd like that. All I need is my night shirt, sponge bag, change of clothes, clean underwear and my paints.'

'I was looking at some of your paintings. They are really good,' said Francesca. 'Does painting help you?'

I nodded, not sure if I could explain how. I took a long lick of my ice cream, while I tried to find words. 'There is a lot . . . of tension in me right now,' I said.

'Well, that's hardly surprising,' said Francesca.

'I often feel as though I don't belong in my own skin, really restless and twitchy and tense. Sometimes I feel as if I could explode.' Francesca was listening intently.

'At the same time I don't have the energy to actually explode.'

'I'm glad about that,' she managed a smile.

'I don't have the energy to run or walk much or ease the tension that way, so it explodes onto the paper. When I paint, the tension comes out and spreads itself in colour flat before me. It's out where I can see it and it's less scary.'

'Wow! That's amazing!' said Francesca.

To me it didn't feel amazing, so much as essential.

'Have you spoken to Alberto lately?' she asked. I nodded.

'He called yesterday to see how I was, when you were out getting provisions.' I smiled. Francesca was so good; she had bought me my favourite pasta and chocolate cake 'for those moments when you really need cheering up.' She knew exactly how to be supportive.

'He says the children are fine, loving it down there. Beppe is, I know, but I worry about Michela, although she sounded okay when I spoke to her. She's been going to the beach with friends most days. Alberto gets her older cousins to keep an eye on her. I guess they're fine.' I sigh, 'I miss them.'

'How are things . . . between you and Alberto?' asked Francesca tentatively. 'I know it's difficult at a distance.'

'Okay, well . . . it's hard to tell, to be honest. I want to feel close, safe, protected. He used to make me feel like that. I hate this distance. He says he misses me but I can't tell if he really does. Truth is, we were a bit . . . distant from each other before the cancer.'

Francesca nodded, 'I remember you saying that.'

'Yeah, well . . . when I was diagnosed he seemed so supportive at first but it didn't last long. Now I don't know. He's so far away, in so many ways . . ..'

'I think he really wanted to be supportive,' said Francesca, 'I think he wanted to make everything okay for you and found that he couldn't.'

'Yeah, I guess. I really only wanted him to hold my hand

Colour me in

and listen and take care of the children. Why was that so hard?'

'People react differently to these things, don't they?' She leant over and squeezed my hand, the one not holding the ice cream. 'I know everyone says that and I know it's hard not having him here but . . ..'

'Do you know, in some ways it isn't,' I interrupted her. 'In some ways it's easier having just myself to worry about and being able to put Alberto on hold between phone calls. There are times when I really need a hug.' Francesca nods. 'But I get lots of hugs from my friends, plus I get understanding from them.' I felt the cool ice cream slide down my throat.

***

Alberto stood at the front door holding a bunch of flowers. I was still in my dressing gown. He was half an hour early for a 10 o'clock lesson, which was early enough for me anyway. I stared at him sleepily for a moment, not sure what to do.

'These are for you,' Beaming, he thrust them into my hands.

'Ah, thank you. What a surprise!' I stared at the flowers completely taken aback. 'Um, I'll get a vase.' I began to walk to the kitchen, then remembered Alberto in the doorway. 'Come in, Alberto.' I dug around in the cupboards until I found a vase, filled it with water and plonked the flowers rather unceremoniously into it. 'Well, they're lovely thank you.' I felt myself blushing and I didn't want to blush.

'Look, um, could you wait here? I'll go and get dressed. You're half an hour early, you know.' I ducked out of the room realising that I sounded a bit peeved. Why had he brought me flowers? I worried that it may be more than just an apple for the teacher.

***

'I feel sick, I feel sick, I feel sick!' It was my voice. The room was zooming in and zooming out. Millions of tiny bubbles were dancing before my eyes. The nurse, having hooked up the drip, had just reached the door. She came running back, shooing out the visitors, including my poor mother who had come over to be with me for my sixth chemo. Her horrified expression is still imprinted on my memory.

My face felt hot and prickly as if it were bursting out of its skin. Oh my God, I'm swelling up, like the incredible hulk. Such a weird feeling! The tiny bubbles were all still there, floating in their thousands before my eyes. A nurse brought a bowl and I gratefully threw up.

I could feel a blurry whirl of activity around me. The bubbles still floated in front of me and I couldn't stop being sick. It seemed like ages before it all finally subsided and, as I lay back on the pillows, exhausted, the room gradually stopped spinning. The nurse was hooking me up to another bottle that I later learnt was cortisone to calm down the reaction. Gradually it did; slowly the bubbles floated away.

Gradually the buzz subsided as the room emptied out, leaving just us three patients. I closed my eyes, finally feeling a kind of calm.

Dr Mori came into the room and gently asked me how I was. He told me I'd had a 'toxic reaction to the Taxol'. He suggested that my immune system was maybe too strong and had therefore rejected the drug.

'Surely that's a good thing?' I asked 'Surely it means I don't need it anymore.' He was non-committal about that and said he was going to talk to my mother to reassure her that I was okay. I thought that was kind but I supposed it was part of his job, and a chance to practice his English. He left the room and I closed my eyes again grateful to be in bed, my body felt very strange and totally exhausted. I so hoped that I would never have to have chemo again as I didn't know how I could possible cope with it. I felt sure that my body was saying, 'Enough, I don't need this any more.' Mum popped her head around the door for a few seconds and then disappeared again.

The Doctor reappeared after a while. 'Ah, you're returning to normal'.

'What's normal?' I asked, managing philosophy in my blurry state.

'Well, you were bright red before,' he explained. 'You're more of a pink now.'

'Bright red? Really? I know I was swollen, but red? I didn't know.'

'It's calming down now,' he said. 'You'll be okay. I'm going to talk to Dr Crispi, about your further treatment.' Doctor Crispi was Head of Oncology.

'I really don't think I need any more,' I managed to say as he left the room.

Mum's head appeared round the door. Slowly she stepped into the room, hardly able to look at me.

'Mum, am I really red?'

She hesitated, 'You were earlier, dear, very red. You've calmed down a bit now.' She tried to smile.

'Am I swollen and puffy?'

Mum nodded, 'Very much so, I'm afraid.'

I'm trying to build up a picture. 'So I was bright red and swollen and puffy?'

'Just like a red Michelin man.'

I was horrified but managed a chuckle. 'Thanks, Mum, I get the picture.' I motioned to the chair next to me where she had been sitting before. I wanted her to sit down, hold my hand and be there quietly while I tried to settle and feel real again, whatever that was. She came and sat down, getting used to the sight of my swollen, puffy face. I held out my hand and she took it in hers.

'Well your timing was unfortunate,' I grinned. 'Of all the cycles of chemo you could have picked, you had to pick this one!'

'It sounds strange but I'm glad to be here.' She squeezed my hand again. 'Listen darling, I was thinking, perhaps I'll go and ring Jenny. It would be nice if she could come here.'

'Why?'

'We need support.'

'Do we need support?' I wondered. Mum paused and then swallowed, looking a bit pink-eyed.

'Well, we know her. She's a familiar face and someone I can talk to.' I realised through my fug that she felt very isolated, not being able to understand what people were saying, and she must have been very frightened.

'Fine, that's a good idea ring Jenny,' I agreed. She slowly got up and moved out of the ward. I felt guilty that she had had to witness this.

***

These paradise seagulls look much better than my last attempt at a bird of paradise. I have painted two of them standing proudly on the rocks, gazing at each other as if in conversation, or maybe they're in love. If only I could paint my own love story.

***

A Buddhist monk stared at me from the mirror. A friend had once brought me back a caftan from Tunisia. It wasn't orange but one of the pale grey ones the men wore. It was perfect for the sticky August heat. I had changed into it as soon as we got home from the hospital. I looked at the bald, puffy-faced creature with black bags under her eyes looking back at me, definitely more like a Buddhist monk than anything else. At least the tomato-faced Michelin man look had finally worn off. I really must put a big towel over this mirror.

The doctors had decided that after the reaction I had had enough chemo and didn't need any more. I was over the moon, no more chemo, hurray!

So why did I feel so heavy? I wanted to feel happy and rejoice but couldn't.

I picked up the phone and dialled my mother-in-law's number. It was seven in the evening. They should be back

Colour me in

from the beach by now.

'Pronto,' it was Michela's voice. Bless her; she must have been waiting for the call.

'Hello, darling, it's me.'

'Mamma, how are you? How did the chemo go?'

'Well . . ..' I felt sick thinking about it. I focused on a photograph of the children I had hung on the wall opposite the telephone. Michela was about eight and Beppe just one. Michela had a broad almost angelic smile on her face and little Beppe was looking up at her with what seemed like adoration in his eyes. It was a beautiful photo and never failed to cheer me up.

'The good news is, I don't have to do chemo any more!'

'Really? Wow Mamma, that's great! Are you coming here, then?'

'Yes, I'll come in a few days. I need to get my strength back first.' As I sat on the chair in the hallway by the phone, I felt that restless tension in my legs again. It seemed to spread to my arms and throughout my whole body. It was hard to stay still. I felt twitchy all over, tense and heavy. I had an overwhelming longing to cry. I focused hard on Michela's words as she talked cheerfully about the trip she'd been on a few days before with some of her cousins.

'Oh Mamma, I'm so glad you're coming. But why have they stopped your chemo? Are you okay? Has it worked?'

I had to smile. 'I expect it has worked but I had a reaction to it. I was sick so I think that means my body rejected it and doesn't need it any more.'

'Oh Mamma that must have been horrible, are you feeling okay now?'

'Yes, thanks, I'm fine now and glad it's over.'

'That's great news; thank god you don't have to have it any more. It must mean you're getting better, mustn't it?'

'Yes, I'm sure it does.'

'Is Granny still with you?'

'Yes, she's here until next Tuesday. If I'm feeling okay,

I'll probably come down a few days after she goes.'

'Oh good, I miss you, Mamma.'

'I miss you too, darling. Is Papà around? I need to talk to him and is Beppe there?'

'Beppe is, I'll tell him to get Papà and then you can speak to them both.'

'Fine.' My mother had come into the hallway.

'In the meantime, darling, your grandmother would like to talk to you.' I handed my mother the receiver and stood up trying to stretch out the tension in my limbs.

***

As the first impact of the pain over Leo softened and spread into a more general depression, I badly wanted to know if he had really cared about me or whether it had all been an act. I could not really believe that it had just been superficial fun for him; it had all felt very real to me. But Leo could be distant sometimes, maybe that was guilt over Cassandra it all made so much more sense now.

I fantasised about seeing him, going over and over the conversation in my head. Playing it out night after night as I lay in bed. In my favourite version of the fantasy, Leo realised that he couldn't live without me and was willing to finish with Cassandra. All I had to do was find it in my heart to forgive him, and somehow I did.

In the cold light of day, though, I asked myself if Leo would ever be trustworthy. Would I want a relationship with someone so sought-after and popular that I felt in competition with everyone else for his attention?

I finally realised that I had to try and see him. There was no way I felt able to ring him so I enlisted Sandro's help. I asked him to arrange to meet Leo for a coffee one morning and I went instead.

The expression on Leo's face was not really surprise, more pained resignation. My stomach turned over. He hardly looked at me. The silver-tongued charm had disappeared.

Colour me in

I couldn't think of anything to say. All those nocturnal practices had been for nothing. Luckily the barman turned to me and asked what I wanted. I ordered a cappuccino and Leo asked for an espresso. I couldn't stomach a pastry. We stood in silence until the coffees were placed on the counter. I took a sip of my cappuccino and finally found my voice.

'Well, now you can tell me about your relationship with Cassandra.' I was amazed at how calm and collected I sounded. Leo looked as if he were about to say, 'It's none of your business,' but he didn't. His face softened a little. 'Look, Lori, things got out of hand. I didn't mean things to happen between us as they did.' A chill went right through me. I'd just been a big mistake to him. To make it worse, Leo added, 'I shouldn't have done it, I know.'

I didn't want to cry in front of him. I kept telling myself, 'Don't cry, do not cry.' I managed to look up at Leo and say as calmly as I could, trying to keep the shake out of my voice, 'So I was just something you weren't supposed to do?' He didn't reply. I stood in front of him clutching my coffee cup. Leo finished his coffee and pulled his wallet out of his pocket.

I had to say something. I cleared my throat but my voice still came out squeaky, 'Leo, I don't understand. Why did you turn up with her at a barbecue that you and I had planned together?' Silence. 'Why didn't you at least tell me? Turning up with her like that was a horrible thing to do.'

'I had no choice. She'd arranged to go away with friends for Easter but their plans changed at the last minute so she was home. I had to bring her.'

'Why didn't you call to warn me?'

'I didn't know what to do. I didn't know which way would be . . . least bad for you.' The tears were threatening again.

'I should have called,' said Leo. I managed to nod. My fantasy was not going to happen. He called the barman over and paid for the coffees.

I picked up my bag. I would have liked to say something profound, something he would remember forever, but of course nothing came to mind.

'Goodbye, Leo.'

'Goodbye, Lori.' I glanced back as I turned out of the door. He looked sad.

Chapter 12

Everything looked muted. Colours looked paler, greys looked greyer, even the beautiful medieval redbrick looked faded. The colour had drained out of the sky and the flowers looked washed out.

I was standing in a big square near the centre of town. It was essentially a car park surrounded by tall buildings. I looked up at the big grey building in front of me, it jarred against the soft redbrick medieval buildings surrounding it. Built during fascism, it was sharp and austere.

'I'd paint it blue,' I said. 'A fresh sky blue.' I stepped away from the building so that I could look up at it more easily. I was standing in front of a row of parked cars. A couple walked passed me.

'That's it!' As I craned my neck, it came to me. 'Birds. I will paint birds, flying across the blue sky.' What a wonderful idea. 'They could be any sort of bird. They could be big birds, colourful birds, birds of paradise.' A woman stopped and stared at me. Perhaps I'd been talking out loud.

'Are you all right?' she asked. I nodded. She walked away, glancing back at me once or twice. I don't know what she'd thought I'd do.

'There could be a whole flock of birds of paradise, flying down from the top floor to the bottom,' I said, more quietly this time.

I decided to go home. My mother had returned to England and Francesca, who had stayed with me for a couple of days after she had gone, was at work. I'd told her I would be okay on my own now, but I'm not sure she was convinced.

I walked into the flat, desperate for colour. I couldn't paint that big grey building but I had to paint something. There were piles of my pictures on the kitchen table and on the work surfaces. I didn't want to paint on a small sheet of paper. I looked at the kitchen wall. It was a nasty, dirty mustard colour. It had been that colour before we moved in and I had always wanted to change it. We had some white left over from doing the bedroom so I hunted it out. We had one expanse of wall over the kitchen table with no cupboards, shelves or kitchen implements hanging on it. I pulled the table away, stood on a chair and started covering it. The white was lovely and clean, but colourless. I opened a cupboard door and pulled out my treat to myself, a box of acrylic paints and new brushes of different sizes.

My bird of paradise had blurred edges because I was too impatient to wait for the white background paint to dry completely. I wanted to paint him swooping down to the table from the ceiling. I started with a beautiful crimson and then added bright azure blue followed by a brilliant green. How lovely to have such colourful feathers!

After a while I climbed down from the table and stepped back to the other side of the room to see my handiwork. My bird of paradise looked very bright, but lopsided rather than magnificent, and he seemed to be heading for a crash landing rather than flying. Nothing like the glorious, proud bird I had in my head. My arms ached. I sat down, feeling deflated. Then the tears came.

When I heard the door buzzer I got the impression it had been buzzing for some time and I hadn't registered it. I struggled to my feet and went to press the intercom button. Francesca's voice floated out of it so I pressed the button to let her in. I heard another voice, which sounded like Simona. I hunted for a tissue to dry my eyes. I wasn't sure whether I was pleased they had come or not.

Francesca took one look at my blotchy face and engulfed me in a hug. As I came out of it I heard a gasp from Simona. She was staring at my bird. Francesca looked up and gasped too. They both stared, speechless. I slumped onto a chair at the kitchen table, which I had moved away from the wall so that I could paint.

'Shall I make coffee?' asked Francesca, reaching for the coffee machine. I nodded.

Colour me in

'You're painting a mural,' Simona spoke at last. 'It's very colourful.'

'It is that.' I managed a pale, rueful grin. 'It hasn't turned out as I wanted. I was aiming for a bird of paradise.'

'Oh I don't know, it's very exotic,' said Simona. She looked a little awkward, then added 'Lori, this probably isn't a good time to bring this up . . . don't you think you should have the x-ray to check the lumps on your lungs before you go down to Calabria? Didn't they tell you to have it done after the chemo had ended to see if that had changed them at all?'

I sat at the table wringing my hands. I looked up at my awkward wonky bird. My bubble began to wrap round me. I hadn't felt it for a while. Simona was talking and I didn't want to hear her words.

'Honey, I'm sure everything is okay. You will feel better knowing, surely? And if it isn't, then the sooner you get the lumps removed, the better.' I loved Simona, but I wished my bubble could blot her out.

'Would you like me to ring the hospital?' I managed to shake my head slowly.

'No, its okay, I'll ring the nurse at Ospedale Maggiore. She will get me the appointment.'

Simona leant over and touched my hand. 'Lori, I don't mean to hassle you but . . ..'

'I know, it's okay, I'll do it.' I managed a watery smile.

I wanted to sink back into my bubble and be left alone.

Francesca turned on the gas under the coffee pot and looked up at my bird.

'You know what you said to me before about tension? Well you must have released some here.'

'I suppose I did but I felt bad because it's not what I saw in my head.' The distress returned as I spoke. 'I couldn't get it to be the proud, soaring, free-flying, strong, beautiful bird that I wanted.'

'Well, I'm sure that, with practice, you will,' said

Francesca.

'I needed a larger space to paint on,' I went on. 'The tension is still building up. There's so much of it, I don't know where to put it and I need to paint more and more on larger and larger spaces.' I swallowed, watching their faces, did this sound crazy?

'I need colour,' I said. 'I have to paint to make up for the lack of colour. I'm colourless and the world around me seems colourless too. The colour seems to have drained out of it.'

Simona looked thoughtful. 'Lori, would you fancy doing art therapy?' she asked. 'An art therapist may be able to help you express some of the tension and other emotions, perhaps help you to understand more about how you're feeling, what's happening inside you.'

I knew she probably had a point, but I didn't want someone else guiding my painting. Even when I disappointed myself, painting was mine and I wanted to keep it.

***

My paradise seagull's eyes have come out a kind of lilac, an unusual colour perhaps but I like them, they suit her. I don't know why I think of this one as female but I do. She's deep purple with pink tips on her wings and a white beak. Her eyes seem to be looking at the male seagull, but he's gazing out to sea and, although they are standing very close, he doesn't seem to be aware of her.

***

'Oh Jen, you're kidding me. Don't tell me you're trying to get me to come on a blind date.'

'Well, it's not exactly a blind date. You don't have to go out with him or anything, just come along.' I wondered why people couldn't just leave me alone to be miserable over Leo.

'Jen, I'm glad you've met someone you like. I'm really pleased for you, but why can't you go out with him on your own, on a normal date?'

'We only met a few days ago. We spent the evening chatting in La Vareda with friends and he's really nice but I don't want to go on a real date yet. I want to make it casual.' She looked me straight in the eyes. 'I really like him but I don't know if he fancies me or not. Lori, please, I would feel more relaxed if you were there. It's a concert, so there'll be loads of people we know. You won't even need to talk to his friend. We'll all be listening to the music and dancing.'

'Okay, of course I'll come,' I agreed. 'You deserve to meet someone nice. Have you met Carlo's friend?'

'No, I haven't, but if he's anything like Carlo, he'll be lovely.'

'You've got it bad, girl.'

'He's great. Not drop dead gorgeous, but nice and sweet and funny and clever and we've got loads in common. He's also studying languages and he loves skiing.'

'Since when did you love skiing?'

'Well, I've never had the chance to go but I'm sure I could love it.'

***

It was the last week in August and the weather was still hot and sticky. I arrived at Bologna station at nine-thirty in the morning and already I could feel beads of sweat trickling down my back. It would be good to get out of the city.

I tried to focus on Alberto's village and feel happy about going there but every time I saw his mother's house in my mind's eye, the chemo sickness feeling came back again. The antidote was to focus on the children. I kept a picture of them in my head.

My train was due on platform three, heading down to Reggio Calabria. Francesca had bought my ticket for me at the travel agent's near my house. The platform was packed. I was glad it was a Eurostar train and that I had a seat booked. When the train came, it seemed to take me ages to struggle down the corridor with my suitcase and find a place to stash it behind a nearby seat.

I got lots of stares. I was wearing my lovely blue-fringed scarf and had made my eyes up bright blue, with very dark blue eyebrows and I wore bright pink lipstick. I hadn't drawn any other decoration on my face. Very restrained I thought, partly because I was aware that if I sweated the face paints might run and I didn't want to be covered in multicoloured streaks.

Mercifully, the train was air-conditioned and after a while I felt more comfortable. The train started and I dozed off. Every now and again I opened my eyes and looked out of the window at the beautiful Apennine Mountains. I had travelled this route many times but I never tired of gazing at their rugged beauty. I longed to be out on the rocky slopes, peppered with cypress trees, where the air was cooler and fresher than the city and where there was no one to hassle or have expectations of me.

In my shoulder bag I was carrying a picture I had drawn when I was pregnant, the day I'd found out that Michela was a girl. Alberto had dropped me off at home after the scan and had gone to a lecture. When I entered the flat, there on the kitchen table was a packet of felt tip pens one of his flat mates must have been using for colouring something. I had lost the habit of drawing but that day I rummaged in the bag of things I had tucked under our bed and, to my delight, found my old sketchpad. I sat down at the kitchen table, took out the pens and began to draw a fantasy picture of a baby girl, beautiful and happy, surrounded by birds and flowers. Michela really loved it. I often think about framing it and giving it to her. Its happy colours lifted my spirits and reflected the excited anticipation I'd felt when I'd painted it. Sitting on the train, looking at the picture, an idea came to me.

***

I wanted to kill Jenny. How could she do this to me? I

Colour me in

could feel the fury blazing in my eyes as I looked at her.

'You don't listen to me, do you?' I turned on my heels and began to weave my way back through the crowd to the exit.

'Lori, wait!' Jenny was right behind me. She grabbed hold of my arm, which I tried to wrench away from her.

'Leave me alone!'

'I didn't know, Lori, I swear I didn't know that Carlo's friend was Alberto.'

She loosened her grip on my arm and I pulled it away. I tried to carry on towards the exit but the crowd was solid. Jenny wriggled between a few people until she came in front of me and put her hands on my shoulders. 'I told you I didn't know Carlo's friend and I honestly didn't, I swear! Listen, Lori, we arranged it very casually. I said to him, "Let's go to the concert and let's bring friends." Though now I come to think of it, I remember him asking me if my friend was English.'

'Ah, so that's how Alberto knew it would be me.' I felt bitter. 'He and Carlo cooked it up together so I would be forced to go out with Alberto,' I continued angrily.

'I'm sorry I would never have done this to you, really I wouldn't. I know you don't want to go out with Alberto. I would never have forced him on you.'

I calmed down. 'Okay, I guess you wouldn't.'

'Carlo didn't know your feelings about Alberto. How could he? He would just have known that Alberto likes you.'

'So it's down to Alberto's scheming and conniving.'

'He likes you Lori, a lot it seems, even after you turned him down the other day. Maybe he has a dream that one day you'll decide he's the one for you.'

'Oh please.'

'Of course you never have such dreams about anybody!'

'Oh, Jen, that's not fair!'

'Why not? We're all human. He is too, you know.

Different on this end, isn't it?' Maybe she had a point.

'Oh well, okay, let's go and hear the band.' We linked arms and walked back into the throng.

The rest of that night is blurry in my memory. I know I hit the bottle, having decided to have a good time. I do remember being surprised at how groovy Alberto was on the dance floor. He even looked quite cool. I loved the band and I think it was a good night.

The next day Jenny couldn't stop talking about Carlo. He clearly liked her a lot too. I was very happy for her. I also had to admit that Alberto wasn't exactly ugly either, not gorgeous by any stretch of the imagination but lovely big brown eyes, long curly eye lashes and a nice smile.

We ended up going out quite often as a group and I started getting used to Alberto's company. He had a good sense of humour and I warmed to him but still had absolutely no desire to go out with him.

I couldn't get Leo out of my head. Whenever I got ready to go out, I dressed with bumping into him in mind.

***

It came out a little differently from the original picture. Some of the paint colours did not correspond exactly to the colours of the felt tips, but it looked okay. I was really pleased because this was a far greater success than the parrot bird I had painted on the kitchen wall in Bologna. It was quite an emotional process painting it, remembering the hope and joy I had felt knowing that I was going to give birth to a baby girl. This baby Michela looked better than my original drawing I was pleased with it. I added more birds and butterflies than were in the original picture. In fact, I almost covered her bedroom wall with them.

Three weeks had passed since my arrival in Calabria. The weather had cooled down as August turned into September and was much more bearable. I had had the house to myself all morning. Alberto was at work, the children had recently started at local schools and Assunta had gone to the market

Colour me in

with a couple of her friends.

As soon she left the house, I dashed to the local newsagent shop, which sold sketchpads and paints. I bought a really nice set of gouache paints. The make was called Giotto, named after the famous Italian painter of the late thirteenth and early fourteenth century. His murals can be found in a number of chapels and churches in Italy. He developed the most amazingly magical blue. Soon after I first arrived in Bologna as a student I went to Padua to the Arena Chapel (Cappela Scrovegni), which has Giotto frescoes all around the walls, depicting scenes from the life of Christ and the life of The Virgin Mary. One scene, which has always stayed with me, was the visitation of the Virgin Mary, where the Angel is peering into Mary's face, more like a concerned neighbour than an angel. Three other women are standing around looking very calm, one of them pregnant. I felt that the scene had a strange air of normality about it but behind them was that amazing blue. The whole chapel was breathtaking and well worth the hour and a half train journey from Bologna.

These paints seemed to be a sign that I was right to do this. I bought a couple of brushes and back at the house collected an old tin jug of water from the kitchen, then went upstairs to the room Michela was using. It used to be Alberto's younger sister Antonella's room and she still slept there whenever she was back, but she wasn't there just then and I was sure she would not have objected to a mural. My painting style seems to be getting looser so luckily it only took a couple of hours to paint it.

I was just finishing when I heard Assunta come in. I listened for a moment and heard her go straight into the kitchen. Relieved that she hadn't decided to come upstairs I tidied up, cleaned the brushes in the bathroom and then went downstairs to help her with lunch.

Beppe arrived home around five past one. The primary school was close by and he preferred to walk home by himself rather than have me come and meet him. It was nearly half past one by the time Michela arrived. She was full of complaints about her new school.

'The French teacher is useless. She doesn't even know all the verbs herself. She made a mistake this morning. Can you believe it? She speaks so quietly you can hardly hear her and all the kids chatter while she is talking, it's terrible.'

'Not all your teachers are that bad, are they?' I asked, feeling guilty about her having been forced to change schools. Luckily Beppe seemed to be settling well into the village school where he knew most of his classmates from playing together every summer.

'No, some of them are okay,' she sighed.

'You go up and put your things in your room and then come down for lunch,' I suggested.

'I'll wash my hands down here and go up after.'

'No, go up now.'

'Mamma, why?' I could hear the beginnings of protest in Michela's voice.

'Because there is something in your room I'd like you to look at and tell me what you think.'

Curiosity aroused, she ran upstairs, Beppe on her heels. Assunta came in from the back yard where she had been picking tomatoes. 'Where are the children? Why did you let them disappear when lunch is almost ready?'

'They'll be down in a minute.'

'Oh wow, Mamma!' Michela's voice drifted downstairs.

'I want . . . Mamma, I want a picture on my wall. Mamma, you painted a picture for Michela. Can I have one too?' Beppe appeared breathless, having rushed downstairs.

I was about to reply, 'Of course you can,' when I saw my mother-in-law's face.

'A picture?'

'Mamma, come up here.' Michela's voice again.

I walked to the stairs.

'Come and see, Nonna.' I turned to see Beppe take her

by the hand to lead her up the stairs. She looked confused and a little cross at the delay to lunch. They followed me upstairs. As I entered Michela's room she flung her arms round me.

'Mamma, it's amazing. It's thatfantasy picture you drew of me as a baby, isn't it? What a wonderful idea. You're so clever!'

'It's a simple picture. I didn't do anything complicated, otherwise it could have taken weeks.'

Assunta came in, breathing hard from her climb up the stairs. She stared at the wall and then stared at me.

'Nonna, don't you think it's lovely?' asked Michela, 'It's a painting of a drawing Mamma did when she found out I was going to be a girl, all those years ago.' She smiled happily. 'Go on, Nonna, you've got to say it's beautiful.'

'This is Antonella's room. Did you ask her permission?' Michela looked taken aback.

'No, but she'll love it, you know she will and, if not, I'll paint it over when we move out,' I said as calmly as I could, leading the children downstairs.

'Mamma, can I have a painting on my wall, too?' asked Beppe.

'Of course you can, darling,' I replied.

That evening I heard Assunta saying to Alberto, 'She paints everything; the wall in Anotonella's room and now she's going to paint the wall in Beppe's room as well, and she paints herself with all those bright colours. There's something not right with her.' She sighed, 'Oh Alberto, if only you'd married Maria Teresa.'

***

'Are you sure your father has a job for each of us?' Jenny asked Alberto. It was June and the city was already heating up. The term was nearly over and soon we would have to go back to England to start our final year in October.

We were sitting on the edge of the raised pavement in piazza Verde at the centre of the University, basking in the sun. There were students all around us, sitting and sprawling on the pavement. A large black and brown Alsatian, presumably belonging to the guy curled up asleep next to us, was lying in front of our feet.

Carlo and Alberto had come up with a plan to keep us in Italy a little longer. Alberto's father ran a pizzeria on the beach in Calabria and needed extra help throughout the summer.

'I'll check that he hasn't got all the people he needs, but I'm pretty sure he won't have yet.' Alberto spoke fast, sounding a little nervous. 'He will be expecting me and Carlo as usual but he always needs quite a few extra people in August as it's a big place and open all day until the early hours of the morning. Besides, if there are more of us, we won't need to do every night. We can take it in turns with some of the others to have a night off.'

Jenny and I looked at each other. I could tell she was dying to go. She had been fretting about the imminent separation from Carlo and they had been trying to work out how they could stay together as much as possible.

'Well, if there is definitely work, that would be good,' I said, a little cautiously. As I spoke, I realised that this could be the perfect solution. I had been feeling really torn these past few weeks. On the one hand I wanted to run away from the source of my pain and take my broken heart back to England; on the other, I didn't want to spend the summer holidays with my parents. This would be a good way of getting away from Bologna, without going back to England, earning some cash and getting sun and sea into the bargain.

That evening Jenny and I phoned our respective parents to tell them about our plans. They were glad we had work for the summer. My father reminded me that I had to be back for university in October. As if I could forget!

Chapter 13

I stared at the picture I had painted on Michela's bedroom wall. It seemed to anchor me, maybe because it reminded me of my decision to keep her. It took me back to when Alberto and I were working together, sharing something special, sharing imminent parenthood.

I had never felt a sense of belonging in my mother-in-law's house. Sitting in Michela's room looking at the picture gave me the closest to a sense of being at home I had experienced there.

'I thought I would find you here.' Alberto came into the room and stood a little awkwardly in front of me before sitting on the bed beside me.

'You like this picture, don't you?' His voice had the tone of someone who was really trying to understand. I had felt very distant from him since coming down to Calabria. It had been hard to talk. We had both been friendly and pleasant but careful with each other, polite almost. If Alberto shared his mother's horror of my need for colour he hadn't said anything to me. It was nice feeling him sitting next to me on the bed, paying me attention, with no one else around. Even at night, alone, we hardly talked. He would fall asleep straight away and I would lie awake watching the thin shafts of light from the partially open shutters play across the ceiling.

'Yes, I do, I love this picture.'

'Why is that? Why is it so special to you? Does it remind you of when you first drew it, when you were pregnant, or of when she was a baby?'

'It takes me back to both those times, to when we were happy, when we were communicating, talking, being together.' He turned and looked at me.

'Lori, I'm sorry. You've come down here, you're here now and I'm so glad you are.' His words came out like a sigh of relief. 'But . . .' he went on, 'I never really know what to say to you. I . . . you are . . . well, different somehow. I suppose that's not surprising, but I always seem to get it wrong. I'm always afraid that you're not happy here. I've been afraid to ask you . . . I know my mother can be difficult.'

'Alberto, we must talk more . . ..'

'Yes, of course, we must.' Assunta's voice came up the stairs calling us for dinner. I put my hand out towards Alberto. He reached it and gave it a squeeze. I wanted to cry with relief.

***

I think these birds will do for now at least. I've brought the sea inside to cheer me up, to cheer up the room, the house. The children will love it. I'm sure they will.

I need to paint a flying bird. My sky is dry now, waiting for a magnificent bird to spread its wings across it. I really hope I can capture flight this time. I think there are birds pictured in flight in Beppe's book. Last time I tried to paint a bird flying it looked as if it was drunk, floppy and misshapen. It will be much better if I have some pictures as reference.

***

'Two Margaritas and a Four Seasons with extra ham.' My throat was dry and I was going hoarse from all the shouting. Pietro, the pizza chef, slid two huge pizzas across the counter at me accompanied by a huge wink. I picked them up and wove my way between the tables on the large wooden terrace overlooking the sea.

It was getting on for midnight and the place was still packed. I had to duck around a group of slightly drunken teenagers getting up to leave. Taking the right pizzas to the right table in one piece always seemed like a great achievement. The customers had no idea what we went through for them.

'How are you doing? My feet just want to soak in a cool bowl of water, they have had enough,' Jenny whispered in my ear.

Colour me in

'Mine too. We should have run away to the circus; it would have been easier.' She laughed and looked very cheerful in spite of the tired feet. She and Carlo seemed to manage to cross each other's paths all the time, exchanging meaningful glances and whispering comments which sent them giggling off across the terrace with pizzas held high. Alberto had spent most of the time at the cash desk that night where he often filled in for his father or sister when they were not around. We envied him the chance to sit down.

I had to admit that, on balance, I was having quite a good time. I wished that Leo were there and that we could be happy together like Jenny and Carlo, but in spite of the sad moments, living and working on a beach for six weeks was definitely not bad. We had arrived in the last week of July and were due to work until the first week of September. We were hoping to stay another week after that, to rest up and relax before returning to Bologna and then England.

At last the best part of the night arrived and we walked away from the terrace, bottles of beer in hand, down to the sea. I plonked myself down on my favourite rock, kicked off my sandals and dipped my feet into the water. What a blissful feeling! My feet seemed to sigh with relief. Then came the lovely shshsh sound as Carlo prised the top off a beer bottle and handed it to me. Heaven! As the cold beer soothed my throat, I looked up at the gorgeous starlit night and couldn't help wishing that Leo were with me. Carlo put his arm round Jenny, who snuggled happily against him. I tried not to feel jealous. Alberto was sitting on his hands, gazing out to sea.

'You fancy the concert tonight?' he asked. 'Or alternatively, my friend Gabrielle is having a party at his granddad's old place up the mountain. We could go there. His mate Michele is a DJ and has a great sound system.'

Jenny and Carlo were silent. Normally we all went out

after work. 'I'm really tired,' said Jenny. 'Tonight I think I'll take it easy. I'd rather just sit here and drink my beer slowly and then go back and crash.'

Carlo nodded, 'You two go.' Alberto looked at me with a question in his eyes. I had got used to the nocturnal lifestyle but did I want to go out alone with Alberto? On other occasions, when Jenny and Carlo had not come with us, there had always been other friends around. I didn't feel like going back to the chalet just yet. I said to Alberto, 'Lets go, these boring old farts can go to bed. We're going to party all night long!' I caught his broad smile out of the corner of my eye.

***

'What about sleeping tablets?' Alberto was beginning to sound impatient.

'I've tried them you know I have. They don't seem to help.'

'Lori, you haven't slept properly in ages. At least, when you were going through chemotherapy it wore you out and you slept, but, since finishing it, you have seemed so . . . down and listless and yet wired up at the same time. You need sleep.' His voice was heavy with sleep and he was disgruntled, as I had inadvertently woken him up.

'It would be nice to be in my own bed again and maybe I could go and see my own doctor in Bologna. I'll do that when I go back for radiotherapy.'

'Lori, there are perfectly good doctors here. Dottore Bernardini is fine. He has been our family doctor for years.'

'I need to paint,' I said quietly, 'I really do need to paint.'

'Okay then paint,' he sighed. 'Lori, if that's what you need, then do it. They sell pads in the village shop, don't they? Better you paint on a pad than cover any more walls. You can get one in the morning.' He sighed as he began to turn over, away from me, adding, 'Be sure not to make a mess on my mother's floor. You know how she hates that.'

I sat up and swung my legs over the side of the bed. I

Colour me in

needed to go downstairs and fetch some more water. Alberto and I were making an effort to talk to each other but it was a struggle. I tried to explain to him how I felt - my sense of distance from everything, the tension in my body, my desperate need for colour - but he usually just ended up looking puzzled.

I stood up and stretched. If it weren't for the fact that I was delighted to be with my children, this spell in Calabria might have felt like a prison sentence.

***

I could feel the presence of the mountains towering above us in the dark. At certain moonlit moments their outlines appeared against the sky, overshadowing us as we chugged up the winding dust track in Alberto's little Fiat 500. After a while we came across a plateau surrounded by olive trees, their leaves shimmering silver in the starlight. The rhythmic beat of a drum floated across to us and as we approached we could make out the sound of reggae music.

'Good old Michele,' Alberto grinned. 'You can hear his sound system for miles.'

'You mean we've still got miles to go!' I hoped I was joking. It turned out I was. The trees opened up into a clearing full of cars. We parked and followed the sound of the music down a stone-covered driveway which suddenly curved round to the right and brought us in front of a beautiful old building with three tall palm trees standing majestically on the right-hand side of it. The entrance to the building was a high stone arch. We walked through it into an entrance hall opening out through another arch into a large courtyard full of trestle tables covered in food and drink, sound systems, speakers and people. Everywhere you looked, people were standing around talking, dancing or sitting in groups smoking joints.

The beat of the music underpinned everything. Dancing and chatter floated above it in layers. I breathed it all in. I couldn't get over these amazing outdoor parties. All summer long old houses, fields and beaches were taken over and lit up with colour and sound.

We carried our bottles of beer to the drinks table. Alberto was greeting every other person as we wove our way among those standing and chatting around the edge of the dancers. I said 'hi' to a lot of people too. Working in a beach pizzeria and partying every night certainly gets you known. I touched Alberto's arm and indicated that I was going to dance. He nodded and continued his conversation with an earnest-looking lad in dreadlocks and round glasses.

I alternated dancing and drinking, often dancing in groups with people I knew, then I would sit down on the ground with a bottle of beer to cool off and catch my breath. To my great surprise I was enjoying Alberto's company. He was a solid, reassuring presence. I didn't feel alone with him there. He came over to me as I held onto a table to steady myself as all the alcohol I had been knocking back suddenly took hold.

'Are you okay, Lori?' He looked at me with concern in his dark eyes.

'Yeah, fine it's a grrreat party. Oops.' I nearly knocked a bottle over.

'Maybe you should switch to water.' He swapped my beer bottle with one of water. I was thirsty and it tasted good.

'You don't want to work with a hangover tomorrow. Do you remember the other day?' Alberto chuckled.

'Yes, I remember.' A vivid image of myself throwing up popped into my head and I shuddered, 'I don't want another hangover, but I feel fine right now.'

'Well, I'm glad,' he smiled and looked at his watch.

'Are you going to tell me we should be going home?' I leant heavily against his shoulder.

'It's getting on for four o'clock.'

I didn't want to go but I was unsteady on my feet, tired as well as drunk.

Colour me in

'I s'pose we better had,' I conceded.

'Tell you what,' Alberto spoke carefully, trying to sound casual. 'We could prolong the night a little bit. I've got some nice grass so we could have a goodnight smoke on the beach. That'll ensure we sleep well!'

'Hey, great idea.' I loved sitting on the beach at the end of the night. I couldn't take much grass but just a couple of puffs would be fine and, as Alberto said, it would prolong the beautiful starlit night.

We left the party and drove back down to the coast, parked the car by the beach and settled down at our favourite spot. I took a puff of the joint Alberto handed me but it made me feel a little queasy, so I handed it straight back to him. I moved off the rock and onto the sand, my feet touching the edge of the water. As the waves came inwards they lapped right over them. 'I won't need to wash my feet tonight,' I chuckled.

Alberto settled close beside me. I could hear the sound of his breath close to my ear as he inhaled the joint and slowly breathed the smoke out. I was propped back on my elbows high enough to watch the sea but almost lying down. I felt something light touch my arm sending a shiver up to my shoulder. It happened again. I turned to Alberto. He was stroking my arm. He lifted his head to look at me. As I looked back at him, he slowly moved his head towards mine. I saw his mouth and then we were kissing. Oh my God, I'm kissing Alberto! It was okay though, an okay kiss. We stopped and looked at each other for a moment. I thought about moving away but he moved in again and I found myself thinking, 'Oh, what the heck, enjoy it', so I sank hazily into the quite delicious tingles I was feeling.

I tried not to think, "Oh my God, this is Alberto!" but tried to focus on the nice feelings. I felt my dress move up round my waist and his hand dive between my thighs. I lay back and enjoyed the shivers running down the insides of my legs and the waves lapping on my feet. Every time I opened my eyes there were stars, it seemed like millions of them shining above us. "Sex on the beach." Jenny would be proud of me.

Alberto was frantically trying to pull off his jeans, I sat up, trying to suppress a giggle, as he looked so funny.

'Hey, take it easy, there's no rush.'

Leo's face suddenly appeared in front of me and I was lost for a few seconds. Alberto took hold of my shoulders and kissed me again, pushing me down onto the sand. He kissed me all over very quickly and breathlessly.

'Is it okay?' he mumbled. I think I must have nodded and he began to enter me. Within a few seconds he was pumping away frantically. I wanted to tell him to take it easy and slow down but couldn't find my voice.

The sand was hard and grainy and, although Alberto hadn't taken my dress off, my back and especially the backs of my legs were getting quite rubbed and the sand was getting everywhere. "I'm going to have to shower when I get in," I thought. Alberto came with a long moan and then flopped on the sand next to me. After a minute or so he rolled over to me and stroked my arm again.

'Lori, how are you?'

'Okay.'

'Okay! You're just okay?'

I nodded, I felt okay but confused. 'Well, it was a bit of a rush.'

Alberto looked dismayed, 'I'm sorry Lori. I've wanted this for so long I got carried away. Let me make it up to you.'

He looked questioningly into my eyes. I found myself looking back into his and he moved in and kissed me again, this time slowly and gently but very firmly. It was actually very nice.

'Lori, you have made me feel amazing, fantastic. I want you to feel like this.' He looked into my eyes. 'I'm sorry, Lori, I'm not so experienced you tell me . . ..' He tentatively

Colour me in

stroked my breast, it felt nice, but I felt confused and covered in sand. I needed a shower and I needed my bed.

'Look Alberto it's incredibly late and I'm really tired. I have to sleep. We have to work in a few hours.' I rose to my feet, shaking the sand from my dress. I found my knickers partially buried in the sand near my feet and decided not to put them on. Alberto found his and spent ages shaking the sand off them. He looked worried. 'Won't you let me try? It's your turn now. I'm sorry, I've been selfish.' He walked up to me and gently stroked the side of my face. 'You know I think you're wonderful. Since I met you on the train nearly a year ago, I have wanted this to happen.'

I managed a smile and may even have blushed but all I knew was that I needed to get away from him and be on my own to make some sense of this. 'Thank you but right now we must go home. Your car is parked over there.' I waved a hand towards it in case he had forgotten. 'Are you okay to drive?' He nodded, suddenly looking sad. 'Bye then, see you in the morning.'

'Lori, let me walk you . . ..' I shook my head and carried on walking up the beach. 'A drink of water,' I thought, 'that's what I really want, a drink of water.'

Chapter 14

Dottore Franceschi was a big man, not typically Italian at all, with large hands and a booming voice. 'We give radiotherapy to women who haven't had the whole breast removed,' he said. To my astonishment, when he said the word 'breast' he cupped his hands in front of his chest. As if we didn't know what breasts were! I glanced sideways at Gina. She was staring down at her knees trying to keep the amusement from her face.

I had come back to Bologna several days before and now Gina and I were sitting listening to the Head of Radiotherapy explaining why I had to have this treatment. It was a cold January morning, the hospital was draughty and I had kept my coat on, but somehow this big man warmed the room with his presence. 'The idea is,' he went on, 'that if there is any remaining cancerous tissue in the area, the radiotherapy will destroy it.'

He then talked about how the angle of radiation was calculated, taking into account the need to avoid hitting the patient's heart and lungs as much as possible. In my case it was my right breast so thankfully I didn't have to worry about my heart. My lungs were going to be caught, apparently, but they would minimise that as much as possible.

Dottore Franceschi illustrated his point by drawing breasts on a piece of paper on the desk in front of him. He then drew the angle at which the radiation beam would strike my right breast and drew my lungs to show how much would be hit.

'This is only a rough diagram,' he explained. 'You will have to come in before starting therapy to be measured and we will mark your breast so that the beam is lined up properly and always in the same place each day.' He explained that I would have to come in every day for twenty-eight consecutive sessions, with Sundays off.

I appreciated his attempts to make it all as clear as

Colour me in

possible. It worried me that my lungs would be radiated as well, but he seemed to suggest that it was a small price to pay for ensuring that any remaining cancerous tissue in my breast was destroyed. He then continued drawing pictures of breasts on the paper in front of him, almost absentmindedly, as he talked. I noticed out of the corner of my eye that Gina was biting her lip.

Dr Franceschi stopped talking and looked at me with a pleasant smile. 'Well, I think that's about it. Do you have any questions?'

Although he was smiling I found his presence a little intimidating. I swallowed. 'I have had chemotherapy and apparently the point of that was to kill any remaining cancer cells that may be in my body. If it has done that, then why do I need radiotherapy?'

'Statistics show that women who have radiotherapy as well as chemotherapy have a higher survival rate.' He went on to quote some statistics. I had to hand it to him, he was very thorough but I still didn't understand why.

'They only have statistics to go on,' said Gina, as we drank coffee in the hospital cafe afterwards. 'Maybe they are not totally sure how it works but if statistics show a higher recovery rate as a result, then they have to do it.'

'I guess so,' I said. I wanted to know more about how these treatments were actually going to work. Maybe I needed a serious medical book.

'That doctor sure loves his job,' giggled Gina. 'He sure loves drawing those diagrams.'

'And talking about breasts,' I said, cupping my hands in front of mine as I said it. We collapsed in giggles for a moment then Gina got serious again.

'That phrase 'survival rate',' she said. 'That's what it's about and it's a good criterion. They want as many people to survive as possible. If you're going to be a statistic, Lori, then you want to be in the 'survival rate'.' I wrapped my hands around my cappuccino cup. 'In fact, it is where you are,' she added. I wished I had her confidence.

***

I was painting breasts, breasts with big ugly scars right across them, breasts bent over in the middle with the sad skewed nipple pointing sideways. I painted and painted and painted. Well over an hour and a whole pad of paper later, I finally came to a halt and flopped over the kitchen table, my head on my arms.

I had just come home from my fifth radiotherapy. Five days of waiting in a corridor for my name to be called, to then walk into the room containing the radiation machine. There was no changing room so I had to take off my coat, jumper, tee-shirt and bra in front of two nurses, usually male, who were waiting impatiently for me. Then I had to lie on the machine while they lined up the dots they had drawn on my breast as a guide. Then they switched the machine on and went out of the room. The machine whirred, stopped, and whirred again. Just a few seconds and it was done. The nurses came back and one helped me up. I put my bra, tee-shirt, jumper and coat back on, under the watchful eyes of the male nurses who were impatient for me to go so they could call the next patient.

Peeling off my clothes under the clinical gaze of a young man, allowed to stare at me because he was a nurse, made me feel invaded somehow even though his stare only showed impatience. Obviously I didn't want desire or any other kind of interest but this clinical coolness also made me feel exposed. I felt sordid and inhuman. I didn't want to take my clothes off in front of any man ever again, in any context.

***

I woke up, gripped with fear, and slowly my nightmare came back to me. I had been with Michela, talking to a couple of men, I don't know where or what about, but then I lost her and when I found her again she told me she'd been raped! I held her in my arms and rocked and rocked her. Tears poured down my face as I remembered the dream and I felt so angry with myself. How could I have let this happen?

The fact that it had been a nightmare and hadn't really happened slowly crept over me. The horror and guilt gradually gave way to relief but they didn't quite leave me, an after shadow of them remained. I got out of bed, picked up my mobile phone and sent Michela a good morning message. I got one back immediately. She was on the bus going to school.

I wondered how I could have had such a terrible nightmare. I got out my paints and paper. There is only one way for me to get this nasty fear and guilt out of my system.

***

My bird's wings are spread wide across the wall and he's flying towards me, as if coming out of the picture. How wonderful if he could just fly onto the dining room table. I must make him bright. I don't want a crow-like bird to remind me of my mother-in-law. What will she think of him? I look round at the dresser, butterflies rising in my stomach, I can't think about her now. I must finish my picture.

***

Although it was around six o'clock in the morning when I finally collapsed into bed, hopefully having showered off all of the sand, I was afraid that I wouldn't be able to sleep.

I had totally surprised myself having sex with Alberto and had to admit that some of it had been nice. I fell asleep amid confused thoughts of Alberto and Leo and when I woke up later that morning I had the memory of a dream.

I was floating on the sea in a little dinghy feeling all alone and lost. Then I saw two figures standing on the shore. I waved and shouted at them for help, but they stayed where they were and I noticed that they were laughing. At first I didn't know who they were but when I saw their faces I recognised Leo and Cassandra. They laughed at me as I drifted away feeling very scared. Then I felt arms wrap themselves round me and I realised that someone else was in the boat with me. A reassuring voice said 'Hey Lori, it's okay, I'm here.' It was Alberto's voice.

***

As I arrived at the pizzeria for the lunchtime shift, Alberto was sitting outside on the low terrace wall. He stood up as I reached him.

'Lori, can we talk for a moment, please?' The urgency was audible in his voice.

'Yes, okay.'

'Let's walk.' He started along the beach.

'We'll be late for work.'

'Only a minute.'

I followed him. He was walking with his head down, looking very awkward. A few yards away from the pizzeria he stopped.

'Listen, Lori, for me last night was . . . very special. I don't want you to think . . . I don't want you to think all I wanted was . . . sex.' I didn't know what to say. 'Lori, I really like you. I want you to be my girlfriend.' He swallowed. It sounded really sweet. I think a little smile must have played about my lips. 'I would love to ask you out on a date.' He looked down, shuffling his feet in the sand. I had said 'no,' to him before but now things felt different. It was really nice to feel so wanted. I looked at Alberto still shuffling his feet nervously.

'Yes,' I replied and smiled at him, 'let's go out.' Alberto breathed out a great sigh of relief, making no attempt to hide it and grinned broadly. 'That's great, Lori, really great.'

***

How wonderful to fly, to take off, to soar above everything, to leave earth behind. I envy my flying bird.

I've painted him strong and fearless. His feathers are a range of shades from deep purple to pale pink with different blues in between. His beak is pink and his eyes are

Colour me in

very bright blue. He seems to be looking straight at me. He is too magnificent to be a seagull; he is a bird of prey, powerful and regal.

Chapter 15

The lights from the shops were blurring into the mist. It was good to see lights but they had no shape. Early evening shoppers crowded the pavements. I loved this time of day, people coming out from work, meeting to have an aperitif in the bars, shopping, strolling in couples and groups, chatting and laughing. It was a cold evening in late January and I was halfway through radiotherapy.

The fog gave a surreal feel to the evening. Shapes emerged from it, coming into sharp focus for a minute as they passed me and then disappearing again, engulfed once more.

It seemed to me that the fog was here to blur everything, to blur me, to make me shapeless. I didn't want to be shapeless and lost in the grey fog. I needed a shape. 'What shape shall I have?' I wondered. The shape of a bird came the answer. I knew it really. I knew I wanted to be a bird, so that I could soar above this fog, so that I could soar away and be alone, free in the sky with no one to ask anything of me.

I walked down via Independenza. 'There are too many people here,' I thought. I could easily be bumped into, knocked over. I turned left down a narrow street and found a quiet section of pavement, just wide enough for people to pass me.

I opened my wings as wide as I could and leant forward from the waist until I was parallel to the ground. I felt too static, so I lifted my left leg backwards off the ground a little. I closed my eyes. 'I'm soaring,' I thought. I tried to picture myself flying across a beautiful blue sky, over mountains, over the sea, but at first I couldn't picture it. The vision eluded me. Slowly I opened my eyes and saw the grey pavement below. 'I need sky.' I closed my eyes again and breathed deeply in and out, in and out. Gradually my body relaxed and I flew away from the foggy evening and up into blue sky. I could see the city below getting smaller

Colour me in

and smaller as I flew towards the mountains. It was a wonderful light feeling and I had a real sense of gliding into the blue.

I felt a presence somewhere behind my right wing. Someone was casting a shadow over my vision, someone tall. It felt like a man. I could feel him watching me. I couldn't turn to look but I felt all right. I was in flight position. I could flee from danger, but he didn't feel dangerous. I stayed in my flight position, frozen still. He was frozen still, watching me.

"Best not to move he will go away soon." I kept my eyes closed and tried to soar away but I felt a step towards me. I could feel the shadow bend towards me. My heart started pounding.

'Lori, is that you?' My heart seemed to stop. That voice.

'Best not to move he will go away.' I was still; he was still. Then I felt the shadow bend towards me again.

'Lori, are you okay?' My eyes were open now but I could only look down. The cracks in the pavement seemed to widen. Perhaps they will swallow me up. I wobbled. My leg lowered itself to the ground. My wings ached. I knew that voice.

'Lori, is there anything I can do?'

A hand touched my wrist. I jumped.

'Sorry, I didn't mean to startle you but maybe you should stand up.' He held my wrist and gently pulled my arm up.

'Can I take you to the hospital? Are you hurt?'

My left arm went down by my side and I stood up.

'It is you, thank goodness!' he said. 'I thought for a moment I might have grabbed a stranger, though we have been strangers . . .'

Embarrassment rose up from my feet, in a big wave through my whole body up to my face, which blushed hot, bright red. 'Leo.'

***

My mixing of the nurses' uniform green into different

shades has used up every old container I could find in the house. I have a very pale green and some beautiful palm tree greens and some luscious dark greens, just what I need for a jungle. I have a little yellow left, enough for some flowers and hopefully enough to mix with red to make orange. I found a fabulous picture in Beppe's book of two bright orange birds sitting on a branch. They have what look like orange fluffy balls on their heads and brown wings. I'd love to paint them.

I still have a few shades of blue so I can mix them with some acrylic red to make some more shades of purple and deep cool pink for my orchids. I'll paint plenty of big green leaves to create cooling shade to sit in, beautiful flowers to gaze at and birds to remind me of freedom.

***

Another hangover! We'd crammed three leaving dos into one week, culminating in a party the night before, and I was feeling rough. That morning I could not get my head out of the toilet.

'What's wrong with me? I didn't drink that much last night, did I?'

'It has accumulated,' explained Jenny, ever the wise expert. 'Several nights of heavy boozing, you need a couple of nights off the booze.'

'Well, that's going to happen before we go back,' I retorted a little sharply. My, I was feeling rough!

We had planned to go out every night until we left, but I didn't know how I was ever going to face another sip of alcohol again. Exhausted from throwing up, I struggled back to bed, feeling miserable. We hadn't even started packing and we were due to leave in three days.

Leo had shown up at last night's party. Sandro had told him that we were leaving and he'd come to say goodbye. Did I see regret in his face? I had studied it for signs. He had seemed friendly, not as cool and distant as I had feared, and I was really glad that he had come. I had so wished that

Colour me in

I were good with words so that I could have detained him with my stunning witty conversation but I hadn't managed it. He had walked away from me after a few minutes, chatted to a few people and left.

Alberto had hung around me quite a bit at the party, perhaps sensing Leo's presence as danger. Had he ever seen us together? I didn't think so, but couldn't be sure. I had been having fun with Alberto and liked him but I wasn't sure how I felt about leaving him. Maybe it was a good thing I was leaving, maybe it would be better to bring things to a natural end.

***

'How did you stand on one leg for so long?' Now I was on two legs but I felt unstable under his intense gaze.

'Did I stand for long?'

'Well, I watched you for quite a few seconds.'

'I felt you watching me.' What else could I say? The eyes were the same; warm, concerned and melting.

'Are you sure you're okay? I think maybe I should take you to a hospital or doctor or something.' I shook my head. 'Well, what about a drink then? I'd love to talk . . ..' His voice tailed off. He seemed awkward. I nodded.

We walked in silence back to via Independenza, among the blurry lights and the shoppers emerging from the fog.

'I want to get colour back into my life. I want to fly . . ..' Silence. 'Leo, I had breast cancer.' I hated the shocked look on his face. I hadn't wanted to do that to him, but didn't know how to make conversation. We carried on walking and he gently put his hand in the middle of my back to guide me in front of him across the road. We entered a crowded cafe and found two stools at the far end of the bar.

'Frizzantino?' Leo asked me if I wanted sparkling wine, a popular local aperitif. I nodded.

As I moved to take off my warm woolly hat I wondered how he would react to my incredibly short hair. As he passed me my drink he smiled, 'It suits you, shows off those cheekbones.'

'Thank you, I'm so glad it's growing back, I hated being bald. Even though it is growing back the same colour as before, I quite fancied being blond.'

Leo smiled. 'I always loved your red hair, it's unusual in Italy.'

I sat caressing my glass and then took a sip. I loved feeling the bubbles on my tongue. I looked at Leo, not sure that he was real. Flying over the mountains had seemed more real than this.

'Do you want to talk about it?' I could hardly stand the intensity of the concern in his voice and his eyes. I shook my head.

'Not right now, you tell me, how are things with you? Life, family, children?' I couldn't say Cassandra's name, even after all this time.

'Well, I have two sons.' He grinned and his voice struck a cheery note. 'They are fantastic, so bright, so amazing, so much more together than I was at their ages.'

'How old are they?'

'Giorgio is ten and Sandro is eight.'

'Sandro?' I laughed.

'Yes. I had to name one of my sons after him! Well, actually it's Cassandra's grandfather's name. He had just died, so it seemed like a nice gesture, the cycle of life and death and all that.' So he married Cassandra. 'You have a son, don't you?' He hurried on, covering the brief pause. 'I bumped into Francesca, must have been about three years ago, she said you had had a second child, a boy.'

'Yep. I managed one of each.' It was my turn to grin. 'Beppe, he's great too. He's seven now.'

We had to move our stools together as a group of people jostled in next to us at the bar. Our knees were almost touching. 'Your daughter must be . . . fourteen.' He could do sums.

Colour me in

'Yes that's right.'

'How is she?' He suddenly looked embarrassed. 'Sorry, silly question, all this must be really tough on them.'

'They are . . . coping. They just want to know that I'm not going to die. They want assurance that I can't give them. Everyone does, everyone wants you to tell them that you're okay, that you're going to be fine, like an exam result; you've passed and all is well.' I stopped. I had not expected that outburst. 'Sorry Leo, I . . .'

'That's okay. It's great hearing you sound so spirited. This is the Lori I knew.' I looked down at the floor.

'The Lori I met earlier was much harder to recognise.' I slowly lifted my head up.

'Sometimes I'm not sure I recognise her either,' I said. I didn't add that at other times she seemed more real than the person he was talking to now, the one who could just about hold an adult conversation.

'I'm not saying you don't have the right to react in any way you feel.' He spoke quickly, then hesitated, and looked at me with intense concern again. His eyes were just as beautiful as ever. He had a few grey hairs giving him that lucky distinguished look that many men get, a few lines, shadows under his eyes. He looked tired. His voice was gentler than before and he sounded a little worn down. I wanted to stay there among the soft lights and the bubbles and listen to him for a very long time.

***

These leaves are lovely, big and shady, such a rich green. This is gorgeous, I can paint in big sweeping brushstrokes, at this rate it won't take long to cover this wall. I must leave room though for orchids and some birds in the trees, a Toucan perched on a high branch, hey there's an idea!

***

'Yours or mine?' Jenny was holding up a Bjork cd.

'Mine, definitely. You don't even like Bjork!' It was the following morning and, in spite of having had a relatively quiet and fairly early night the night before, I had still thrown up that morning. Feeling pale and fragile, I was sitting up in bed, cardigan round my shoulders, watching Jenny packing, with no inclination to move but knowing that I was going to have to.

'I can't believe it; I've got twice as much stuff as I came with. Where does it all come from?' Jenny was cramming clothes into a rucksack.

I shook my head. 'It's not as if we've had any money to buy things with, is it? I mean, we've hardly bought anything and yet . . .' I gazed around the floor at the piles of clothes, books and cds.

'Oh my God!' I felt sick again. I scrambled out of bed and raced to the loo. Luckily no one was in it and I got there just in time. As I walked slowly back into the bedroom, feeling very weak, Jenny came towards me and helped me into bed.

'Lori, did you really drink that much last night? I mean, you do throw up from time to time but . . . .'

'I've got a really sensitive stomach, it seems.' Jenny looked worried, sat on the bed and picked up my hand.

'Lori, have you thought . . . ?' At that point the doorbell rang and she went to answer it. Simona and Francesca walked in.

'Hey Lori, feeling rough?'

'Yeah, can't seem to take my drink.'

'Well, you've been hitting the bottle hard for several nights in a row. It's not surprising,' laughed Simona.

'Maybe I'll become teetotal when I get home.' I grinned.

Francesca sat down on the bed and took my hand. 'I don't think you should go back to England. Stay here and recover.'

I smiled. 'That's a nice thought. Right now I have no desire to get out of bed and pack.'

'Seriously, though,' said Simona, 'what are we going to do without you two? I shall miss you so much!' That immediately led to hugs all round.

'Come and visit,' said Jenny.

'Oh yes, please do come as soon as you can.' I hated the thought of leaving them.

'Hey, guess who we've just bumped into?' asked Simona.

'Oh, yes,' Francesca added, 'such a surprise.'

'Do you remember Gina, the student we were talking to the other week?' asked Simona. 'She teaches Italian at the language school where you two were thinking of asking for work.'

'Oh yeah,' replied Jenny, 'She was really helpful when we thought of working there but there wasn't really time. I'm going to get in touch with her when I come back next year. She's a good contact for work. She translates too, doesn't she?'

'Guess what,' said Simona, 'she's pregnant!'

'Really! An accident or planned? I didn't think she was in a relationship,' said Jenny. I couldn't speak.

'I think it was an accident but she has recently got together with this guy and they have decided to keep the baby.'

'That's a bit mad,' commented Jenny, 'I mean she's only, what, early twenties? I know she's a year or so older than us but still young, and she obviously doesn't know him very well. How's she going to manage financially? What's she going to do about studying?'

'She seems really happy,' said Francesca. 'She says she'll carry on studying for as long as she can before the baby is born. She may even manage to finish her exams. She's got four more to do. That would be pushing it a bit, especially as she works as well, but she may do it. Then she'll do her thesis and any remaining exams after the baby is born. She seems to have it all worked out.'

'Wow! Well, what about money? I know her parents haven't got much. She said she's worked since she left school to put herself through university.'

'She says she'll carry on working, but less until the baby comes, so she can finish her exams. After the baby is born she'll teach a few hours a week and she'll be able to translate from home. Also her man has just finished his thesis and is looking for work, they'll move in together which will reduce the rent.'

I struggled out of bed. I couldn't listen to any more of this. I felt sick again, this time accompanied by a low down tension in the pit of my stomach.

Chapter 16

I found a table near enough to watch the band but not too close to the dance floor. I nursed my glass of red wine and watched Jenny and Carlo dance.

'I'm not sure what dance Jenny's doing.' It was Simona who sat down with me. 'But she's certainly having a good time.'

'Yeah, Francesca's band is really great isn't it?'

'Really good,' agreed Simona I'm so glad they could play they're very much in demand these days. Francesca was playing piano in a band that played a mixture of jazz funk and soul dance music. She was a talented musician and played several instruments, quite a contrast from her day job teaching economics.

'Do you fancy joining me on the dance floor ladies?' Sandro appeared, smiling at us both, Simona had been so glad when she had managed to get hold of him. None of us had seen him for ages. He was as much fun as ever and had given me lots of lovely bear hugs that evening. I shook my head. 'Simona will dance with you.

'Are you sure you don't want to?'

'Yes thanks, you birthday girl are not going to be a wall flower at your own party.'

'Just as long as your big strong husband doesn't come over and bop me one,' laughed Sandro.

'Oh he's too busy propping up the bar,' laughed Simona. 'I haven't seen him dance in years.' She got up from her seat, took Sandro by the hand and led him into the middle of the dancers.

Simona had hired a large room in a hotel for her fortieth birthday party. The area in front of the stage had been cleared for the dance floor but the rest was covered in tables where the party-goers were eating and drinking.

Francesca's band was creating a lively party atmosphere and the dance floor was full. After a while they stopped for a break and a DJ took over.

Francesca came over to join me.

'That was great, your band is so good, great music.'

Francesca flushed and smiled, 'thank you Lori we rehearsed specially for tonight. I wanted it to be really good for Simona.'

'It is, she's loving it.'

'I'm so glad. How are you? I notice you haven't been dancing.'

'No, but I've been loving the music and the atmosphere.'

I was glad she had come to join me I really needed to talk to someone about what had been burning on my brain.

'Listen, I have something to tell you.'

'Ooh, sounds intriguing.'

'Could you keep it to yourself for the moment? I'm not ready to tell the others just yet.'

'Of course.' I took a deep breath and told her about my meeting with Leo. I told her about the need to fly, about my desperation to soar above the world, everything. When I finished, there were tears in her eyes. 'Oh my God, Lori, what a story!' She took hold of my hand.

'It's just that sometimes I need to . . . I don't know . . . escape.' Francesca squeezed my hand and we sat listening to the music for a moment. Then she spoke.

'How incredible, though, seeing Leo after all this time. I saw him, um, a couple . . . no, it would be at least three years ago now. I'm sure I told you at the time. He asked about you. How was he?'

'He seemed okay, worried about me,' I laughed, embarrassed. 'Understandable under the circumstances.' I cleared my throat. 'Oh Francesca, he was so lovely, such warmth in his voice, such concern, it melted my heart.'

'How did you feel seeing him?'

'He seemed very tired, quite worn down. I think there was a kind of sadness in him.'

'That may have been seeing you . . . you know, in a rather unhappy state.'

Colour me in

'Maybe. It must have been a shock for him. It was a shock for both of us, bumping into each other. To think I haven't seen him for all these years and then he picks that moment to walk past me. I was in a tiny little side street.'

'That is amazing,' says Francesca thoughtfully. 'There are a couple of old flames from our student days I wouldn't mind bumping into again. It's hard meeting nice, single men nowadays.'

I smile at her. 'You deserve someone nice, I'm sure you'll meet someone soon.'

'Thank you, I hope so. Well, Leo, how do you feel about him now?'

'I really . . . I wanted to stay there in that warm little bar talking to him forever. Afterwards we walked to his car and he gave me a lift home. Luckily he had to rush back or I would have been tempted to ask him in for tea, but I didn't.' I looked at the question on Francesca's face. 'Just to talk, just to be in his company.'

'The old magnetism?' she asked.

'Yes, I suppose so . . .. But, do you know, there is a new magnetism, much stronger and more human.' Warmth crept through my body as I remembered the concern in Leo's eyes.

***

Toucan looks more like a bee than a bird . . . he looks ridiculous. I've nothing against bees of course but it was not what I was going for . . . chubby and floppy. I can't do this, I really can't . . . a jungle scene was much too ambitious. I was stupid to try.

***

Pregnancy tests then were more complicated than they are today. I had to warm up my pee in the little test tube provided, along with some chemical from the kit, then put in a little white spatula. If the spatula went pink, you were pregnant. I stood in the kitchen first thing in the morning, eyelashes glued together by sleep, trying to peer at this tiny spatula in my hand and make sense of it. Jenny walked into the kitchen, wearing lilac striped pyjamas, also looking bleary. I held the spatula up for her to see. It was pink.

'I'm pregnant!'

'We'll have to sort this out.' Jenny took the spatula from my hand, went over to the sink, got some heavy-duty bleach from the cupboard and started scrubbing. The spatula turned white again.

'There, now you're not pregnant any more!' Jenny was holding up the now white spatula, grinning triumphantly. I had to laugh. We both giggled helplessly for a moment and then I collapsed in her arms. As I pulled slowly away from her, I was both laughing and crying.

Jenny turned the little spatula over in her hand. 'Well, it's a good thing we're going back to England. You'll be in time to get an abortion there. It will be much easier than here. In Britain you need referrals from two doctors: your GP and a doctor at the hospital. It depends on the hospital but if it goes through quickly enough you can have it on the NHS.'

I stared at her. It was as if she were talking a foreign language. She was really into her subject. 'I think St George's Hospital is quite good. I know the central hospital is much slower and people often end up having to go private. Do you remember Sally Wilson? She went to a clinic in South London. She said it was great, they treated her really well, counselling and everything, and it wasn't extortionate. If you need to do that I'll help you with the cost, you know that, Lori.'

'You know something Jen? I have to lie down again. It's early and I'm feeling a bit dizzy.'

'Sure, you go back to bed. I've got to get moving, I've got an appointment with my course tutor.' She left the kitchen and I stood where I was, dazed, unable to sit down. I'm pregnant! I'm going to have a baby!

I'm not sure how long I stood there but Jenny came back into the kitchen fully dressed, looking worried.

'Hey Lori, you okay? You look as though you're in shock.' She took me by the arm. 'I'll help you back to bed. Maybe we should make you some sweet tea.' Maria entered the kitchen at that point. Jenny had clearly told her. She hugged me and then went over to the stove to heat some water. One thing I missed in Italy was an electric kettle. It made an emergency cup of tea so much more quickly.

***

I've painted over Toucan, there's a damp greyish patch where he once was. I'm tempted to walk away . . . to go out and not be here when they come back. But I do want to finish. I'm not sure whether to try Toucan again or go for the orange puffball head birds. Whichever I do I'll follow the picture in Beppe's book closely. Patience Lori . . . calm and patience is what you need.

***

It was rare to see Jenny lost for words but now she stared at me, incredulously.

Our packed bags were all around us. Our flight was booked for the next morning. We were ready to leave, just one last night of goodbyes. Jenny was spending it with Carlo and I was spending it with Alberto.

'Why not come back and think about it there?' Jenny wanted to know. 'Lori, you have got some time. You can't be more than six weeks gone.'

'It is almost exactly six weeks,' I said. 'I know because that first time on the beach was the only time we took a risk. After that we always used a condom. I know they are not a hundred percent, but still it's most likely to be then, isn't it?'

'Maybe you need some distance from it, Lori. Why waste a perfectly good ticket?'

'Jenny, I have to stay here if I'm going to have the baby. The baby's father is here.' I looked at Jenny standing very tensely in front of me. 'I'll talk to Gina,' I went on, 'She can help me get work at the language school. We can be expectant mothers together.' A warmth crept up from inside at this thought.

'You're not seriously thinking about having this baby?' Jenny looked me straight in the eyes.

'I am.' There was a kind of pride in my voice as I replied, 'I'm going to stay here to be with the father of my child.' How good that sounded, "my child." I felt as though I were surrounded by a warm glow. I was going to be a mother. I didn't have to worry about what to do with my life. I didn't have to go back to university, to boring old England or to my parents. My parents! Not a good thought. Jenny read my mind.

'Your parents are going to go ballistic.'

I didn't like the tense feeling in my stomach that sentence evoked. I tried not to focus on it.

'All the more reason to stay here then.' I fancied that the earth mother glow was already emanating from me. I expected Jenny to see that and understand, but she didn't.

'Lori, please think very carefully. You're bound to regret this. You're only twenty-one and you don't even know if you love Alberto.'

'Nearly twenty-two,' I mumbled.

'You haven't finished your degree yet. Do you really want to live in a country you don't know that well, with a man you don't know that well, bringing up a baby without support?'

'I'll have support. Alberto will be supportive and there's Simona and Francesca and I'll get to know Gina better. That will be great. We can help each other.'

As I spoke, the idea of staying in Bologna bringing up a baby, teaching English and translating to earn our keep, seemed like the ideal life. No longer would my every decision be subject to my parents' scrutiny, no longer would I have to struggle for ways to earn my father's approval. Still there was a tight knot of fear at the thought of my parents and how they were going to react.

Colour me in

***

Looking back, I know that I wasn't feeling as secure and calm as I tried to appear. What I really felt was a kind of defiance. I had found something that was mine at last, something that gave me an identity of my own. Deep inside, though, there was a scared feeling which I couldn't show anybody. In fact, as far as possible, I kept it hidden from myself.

Now, as I wipe my sticky, paint-stained hands on my shorts, I know that I was not following my dream by becoming a mother. I was running away from the fear of never being able to live up to my parents' expectations of me. The baby gave me the opportunity to do that and I took it.

***

'Lori, I don't know how you could see him again after what he did to you. He is married to Cassandra and . . ..'

'I know, Jenny, I know,' I sigh. The last thing I want right now is to be told off. Jenny had taken me to the station to catch my train back down to Calabria after my radiotherapy had finished and I was wishing I'd caught a cab.

'Jenny, all I know is that he asks me how I feel and seems to understand my answer. The way he found me on the pavement that evening didn't really faze him. He took it in his stride. He took me seriously.' Jenny looked sceptical. 'Being with someone who really looks at me,' I went on, 'and really listens to me, is so great. It seems so long since Alberto has done either of those things.'

'Lori, I understand that but Leo is not the answer to your problems with Alberto. He will just hurt you again. This time the happiness of lots of people is at stake. You both have families.'

'Jenny, I only met him for a chat, for God's sake. Stop lecturing me, especially about something I haven't done.'

I was relieved that in a few minutes I had to catch my

train. Much as I loved Jenny she could be really hard to take sometimes. Her brand of in-your-face reality was not what I wanted to hear. I wanted to sink into my bubble and take Leo in there with me, away from harsh light and complications.

Leo had come round two nights before. We had popped out for an aperitif down the road and chatted for a couple of hours. He could be just as charming as ever but seemed much more genuine now and a much better listener than he had been all those years ago. His slightly sad air of world-weariness was quite endearing, making him much more gentle than the determined fighter I had known and loved back then. Meeting him again made it even harder to leave Bologna. We had promised to keep in touch and I wondered if that were going to happen.

Chapter 17

'Lori, fetch the coffee, would you?' I put the little coffee maker on the table. As I poured some out for Giuseppina, Assunta's next-door neighbour, I heard a voice saying dreamily, 'Green swirls, I'd paint him in green swirls, like a skirt I had when I was sixteen. Green swirls with black lines between them, that's what I'd paint on his back.'

'What? Whose back?' Assunta stared straight at me, with her grimmest thin-lipped look.

'Roberto's,' I replied automatically naming a friend of Alberto's from the village, I had seen him recently because I was teaching his daughter English. 'A big green swirl from his left buttock up to his right shoulder, covering most of his back with fronds running off it down his left leg and along his right arm. He's very slim, very light, you could almost imagine him blowing in the breeze.'

Open mouths, the sudden clatter of spoons in coffee cups, I stared at their faces as it slowly dawned on me that the voice was mine. I had spoken my fantasy about painting Roberto's back out loud, in front of Assunta, Antonella my youngest sister-in-law, and Assunta's neighbour Giuseppina, who just happened to be one of the village's greatest gossips. The momentary peace was bliss, all three of them with their mouths open, their eyes bulging with incredulity.

Then Assunta found her voice, like gunfire across the table. 'When did you paint him? He's a father of three! His poor wife, poor Viviana! You whore, how could you?' It was my turn to stare, incredulous.

'You can't call me a whore! I only talked about painting him.'

'You mean a portrait?' Poor Antonella was trying to make sense of it all, but her mother didn't need sense, she went straight to judgement.

'I knew it, she's an adulterer! Poor Alberto.' Assunta could hardly spit the words out. 'And poor Viviana, fancy her husband . . ..'

'Mother, Lori is talking about painting, not adultery.' Antonella almost had to shout above the shocked protests.

'She is a good woman, is Viviana. She doesn't deserve this. How could you, you . . . ?'

'Mother, she's talking about fantasy, not reality.' That word really sent Assunta off.

'Fantasy! She has fantasies about Roberto! Oh Holy Father!' She cast her eyes heavenwards and crossed herself.

I was washing up the breakfast things, carefully stacking clean plates in the draining cupboard above the sink. Antonella came over to me and took hold of my arm, desperate for my attention.

'Lori, please tell them quickly or their versions will be all over the village by this evening.'

I wanted to distance myself from my own words and from their reactions. I didn't know what to say.

'Tell them what?'

Antonella was exasperated. 'Tell them what you said before, about painting, about fantasy. Lori, they think you're having an affair with Roberto and if you don't convince them otherwise, it will be all over the region by sundown and it won't matter a jot that it's not true, your names will have been dragged through the mud.'

I was shocked. I had said something out loud that I'd only ever thought before and now my mother-in-law and her neighbour condemned me with my own words.

'I imagined painting him with green swirls,' I said.

'That's all,' interrupted Antonella, 'isn't it, Lori? You were just talking about imagining?'

'You, signora,' I turned to Assunta, 'You should be painted as a black crow with a big sharp and treacherous beak!' Assunta flew across the kitchen table.

***

As I approached Alberto I began to realise how nervous I was. I had lain awake the night before, worrying about his

Colour me in

reaction. We met outside a trattoria and kissed each other tentatively.

'Can we walk a while before going in?' I wanted to talk somewhere less public.

'Sure, it's still quite early.'

We wandered down the road and into Piazza San Francesco. We had to walk round the edges of the piazza to keep out of the way of a football game going on there among much shouting and excitement. When we reached the benches in front of the old church, we sat down. I gazed up at the magnificent building and tried to calm the butterflies in my stomach.

Alberto also seemed nervous. I was banking on him being relieved when I told him I was staying and hoping that becoming a father would seem like a small price to pay for my continued presence in his life. Dream on, Lori!

He looked good, handsome almost. He still had his summer tan, his dark curly hair was tousled and his deep, dark eyes had a serious, worried look in them. If I hadn't been pregnant I doubt that I really could have ended it then and there. Instead I felt very scared about what I was about to reveal. What if he just said no, he wanted nothing to do with becoming a father? What would I do? My mouth felt very dry. Maybe Jenny was right and I was being unrealistic and pig-headed.

Alberto tentatively took hold of my hand. It felt nice and I smiled at him. 'I'm sad we haven't been able to spend more time together in the last few days,' he said. 'I really am going to miss you, Lori.' I wondered how on earth to begin. 'It's been a great summer, for me anyway,' he went on.

I nodded. 'And for me.'

'Really?'

'Yes, it was . . . a summer of surprises.'

He squeezed my hand. 'It certainly was, and it was a wonderful surprise for me . . .' As he trailed off, he looked at me anxiously. 'Lori, I do want to come and visit you in England, if that's okay with you.' I started nodding and said, almost automatically, 'Yes, yes, that would be great.' Alberto looked relieved and visibly relaxed. I felt my heart beating. I turned towards him on the bench.

'Alberto, I have something to tell you.'

'What's that?' He moved closer to me and squeezed my hand. I wondered what was going to happen to his expression next. I stared at the ground.

'The thing is, Alberto . . . I'm pregnant.' He gasped and dropped my hand. He looked astonished, as if it had never occurred to him that it could possibly happen.

'Alberto, we took a big risk that first time on the beach.' He sat very still staring in front of him. I began to feel anxious. Why wasn't he saying anything?

'It was just the one time. I . . . I'm sorry, Lori, I thought I'd asked you, I thought it was okay I didn't think of it as a risk. I was stupid. What do you want to do?'

I swallowed, 'I want to have the baby.'

Alberto's tanned face paled visibly. 'Really? You do?'

'Yes.'

'But Lori, your studies . . . you're not Catholic. You don't have a mother like mine. When my eldest sister got pregnant it was straight up the aisle, no hesitation. She would never have allowed an abortion. But your mother is not like that. You have choices.' Alberto swallowed and then said more slowly, 'I have heard you, Jenny and Simona talking about a woman's right to choose to have a career and a family. Are you sure you don't want to finish your degree and work for a few years before starting a family? You said you wanted to travel.'

'I know I did and maybe I will someday, but Alberto, I've been thinking about it over the last few days and I do want this baby, I really do.'

I wasn't sure whether I sounded courageous or just stubborn. Alberto took hold of my hand again, which was a relief, and turned to look straight at me.

'Lori, I think you should consider everything very carefully. Don't rush into a decision. You don't need to decide now.' I'd heard that a lot in the last few days.

We sat in silence for a few seconds, although it seemed longer. I realised what I needed urgently to ask him and suddenly felt very nervous. He clearly thought I was being far too hasty as it was.

'Alberto, how would you feel if I didn't get on that plane tomorrow?'

'Is that what you want, to stay here?' His voice sounded tentative. I suddenly had an urge to hug him, to feel his arms around me, maybe because his response was so important to me. I really didn't know if I could have this baby alone.

I nodded, 'Yes, I do.'

'Do you want to stay to have the baby or do you want to stay anyway?'

'I . . . I haven't thought about not having the baby. I want to stay here and have the baby.' Alberto looked out in front of him again, gazing at the last few footballers who having finished their game, were walking away across the piazza. I squeezed his hand. 'I'm glad,' I added, 'to have a reason to stay here with you. Look I know this is a big shock. I would like to stay here with you and bring up the baby but you have to decide if that's what you want.' My voice faded as fear began to shake it.

Alberto looked at me and I couldn't work out his expression. I felt cross with myself for not having thought enough about how he would feel and react. I think that inside my earth-mother glow I had simplified everything, hoping that Alberto would be glad to stay together and play happy families. He, however, seemed well aware that the situation was much more complicated.

We stayed on our bench talking while the sun went down over the red tiled roofs of the buildings across the piazza.

Alberto wanted me to consider not keeping the baby and I promised I would think about it some more.

Alberto thought it would probably be well over a year before he had completely finished his last two exams and his thesis and pointed out that neither of us could ask for any financial help from our parents. I said that I wanted to give up studying and get work as an English teacher, that my friend Gina, who was also pregnant, was teaching Italian to foreign students and doing translations into Italian. She was helping me get a CV together and thought that I should be able to get translation work into English once my Italian was better.

We talked and talked. Alberto was very worried and, looking back, I guess it was just as well one of us was capable of being realistic. We strolled through the town as dusk deepened to dark, neither of us remembering that we hadn't eaten.

Under the portico in via Ugo Bassi, Alberto stopped and turned to face me. He took hold of my hands.

'Listen, Lori, I can see you're serious about this. I still think you should think it all over very carefully. You have time to change your mind but, in the meantime, stay. You can move in with me and we can see how we get on.'

I stepped forward and slipped my arms around his waist. As his arms wrapped around me I told myself that Alberto made me feel safe and secure and that he was the one person I wanted to bring up a child with.

***

'Lori, I tried.' Antonella looked really unhappy. 'You should have defended yourself. You know what a gossip Giuseppina is and my mother is always ready to believe the worst.'

'Especially of me.' I said wryly.

'Well, you make it easy for her to . . ..'

'Hate me.' I finished her sentence.

'No. I was going to say wind you up. She doesn't hate

you, Lori. She just can't understand you.'

I sighed. 'You're right. I should never have called her a crow.' I couldn't suppress a giggle at the memory. 'She did look . . ..' I stopped. 'I'm sorry, Antonella, she is your mother. I . . . she just . . ..'

'Winds you up,' Antonella smiled.

She had suggested that we go for a walk round the village to let her mother calm down. It was a lovely sunny spring morning and bougainvilleas were in flower everywhere. I loved them with their bright pink petals and soft scent. Although I really liked Antonella I felt a little fearful of what she was going to say. I had always considered myself very lucky that Alberto's sisters were all so easy to get on with. Rosanna, who lived nearby and ran the pizzeria with her husband; Sara in Bologna and Antonella, who was a teacher in Saluzzo in the north, were always very kind and thoughtful. They were all good humoured and sunny like their father. Alberto, on the other hand, was much more like his mother. He had once had a great sense of humour but I had seen little of it for a long time.

Antonella linked her arm through mine. 'You're obviously under a huge strain at the moment.' We turned off the main village street and after a few metres the asphalt and the houses ended and the road became a dusty lane leading us across a field littered with rocks, stones and cacti. I leant into Antonella for comfort.

'Do you,' I swallowed, 'do you think I'm losing my grip on reality?' I shivered as I said those words. Antonella was silent, just for a few seconds but it felt as if she were confirming my fears.

'Lori, I . . ..' She squeezed my arm. 'Do you think talking to someone, I mean, someone professional, would help?' I hated the word "Professional." I couldn't imagine being able to explain how I felt to such a person. Would they think there was something wrong with my mind? I shook my head.

***

Shocking pink orchids! They're looking okay, at least I think they are. I was shaking, I don't know why . . .. I was holding the dish of paint and managed to splash bright pink all over the floor. I must clean it up now. I'll do some paler pink ones too, hopefully once they're done the patch that was Toucan will be dry and I can paint him again. The tension knots in my stomach as I think about him. For some reason I feel as though I can't give up on him although I think the orange birds might be more fun.

***

Assunta, Alberto and I were sitting in the back yard under the tall palm tree having coffee after dinner one evening, watching the children playing bowls. All along the edge of the courtyard were beautiful flowering succulents throwing up their soft scent.

'Why are you still paying rent on that flat in Bologna?' asked Assunta. I wasn't sure what to say. 'Why not just let it go?' she continued. 'You are here now and soon you will move into Zio Donato's house.' She looked at Alberto, 'Your job is here.' She turned to me, 'Your family is here and your life is here.' I felt a shiver run down my spine as she spoke.

'Lori isn't quite ready to let it go yet.'

'Alberto, it's about time you stopped pandering to her.' She spoke as if I were not there.

'Mamma, Lori needs time to get better.' He leant towards me in his chair. Assunta looked at me this time but still addressed Alberto.

'But don't you see? She's not getting better; she's getting worse. Her behaviour is getting stranger and stranger. Alberto, she insulted me, I told you she called me a crow, in my own house!' She turned towards me now, anger on her face and indignation in her voice.

'Mamma, the cancer has been a big strain, hasn't it, Lori?' Alberto was struggling. I couldn't speak.

Colour me in

'Maria Grazia had breast cancer a few years ago and she didn't do these things. She would never ever have insulted the person whose house she was living in.' Still looking pointedly at me, 'Your Zia Pasqualina, do you remember?' she turned to Alberto. 'A few years ago she had both breasts removed. She stayed perfectly sane. Not a sign of madness.' She turned back to me. 'She wasn't even sad. She always joked that her breasts were too heavy anyway. She used to say, "Well, at least now I'm not in danger of falling over!" She always looked on the bright side.' Assunta shot me a look. I didn't want to rise to the bait. She had accused me of being mad and I couldn't challenge her.

***

Long fronds of palm leaves, once I've done these the wall will be quite covered. I can fill in the gaps with more flowers. The Toucan patch isn't quite dry but once I've done this palm it should be. It has to be . . . time is running out. The soreness in my gut is a hot nervous feeling that won't go away. This has to be finished, maybe I will go out, maybe I don't want to be here . . . but the children will love it. I hope they see the magic.

***

The middle finger of my right hand moved slowly from my cheek over the line of my jaw and down the side of my neck, over my collar bone and down towards my right breast. A bright electric-blue streak. I have to take my tee-shirt off.

What started as a blue bird just below my eye had now travelled down from my face to my body and I didn't want to stop. I pulled off my tee-shirt and dipped my finger again in the pot of blue face paint on the dressing table. It was a hot June afternoon and the whole household was sleeping.

Soon after I had arrived, Alberto had dragged the spare single bed into Beppe's room as my erratic sleep patterns drove him crazy.

Standing in front of the dressing table mirror, I let my

fingers roam where they wanted to go. I had to take my bra off. 'Oh stupid,' I mumbled, as I'd already covered the middle finger of my right hand with fresh blue paint. Oh never mind, I can wash it. It landed on the floor.

My right breast looked so much smaller than the left. All the flesh was gone from underneath it, the soft oozy part you can cup in your hand, gone! The scar ran from the inside of my breast, from where I had once had cleavage, right up to the edge of my nipple. It dipped down in the middle, caving in my breast and causing my nipple to point inwards. It looked so sad and forlorn. Usually the sight of it made me cry, but now I wanted beauty instead of sorrow.

Still with the blue paint on my middle finger, I gently traced the scar, from the inside towards the nipple, a little river winding its way up a bumpy hill with a crooked peak.

Time for more colour. There's red, there's pink. I laid the little pots out in a row in front of me yellow, purple . . . .. I had finished Beppe's birthday paint sticks long ago. These little pots held much more paint and could cover whole bodies, rows and rows of them. I closed my eyes and saw beautiful bodies covered in fields of poppies, gothic spires and Rubenesque cherubs.

I opened my eyes and returned to my body. We are in the countryside: flowers, I think, along by the river. Violets, and then, stretching out below, a wood full of bluebells. Purple paint, followed by green and then brown, I have violets all over my right breast and a bluebell wood across my rib cage. By now I was used to painting while looking in the mirror. Up to then I had done only my face and head. This felt different but I was getting there. The bluebell wood took some doing but I loved the effect I achieved with different shades of brown and green. Then the deep purple blue of the bluebells splashed over the top and the wood came to life. The texture my fingers created worked well for the flowers and leaves as they ran down over my stomach. I had undone the fly of my cotton trousers. Now

Colour me in

they had to come off. I tried to wriggle and jump out of them without touching them too much, but they ended up on the floor in a scrunchy, sticky mess of cotton and paint.

I slipped my left hand into the top of my knickers and pulled them down. They slid off more easily and I stepped out of them. I wanted a meadow beyond the wood. My left breast was still bare and shiny-white amidst the colour. 'A flower garden for you, my love.' I dipped my fingers in flaming orange, tracing the curves of my healthy breast. 'Be glad you still have one whole and beautiful,' I whispered to myself. The tears came.

I didn't hear the door open. I had managed to create an entangled trellis of woven orange and yellow flowers all over my left breast, which curved down my left side and across part of my back. Even using the mirror, I had had to turn my neck as far round to the left as I could. It was awkward painting that way, but I loved the effect.

Beppe stood with his mouth open: 'Mamma, what have you done?' I smiled, 'What do you think?' I spread open my arms to show him just as Alberto appeared. 'My God, Lori! Whatever will you think of next? Wash it off at once!' He gripped my wrist very tightly and started pulling me out of the bedroom and into the corridor towards the bathroom. Assunta's door opened. Nothing escapes her radar. She stood in front of me, arms folded, a triumphant smile quivering across her lips. 'Well, well, she really does paint bodies.' She leant forward and whispered in my ear, 'Is this what you do to Roberto, eh?' I said nothing. Beppe was behind Alberto. Assunta stepped back and, resuming her full volume, said, 'In front of your son, naked and painted like a whore!'

'Mamma, don't talk like that.' Alberto sounded worn out and exasperated rather than angry.

Alone in the bathroom I didn't want to wash it off. I think Alberto had wanted to put me under the shower but I closed the door firmly and bolted it. The mirror over the basin showed my painted body. The violets were running into the river, my right breast was covered in shades of purple and blue and looked bruised. My knees caved in. I leant against the wall and slowly slid down to the floor.

As I emerged from the bathroom wrapped in a towelling bathrobe, my beautiful painting washed down the plughole, I felt a breeze come through the open window at the end of the corridor. I stopped to look out: the afternoon sun was slowly sinking and the sky around it was a soft peach colour, ready to deepen and spread as sunset approached. Alberto and Assunta were sitting in the backyard just below the window. Their conversation drifted up to me.

'You have to come,' Assunta was saying. 'She is your cousin and it's her baby's christening. You must come, and bring the children.'

'I don't want to leave Lori alone, Mamma. You've seen her she's unstable right now we can't leave her.'

'I am not taking her with us!' Assunta barked, spit flying out of her mouth in her determination to get her point across. 'She'll be okay Giuseppina can look in on her. She's only next door I'll tell her to watch the door and make sure she doesn't wander out naked and painted!' Alberto was silent.

I felt a long sigh breathe out of me. Tomorrow I was to be left alone while they went to the christening.

***

Toucan two is better, yes, I believe he is, his beak is good that's what matters . . . oh god I really don't have much time. I'll stand in the middle of the room in a minute, take stock, see what still needs touching up. I want to get a good look at it before . . . .. I don't know though maybe this beak isn't really . . . actually there is a space by the pink orchids. I must paint another flower, something red . . . do I have enough red?

I sink to the floor my arms aching. My stomach feels so tight. I must get on . . ..

Colour me in

***

I sat down at a table in a patch of sunlight by a large arched window in the student coffee bar at the end of via Zamboni overlooking piazza Verdi. It was a beautiful room with high ceilings and sun streaming in through the windows.

I put my cappuccino and pastry on the table and looked out at the piazza, which was full of students clutching bags and files on their way to and from lectures. I decided to keep my coat on for a moment. It was a cold January morning and even inside the café it was chilly. It felt strange being surrounded by students and yet not being one of them any more.

To think that a whole year had passed since we came back from the holidays to find the university in occupation. The excited Lori who had rushed through the streets in search of Leo seemed a long way from the pregnant, married woman gazing out of the window now. I sighed and sat down. Would I get used to feeling that student life was no longer mine and that Leo was just a memory?

I had come here to meet two students who wanted private English lessons. As I put my bag on the chair beside mine, I felt someone standing right behind me and turned my head expecting to see the students I was waiting for.

'It is you! Hi, Lori.' Leo stood awkwardly looking down at me. My heart jumped into my mouth. I didn't know what to say. 'Are you waiting for someone? May I join you for a moment?' I nodded. I hadn't seen him since the goodbye party before we were supposed to leave for England last September.

'Um, yes, yes. I'm waiting for two students who want English lessons, but fine, sit down . . ..' My voice trailed off. I watched him take off his coat and scarf and settle into the seat opposite me.

'What a surprise I thought you were back in England long ago.' I was surprised that he hadn't heard. I would have thought that Sandro had told him.

'No, I decided to stay I'm working now.'

'Teaching English?'

'Yes, I've been doing a training course at a private language school. They're gradually giving me more hours. I'm starting a new course with them this week and I'm going to start translating soon.' I smiled, determined to show him that I was doing fine without him.

'Wow! So you're staying here?'

'Yes, I am.' He looked at me steadily for a moment.

'Lori, I'm very glad to see you. I've thought about you a lot over these past few months.' He had his "I'm really sincere" look on his face.

I didn't know what to say. He seemed to mean it. I felt a lurch of excitement in my stomach and wished I could stop it. Leo looked as beautiful as ever, especially with that smile. As if he had read my earlier thoughts, he said, 'Just think, this time last year we were in occupation!'

'I know, sometimes it seems like yesterday.'

'A lot has happened, though,' Leo went on. 'I guess you've heard the University is really on the offensive now. They've started limiting the numbers on a lot of courses and closing down others altogether.' He sighed and shook his head, 'I know we were expecting it but they are on the attack, already directing some courses towards the needs of big business. I wish we could have fought for longer.'

'You did . . . we all did our best.' I smiled at him and he suddenly seemed embarrassed.

'Listen, Lori, last time we met I didn't tell you but I . . . wanted to say . . . I'm sorry. When we met for that coffee, I felt so guilty, so bad, I didn't know what to say.' Wow, he was actually apologising.

My stomach lurched again and I tried to speak, 'I wish you . . . I wish . . .' What did I wish? That he'd been honest with me? Well, yes, but what I really wished was that things had been different, that he had been single when we met and that we were still together now.

Colour me in

Did I wish that, though, now I had a baby on the way and a man who made me feel safe, not insecure?

'Lori, I want you to know that . . . I miss you.' My heart started thumping. What could I do? I took a deep breath, then remembered my cappuccino and lifted it and took a sip. I put the cup back down.

'Leo, why do you say that? Surely you are still with Cassandra?' I managed to say her name. He nodded, a little reluctantly it seemed.

'We are together.'

'Good,' I said. 'That's fine.' He looked unnerved by this.

'Lori, I really want us to be friends. Can we be friends? You are here in Bologna. I will need more English lessons.' Now what did that mean? I couldn't reply.

It occurred to me that my students were late. I was warm now and decided to take my coat off. I stood up, undid the buttons and slipped it off. As Leo watched me a puzzled look crept across his face. I was now five months pregnant. He stared at my stomach, then up at me, and then back to my stomach again. He looked quite shaken.

'The baby is due in mid May.' Leo's mouth was open but no words came out. He swallowed and then found his voice.

'Who's the baby's father?' At that point I spotted my students and waved them over.

'Alberto, the guy I married.' He looked confused and maybe a little sad.

Chapter 18

I don't know what flowers these are, a rough copy of some in the book . . . I'm doing them red. I must get back to Toucan and finish him properly . . .. A car door slams - that reminds me, I don't have much time, I must tidy up and wash the brushes before they get back.

The front door opens. I'm squatting, I stand quickly and the blood rushes to my head. I stop, rooted to the spot, brush in hand, dripping red paint, staring down at the half-finished flower.

I hear footsteps rushing into the room. I feel Beppe hurl himself at me, wrapping his arms around my waist. Then he lets go. I hear his steps retreating across the room. I stare at the red paint on the wall. I can't lift my gaze.

Other steps come clicking in. A sharp intake of breath, then a strangled shriek, Assunta's voice comes out in breathless bursts, 'Mad! Mad! Completely mad . . . to do this! To do this to someone else's house! You have ruined, ruined my beautiful house! Alberto, Alberto, your wife is mad. I knew it. She's gone mad.' I hear her rush out of the house. Then lighter steps run across the room and arms wrap around again. This time it's Michela.

'Oh Mamma, what have you done? Nonna is going completely crazy.' I hold the paintbrush away from her and remain staring at the red flower. Little rushing steps enter the room, followed by larger, slower ones, followed by the click of Assunta's heels.

'Oh my God, Lori!' Alberto's voice.

'I told you she's mad, completely mad. Alberto, your wife is mad - I told you. Now do you believe me? Huh? Now do you believe me?' Assunta's clicking heels echo all around the room. 'She has ruined my dining room!' Her voice rises to a wail. She's covered these two walls, completely covered them with her ridiculous paintings. How can we use this room? How can we eat dinner in here? We can't.'

The clicking heels come close. I feel her breath on my

Colour me in

neck and a sharp prod in my right shoulder. 'Look at what you've done to my house,' she hisses in my ear. I have to look up and step away from her. There is desperation on her face as she throws her hands in the air.

Suddenly she catches sight of the dresser. 'Oh no, not the dresser too! It was my mother's.' Assunta recoils in horror at the sight of my bright orange sun. She looks near to tears. I feel sorry for her, as if I have nothing to do with her pain.

Assunta turns to face me. 'You're mad! I've tried to understand. I've taken you into my home. You've painted bedroom walls, you've painted yourself, you've talked about painting Roberto and goodness only knows what you got up to with him. This is enough. I'm not putting up with you any more. You need help. We can't deal with you. You're mad.' She marches out of the room and into the kitchen.

A white, worn Alberto follows her out of the room. The children hold each other's hands. Beppe looks scared.

'Oh Mamma, why did you do it?' asks Michela. I want to give her a proper explanation but all I can do is shrug and say, 'I had to.'

'Why?'

'This house needs colour.' Michela looks puzzled.

'Children, go into the kitchen with your grandmother please. She's preparing dinner.' Alberto returns, his voice sounding unusually authoritative. He comes over and takes hold of my shoulders. 'What on earth are you playing at?' I step backwards out of his grasp. For the first time ever, I'm afraid of him. He isn't shouting but anger is seeping out of every syllable. 'What were you thinking of?' He looks around the walls. 'I can't believe that you've done this! After everything my mother has done for you! She has let you stay here to recover and rest and look how you repay her!'

I step back again, well away from him. I lean against my sea-covered wall. Some of the sticky paint adheres to my hair. I lean harder, wanting to become part of it, to disappear into it. I had been happy all day painting a mural and now they come home and take it away.

Alberto sits down on one of the dining chairs I have pushed against the far wall. He puts his head in his hands and stays still for what feels like a long time.

'I don't know what to do with you.' It comes out muffled, and then he lifts his head slowly. He looks lost. 'My mother says you need help, she's right. We must find you help,' he says quietly.

'Finally,' I mumble, looking away from him. 'Help at last.'

Alberto looks shocked. 'What do you mean?'

An overwhelming exhaustion comes over me and I can't find any words.

'I've helped you as much . . .' His voice fades out. 'I tried, I guess it just wasn't . . .' He looks at me for a second and then looks away again. 'Lori, this is not sane, normal behaviour. It's wanton destruction of someone else's house.' I have to sit down. 'I don't know how you could do this, I really don't.'

I find my voice. 'I think it's beautiful. I've brought the sea, the jungle, birds and flowers into the house.'

Alberto stands up and looks at the wall. 'It should be in a gallery, not here. You've lost your sense of what is . . . appropriate behaviour. You have a problem.'

'Do you think I'm mad, Alberto?'

'I . . . don't really know what to think.' He looks around at the walls. 'Lori, this is not exactly sane.'

He sounds very sad. I really want him to hug me, to hold me in his arms, but he walks out of the room. I hear his footsteps go into the kitchen. I lean into the sea-covered wall flattening my hands against it.

***

From the bedroom I can hear Alberto's voice floating up from the hallway. I know he has spoken to the doctor and is now talking to someone else. The knot in my stomach

Colour me in

tightens and I feel sick. I walk to the top of the stairs where I can hear more clearly.

'Definitely, that would be good. We need your opinion.' Then a pause, 'Yes, I think that would be best. My mother can't cope with her in the house and our children are upset.' Pause. 'Mmmm, that would be excellent, an assessment, to decide her treatment. Would that be drugs?' Alberto is looking down, concentrating, and has not seen me.

'Great, so we bring her in tomorrow morning and you will do the assessment then?' Pause. I can just see the anxious expression on Alberto's face. 'Ahh, well I don't know how long we could wait around she may not stay. She is not really . . ..' The relief in his voice is discernible as he says, 'A bit later, thank you, yes. That's fine. So we bring her in at midday and you will see her then? Right, and you will keep her in for a period, to be decided on the basis . . .. Oh yes, of course. Thank you very much, Doctor. It's so kind of you at such short notice. Yes, thank you. See you tomorrow at midday.' He puts the phone down and goes into the kitchen.

***

'Keep her in.' I'm carefully folding my favourite dress and putting it into my suitcase. 'Keep her in,' all the clean knickers I can find go in beside it. I go into the bathroom for my sponge bag. 'Keep her in,' indeed. I put my toothbrush and toothpaste, shower gel and shampoo in the sponge bag. I return to the bedroom and pick up the little pots of face paints and put them in a plastic bag, which I stow safely in the suitcase.

Bending down I fish a sketchpad and some loose sheets of paper with paintings on them out from under the bed. These must come with me. I won't worry about the paints, there are plenty at home. Finally the suitcase is full and everything I can think of is packed. I plop down on the bed, shattered and shaking, tears rolling down my face. The blotchy character in the mirror looks distraught.

Nicola Sellars

'My husband is trying to put me in a psychiatric hospital, a loony bin. My husband is trying to put me in a loony bin.' It dawns on me that I'm still wearing my paint-covered clothes, so I slip them off. Taking my sponge bag out of my suitcase again, I go back into the bathroom to shower.

I dress in clean clothes taken out of the suitcase and repack my sponge bag. The others are down in the kitchen eating dinner. I'm not hungry. I close the bedroom door and, taking my phone out of my handbag, call the local taxi. I hope to be in time for the night train. My suitcase is still open on the bed and I pull out one of the loose paintings and write a note to the children on the back of it. Writing is difficult as my hands are shaking with fear. When will I see them again?

***

'Are you alright?' The man sitting opposite me on the train is peering at me with an anxious look on his face.

The tight band across my chest that I've been feeling for a while, is getting tighter and I'm not sure how to breathe. I try to take a breath and find myself gasping.

The man sitting opposite becomes a blur. The carriage starts spinning and I feel myself falling . . ..

I'm lying on the floor aware of people around me and hear phrases like 'asthma' and 'heart attack'.

'Are you ready to sit up?' Hands help me up to my seat. Someone suggests I put my head between my legs. I do for a minute but feel wobbly. Gradually I sit up. The carriage is still spinning but more slowly now and I'm shivering. My breath is still coming in gasps.

I hear a voice saying 'breathe in as deeply as you can . . . now breath out.' I try to follow her words but I've forgotten how to breathe. A hand takes hold of mine and the words 'breathe in . . . breathe out' continue, she speaks slowly and rhythmically saying, 'breathe in . . . breathe out' and I follow her words. I am breathing. It feels amazing. The carriage is still moving slightly but as I continue to

Colour me in

breathe, it gradually rights itself. I am aware that I'm sitting in my seat, a woman beside me holding my hand and the man opposite looking concerned. He hands me a plastic bottle. 'Would you like some water?' I nod gratefully as my mouth feels very dry. I sip carefully, aware that my stomach feels wobbly.

After a while I manage to thank them for their help. They had helped me off the floor and onto my seat. The woman says that she used to suffer from panic attacks and learnt that deep breathing was the best way out of them and the best way of preventing them.

'Well I've never fainted like that before,' I say. 'I don't know what happened, but I couldn't breathe and you got me breathing again, thank you so much.'

I feel very tired, the woman returns to her seat nearby and I spread out across the two seats and fall asleep.

***

As soon as Jenny sees me, she starts running. I'm enveloped in her embrace and I burst into tears. 'Oh Lori, whatever has been going on?' I hold her tight. She phoned me just after I got on the train, saying that Alberto had called her and she wanted to check where I was going. When I told her, she asked what time I would be arriving in Bologna. The line was too bad to talk but I was pleased to hear her voice.

'I got a garbled call from Alberto that I couldn't fully understand, he said you ran away.' Her voice sounds incredulous. 'It sounds as if you were a prisoner.' She looks at me, puzzled.

'He was going to put me in a psychiatric hospital!'

'He told me he had arranged for you to see a psychiatrist, but didn't mention a hospital.'

'I heard him on the phone to a psychiatrist arranging an appointment for an assessment and then he said "and you will keep her in for a period." My own husband wants to have me committed!'

'Oh Lori. You look very pale let's get you home.' She starts to lead me towards the station exit.

'I fainted on the train.'

'Oh no . . ..' Jenny stops walking and turns to look at me. I stop too.

'I had a tight pain in my chest, couldn't breathe and fainted. Some of the other passengers helped me. I was lucky.'

'Oh Lori, and you were on your own. Thank God you got here safely.'

She hugs me again. 'This whole thing must be stressful how are you feeling now?'

'Okay, just weak and very tired.'

'Well let's get you home and then you can sleep.'

She takes my hand and we continue towards the exit.

Once we are settled in Jenny's car she says, 'Alberto was ranting on the phone. He said something about you painting walls. Did you really paint a mural in Assunta's house?' I nod.

'I bet she liked that,' she chuckles. 'I would love to have seen her face.'

'It was lovely, Jenny, I managed to get the sea . . ..' Seeing her expression my voice goes quieter, 'It looked so real.'

'The thing is, you're supposed to paint murals when people ask you to,' says Jenny, 'not cover their walls while they're out.' She chuckles nervously as she drives out of the car park.

As we enter the morning rush-hour traffic on the viale, the Bologna inner ring road, I say, 'I'm not mad you know Jen.' She looks in her mirror and does not reply.

'I am not mad.'

'Your behaviour has been . . . strange.' I stare out of the window. Not her too.

***

On the way home we stop at a shop and Jenny pops in to buy me some food. I stay in the car; my body feels heavy

Colour me in

but fragile at the same time. I want Jenny to say something to reassure me that she's on my side, but nothing.

We drive home and she makes sure I have everything I need. She's worried about leaving me but I assure her that I'll be okay. I just want to sleep.

I fall asleep as soon as I get into bed. I awake after a couple of hours and drift in and out of consciousness with strange snatches of dream. A grey mist surrounds me and figures are walking towards me. As they come nearer, I think I can make out the silhouettes of Michela and Beppe, but just as I'm about to call out and run to them I realise that now they are walking backwards away from me. I run towards them but they are so far away I'm never able to get near them. Then I wake up, a horrible fear gripping my stomach. I struggle up and lie propped against the pillows blinking away the mist.

After a few minutes I stumble into the kitchen to make coffee to wake myself up. I roll up the blinds and throw the balcony doors open, letting the sun stream in. I gaze out at my familiar view of the car park and the buildings beyond, squinting through the afternoon heat-haze at the church spires and towers in the distance. I let out an involuntary sigh of relief. At last I'm in my own home again! My stomach clenches when I think about the children and wonder what I'm going to say to Alberto.

This thought takes me to my handbag where I fumble around for my mobile phone. Alberto has called. I hold the phone in the palm of my hand. Best call him on his mobile rather than on Assunta's house phone. He called me while I was on the train and left a message saying that he just wanted to know that I was okay. I texted him saying I was heading to Bologna and would talk later. I click on Alberto and press the little call symbol. My stomach clenches again and my hand is shaking.

'Hi, Lori.' He speaks quietly and a sigh comes out with the words. 'Are you okay?'

'Not too bad, I dozed a little on the train and have just had a couple of hours' sleep.' I decide not to tell him about the fainting.

'Right, I'm glad you managed to sleep.' Silence. I can hear his breathing at the end of the phone, strangely reassuring. I'm angry with him but I just want to stand there in silence and not say anything.

'The children are worried about you.'

'Tell them I'm okay. I didn't leave to worry the children.'

'I know.'

'I left because I had to, not because I wanted to leave my children. I don't want to be apart from them, Alberto.'

'Lori, I know you don't. I would ask you to come back but . . ..'

'Not if the only option is a psychiatric hospital.'

'Oh, so you did hear. '

'Yes, I heard you talking to the psychiatrist, "so you will keep her in for a period."' The shaking seems to spread from my hands and down my arms to the rest of my body.

'I don't need to be locked up,' I gasp, as the tears take hold.

'Lori, you can't go on like this. You need help.' I manage to take a deep breath and reach for a tea towel to wipe my eyes. The voice of the woman on the train comes back to me, "Breathe in . . . breathe out."

'Alberto, I do not need locking up!'

'Maybe not, Lori, maybe Mamma went . . ..'

'You called the doctor and talked to the psychiatrist.'

'I didn't know what to do. Mamma said you had to leave her house.' He sounds tense and tired. Silence descends on us again, broken only by the sound of my breath as I continue the deep breathing.

'Listen, if we'd been in our own house, if we'd moved into Zio Donato's house, you could have seen a psychiatrist for sessions and stayed at home. But my mother . . ..'

'Okay, I know. I just wish you could support me

sometimes instead of . . ..'

'What could I do?'

'Just make me feel that you understand.'

There is silence. I hear his breathing again, and then he says quietly, 'I don't understand.'

***

'I'd have loved to have been a fly on the wall when Assunta walked in and saw the mural in her dining room,' says Francesca. She, Jenny and Simona have come round in the evening, bringing pizza.

'What made you paint a mural?' Simona asks. I swallow, I really need to make them understand. 'I wanted to do something that was mine. I wanted to bring colour into a house full of darkness.'

'Full of darkness?' There's surprise in Francesca's voice. She squeezes my hand.

'Did it work?' asks Simona.

'Well yes, until they came home I felt great. Then Assunta was angry, Alberto was angry and it was all ruined.'

We concentrate on our pizzas, for a moment no one seems to know what to say. I swallow down a mouthful. The words "I have to make them understand," are reverberating round in my head.

'Sometimes when I painted pictures or when I painted the children's walls I felt a lot better afterwards. I felt alive while I was painting and then relief.'

'Alberto said you painted yourself and flashed to Beppe. He was outraged.' Jenny sounds accusing. I feel myself shrinking into the sofa. I struggle to find my voice.

'For months I have felt judged by Assunta and Alberto and now you are judging me too!'

'I'm not. I don't mean to. It's just that, well, it's unacceptable behaviour.'

'You sound like Assunta.'

'I don't.' It was Jenny's turn to sound hurt.

'Then stop judging me.'

'I'm not judging you.'

'Then tell me you don't think I'm mad.'

'Lori, your behaviour has been . . ..'

I can't bear it. Jenny too. She doesn't hear me. It makes me feel very scared, very alone. Maybe I am mad. I can feel myself shaking.

Francesca is sitting beside me on the sofa. She puts her arms around me and cradles me like a child. I want to sink into her arms but feel too tense. I sit up straight, moving out of Francesca's embrace. Alberto has told me that he doesn't understand me, and now Jenny thinks I'm at fault. If I can't explain myself to my friends then I really am totally alone.

Jenny is sitting in my rocking chair, her arms folded. It seems to me that she has a tight, Assunta like, judgemental expression on her face.

I get to my feet and looking straight at Jenny I say, 'I painted a mural okay. So I painted a mural in Assunta's house. It was beautiful. Sometimes we do things that aren't "acceptable" behaviour.' I make the quotation marks with my fingers. 'Well I needed to do it and it didn't do anyone any harm!' My voice is shaking and I have to sit down again.

Jenny is silent. I was expecting a tirade back but nothing, just that tight expression on her face.

I look at Francesca; I'm shaking, she takes hold of my hand. I take a deep breath and sit upright, still holding her hand.

'Since he went down to Calabria, Alberto seems to have fallen increasingly under his mother's influence. We have talked, we have said that we must communicate better, but it feels as if he doesn't really want to know or just doesn't get it or I don't explain myself clearly. Oh, it's just a mess.' The tears take over. Francesca hands me a tissue. 'I do what is expected of me. I am dutiful and I am numb. I can't feel and no one hears me.' There are tears in Francesca's eyes. 'Inside I'm screaming and no one listens. For months and

Colour me in

months no one has listened to me. I can't make anyone understand me.'

'This sounds like a cry for help,' says Simona quietly.

'Is that what it was, Lori?' asks Francesca. 'Were you trying to get them to notice you, to listen to you?'

'Maybe, I don't know.' I take a deep breath. 'Do you think they will use this to take the children away from me?'

'No, surely not!' Francesca sounds appalled. 'They can't. I'm sure Alberto wouldn't want to . . . .'

'But he thinks I'm mad. He can say I'm not fit to be a mother.'

'What, because you paint walls?' says Simona. 'No, Lori, he can't say that.'

'But I have run away. Was that the wrong thing to do? They could say I ran to avoid going to psychiatric hospital when they were just trying to help. Oh my God! Have I lost my children?' The tight feeling grabs me across my chest, just as it did on the train, as I gasp for breath, the band tightens around my chest and I cannot breathe. Francesca tries to take me in her arms but I shake my head, 'I can't . . . .' I cannot tell them that I can't breathe. I try to take a deep breath, but the band tightens and I gasp again. The room starts spinning. How can I tell them that I need to take deep breaths?

Then Simona is beside me holding a paper bag. 'Breathe into this, breathe in . . . breathe out.' I follow her instructions; I nod at her to continue, silently begging her, "Please keep talking." She gets my message and continues saying, 'Breathe in . . . Breathe out.' Gradually my breathing restores and slowly the room stops spinning. I can still feel the tight band around my chest so I continue with the breathing. After a while I indicate to Simona that she can stop speaking.

Francesca slips a blanket over my shoulders as I'm shivering. I can hear her voice. 'Lori, it's okay, it's okay.' Jenny is in front of me, handing me a glass of water. I lean forward and take it. I slowly lift the glass to my lips and drink. My mouth is dry, so it feels good. I look at Jenny trying to see what's in her face, but I can't read anything in it.

I don't know what's happening and feel very scared. 'I . . . told Alberto today on the phone that I don't want to leave the children . . . that I want to be with them. He says he knows that but he says he doesn't understand me. He thinks I'm mad, just as Assunta does.'

'I'm sure he doesn't,' says Francesca.

Simona comes and sits on the other side from Francesca. I feel comfortable sandwiched between them. It's a warm evening but I feel shivery. Simona takes my hand.

"Are you okay now?' I nod. 'Is your breathing okay?'

'Yes, thanks . . . it . . . happened on the train. I seem to have a problem breathing. I have a tight band around my chest.'

'It happened on the train, when you were alone?' Francesca sounds appalled.

'Some passengers helped me . . . actually I was very lucky . . . I fainted.'

Simona squeezes my hand. 'Honey I think you have had a panic attack.'

Something cold hits my stomach. 'What, just now?'

She nods, 'and on the train.'

I don't know what to say to that. Then I remember, 'the woman who helped me breathe said she used to have panic attacks. I didn't realise . . ..'

'Lori, you've just had a terrible shock and on top of everything you've been going through . . ..'

'A panic attack?'

'I think so.'

'It was very scary. I don't want to do it again. I really don't.' The thought makes me feel shaky again. I squeeze Simona's hand and start deep breathing.

'Lori, you need support, all the support we can give but

more than that. I think it would be a good idea if you saw a therapist or counsellor.'

'Would they help with the panic attacks?'

'Yes, they could help you work out what's causing them.'

'I might lose my children . . . I may have lost my children.' I feel shaky again.

Lori, I think it would be good if you could talk to someone . . ..'

'Professional,' I remember Antonella's words.

'Well, yes. Lori you've had cancer and you've been through such a lot. Fear of it spreading, fear of . . .. I really think that professional support could help you to deal with the panic attacks and find a way to gradually release all the hurt and pain you're feeling.' She keeps hold of my hand as she goes on. 'Listen Lori, I'm sure Alberto won't try and take the children, but it would be useful to have someone who can say that you are fit to look after them if need be.' I feel shaky again and clutch tightly onto Simona's hand. They are all watching me.

'Simona,' I say.

'Yes.'

'Do you have someone in mind?'

Chapter 19

I stare at the wall. It's hard to look at the two women sitting in front of me with their concerned and friendly faces. As I answer their questions the thought "They must think I'm mad," bounces around in my head. When I describe how I felt painting my own naked body it's as if I'm seeing myself for the first time. I stop, feeling very self-conscious. 'It sounds mad, doesn't it?' I look down at the floor. I would like to drop through it into another world. Out of the corner of my eye I see Luisa, the psychologist, shake her head.

'No, it doesn't sound mad at all.' She says it as if she means it. I manage to lift my head. 'It's very moving,' she continues.

I feel so awkward talking about it, my stomach clenches and I want to run out of the room.

'What was in your mind as you painted yourself?' asks Luisa.

'I wanted beauty among the ugliness.' I surprise myself.

'Did you feel ugly?' I nod.

'Did you feel like that before or was it the cancer that made you feel ugly?' asks Marina, the gynaecologist.

'Well, losing my hair made me feel ugly and sexless in a way. Then having a big scar on my breast and being bloated from the steroids they gave me after the reaction to the chemo.'

'I understand all that would . . .,' says Luisa.

'But, looking back I've felt pretty drab for a long time.'

Luisa, a psychologist who used to work with Simona, and Marina, a gynaecologist, run a group for women who have had breast cancer. Simona felt that they would be a good starting point to get me support. Their group is every Friday afternoon, but to start with they see women individually. Marina deals with all physical problems arising from the cancer or treatment and can give on-going gynaecological care, free to women who have had breast cancer.

Colour me in

Otherwise, in Italy, you have to pay a gynaecologist. Luisa gives counselling and guidance and also refers women to other practitioners for various therapies, including psychotherapy, dance therapy and art therapy.

For the two days since my return from Calabria, Simona has been looking after me. She seems very worried and determined to find me the support I need.

'Did you feel better after you had painted yourself?' asks Luisa.

'I felt great while I did it, totally absorbed in what I was doing and very alive, yeah, alive.' It feels strange talking about it. I swallow. 'Then Beppe my son came in and I showed him because I was proud of it and Alberto appeared.' A big shiver runs through my whole body. I suddenly feel shame grip hold of me.

'I'm a terrible mother. I'm a terrible mother and they will take my children from me.' My teeth start chattering and tears flow down my cheeks. I feel myself shaking.

'No, you're not a terrible mother.' Luisa gets up from her chair.

'I'll lose my children I should never have left them.' I have an urge to wail, to yell, to beat my fists on the floor. It takes a huge effort to stay on the chair. Fear engulfs me and I shake. 'I am! I have been so . . . so wrapped up in trying to get colour back in my life. I don't want to lose my children!'

I feel the panic rising again and the band tightens around my chest. "Oh no not again" echoes round my brain. I gasp for breath and manage to gasp 'Simona.' Luisa comes from round the desk and starts rubbing my back. Marina leaves the room.

I gasp for breath and can't stop shaking. The room starts moving and everything goes blurry.

Then I hear Simona's voice, 'breathe in . . . breathe out.' I follow her words. She continues until I'm breathing normally and slowly the room stills itself and I can focus again. I'm still shaking and feeling incredibly weak.

All three of them are looking at me anxiously. 'Thank you for fetching Simona.' I say to Marina.

'That's okay, she was in the next room catching up with an old colleague.'

Simona used to work as a psychotherapist attached to the clinic where Marina and Luisa work. When she had her first child she moved to another clinic where she works part time.

'I can get you something to calm you,' says Marina. Her surgery is just along the corridor.

'No! Please don't.'

'A short term solution to calm you down, to stop the shaking.' I shake my head.

'Please don't give me any drugs.' Marina pauses and looks thoughtful, then says, 'right, I'm going to get you some tea.' She gets up and leaves the room.

'Well,' says Luisa has that happened before?' I nod.

'Yes,' says Simona 'the other evening when Lori got back to Bologna and on the train coming up.'

'Was the train the first time it happened?' Asks Luisa. I nod. 'So as you were leaving your family to come here?'

'Yes.'

'In distress about being submitted to a psychiatric hospital.'

'Yes, and worried about leaving my children.'

'When you described it earlier I did think it sounded like a panic attack and that's what it looked like just now.' She looks at Simona. 'Is that what you thought?'

'Yes, it is. It was the same the other night wasn't it Lori?'

'Yes, each time I feel like a band tighten around my chest and I can't breathe properly and I feel very scared and . . . well, panic rises and the room starts moving and I feel . . . faint. I did faint on the train. What seems to stop it is the breathing.'

Luisa nods, 'Start the deep breathing the minute you feel the slightest indication . . . or even if you are in a situation where it could happen. The thing is Lori while you are breathing deeply in and out like that you can't have a panic attack, as you've seen, breathing can calm an attack but it can prevent one too.'

'It seems to happen so quickly and then I find myself gasping and I just can't breathe.'

'Yes that is hard, but you can do it, you can breathe.'

'I seem to be able to do it when someone else says, breathe in . . . breathe out, not on my own.'

'You can learn to do it on your own Lori,' says Simona. Luisa nods.

Luisa keeps hold of my hand and I feel calmer but the underlying shivery feeling won't go away.

'So do you think the panic attacks are caused by my fear of losing the children?

'Do you think that's what triggered them?' Asks Luisa.

'Well, yes and fear of the psychiatric hospital and being labelled mad by my mother in law and husband.'

Luisa looked shocked by this.

'Does this mean I'm mad? Having panic attacks, something is wrong with me isn't it?'

'Lori the panic attacks are completely understandable, you have been through a lot, cancer, the treatment, fear of death. . ..'

That word strikes me, few people actually say that word, but yes, fear of death.

'The band round your chest when you feel it do you feel fear?

'Yes.'

'It could be fear of death too, when it happens try massaging your heart. That will usually release the fear.' I nod. I can do that, but I don't want it to happen again.

'Hopefully now you're getting support you won't have another one,' says Simona. 'But if you do have another one and manage to deal with it, then you won't need to be afraid of them.' That makes a lot of sense to me it seems I have enough to be afraid of without panic attacks too.

Marina then appears with a cup of tea. 'Are you okay to hold this?' I nod. The shaking has subsided and I take the cup from her. 'Are you sure you won't let me get you something to calm you down?' she adds.

'Yes, honestly, I would rather not take any more drugs if I can avoid it. They scare me. I had a toxic reaction to Taxol during chemo therapy and I really can't cope with serious drugs anymore.' Marina looks as though she is about to say something else, then changes her mind. I'm glad; I really don't want to argue with her about it.

I sip my tea gratefully. The sweet heat warms me from inside.

Luisa goes to her desk and writes a name and number on a piece of paper. She hands it to me. 'This is the number of an excellent psychotherapist. She is also an energy therapist and can teach you a deep relaxation method called Autogenic Therapy which will help you to learn to relax and help prevent panic attacks.' I take the piece of paper. The word "relax" resonates. I don't remember when I last did that.

'The method was developed by a German doctor to help soldiers suffering from shock after the First World War and is a good relaxation technique which I think will help you a lot. She also uses things like writing and painting to help people to get in touch with and express their emotions. I think she will be ideal for you.' Luisa looks at Simona, who nods.

'Thank you so much, Luisa.' She says and looks at me. 'Are you okay to go? My car is parked just round the corner.'

'Yes, I'm fine now. Thank you both very much.'

'Do call again if you'd like to talk to us,' says Luisa. 'And once you're feeling up to it, you might like to come along to our group. It's every Friday afternoon at 3 o'clock.' I nod. 'While I think about it,' she adds, 'we talked earlier about

Colour me in

Art Therapy, I'll see if I can book you in for a series of sessions. I'm pretty sure that Luca who runs the courses is starting a new one very soon but I'll have to check whether he has any places left. I'll let you know.' I thank them again as Simona and I leave the room.

I have to grip the banister rail as I gingerly step down the winding staircase to the ground floor. Simona looks behind her to ensure that I'm okay. As I get to the bottom, my knees start to give way, tears begin to flow and I start shaking again.

'Hey, hey, just let it all out.' Simona envelops me in her arms. 'You have so much shock and pain inside, just let it out.' Still holding me, she ferrets around in her bag. After a few seconds she produces a tissue and hands it to me. Gradually the tears and shaking subside and, blinking back the last of the tears, I manage to ease out of the hug and start walking towards the front door. We are in a local health centre in a large old building quite near the centre of town. I take Simona's hand as we walk.

'Do you want to walk round to the car with me? It's only a few yards. Or wait here while I fetch it?' She asks.

'I'll come with you, thanks.' I feel completely drained and don't want to let go of her. She feels like the lifeline that I need to stop me from drowning.

***

Once safely in Simona's car, the shaking comes back and I sob uncontrollably. Simona returns from paying her parking ticket. 'Oh honey!' She leans over and picks up a box of tissues from the back seat and hands it to me. 'Go for it girl! We are equipped in this car. Used to driving small children around.'

'Hey,' I manage between sobs, 'you'll need to get back to the children.'

'It's okay. My niece Monica is staying at the moment until she finds a room in a student flat. She's happy to babysit. As it's the summer holidays, she has no classes.'

'Thank you so much Simona. I don't know what's wrong with me.' The tears continue and my body aches from shaking and sobbing. Simona leans over the gear stick and puts her arm round me.

'Lori I think you're suffering from shock, that could explain the shaking and tears.'

'Yeh, could be,' I mumble through the tears.

'Listen, honey, I understand why you don't want to see a doctor and don't want to take more drugs, but there is someone who I think could really do you good.'

'Okay.'

'Well,' says Simona, 'he's the father of an ex-colleague of mine and is a homeopath and naturopath. He used to be a doctor but changed years ago to homeopathy and then trained as a naturopath as well. He works with people who have cancer. He's a lovely man.'

'Well, if you think . . ..' I blow my nose. At last the tears seem to be drying up.

'I think you need to see him as soon as you can. He'll probably give you something for the shock. It will be okay. He uses homeopathic medicine and herbs.'

Simona withdraws her arm from around my shoulders and reaches in her bag for her mobile phone.

'I wonder if Gaetano could see you today.'

'I'm in a mess, aren't I?'

'Lori, you've coped with so much over the last year and a half; the shock of the diagnosis, the chemo and reaction to it, Alberto leaving and now the psychiatric hospital threat.'

'And the fear of losing my children.'

Simona is about to press a button on her phone but stops.

'I feel bad,' she says.

'Why?'

'I was worried about you before you went back to Calabria. Having to live with Assunta. It seems you've had to cope without anyone you could really talk to . . . I guess I thought Alberto would be able to support you more. I wish I'd seen it coming. I wish I'd tried to stop you from going back, or at least come down to visit.'

'Simona, you can't blame yourself. I had to go back to be with the children. You couldn't have stopped me.' The tears subside but I'm still shaking. Simona presses the button on her phone.

***

The character sitting behind the huge old desk covered in piles of files and books reminds me of a cross between an old rock star and a past incarnation of Dr Who. He must be well into his sixties with wild, curly, grey hair. He is wearing a big, baggy, black jumper and a deep-red cotton scarf wound around his neck. His presence is both attractive and overwhelming.

When Simona called Gaetano Grandi she was told to hurry round as he had a last- minute cancellation. 'This was meant to be,' she said and drove me straight there.

Now I'm sitting in a large room in an old building across town from the clinic where we were before. Behind Gaetano are dark wooden shelves, every millimetre of them stacked with books. On one side of the room is an examining bed with a table next to it covered in test tubes and glass bottles of liquid. The shelves along that side of the room contain jars of herbs. Below these are three sets of small, important-looking drawers.

"Eccentric professor" is the phrase that springs to mind. Gaetano has a very engaging smile. 'Well, my dear,' he says, 'Simona informs me that you have been through some very difficult experiences. Tell me what has brought you here.' Biting back a flippant urge to say, "Simona, in her car." I take a deep breath. Strangely, the shaking has already calmed down. I speak slowly, trying to sound as together as I can. When I describe the doctor walking away from me while she tells me I have cancer, I burst into tears. Gaetano leans across his desk, picks up a toilet roll and hands it to me. I tear some sections off and dry my eyes. Gaetano smiles. 'That's better,' he says, 'Now you have removed the mask hiding your depression.'

'Depression?' I'm surprised. 'I know I felt low after the chemo ended, although I don't understand why I felt like that. I had expected to feel like celebrating but I hadn't. Now though . . . I thought I must be okay by now.'

'How do you feel after crying?' he asks. I pause.

'Lighter,' I say. 'Better, I think.'

Gaetano nods and then asks me exactly what treatment I've had for cancer and whether I'm taking any medication now. 'I'm supposed to be taking Tamoxifen.' I gaze down at my hands, suddenly feeling awkward and self-conscious.

'Supposed to be?' To my surprise Gaetano is smiling, no look of reproof on his face at all.

'Yes, my doctor at the Oncology Department gave me a prescription for it. He said to start taking it while I was still doing radiotherapy but I couldn't. I just put the prescription in the drawer and thought, "I will get it sometime," but I . . . I haven't been able to.'

'Why is that?'

'I'm scared. After the reaction to the chemotherapy, I'm scared of serious drugs with side effects. I know it's supposed to protect me from further tumours in my breast but I can't take it.' Tears are streaming down my cheeks again. 'Oh, I'm sorry.' I help myself to the loo roll.

'Don't apologise, my dear. This crying is good, very good. You let it out, my dear, you let that mask drop.'

'Do you think I should have taken the Tamoxifen?'

'Not if you didn't want to. Tamoxifen will block estrogens from entering the breast and as the majority of breast cancers feed on estrogens to grow, it prevents them from developing, at least for a time, but it won't necessarily stop cancer from developing elsewhere in the body.'

'I just can't face any more drugs.'

'That's quite understandable my dear, western medicine's

treatment for cancer just chews you up and spits you out when it's done, feeling exhausted weak and vulnerable, precisely at the point when you really need support.'

'Chewed up and spat out! Yeah that is how I feel.' Gaetano smiles encouragingly and I manage to continue my story, explaining about the reaction to the chemotherapy and Alberto leaving. I even manage to tell him about some of my painting incidents. I finish with the train journey and the panic attacks. I glance up at Gaetano who is looking at me thoughtfully. 'It's not surprising my dear that you are overwhelmed by panic and sorrow. I'm going to give you something to deal with your current state.'

He smiles, gets up and goes over to the shelves full of herbs. He opens one of the drawers below them and picks up a small bottle of pills. He takes a tiny plastic self-sealing bag out of another drawer and drops three pills into it. He comes over to my side of the desk and hands me the little bag. 'These are Ignatia,' he says. 'They will help you deal with the overwhelming sorrow and the shock and will make you feel a lot calmer. Take them all within a 24 hour period. I would advise you to take one now, one before you go to bed and one when you wake up in the morning. However you do it, take all of them by this time tomorrow.'

'Thank you.' I look down at the little packet, wondering how these three tiny pills are going to deal with all the shaking and sobbing.

'Do you know how to take them?' I shake my head. I've never taken homeopathic medicine before. 'Put one under your tongue and let it dissolve.'

'Okay.' I put the little packet into my purse so I won't lose it.

'Now, young lady.' I have to chuckle at that. 'I would like to see you again in a couple of weeks if possible. We need to monitor your progress. There are a lot more things to do. We need to see how your immune system is faring. The chemotherapy will have dealt it an enormous blow. I do my own tests for that. Then there is the depression . . ..' I think I must be looking alarmed because he gives me a reassuring smile. 'Don't worry, my dear, these are all normal reactions in cancer patients and there is nothing we can't deal with.' He walks to the door and opens it for me.

'How much do I owe you?' I find myself thinking, "I'm going to have to get well and go back to work full-time to pay for all this treatment."

'Let's leave that for the moment, shall we?' he smiles kindly. 'I'll work something out with Simona and let you know next time.'

'Well, that's very kind, thank you.' I walk out into the reception area where Simona is waiting.

***

'So what did you think of him?' Simona walks into my living room with a tray bearing two mugs of tea and a plate of biscuits. Having driven me home, she has come up to my flat to settle me in and make sure I'm okay.

'Oh, I want to marry him and have his babies!' I joke, grinning.

'Well, he must be about sixty-three' she laughs. 'Oh Lori, it's great to see you smile. You've looked different since coming out of his office.' She puts the tray down on the table.

'He's made me feel looked-after and it's a good feeling.' I look at Simona. 'You know, all this time I've been telling myself I should be fine and wondering what's wrong with me. It's great to be told that it's okay and normal to feel the way I've been feeling.'

'Oh, I'm so glad.' She hands me a cup of green tea and I curl up gratefully on the sofa with a blanket over my knees, a strange thing for late June but, although the shivers have eased, I still feel chilly.

'Did Gaetano say he would work something out with you about payment?'

'Don't worry about it for the moment.'

'Hey Simona, you can't pay for me. He must cost quite a lot. He really knows his stuff.'

'He is very experienced and teaches on training courses for homeopaths and naturopaths, but don't you worry. I saw his daughter for some sessions a while ago and wouldn't take a penny. That's what he's thinking of.'

'Oh Simona, then you must let me . . ..'

'Honey, leave it be for the moment. There is still the therapist, remember. I really think you should see her as well. She'll teach you to relax and with her you can gradually work through a lot of stuff. Keep your money for her.' A shiver comes back as I think about having to talk to a therapist.

'Do you really think I need to see a psychotherapist?'

'I think she'll help you look at the fear and trauma the cancer, Alberto's reaction and everything else has caused you.'

'Because it's all made me a bit mad?'

'No, Lori. Not at all, you're not mad, you've just reacted to a really tough situation. You need support honey that's all, support from someone who knows what she's doing. From what Luisa said she'll be ideal for helping you deal with the panic attacks and to learn ways of releasing the pain.'

I nod. 'Okay, I do feel like I need all the support I can get right now.'

'Do you want to ring her or would you like me to?' asks Simona.

'I'll call her. I do need this and I want to be trusted with my own children.'

'Oh honey, you can be, no one doubts that. Maybe now that you're recovering physically, you are strong enough to take everything else in.'

'Maybe.'

'It could be, Lori, that at least part of why you left is because you're ready to deal with the shock and trauma of the cancer and treatment, and to really start recovering.'

'That's certainly another way of looking at it.' As I think about it I realise that I like Simona's take on it. I hadn't run away. I had come to sort myself out and take control of my life again. Simona is standing looking at me.

'I'm fine if you want to go home.'

'Are you sure?'

'Yes, I feel very comfortable now. If the shivers come back, I'll just get right under the blanket.'

'Have you taken your first tablet?'

I nod and grin. 'Yes Mamma!'

She chuckles, 'and remember the deep breathing if you need it.'

'Yes, I'm fine, really.' It was so nice to be able to say that.

'Well, if you're sure you're okay, I'd better get back. Monica has been looking after the children since quite early this morning.' She makes sure that I have everything I need to hand.

'I can get up, you know,' I say, chuckling. 'Simona, thank you so much for everything you've done for me, without you I don't know . . ..' tears well up again.

'Oh, come on honey it's fine, I'm so glad I could help. You will ring if you need anything?'

'Yes, of course I will but I'm sure I'll be fine. Francesca said she'll pop round later. Right now I'm going to read a crappy magazine. Bliss!'

***

I stare at the ringing phone. Jenny's name is on the screen. I'm worried about answering it, as the prickly tension between us at the moment is difficult to deal with. But on the other hand I hate the fact that we seem to have fallen out and would love to clear it up.

'Hi Jen.'

'Hi Lori I just wondered how things are going. How are you feeling?'

'Yeah, good, actually a lot has happened today.'

Colour me in

I tell her about my session with Luisa and Marina and about the amazing Gaetano. We manage to laugh about me falling for a sixty three year old eccentric.

'Lovable eccentric, uses loo roll instead of tissues,' I chuckle. 'Very attractive in his own way.'

'I'm really glad you're getting help Lori. What about the children when are you going to see them?'

I feel myself tensing at this question. 'I don't know, soon I hope.'

'Well, if you hadn't left them there would be no need to . . ..'

'Jenny, I had to leave. Alberto was going to put me in a psychiatric hospital.'

'Oh come off it, you over reacted, he would never do that.'

'How do you know? I heard him on the phone. How come you know everything all of a sudden?'

'I just don't understand how you could leave the children. I know that Alberto took them down there and that you had to finish your treatment here but now there's no need . . ..'

'You think I should stay down there, that's what Alberto wants and I can't bear it any more.' Tears well up in my eyes.

'Alberto is right you do need psychiatric help. I just think if you'd stayed down there and got help while being with the children instead of abandoning them.'

'I did not abandon them. I left them with their father and grandmother.'

'It probably feels like abandonment to them.'

'Oh Jenny how can you say that! I've spoken to them every day since I left, they're fine. Michela is worried about me, but they're coping fine. Will you stop telling me what I should do.'

'I have resisted telling you until now.'

I feel as though I've been punched in the stomach. The

way she says it sounds smug. 'Oh . . .. What? So all along you've thought I was doing the wrong thing.' Silence. 'You have no idea what it's been like.'

'I know you've been through a lot Lori but . . ..'

'You've made no attempt to see things from my point of view. The last thing I need is to be judged by you again. After all these years I'd hoped you'd stopped doing that.'

'What do you mean?'

'You didn't think I should have had Michela. According to you I should have had an abortion and followed a serious career like you did.'

'Well I . . ..'

The tears that were threatening to come are dried by the anger and hurt I feel. 'Just stop it . . . stop it . . .. Your way of dealing with things is not the only way.'

'I know that Lori I just . . ..'

'I don't need this,' I say quietly. 'I can't cope with anything right now let alone with my oldest friend judging me.' I'm shaking and can't bear to hear any more so I put the phone down and take some deep breaths.

Chapter 20

We're sitting in a large light room on the fourth floor in a leafy suburb of Bologna. Through the window I can see a palm tree. Maybe I don't need to talk. Maybe my therapy could be to stare at this tree for an hour every week.

Rina, the psychotherapist, and I are sitting on adjacent chairs at a slight angle to each other so that we can see each other comfortably. The chairs are a cross between dining chairs and armchairs - comfortable, with wooden arms, but not too cosy. Rina hands me a glass of water and then sits down and smiles. 'Well, Lori, would you like to tell me what I can help you with?'

I take a sip of the water and then put the glass on a small table next to my chair. I have no idea where to begin. I open my mouth and close it again. I look at the tree. I take a deep breath.

'I had breast cancer early last year and, well, I've been shaking a lot recently and am scared of losing my children. Luisa, the psychologist who runs a group for women with breast cancer, said you could teach me a technique called Autogenic Therapy, which could help me to relax. My . . . homeopath prescribed me something that seems to have worked but Luisa thought it would be a good idea to ask you to teach me your method of relaxing.'

'You're afraid of losing your children?'

'Well, they're with my husband.' I don't want to explain. I feel shaky; I blink and swallow, take a breath and manage to go on. 'I want to get well, to stop the shakes, to be able to have my children with me.'

Rina nods and indicates my glass of water. 'Do have a sip if you need one.' She waits while I drink some water and somehow I feel calmer. I inwardly send her a message, "please change the subject."

'Would you mind telling me a little about how you found out that you had cancer and how you felt?' Not what I'd had in mind, and as soon as I start telling her the tears well up again. As I describe the time Dottoressa Calchi walked away from me down the corridor I feel sick, as if it were happening now. The smile drops from Rina's face and she looks horrified.

'My goodness, that's disgusting. I know some doctors can be extremely insensitive but that's terrible. Didn't she ask a nurse to sit with you, to talk to you after she'd left?'

'No, she just walked out through the double doors leaving me standing in the corridor thinking, "I have breast cancer, I have cancer in my lungs, maybe I'm riddled with it."'

Rina tells me how appalled she is that a doctor anywhere, but particularly in Bologna, renowned for its high level of medical training, could treat a patient so insensitively.

'No wonder you're suffering from shock,' she says.

She leans towards me with a box of tissues. 'We can help you get over the shock.' She pauses for a moment then says, 'Lori, if you can manage it, I would like you to tell me more about this doctor and if there were other incidents which caused you shock.'

I blow my nose and tell her about the casual way Dottoressa Calchi told me I was to have chemotherapy and how terrified I was. Then I go on to describe the reaction to the chemotherapy. As I describe the feeling of swelling up like the incredible hulk, feeling desperately sick and seeing millions of tiny bubbles before my eyes, I'm back there living through it again. The tears come out in big sobs this time. I'm shaking and crying so much that I bend forward in my chair with my head close to the ground.

Gradually it eases. Rina is in front of me with the tissues. I dry my eyes and she hands me the glass of water. I sit up and take a sip. Rina returns to her chair and I put the glass back on the little table beside me. I take a deep breath.

'It's very present, isn't it?' says Rina. I nod. She looks very thoughtful and says,

'Lori, have you ever heard of Thought Field Therapy?' I

Colour me in

shake my head. 'Have you heard of shiatsu or acupuncture?'

'Yes, I had shiatsu some years ago. A friend was learning it and practised on me. It was very relaxing.'

'Well, as you know, in shiatsu the practitioner presses on certain pressure points on the body which are connected to meridians flowing through the body to our organs; heart, lungs, etc.' I nod. 'Well, when something traumatic happens to us, very often the emotions we felt at the time get trapped in different parts of our body or in our energy field. These emotions can be released by tapping on certain pressure points.'

'I feel as though I have a lot of emotions trapped inside me,' I say. 'I feel so full of them, sometimes I feel as if I could explode. In fact I have exploded . . ..' I stop, as I remember painting the mural.

'The beauty of Thought Field Therapy, also known as energy tapping,' explains Rina, 'is that, once you have released the emotion attached to a memory, you can still remember whatever happened but it's not painful in the same way any more because the emotion has gone. For example, a rape victim can't bear to remember being raped because she relives the fear, terror and other emotions she experienced during it. If she can release those emotions, then, whenever she remembers the rape, she no longer relives the fear and terror she felt at the time and does not have to go through it all again. The memory no longer has power over her.'

'It sounds amazing.'

'I wonder if you would like to try it, to release the emotions attached to the reaction you had to the chemotherapy. It would mean remembering and reliving the emotions at first but as we go through the exercise you will gradually release them.'

I feel very scared but agree to try. Rina tells me to close my eyes and picture being in the hospital and to bring the reaction to the chemotherapy into my mind. It comes quite easily. She asks me how I feel on a scale of 1 to 10, with 10 being very bad. I say 10. Rina then takes me through a little ritual where, following her, I tap my eyebrows a few times then my cheek, then the back of my hand. The ritual also involves rolling my eyes right up and down and singing a snatch of "happy birthday". I'm grateful that no-one can see me but if this helps take away the pain of remembering, then great.

We finish and Rina asks me to continue focusing on the reaction to the chemo but to say how I am now feeling on a scale of 1 to 10. To my surprise the number is 8. We repeat the ritual again and the number goes down to 7 then 5. We continue until it is 0. I'm astonished. By the end, I can clearly remember what happened without bursting into tears or feeling sick. As I reach for my water, I feel tired but much calmer.

'Can we do this for everything?' I ask. 'For the time I was told I had cancer and for other situations like that?'

'For most things,' she replies. 'We'll look at each situation and see how best to deal with it. We talk some more about Dottoressa Calchi and she suggests that I sit down on my own quietly with an empty chair in front of me and imagine that Dottoressa Calchi is in the chair.

'Oooh,' I say, 'I don't want her near me.' Then I laugh, 'Gosh, it is real, isn't it? The idea of imagining her in front of me is really scary.'

'You can try it if you feel able to,' says Rina. 'You can say whatever you like to her. You can tell her what you think of the way she told you that you had cancer and the effect it had on you. You can shout and yell and release your anger at her if you want to. The fact is your subconscious does not know the difference between visualisation and reality, so you will feel as if you had really spoken to her. That's why visualisation is such a powerful tool in healing. When you feel able to we can do it together in a session.'

We don't have the time to start the Autogenic Therapy

but we agree to start it next time. She also suggests that I write a list of the emotions I feel when I think about the cancer and treatment - I think I can do that.

***

'She's a psychotherapist and she seems good. She has helped me to release the trauma from the reaction to the chemo.' There is silence on the other end of the phone.

'And she's going to teach me relaxation to stop the shaking, although the homoeopathic medicine seems to have done that pretty well. Alberto, I feel so much better already, really I do.'

'I'm glad, Lori.'

'She was shocked when I told her about how Dottoressa Calchi gave me the diagnosis. She says that I'm still traumatised by that.'

'Oh, really?' He sounds surprised. 'Well, I suppose you would be. It was shocking.'

'I'm apparently suffering from shock and trauma.'

'I can see that makes sense. You're okay up there.' It was a statement rather than a question. 'You're getting support from your friends and now you're getting professional help.' I think he wants to reassure himself.

'Yes, yes. I guess I should have done that earlier.'

'Well, you're doing it now. That's what counts.'

'How are the children?'

'Fine. Michela wants to talk to you but she's out at the moment. She can ring you later. Beppe's here somewhere. I'll call him in a minute.' He stops for a few seconds. 'Lori, I would not have left you . . ..'

'What?'

'I would not have left you in a psychiatric hospital. Maybe for a night or so, but no longer, just to get you the help you needed. There are not so many choices here. In Bologna there's every flavour of therapist, psychologist, counsellor, but not here. I didn't know what to do and my mother . . ..'

'I know, I wish you'd talked to me first and told me what you wanted to do. I had to hear you on the phone.'

'I did tell you that I was going to get you help.'

'I guess so, but . . ..' I stop, I don't want to argue with him. He's trying to explain himself and I'm glad.

I want to ask Alberto if he loves me. Once upon a time he used to say that he did. I really need to hear it again, but I hesitate. I don't know what I would say if he asked me . . .. I've told him a few times but it must be years since I last said the words to him, to the children often but not to Alberto.

'Ah, here's Beppe, he wants to talk to you.'

'Okay.'

***

I'm not sure how long I've been awake. It's dark apart from slats of light cast across the ceiling from the partially open blinds. I'm lying completely still, increasingly aware of the band tightening across my chest and the rising feeling of panic and fear.

I try to breathe in and it hurts. I lie very still because I can't breathe without hurting. I'm afraid to move and aware that I'm absolutely rigid with fear. I don't know what to do. Every time I breathe in it hurts but I need to take deep breaths. The band around my chest tightens. Then I remember Luisa telling me to massage my heart. I'm glad to have something I can do. I move my left hand slowly up off the bed and massage just under my left breast. I somehow know that this is fear of death.

'It's okay,' I whisper. 'It's okay, heart, you're not going to die, you are not.' I lie very still and gently continue to massage. I breathe in slowly and it doesn't hurt too much. I continue to massage and breathe slowly out. I continue to massage and breathe in and out. 'It's okay, it's okay, I'm not going to die. I'm not going to die.' Gradually my breathing becomes smooth, regular and without pain as the tight band around my chest gradually loosens. I feel calmer and

Colour me in

eventually nod off to sleep.

***

This morning, after being gripped by fear the night before, I felt strangely light and happy. It's as though the fear had come up to the surface and then left my body. I was so pleased to be able to deal with it by myself. All day I've been cheerful and light.

Now, as evening creeps over the city, I'm sitting on my balcony enjoying the view of the rooftops and the gradually darkening sky. The street lamps are on and lights are beginning to come on in the flats, lighting up the dark buildings. Those on the distant hillside are like tiny pinpricks of light and those nearer are like glowing fireflies.

This is my favourite time of day. The sky is streaked with pink and purple and the lights give me a cosy sense of thousands of households coming home from work, discussing their days and cooking dinner. At the same time, I feel lonely and wish Michela and Beppe were here with me.

I go over the session with Rina. It's incredible that I can now remember my reaction to the chemotherapy without fear and sickness. I think about the surgeon: I don't have the strength to try talking to an imaginary her yet but I promise myself that I will try in a session with Rina where I feel safe. If it is as effective as the energy tapping I did yesterday then it will be wonderful to release the anger I feel towards her.

I hear a buzzing coming from inside the flat: it's my mobile phone. I get up and walk into the kitchen. The phone is on the table. Leo's name is flashing on its screen. I haven't spoken to him for a long time. We emailed a few times when I first went down to Calabria but then I found it hard to continue. Being chatty and cheerful in an email became hard work somehow.

I watch the phone buzzing with Leo's name on it. I pick it up.

'Hello, Leo.'

'Lori, hi, good to hear your voice,' he sounds relieved. 'How are you? I haven't heard from you for ages. I've emailed and sent you the odd text but . . . .'

'Leo, I'm sorry things have been . . . a lot's happened.'

'That's fine, Lori, just as long as you're okay. Are you okay?'

'Yes.' It's nice to say that. 'I'm much better than I was, anyway.'

'I'm so glad to hear it. Are you still in Calabria?'

'No, I'm in Bologna now.'

'Hey Lori, that's great news!' I'm stunned by his joyful reaction. 'Is it a visit or are you back here to stay by any chance?' His enthusiasm is quite infectious. I find myself chuckling.

'I'm back, at least I think so but things are . . . well . . . complicated. I'm by myself at the moment and I'm worried about the children. They're still with Alberto. It's all rather a long story.' I tell him about my growing desperation throughout the time I spent in Calabria, about painting myself and about painting the wall in Assunta's house. He listens intently, not fazed by any of it.

'Lori, I would love to see you, then you can tell me properly and I can see for myself how you are.' I don't know what to say.

'How about I come over to Bologna one night? We could eat at Da Vito or somewhere else.' It's lovely hearing Leo's voice, feeling his attention at the other end of the phone.

'Yes, that would be great. You're in Modena, aren't you? Do you mind coming over here? I haven't got the car here as Alberto has it.'

'That's fine, no problem, it only takes half an hour. Give me your exact address and I'll come and pick you up.'

I can't believe that I'm making a date with Leo! 'Well, if we're going to Da Vito, we can walk from here.'

'Shall we do that, then?' he asks. A little voice somewhere tells me that I should worry about taking another man into my local restaurant but I manage to challenge it, telling myself that married women can have male friends.

'Yes, that would be great. When suits you?'

'Um, Friday is best as I don't have to work late. What about you?'

I start Art Therapy this week . . . that's okay it's Thursday evening. I have an appointment with Rina on Friday but that's during the day. 'Friday's fine. I'll pop over there now and book a table. They're often busy on Friday. What sort of time?'

'I can get to you around seven, so any time after that.'

'Okay, great.'

'Bye Lori, look forward to seeing you on Friday.'

I put the phone back on the table and return to my sunset over the balcony. I sit down on my chair and stretch out my legs feeling quite dazed, but with a little buzz of excitement in the pit of my stomach.

Chapter 21

A woman with short black hair is talking about having had surgery six times. She had her breast removed and had to have a second and third operation to finish that properly. Then she needed several reconstruction operations. I feel sorry for her but don't want to feel the weight of her pain and anger coming across the room. I have never been able to face the idea of reconstruction, though maybe I will one day. I'm very grateful that I still have my breast, even though it's small and mangled.

Did I do the right thing coming to this group? I want to meet other women who have also had breast cancer but I feel very uncomfortable. I wonder why so many of the women have hair. Maybe they finished chemo well over a year ago like me. But some of them have long hair so it must have been longer ago than that, or maybe they never had chemo or had the type that doesn't make your hair fall out. Absorbed in my own thoughts, I didn't hear Marina introducing me to the group. She is smiling in my direction. All eyes are on me. Am I supposed to say something? Butterflies suddenly float up from the pit of my stomach. I take a deep breath and manage a weak smile.

'I'm Lori,' I say. 'I'm still trying to put the colour back into my life.' I don't know why I said that. Blank faces greet my words. I want to crawl under my chair. I look down at my knees and feel very shaky.

Then I hear a voice, 'What caused it to go? Was it the cancer?' I look up. The words seem to have come from a woman sitting opposite me. She has short spiky blonde hair, large hoop earrings and is wearing a purple scarf with shiny silver threads running through it, loosely draped around her neck. She smiles, 'I'm Carla.'

'Yes,' I manage to reply. 'It was the cancer, although in some places it was fading already but now it has all gone grey and washed out and sometimes covered in darkness.' To my astonishment, a couple of people are nodding. I hear

Colour me in

the odd mumble of agreement.

'I know what you mean,' says the grey-haired woman sitting next to me. 'I felt as if the brightness had gone out of my life for a while.'

'I felt as if there were a grey film separating me from the rest of the world,' said another.

'How do you deal with it?' asks Luisa.

'Music is what gets me through,' says someone.

'I paint,' I say. 'For me it's the only time I really feel okay but . . . I've got myself into trouble doing it.' Marina asks me to explain and they all listen intently to the story of Assunta's wall. 'The thing is,' I say, 'I have wondered if maybe I might be . . . you know, going a bit mad.' I'm amazed at my ability to say this in front of fifteen other women but there are no shocked responses, no sharp intakes of breath, just nods and thoughtful looks.

'I definitely felt as though I went a bit mad for a while,' says a woman sitting next to Carla. 'I'm Donna, by the way,' she smiles directly at me. 'There have been times when I felt I was losing my grip on reality. Like Lori, I find art helps. I also paint, but I usually stick to canvas,' she laughs. 'I'd love to do murals, though.'

For the rest of the session people talk about various ways the cancer has made them feel and how they deal with it. It's amazing to hear other women talking about losing their grip on reality and wondering if they are going mad. A few women in the class paint, sculpt or write, and most of them started after they discovered they had cancer. Carla writes poetry and Luisa asks her if she will read a poem to the group one week.

The session ends and, as I get up to leave, Carla walks across the room to me. 'You were very courageous,' she says.

'Really?'

'Yes. I know it's not easy to be as honest as you were in front of so many people. The first time here can feel scary.'

'I was very scared but it just came out.'

'That's the great thing about this group. You can say anything, and practically anything you say someone else can relate to. It's great to be among people who have been through the same thing, even though we all experience it differently.' I nod and then chuckle, 'I guess it's a good thing that not everyone paints their mother-in-law's house.' Wow, I can joke about it!

'It's probably just as well,' Carla grins. 'Do you fancy a coffee?'

'I'd love one.' I go and thank Luisa and Marina for inviting me to the group.

***

I have painted a picture of a bald woman in a bubble. She's wearing big earrings and looks lost. I paint another of a bald woman curled up small on a very large table.

Looking at the picture makes me feel sick. I want to screw it up and throw it away. I pick it up just as Luca, the art therapist, comes over to me.

'What are you doing with that painting?'

'I can't bear to look at it.'

'Why not?'

'She's so small and helpless it hurts. Let me destroy it please.'

'How does it make you feel?' I take a deep breath. My heart is racing. 'Helpless and vulnerable like being in a hospital bed where all you can do is lie there and they decide what to do to you . . ..' My voice runs out but I want to scream.

'You can throw it away if you like,' says Luca, seeing my distress. 'Or you can put it in the cupboard for a while and get it out to look at some time in the future. It's up to you.'

'How long am I going to be doing this course?'

'The course lasts for eight weeks.' Eight weeks sounds like a long time.

***

Colour me in

Something is pinning me to the chair. My body feels so heavy and relaxed I could easily close my eyes and drift into sleep.

I don't know quite what I was expecting from Rina's Autogenic Therapy but my limbs feel so relaxed they don't want to move. She teaches me the first part - to relax my arms - and explains that we will learn a new piece every session until we have a complete set of exercises to relax the whole body. She gives me a sheet of paper with this week's exercise on it and explains that I need to practice it three times a day. We discuss it for a few minutes and I'm amazed that I can feel so relaxed. I'm looking forward to doing it again at home.

When I tell Rina that I'm doing art therapy she suggests that I draw a picture of the moment Dottoressa Calchi diagnosed me.

'Just paint a rough representation of the situation,' she says. 'Don't worry about details just paint it any way it comes out. Painting is a wonderful non-verbal way of releasing emotions. It gives the subconscious the chance to express what it feels.' I stare at the palm tree; the fronds of its large leaves are fluttering slightly in the breeze.

'So my subconscious has been expressing what it feels.' I tell Rina about when I first started painting all those A4 pictures during chemo and then subsequent paintings on walls, culminating in Assunta's dining room. 'It just happened. At first, I didn't think about why, I just had to do it. The thing is, the cancer made me colourless. I wanted to put some colour back into me.'

'You wanted to replace the colour you had lost,' said Rina.

'I was colourless,' I began, 'especially after I lost all my hair, eyebrows, eye lashes, but even before that, and the world just got pale and washed out and grey, no brightness any more.'

'Does painting help you get the colour back?'

'Sometimes, yes, especially while I'm actually painting. I feel totally absorbed in what I am doing, lost in it, no need to worry about anything else. When I'm painting the colour is back and I feel more . . . balanced again. I am scared though that the grey and the darkness will never go and the colour will never fully return, the darkness is everywhere.' I wave my arms vaguely round the room. 'It lifts a little sometimes: it's better when I'm with my children.'

Rina nods and smiles gently.

'It's worse early in the morning. If I wake up in the night it can be bad, but when I wake up in the morning it feels as if something heavy and dark is hovering over me and I find it hard to get up and move. I want to put my head under the covers and pretend it isn't there. When I'm on my own I quite often just paint myself a little picture while I'm having breakfast.'

'You paint yourself a little picture.'

'It brings me some colour.'

Rina asks me to show her the list of emotions I have written. Anger; I feel that towards Dottoressa Calchi and some other doctors. Hurt; by Alberto, Assunta and Jenny, this last was hard to admit but the hurt was very real. Fear; fear of dying, of the chemotherapy, of never being well again, of living forever in darkness, without colour. Guilt; I feel guilty towards the children, guilty that I have put them through this, guilty about not being a good mother. I also feel guilty towards my own body for inflicting the tumour on it. Grief; I tell her about a conversation I had with Simona about feeling as though I had lost someone close to me. Rina explains that most cancer patients feel grief because they have a sense of having lost the person they were before the cancer.

'Having cancer can change people. It can change the way you look at life. The person you were before probably took life more for granted, was sure of living, of going on. Cancer can make the idea of death much more real and scary. It can make us feel more vulnerable, have a sense of how mortal and fragile we really are. This can be a shock, it can be hard to live with, it can be felt as grief, as a huge sense of loss, losing optimism and hope.'

'Maybe that's what has happened to me, everything has turned upside down and I feel lost.'

'That's understandable, Lori. You're bound to feel lost; your normal goal posts have been moved. It will take time to orientate yourself again. Allow yourself the time and use the tools that will help you.'

'Like the energy tapping; I think I have a lot more that needs to come out.'

'Yes, we can do more of that and the art therapy which, I think is especially good for you.'

I nod. 'I think it will help but it feels very uncomfortable at the moment.'

'Is that because you are triggering uncomfortable emotions?' I nod again and manage a rueful grin.

'I guess that means it's working.'

'Well, probably, in this case.' Rina looks at me thoughtfully. 'I have suggested that you talk to Dottoressa Calchi in your imagination but do say the words out loud because that's a direct way to release some of the anger. What happens is that a diagnosis of cancer can evoke emotions such as anger and fear. Often we don't recognise them at first and certainly don't feel able to express them. They can then be repressed inside. I see it rather like an old car you take to a scrap yard. You go in with a large car, which then gets compressed into a tight, small block. The anger, hurt, fear, guilt and grief get hammered down into a hard little block which feels heavy inside and which you feel as depression.'

'Ahh . . . my homeopath says I'm depressed. I didn't think . . .. So, if I release all these emotions then the depression will go, the darkness will go?'

'Yes, a lot of it will. This may take some time, Lori.

There may be all sorts of things from before the cancer that have also caused the darkness. Gradually we can find ways for you to release them.'

***

I wriggle out of the pale blue dress and throw it on the bed in frustration. Why do I look so crap in all of my clothes?

I catch myself in the dressing table mirror and instinctively move away from it. The comfort-eating, sedentary lifestyle I have been leading has taken its toll. I look pale and puffy, with bags under my eyes, and my hair is a lot shorter than I ever had it before the chemo. I will be so happy when it grows back to a normal length. Some people like keeping their hair short. They discover it suits them and change style, but I need to get mine back. Maybe one day I'll decide to go short again but right now I need to prove to myself that the thick, swinging, red, shoulder-length hair I once had can be mine again. I shake it. There is some bounce in it but it sticks out at all angles.

I force myself to look in the mirror and shudder as I focus on what I see before me. I am wearing an ordinary bra, as opposed to a tee-shirt bra, which evens me up. In this one I can see that my right breast is so much smaller. If I had the left reduced to match the right my bust would be so small! With my short hair and chunky shape I look almost masculine. Leo is definitely just in this for friendship. There is no way I look remotely attractive. I'm still a sexless blob. I sit on the bed, feeling exhausted and miserable. What am I doing? Why am I making any attempt to look feminine? That all went out of the window long ago.

I catch sight of the alarm clock by the bed. 'Oh my God, it's a quarter to seven! Leo will be here in fifteen minutes.' I change my bra and then pull the blue dress back on. It is a bit tight now but it's stretchy and has sleeves, which cover the white, flabby tops of my arms. I must go back to the gym. At least I can wear feminine shoes, so I squeeze my feet into purple high-heeled sandals and teeter into the bathroom to put on some make-up. I resist an urge to paint purple flowers all over my face and stick to lilac eye shadow and a strong pink lipstick! The door buzzer sounds and I go to push the entry-phone button.

'Hi Leo, I'll be right down.' I take a deep breath. 'Slow down, girl,' I tell myself. 'For one thing you don't want to go falling downstairs in your high-heeled sandals. For another, Leo is a friend now, we are both married, this is the beginning of a friendship.'

Friend or not, my heart skips when I see him standing outside, his hands in his pockets gazing up at my block of flats. 'This is quite some building,' he says. 'Seems like art deco.'

'Built by fascists,' I say. 'My landlady's father was a high-ranking fascist colonel who built a lot of property in Bologna.'

'You're looking good, Lori. It's great to see you.' He walks up to me, we hesitate and then we kiss on each cheek. Leo looks at me for a moment then hugs me. He holds me really tightly for a few seconds.

'I'm so glad to see you . . . to see you looking okay.' He lets me go and steps back. 'I'm sure you're still having a hard time but you look well. You are okay, aren't you?'

'I . . . yes, I guess so.'

'Well, let's go and eat.' He holds out his arm, I hook mine round it and we walk round the corner to Da Vito.

Leo asks what my favourite wine is. I hesitate to say. Sergio, the waiter, grins,

'Lori loves our finest Prosecco,' he says. 'It's very dry, just like champagne.'

'Well, we'll have that then,' says Leo. Sergio goes to fetch it.

'Leo, normally I only ever drink it on birthdays and . . . .'

'You are here, alive, getting well. Isn't that worth celebrating?' His enthusiasm makes me feel a little giddy.

Sergio comes back with the Prosecco. As I watch the bubbly liquid fill my glass, I feel overwhelmed. It's almost too much; sitting here with Leo who is being more attentive and lovely to me than he ever was all those years ago. We lift our glasses.

'To life,' says Leo.

'To life,' I repeat. Leo asks me lots of questions about how I've been since we bumped into each other back in January in the fog. I repeat a lot of what I've told him on the phone about Calabria and the painting. I tell him about Alberto's plans to put me in a psychiatric hospital.

'How could he consider doing that? Lori, you were unhappy, confused and overwhelmed, but not mad. Those places are horrible. I can understand him suggesting seeing a therapist but not committing you to a hospital.'

'Well, he didn't know what to do, Assunta desperately wanted me out of her house. It seems to be the only solution he could come up with.' I say sadly.

'Locking someone up for painting a mural on your dining room wall is a bit heavy.' Leo chuckles. 'You can paint, Lori. She doesn't know how lucky she is. It was probably a masterpiece.'

'I doubt that,' I'm embarrassed at his praise. 'But if by any chance it was we'll never know because she had it whitewashed over a few days later. Michela told me, she said that Assunta was on the phone to the decorators the very next morning.' I sigh. Leo is gazing at me intently.

'I bet you looked amazing, painted all over with flowers.' I gaze back at him. Our eyes meet and he holds my gaze, for a moment. A shiver runs across my shoulders. 'The way you describe it, it sounds quite incredible. I would have taken a photograph of you,' he says, leaning over the table towards me.

'Alberto dragged me into the bathroom and made me wash it off.'

'Didn't he even ask you why you'd done it? How you

felt?' A tear trickles down my cheek.

'Sorry, Lori, I didn't mean to make you cry.' I shake my head again and wipe my eyes with a serviette.

'It's okay.'

Sergio brings our pasta. I have my usual *Tortelloni con panna e funghi* and Leo has *Tagliatelle con salsa Bolognese*. I concentrate on eating for a moment. It calms me down.

'How are your boys?'

'They're fine. Giorgio has just installed a new program on our computer. He downloads music all the time. There's nothing he can't do on the computer. I thought I was pretty good with technology but he teaches me how to do things,' he laughs. A warm light shines in his eyes when he talks about his children. Leo puts down his fork, picks up his glass, takes a sip of Prosecco, looks into my eyes and leans towards me.

'With Cassandra and me, well, things have been quite . . . difficult sometimes.' I swallow. 'We don't always see eye-to-eye,' he carries on. 'I know it isn't, well . . . you have experience . . ..' He tails off. 'How are things?'

'You mean what do you do with a husband who tries to commit you into a psychiatric institution? Where do you go from there? Good question.'

'Sorry, Lori, I shouldn't have asked.'

'No, it's okay, Alberto was under a lot of pressure from his mother who wanted me out of her house. I don't know where we are right now.' I take a sip of Prosecco.

'I would like the children to be here with me but I have to get well in order for that to happen, so I'm having psychotherapy. It's difficult going over stuff and reliving memories. But I think it's helping.' I shake my head and take a deep breath. 'I'm going to a breast cancer support group and I've also just started art therapy, which is hard but I think will probably help too. So we'll see.'

'Wow, you're really throwing yourself into this healing process, aren't you?'

'I have to. I have to get well to become sane enough to take care of my children.'

'Oh Lori! You are well, aren't you? Are you seeing your doctor regularly and getting check-ups?'

'I'm seeing a homeopath now. He did some tests recently, which showed that my immune system is getting stronger. He's helping me a lot. I can have tests at the hospital every year so the next ones are due in February. I had an x-ray last year to check the lumps on my lungs and it turns out that there is just one lump and it hasn't changed, so it's almost certainly not cancerous.' Leo looks visibly relieved.

He then talks about the difficulties he's encountering at the university where he teaches, commenting on how much better things could have been if we'd won the Pantera. We drift into reminiscing about our student days.

'Hey,' I say, 'You know when you all went to trial in '97 for organising the occupations?'

'Of course I do,' Leo looks at me. ' I have to say I hoped you'd turn up. It would have been great to see you.'

'Well, I had planned to but Michela suddenly caught a nasty bout of flu and I had to take time off work to stay with her. She was really quite ill.' His hand creeps across the table and takes hold of mine. We sit in silence for a moment. My heart is thumping.

As we walk out of the restaurant, Leo says, 'Lori I want to do this again. It's so great being with you.'

I take a deep breath. 'Leo, does Cassandra know that you're seeing me tonight?' I have carefully not asked earlier but now I need to know. He hesitates and then sighs.

'No, she doesn't. She thinks I'm with some work colleagues.'

This isn't what I want. It was never Cassandra's fault, and I don't want to hurt her. I look up at Leo and in spite of those thoughts I have such a strong desire to kiss him, to feel his lips on mine again, to be held in those arms. I keep

Colour me in

my arms tightly by my side and try to concentrate as we walk back towards my building.

'Which is your car?' I dare not invite him in. He nods in the direction of a pale blue Fiat Tipo under the next lamp-post.

'Lori, listen, I would like to do this again. What do you think?' I breathe in.

'I have to say, Leo, it has been a great evening, wonderful even,' I smile. 'I really enjoyed it, but we are both . . ..'

'I know,' Leo takes hold of my hand. 'But are you going to stay married? To a man who doesn't want to live here with you? To a man who wanted to put you in a psychiatric hospital?'

'To a man who was there for me when my self-esteem was devastated by discovering that you were with Cassandra and had lied to me for five months!' I say, surprising myself.

'Are you still angry with me?' He sounds shocked.

'Maybe I am. I don't know. I'm trying to get things in perspective.' We are standing by Leo's car. He clicks the remote control lock and opens the car door.

'Let's get in. It will be more comfortable to talk in there.'

I hesitate. 'I'm very tired. I think I should just go to bed.' Leo walks up to me, puts his hands on my shoulders and gazes into my eyes. It seems like ages before I manage to step back.

'It's getting late, I don't really do late nights any more,' I grin.

'Okay I'll let you go but only if you promise me that we'll do this again, soon.' He opens the car door, leans in and re-emerges with a diary in his hand. He moves under the lamp-post. 'Right, lets make a date now.' He looks straight at me. I can't say no, I have to see him again. He's out of town on a lecture tour for a few days so we make a date for a couple of weeks' time. I feel a strange mixture of excitement and guilt as I walk across the road to my building.

***

'Mamma, I scored a goal in football today!' The pride and excitement in Beppe's voice is tangible.

'Well done, darling! That's wonderful! Was this a match at school?'

'No, it was this afternoon, with the football team. Matteo was in goal and he saved two goals!' I love talking to my son on the telephone. He always seems to have happy news. We talk for a few more minutes about school, his friends and more football, then he says, 'I have to go now, Mamma, Matteo is waiting for me to go and play football.'

'Okay, darling, we'll talk again in a couple of days. Take care. Can you pass me Papà, please?'

'Okay, Mamma, bye.'

'Bye, darling, love you.'

'Love you too, Mamma.' He's gone. Alberto's voice is not half as cheerful.

'Hi, Lori.'

'Hi, Beppe really seems to love football now, doesn't he?' Alberto's voice comes alive.

'Did he tell you about his goal?'

'He certainly did.'

'He's so proud of himself and rightly so. Nearly all the other boys who were playing are much older than him. They've formed a local village team. He and Matteo are the most promising youngsters, so they've been allowed to join.' Alberto sounds very proud. 'Who knows, maybe he'll be playing for Juventus someday!'

'You're joking!'

'Obviously it's early days yet, but he's very good. If he carries on like this we could think about sending him to a club in a few years' time to play for a junior team.'

'You've been thinking about that?' I feel so out of touch with my own family.

'Well, it crossed my mind. It's just a dream of mine but, if Beppe wants it enough, maybe it could happen.'

'Is he really that good?'

Colour me in

'I'm not sure yet, but he is very promising. Maybe I'm just dreaming.'

'You are a bit of a dreamer . . ..'

Alberto paused for a few seconds then asked, 'How are you?'

'I'm feeling better all the time. My second therapy session was quite a revelation. Do you remember me telling you about when the surgeon told me I had cancer and walked away from me down the corridor?'

'Yes, of course I do, it was terrible.'

'Well, talking to Rina the therapist, I realise how angry I was about that. The thing is I've been holding it down, deep inside. I didn't even want to acknowledge it, let alone express it. She was the person removing the lump and saving my life so I couldn't, but that anger was inside me.'

'I suppose it would have been.'

'Well that's what made me depressed, that and other things I've been holding in and not looking at.'

'Anger caused your depression?'

'Yes, it did. If you hold in anger and fear and other emotions you don't express, they can compact inside of you and turn to depression.'

'I suppose that sounds logical,' Alberto concedes slowly, not sounding entirely convinced.

'The therapy is helping me a lot and I'm feeling much better.' I take a deep breath. 'Alberto, what about the children coming back? I know Beppe is doing well with the football and I'm really glad but there are plenty of football clubs here he could join.'

'Lori, don't you think it's too soon for that?'

'We said they would do a year in Calabria, which they've done. The new term starts in a few weeks, surely now is the best time for them to come back. I know Michela wants to.'

'We said maybe, if you were well. But you're not fully recovered yet are you? Listen, I know you're getting help and support now and you do sound better but . . . would it be the best thing? Beppe is happy here, I really don't think he should be moved and I can't transfer again, not this soon.'

'But the children could come back.'

'Lori, I told you Beppe is happy here and you're not strong enough yet to deal with them. It's far too soon to think of them coming back to Bologna.'

Tears were prickling my eyes, Alberto was being much more definite and unequivocal than he'd been before.

'How is Michela?'

'She's fine. She's been going to the beach with some of her school friends. She's a sensible girl, she understands what's best.' His voice has become tight. I know things are not good between him and Michela, but he clearly isn't prepared to talk to me about it. Tears are trickling down my cheeks and I'm shaking, it's hard to speak but I manage to.

'Alberto, I think we need to talk properly, meet up face-to-face and talk things through.' He pauses for a few seconds and then replies slowly,

'Maybe you're right. Yes, I suppose . . . without the children.'

A cold shiver runs down my spine. 'I want to see them.'

'Listen, I'll see when I can come up. That will be less stressful for you.' Before I can say anything, he adds, 'If I come without the children, then we can talk more easily.'

I find myself wondering if that really is his reason for not wanting to bring them. If it's because he wants us to really talk and sort things out, then okay. But if he wants to keep me away from them . . .. I clutch the phone and, even though he has said he will come up, I feel as if he is pulling away from me.

***

'My therapist says I've been carrying the burden of trying to prove to Alberto and our parents that I'm a good wife and mother all these years.' I giggle at the sound of myself saying "my therapist" 'That sounds pretentious doesn't it?'

'Or American,' says Jenny.

'Oh everyone has therapy these days, it sounds normal,' says Simona.

'What is this world coming to?' Says Jenny.

'I suppose lots of parents do that, don't they?' asks Francesca, handing me a lager 'feel they have to prove themselves.' The four of us have got together in an Irish pub in town for a beer after the others finished work. I'm planning to contact some of my old private students to see if they want to start lessons again in September, but for now I'm finding it strange having so much time on my hands without children to fill it.

'Yeah, but Lori was always trying to justify her decision to keep Michela and give up her studies,' says Jenny.

I look across the table at Jenny, we haven't spoken since our telephone row a few weeks ago and have been avoiding each other's eyes up to then. I had been really worried about seeing her again and now I'm not completely sure if her words are support or criticism, but there is no edge to her voice. She throws me a faint smile.

'And to marry Alberto,' I say.

'You didn't force him,' says Francesca quickly.

'Not exactly, but it was my idea. I didn't give him much choice.'

'Isn't that what your therapist is saying you do?' Asks Simona. 'Take all the responsibility yourself, for your marriage and children?'

'Pretty much, yeah, I assume it's my fault so I have to make everything all right.'

'I think,' says Francesca slowly, 'that you have always felt responsible somehow and believed that the family is more your responsibility than Alberto's.

'Yeah, I think I have. I never really saw it that way until I said the words to Rina. It's funny, isn't it? You can live in a situation and not realise exactly what it is until you say the words out loud, so strange . . ..'

'It's amazing,' agrees Simona. 'I often think that one of the main purposes of therapy is just to hear yourself saying things out loud. It certainly is a big part of understanding what's really going on.'

'I've been feeling trapped,' I say slowly. 'But it's as if I made my own trap . . ..'

'You had high expectations of yourself,' says Simona, 'but not of Alberto.'

'Yes, I suppose that's true,' I say thoughtfully. 'Rina said I felt grateful to Alberto for marrying me and being the father.'

'I think she's right, Lori. You don't need to continue acting out of gratitude,' says Francesca.

'What would you say you want from him now?' asks Simona.

'I want to feel understood, that's what I want.' I'm surprised at how sure I am. 'I want him to listen to me and to understand what I'm saying.' I sigh, 'Is that too much to ask?'

'If you can get that in a marriage you're doing well,' says Jenny. I look at her, surprised. I had always thought that she and Carlo understood each other very well. As if hearing my silent question, she shrugs. 'Every marriage has its moments. Sometimes we're too busy to even think about understanding.'

'I need to listen to Alberto, too,' I say. 'If I want him to understand me, I need to make more effort, too.'

Simona drains her beer and gets up to leave. 'Got to get home to the hubby and kids,' she grins, 'can't stay out drinking all night.'

Francesca reaches for her jacket. 'Can I get a lift Simo? I haven't got my car and it seems to have started raining.'

'Oh so it has, of course you can. You're doing great Lori.' She kisses me goodbye.

'See you soon girls.'

'Bye girls.'

Colour me in

Jenny and I are left on our own at the table. I gaze at my beer. I can feel the hurt at her judgement of me rising again. I need to speak before she hurts me any more.

'Jenny I don't want to argue with you. I'll just say that I had to come back here. I couldn't cope there any more. It's easier to see now I'm here that I needed support, which I couldn't get there. I was losing my grip in some way. I guess the mural was evidence and, whatever you say, it certainly seemed to me that Assunta and Alberto were willing to have me committed. I think maybe it was wrong to leave the children and I did act impulsively but I didn't feel as if I had any choice.'

Jenny fiddles with her glass while I speak. When I finish she looks up at me, she looks sad. 'I'm sorry Lori, I was harsh . . . I wasn't thinking about how desperate you were and how much you'd been knocked off balance. I was afraid that by coming here and leaving the children there that you might lose them. I was judging you, I was thinking, "Oh there's Lori being impulsive again." You're right, I should have looked at things more from your point of view.'

I let out a huge sigh of relief.

'It's all messy though, if I could do it again and not leave them I would. Alberto doesn't seem to want me to see them.'

'What? Oh no!'

'He's being awkward and obstructive, at least that's what it feels like, maybe I've made a big mistake.'

'Lori as you said you had no choice.' She stretches out her hand across the table and takes hold of mine. The tears trickle down my nose.

Chapter 22

The bluebells across her stomach don't look right. Is this really how it looked? I wish I had a photo. Am I completely mad to try and recapture this?

I step back from the large piece of wood Luca has given me to paint on. I'm trying to recreate the painting I did on myself. It's very different doing it from the front. I didn't try to make her look like me, I don't think I could if I tried, but that would feel really scary. The face and body are taken from various pictures in magazines. She has to look real but it's the painting on her body that's important.

I've spent a whole week on this, coming here every spare moment to paint it. But it's not working, something is wrong. I feel such a tension in my arms. If it were paper, I would tear it up.

I look round the room and my gaze falls on a tin of white emulsion by the wall. Without allowing myself to think, I walk over to it and look for something to open the lid with. There are some tools on the table. I go and fetch a screwdriver and manage to prise the lid off. I carry the tin over to my painting and then spot a large paintbrush nearby. I dip the brush in the white paint and, with one broad brush-stroke obliterate her cheek, chin and part of her chest. Gone are a large section of river and some orange flowers. Another brush-stroke and her face has gone.

I carry on in a frenzy of white paint until nothing remains of my painting. The woman and her body covered in flowers are gone.

I sink to the floor and sit.

After a while, I drag myself to my feet and go to make a cup of tea in the little kitchen area off the classroom. By the time I've finished drinking it, the paint has almost dried. I do another coat. I'm not sure whether I feel defeated or liberated.

***

'When will you know?' I sit down on the edge of the

armchair, clutching the phone nervously. My stomach feels tense.

'I'm not sure, it's difficult as we are understaffed so I can't take any time off, and I'm working Saturdays at the moment.'

'Well, in that case, why don't I come down and meet you? If I come to Naples then maybe you could drive there after work on Saturday. We could stay a night and then you could drive back on Sunday.'

I glance at the clock, aware that Leo will be arriving at any minute.

'Are you sure you want to do all that traveling, Lori? I don't want to stress you.'

'Alberto, I'm stressed because I can't see my children. I'm stressed because you and I don't seem to be able to agree about what we're doing . . ..'

'You could see your children if you hadn't left.'

'What, so it's my fault, is it? If I hadn't left, I'd be locked in a psychiatric hospital!'

'No, you wouldn't, and you know it. Things are fine as they are for the moment. You just concentrate on getting well.'

'Oh, right, so you don't want to meet and talk? For you everything is fine as it is. The children are with you and you prefer not to see me until I'm completely well and you can be sure I won't paint any more walls.'

'Lori, you know it's not like that.' His voice sounds worn and impatient. 'Listen, I am only saying wait for a week or two, until I have a little more time, that's all.'

'Okay,' I sigh, 'I'll wait a couple of weeks.' I put the phone down. I'm clearly an embarrassment to Alberto, a problem he would rather not deal with right now. I put my head in my hands.

***

The doorbell rings. I stand, take a deep breath, pick up my bag and head for the front door. I don't feel like going out but Leo is here, waiting for me downstairs.

'Leo, I was in love with you. I went with Alberto on the rebound. I got pregnant on the rebound from you!' I totally surprise myself. Leo looks shocked.

I've been knocking back wine all evening and now, more than a little drunk, I find myself sitting in Leo's car, saying things I have never even said to myself, let alone spoken out loud. Maybe I've been trying to blot out the sense of abandonment I was left with after talking to Alberto.

I feel myself blush and can't look at Leo. I try to open the car door.

'Lori, what are you doing? Don't go just yet.'

'It's time I went home. I . . . I've had too much to drink.'

'Yeah, well, you did manage more than a bottle by yourself.'

'Oh God, I'm going to feel so crap in the morning. I need to get out of the car. I need air.'

'Lori, can we talk about this? I didn't realise . . .. Did I really mean that much to you?'

'Can you open the window, please? I need air.'

'Do you want to go in? Let me take you inside.'

I can't face all those stairs. 'Maybe. Wait a minute until I feel a bit stronger.'

Leo opens the car windows and I take a deep breath. The sick feeling that has welled up in my stomach gradually subsides. I should not have started with a gin and tonic and ended with a brandy, with wine in between. I take another deep breath as the awareness that I'm in a conversation that I can't handle creeps over me. I sit still, staring into the darkness through the windscreen. Leo lets out a long, heavy sigh. I turn to look at him.

'How different things could have been,' he says. 'When I saw you pregnant that time in the coffee bar and you said you were married, I did feel regret, I did wonder . . ..'

The irony of him finally saying that after all these years is not completely lost on me.

Colour me in

I find my voice. 'You never really wanted to leave Cassandra, though, did you?' Leo sighs again and I know the answer.

'Not when you and I were together . . . no.' His mouth curls up as if the words taste bitter. 'I did wonder a bit, though, Lori, but . . ..' His expression is almost helpless for a moment. Then he takes a deep breath. 'Cassandra and I have been together since upper school, apart from when we split for a while during the first year at university.' Leo turns towards me. 'I did think about you, Lori. You did make me question sometimes if I was in the right relationship. Anyway, shortly after the time I last saw you, while I was doing my finals, we found out that my mother had cervical cancer.'

'Oh, Leo, I'm sorry.'

'As is often the case with cervical cancer they didn't find it until it was quite advanced. I don't know how I would have got through if it weren't for Cassandra. I stopped studying to be with mum and so did she, postponing her own final exams to look after Mamma in her last weeks. Her family also rallied round and were a great help taking turns to be with her. She didn't want to die in hospital. I think we made it as good a death as possible and Cassandra was there, by my side, the whole time.'

Leo rubs his forehead. 'It was during that time that I asked her to marry me. I know I had never been convinced about marriage and looking back I can see that it was mainly about gratitude. She was there when I needed her. We both learnt a lot from the experience. It brought us closer together. Having lost my father when I was young, it was hard losing Mamma too, watching her die, but Cassandra and her family made it bearable and became my family. They still are. That's really why Cassandra and I are still together.' He slumps back in his seat and stares ahead again. My hand creeps onto his arm and squeezes it.

'It was wonderful what she did. She must love you a lot.'

'I think she does. I've been lucky but, later, I often thought about you.'

'But that's different. I'm sure that now and then we all look at past relationships and wonder what might have been.'

'Lori, I wanted you to understand why I'm still with Cassandra, but surely gratitude has to stop somewhere? Can we just arrange to do this again, to carry on talking?'

'Gratitude,' I say, chuckling.

'What's funny?'

'Well, I've always been grateful to Alberto for staying with me when I was pregnant, for marrying me, for helping me with my plan to be independent from my parents.'

'That's what it's been? Gratitude?'

'Well, pretty much, it seems. It came out in a therapy session, so it must be true,' I grin wryly. I put my hand on the car door handle again. This time I really must go home.

Leo leans over and picks up my hand. I feel a shiver run down my arm and find myself turning towards him. He's looking straight at me, our eyes meet and my stomach turns over. I don't move.

'Well, I think we should make a pact. Enough gratitude. Gratitude is over. There should be other reasons for being with someone,' says Leo.

Something whispers inside my head, "like love, passion, desire, excitement . . .."

'Gratitude is not enough on its own but other reasons come into play over time, caring for each other, bringing up children together. I'm meeting Alberto soon. We're talking, trying to resolve things.' I slide my hand out of his.

'Do you think you will?'

'We just need to communicate better. Things have been tough. We both need to make a bit more effort to understand each other. Listen, I really must go.'

'I still want to see you again.' Leo picks up my hand and holds it between both of his, then he starts running one

Colour me in

finger gently up the inside of my arm and it tingles deliciously. I take in a sharp breath. I pull my arm away, open the car door and start to scramble out. I nearly fall head first onto the road but Leo rushes round to help me. He pulls me to my feet, putting his arms around me and I lean into his chest. He holds me tight. I let out a sigh and for a moment feel safe.

Leo lifts his right arm and strokes my hair. I snuggle against him and close my eyes. I could blame it on the drink; I just want to stand there. I feel a hand lift my chin until my face is almost touching his. I see his eyes close. He goes out of focus as I feel his lips on mine, soft and warm. I pull my arms more tightly round him as his tongue slips into my mouth. Shivers run down my spine and across my shoulders.

Then I pull back, angry with myself for being so weak and for giving into temptation. 'Goodnight, Leo, I really must go.' I turn and walk across the road to my building, wobbling on my high heels but still managing a fairly straight line. I don't look back, afraid that if I see him standing there I will change my mind.

***

I step back to take a better look at my painting and bump into Giovanni at the easel behind me. 'Oh, sorry! Are you okay?'

'Yes, I'm fine. Hey, that's good!' He stands next to me.

'I think she does look better this time,' I say.

'I didn't see your earlier version but it's great. I can believe that she painted herself as her hand is trailing paint across her skin.'

I'm grateful for his positive feedback. I feel strange looking at her. There is desperation in her eyes. Maybe that was what I hadn't been able to capture before. I have to think about her as 'her' though and not me. I can't do that. I can't even give her a name, she has to be 'painted lady,' an embodiment of my pain, but not me.

Nicola Sellars

I was scared when I started painting her again, but now here she is nearly finished. A life-size naked woman, bald, covered in flowers and bluebell woods. Luca comes up behind me. 'It's coming along really well.' He moves to my side and looks at me, 'How do you feel about it this time?'

'Oh, it's better I think,' I say tentatively. 'What do you think?'

'Oh definitely, there is something more in her eyes; in the way she is standing. Somehow you can feel her pain, and the contrast with the painting on her, which is colourful and cheerful, is really poignant.'

'I've just finished the orange trellis on her left breast and somehow it makes me feel . . . pain. I still have to finish the right breast. I haven't done the scar yet.' I can't stop the tears.

'Hey, Lori, just let it come out. Just paint it and cry or stop if it gets too unbearable.' Says Luca, 'or go back to small sheets of paper and just paint it out again, then come back to the big one. There's no right way. This will release emotions but it's not meant to be torture.' He smiles. 'Some of these are quite remarkable.' He wanders over to the wall behind my easel where I have propped up a number of paintings, a bald woman with big earrings, one of Assunta as a crow, several abstract ones, representations of tumours with needles and shadows.

'You must carry on painting after this course is over,' he says. I feel myself blushing. 'It would be great if these paintings could be seen . . . ..' He's looking thoughtful. 'Maybe we should have an exhibition.'

'An exhibition?' It comes out in almost a whisper.

'I think the emotion in these paintings communicates to anyone looking at them.' I'm flattered, but terrified.

'We've done class exhibitions in the past,' says Luca, 'But not for a while. I think now would be a good time. What do you think?' I can't speak for a moment.

'I agree Lori's pictures should be shown,' says Gianni,

joining the conversation.

'I . . . I really don't think . . ..'

'Come on Lori you have quite a few paintings that would look good in an exhibition,' says Giovanni.

'Really?' He and Luca both nod.

'Absolutely, Lori,' says Luca.

'Well, if you really think so, maybe . . .. Then you have to put some of yours in too,' I turn to Giovanni. 'You've done some great ones. The self-portrait you are doing right now is incredible and really seems to give a sense of what you've been through.' Giovanni came to the class after having treatment for prostate cancer.

'I think we have a workable idea,' says Luca.

'So, it would be a class exhibition with pieces of work from anyone in the class who wants to contribute?' asks Giovanni. Luca nods.

'Oh my god, this sounds real.' I'm feeling shaky at the thought.

'It certainly should be real,' says Luca, 'there's a lot of talent here.'

'Could we invite people from Luisa and Marina's breast cancer support group to join us?' I ask. 'Donna paints, Maria sculpts, Carla writes poetry.'

'Yes, good idea, lets cast the net wider,' replies Luca.

'I suppose that means that cancer would be the strongest theme but the exhibits would all be different,' I add, still feeling shaky.

'The real theme is living through adversity,' says Giovanni. 'Something most of us have to do sometime in our lives.' We exchange grins. I'm amazed that the idea has come out so easily.

'Sounds good,' says Luca. 'Let's put it to the class at the end of tonight's session then arrange a meeting next week to start organising it, inviting anyone who is interested.'

'Great idea,' says Giovanni. 'It would be good to get the ball rolling straightaway.'

'I'm going to the breast cancer support group on Friday so I'll ask if any one would like to come to the organising meeting.' The scared feeling in my stomach is mixed with a flutter of excitement.

***

'Lori, don't take it like that. Try to understand, I can't get away right now.'

My stomach sinks. 'But I need to talk to you. We need to sort things out and I need to see the children.'

Alberto speaks slowly, 'Come down then and visit them. Zio Donato's house is nearly ready. Come and stay for a few days and then we can talk.'

'Alberto when I first asked you if we could talk you said you would come here so as not to stress me, but I said I was happy to meet you halfway. Now you're telling me I have to come down there. It sounds suspiciously like you're saying, "If you want to see your children, you have to come here to see them."'

'Please be reasonable. If you come here you can spend time with the children and we can talk.'

'I'll come down.' I put the phone down. Alberto is making no effort to come and meet me to talk. I can't work out what he's thinking. It's very strange last time we spoke he said we should talk without the children, now he's using them as a way of getting me to go down there. I feel powerless. He seems to have all the balls in his court. If I want to see Michela and Beppe then I must go to where they are. The only way to find out what's going on is to go and visit them. I get butterflies at the thought of seeing Assunta again, but it has to be done. I can apologise to her properly and show her that I haven't gone completely out of my head.

Maybe I should call Alberto back and apologise for putting the phone down so abruptly. I hesitate and then it rings. Maybe he's thinking as I am and is calling to patch things up.

'Hello.'

'Hi, Lori.' It's Leo's voice.

'Hi, Leo.' My mouth goes dry.

'Listen, Lori, I'm in Bologna. We had a conference here at the university today and it went on longer than planned. I wondered if you fancied a quick visit. I could just drop by for a quick chat. Have you eaten? I could bring pizza.' He doesn't mention me walking off the other night.

I hesitate but then think, "Oh, why not? It will save me cooking, and this will be a chance to agree calmly that nothing is going to happen between us. Maybe we can be friends and share the odd pizza." I lick my dry lips.

'Okay, fine, I'd like one with roast vegetables.'

'Great, see you in about twenty minutes.' I try to ignore the flutter of excitement that starts in my stomach and rises to my heart.

'See you then.' I put the phone down and then make myself pick it up again immediately. I dial Assunta's number in Calabria. It's engaged so I call Alberto's mobile number. It goes on to the answer phone. I leave a message asking him to call me. I find myself going over the conversation with Alberto and feeling helpless. He's behaving like a brick wall that I'm forced to bang my head against. He could come up to Naples - it's only a few hours' drive. He could come up late afternoon, we would have an evening and night together and he could go back the next morning if need be. He could easily bring the children with him if he wanted to - we could talk when they had gone to bed. Why is he making it so hard?

Chapter 23

As Leo pries the top off the beer bottle, the ssshhh sound takes me right back to the beach in Calabria with Alberto, Carlo and Jenny, all those years ago. Leo had hurt me then and Alberto was there to comfort me. I knock back the cool beer and pick up another slice of pizza.

'This pizza is good. Did you get it from the place round the corner?'

Leo nods, 'You're lucky, you have some of the best places right on your doorstep.'

I finish the slice that I'm eating. Leo puts his down on the table. He leans forward and takes my hand. I look across the table at him and our eyes meet. Still leaning across the table, Leo strokes the side of my face. It tingles. Then he stands up, holding my eyes in his. I feel my heart pounding as he slowly walks round the table to me. I don't remember getting up, but I'm standing facing Leo, putting my arms around him, leaning in for a kiss. He bends down and then . . . soft warm lips, that fantastic, fluttery feeling. I step into his embrace, thinking, "This man wants to be with me." Then we pull back for another kiss and his hands are in my hair, playing it through his fingers. I kiss his cheek and then move to his ear. I hear him let out a sigh and then we are kissing again, my cardigan is coming off, his jacket thrown onto a chair. We walk out of the kitchen and towards the bedroom. I remember Rina telling me to live in the moment.

I unbutton Leo's shirt as we walk down the hallway, laughing as we bump into walls. Finally we come to the bedroom door, which Leo kicks open with his foot. I pull off his shirt and start kissing his chest and stomach, loving the softness of his skin beneath my tongue. He lets out a sigh and pulls me down onto the bed where we roll in a happy tug-of-war as we pull off each other's remaining garments.

Then Leo reaches to unfasten my bra and my breath

Colour me in

seems to freeze, tears prickle my eyes and I move out of his grasp. He stops and takes his hand off my bra without undoing it and moves around until he is facing me. Kneeling in front of me on the bed, he wraps his arms around me and holds me. 'You can leave it on, if you want to,' he whispers.

'Thanks.' I stay in his embrace for a moment and then move back a little. 'I think it's okay.' I reach round and unfasten it. Leo leans in to kiss me as I pull my bra off. At first I keep close to his chest, scared of exposing my scarred and shrivelled breast, but then Leo leans back slightly and moves down and gently kisses my scar, then my other breast.

Afterwards we curl up cosily and I settle in the crook of his arm, sleepily enjoying the feel of the soft, warm body beside me. Leo drifts off to sleep and I lie musing about how amazing it is being in bed with him again. It had been similar but different, not quite as frantic as in those younger days, and I'm grateful to him for being so understanding about my breast. His skin is as soft as ever but his stomach a little rounder. My body has changed too. Quite apart from one breast being smaller and scarred, they are not as firm as they used to be and my stomach is much rounder and stretch-marked and, of course, there is the cellulite. I sigh and look at the sleeping Leo. It has been lovely and I don't want to regret it.

Leo opens his eyes. A flash of something akin to alarm appears on his face just for a second. He glances at the clock. It's five to ten. He appears to relax, and smiles. 'Hi you, I didn't mean to nod off.'

'It's only been a few minutes.'

He reaches over and pulls me in for another kiss. 'I'm so sorry I fell asleep but it's been a really long day. I bet I never did that in our student days,' he chuckles. 'The years take their toll on us all.' His smile is so endearing that I just want to kiss him again and hold him but unfortunately I know what's coming next.

'I have to go, I'm afraid.' He flings his legs onto the floor and stands up. I watch him pull on his pants, followed by shirt and trousers.

I get up and pull on my dressing gown, 'Would you like a coffee before you go?'

'Oh great, yes thanks, it will help me keep awake for the drive home.'

I make him an espresso and myself a chamomile tea and we drink almost in silence. When Leo gets up to leave, he kisses me on the forehead and then on the lips. 'Lori, I'm so glad this has happened. Are you okay? I really wish I didn't have to leave you right now. We must do it again soon.' I nod and hold on to him for a last hug.

***

'If Jenny were here she'd say, "You absolute idiot! Why the hell did you fall for his charm again? Don't you know any better? Of course he got up and went home to his wife and children and of course he will never leave them. So where does that leave you? Is it worth it anyway? Is this the way to solve the problems of your marriage?"'

Simona grins. 'She doesn't need to, you just did.' We sit down at my kitchen table and I pour the coffee. I phoned Simona that morning, desperately needing a reality check. Jenny is away working in Brussels and I was really glad when Simona said that her husband had taken their children out and she was happy to pop round for a coffee. 'I was telling myself I needed to tackle the washing and vacuum through this morning so you've given me just the excuse I needed to put it off.' Simona tips half a teaspoon of sugar into her cup and stirs it in. 'Well, honey, how do you feel about it?'

'I don't want to feel guilty but of course I do. I had a lovely time. It was fantastic being with Leo after all these years and I felt like a whole sexual being again, after so long.'

Colour me in

'That's great, quite a step forward.'

'Though I have to say I didn't quite have the energy of the old days.'

'Hey, that happens to all of us.'

'I guess so; he was lovely, caring, sweet. It was both passionate and loving. I got upset as he was about to take my bra off and he was great about that. I just felt tearful. The old sexless feeling came back and I thought, "I don't want him to see this." I just felt scared and . . . well, anyway he was sweet and he kissed my scar.'

'Oh, Lori I can only imagine how you felt but I can see that his reaction would be important.'

'It was, very. Alberto has seen my scar but he has never really looked at it. He can't. He always looks away and we haven't had sex since my operation.'

'Really?'

'No, not once, to be honest that's probably more me than him. I haven't wanted it either. I don't remember the last time.'

'Well that does happen doesn't it? A lot of women say their sex drive goes completely when they have cancer, especially if they go through chemo. Although yours is definitely back.' Simona flashed me a wicked grin.

'Well that's true.' A big grin spreads over my face. 'With Alberto it's different, we haven't been close for years and sex has been a rare occurrence for a long time. Now I know that I can still want sex . . . but then I've always fancied Leo. If I'd been with him all this time . . . .'

'Honey you don't know how things would have been.'

'I cannot imagine ever going off sex with him, but you're right I don't know. Things change so much over the years. On the other hand if things had been good with Alberto it would be different. If we'd been in the same place, if I knew whether or not he wants this marriage to continue . . . it sounds like I'm making excuses doesn't it. I have to face it I've committed adultery. Ooo it feels weird saying that, not something I would ever have expected to say, not like me at all.' I get the urge to giggle 'I've committed adultery.' The laughter splurges out of me, I cannot stop it. 'I don't know why I'm laughing.' My laughter is infectious and Simona starts laughing too. It's a great feeling I'm rocking backwards and forwards on my kitchen chair loving the feeling of lightness it brings. As the laughter subsides my sides ache but I feel much more relaxed.

Simona watches me, still chuckling, as I get up to fetch a drink of water. I pour two glasses from a jug I keep in the fridge and pass one to her.

'There's nothing like a good laugh,' she says.

'I don't know why that happened,' I say. 'It just came out.'

Simona nods, 'It's so not you is it? Hard working dutiful wife and mother it just seems incongruous in a way, except that it is Leo, your one Achilles heal.'

'Well, that's one way of putting it. True I suppose, yeah and I gave into it. I shouldn't have let it happen.'

'I don't think you need to feel too guilty though, Lori, but just try and sort out how you do feel.'

'The thing is,' I take a deep breath, the laughter has gone, 'watching Leo get dressed afterwards, something changed. All the way through I was trying to be in the moment and not to feel guilty but, as soon as he got up to go, reality began to kick in. He was going back to Cassandra and I'm married to Alberto, however difficult it is. I did feel cheap in a way.'

'Oh, honey.' Simona takes hold of my hand across the kitchen table.

'I have to admit that over the last few weeks I've been fantasising about how it would be if I were married to Leo and not Alberto. Leo has been so much more understanding.'

'And because things with Alberto are difficult it's not surprising that Leo comes along looking like a saviour.'

Colour me in

'Well yes he does, complete with white horse,' I chuckle.

'I guess he can seem very much like what you need right now.'

'He can and it's scary. I want to stay real, well to be honest maybe I don't, but I know I have to. I could get so caught up in the fantasy. It's easy to imagine that Leo would be perfect compared to Alberto. And it's a way of not facing the problems with Alberto but . . . I can talk to Leo much more easily about how I feel and he seems to understand. I wish Alberto were half as understanding or attentive. But then Leo left and, although I know he had a lovely time too and really does seem to care about me, I saw the anxiety on his face when he woke up. He's married to Cassandra and the last thing he wants is her finding out. He doesn't want to lose her, I know that.'

'Do you think he's had affairs before?'

'Maybe, it wouldn't surprise me.' I shudder at the thought.

'Listen honey it was good for you to have sex after so long,'

'Yeah, to get my mojo back.' I grin.

'Yes absolutely, fantasy can be good for a while . . . but you know the reality.'

'Yes I do.' An edge creeps into my voice. 'He's with Cassandra.'

I gaze into my coffee cup. Would I want him to leave her? Am I just fantasising again, as I did all those years ago, about a relationship that could never be?

***

'Ow!' As I slice into the white cabbage to make coleslaw I catch my finger. A drop of blood lands on the chopping board. I put my knife down and go to the bathroom to fetch a plaster, mumbling crossly at myself for thinking about Leo and not concentrating on what I was doing. I just make it back into the kitchen, plaster wrapped around finger, when the phone rings.

'Lori?' It's Alberto's voice.

'Hi, how are you?' What if he has finally found the time to come to Naples, can I cope with that right now?

'Lori, listen . . ..' His voice sounds dreadful. My stomach turns over.

'What's happened?'

'Michela has left.'

'Left? Where? Do you know where?'

'Apparently she's on her way to you, oh god, I hope so. She went to the station this morning instead of going to school. Mamma rang me in a state, saying that Michela had not come home on the school bus. I rang round her friends and finally got hold of Gemma who said that Michela hasn't been at school at all today. I asked her if she knew where Michela was. She was reluctant to tell me at first but, when I said we were desperately worried and wanted to know that she hadn't been abducted or attacked on her way to school, Gemma relented and said she was sure Michela was safe. She said that she'd been planning to go up to Bologna for quite some time, so I think she's on her way to you. I do hope so.'

'Oh, let's hope so!' The thought of my daughter wandering around somewhere on her own was terrifying. I took a deep breath and reminded myself that she was not a little girl any more.

'I suppose you've tried ringing her?'

'Yes, she won't answer her phone to me. You try her. Perhaps she'll answer you. I guess I'm the bad cop right now. To be honest, she's hardly spoken to me since you left. I just want her to get to you in one piece.' He sounds desperate.

'I'll try her now and I'll call you back. Are you at work?'

'Yes, but call me on my mobile I'm going home now. Mamma and Beppe are both really upset.'

'Okay. Call you back in a minute.'

'Lori . . . call me anyway, won't you? Whether she

answers or not?'

'Yes, of course I will. I'll keep trying her and I'll text her if she doesn't answer.' I put the phone down.

'Please may she be okay,' I pray to an unknown God as I press on her name. 'Please may she be okay and I will do everything I can to get well, everything I can to be a whole person and a fit mother again.'

The number rings. I hold my breath. 'Mamma?'

'Oh darling! Are you all right?'

'Yes I'm okay. Are you okay?' I was stumped for a moment. She sounds so calm and grown up.

'I will be, once I know that you're safe. Where are you?'

'Naples, changing trains.'

'So you are on your way here?'

'Yes, of course where else would I go?'

'Oh god, what a relief, you're safe.' Now I can tell her off. 'Michela, how could you just leave like that without telling anybody? You should have told your father.'

'He would have tried to stop me from coming.'

'I suppose so, yeah that's true.'

'I have to come Mamma. D'you know how many times I've tried to suggest coming to see you? He always says, "No, not yet." What am I supposed to do if he won't listen to me?'

I know she's right. 'Well, at the very least you could have called me straight away the minute you knew what train you were getting. That way we would have known you were safe before they had a chance to worry about you. Your father sounded awful and your grandmother must be desperately worried.'

'I'm sorry that I've worried everyone,' says Michela, 'but I had to come. I've got to be with you, Mamma. I can't stay there. It's like Papà wants us to stay there forever.'

'Did he tell you that I'm coming down?'

'No! You're coming down! Why didn't he tell us? That's so out of order, what's he playing at?'

'Well we'd only just talked about it and I hadn't worked out when yet, maybe he was waiting to be sure before he said anything to you.' I wasn't convincing myself.

'If I'd known, I could have waited for you and we could have come back together but . . . no that wouldn't have worked he would have tried to stop me. No, I think this is the only way. I had to come, I miss you so much. I want to stay with you now, please! I want to stay in Bologna and take care of you, please, Mamma.'

I'm about to say, 'Well, we'll have to see,' or, 'I'll talk to your father,' but I stop; how can I guarantee that Alberto and I will talk? Maybe it's time to make a decision on the basis of what Michela wants.

'Yes, darling, you can. I'd like that very much.'

'Oh Mamma, that's so great! I can't wait to see you!' She sounds relieved and ecstatic at the same time. 'Are you going to ring Papà to tell him I'm okay?'

'Yes, I'll call him straight away.'

'Good I'll say sorry to him later, when I get home.'

'Okay darling, now be careful for the rest of your journey won't you? Have you had anything to eat?'

Michela chuckles. 'If you saw the size of the sandwiches I've eaten! There was a woman from Naples sitting next to me. All the way here she kept giving me sandwiches. She started long before lunch time, wouldn't let me refuse.' She chuckles, 'I'm fine just full of cheese and ham sandwiches.'

'Now darling do promise to be careful. No talking to strange people.'

'What? People who give me sandwiches, you mean?' She chuckles.

'No, well, you know what I . . . use your own judgement and be careful.'

'Mamma, of course I will, I am 15 you know.'

'Only just . . ..' I stop myself. 'Of course you are.' My daughter is really grown up, perhaps more so than her parents at the moment. 'What time does your train arrive?'

Colour me in

'Well, I'm getting the Eurostar from here as it's quicker. It leaves just after three and is due in at seven.'

'Great. I'll be at the station to meet you. I'll call Papà and tell him that you're okay.'

'See you later, Mamma.'

'See you later, darling.' That sounds so good.

***

'I'm sorry that I scared you Papa,' but I didn't know what else to do.' I can make out the rumbling of Alberto's voice at the other end of the phone.

'I tried, oh come on; you know how many times I tried. You refused to talk to me about it.' The voice on the other end is louder.

'You wouldn't talk to me about Mamma at all. About coming to see her, about her cancer. We were all scared that she might die. That's a big thing, Papà, and you never talk to me about it.' She takes a deep breath.

'Papà, I think you should try putting yourself in her shoes for a change.' There is silence from the other end of the phone. Michela sits down looking more relaxed.

'Listen, how would you have reacted if you'd had cancer? Have you ever asked yourself that?' A loud reply from the phone makes Michela chuckle.

'No, I agree, I can't see you painting walls, but you would have been scared, worried, stressed, upset, and Mamma would have supported you and looked after you, you know she would have.' She listens to the voice at the other end of the phone. I can hear that it sounds agitated and I'm grateful that I can't hear his words.

'Papà, I suppose you did, but you never stopped and thought about what Mamma needed, did you? You never asked her and you never asked me and Beppe what we wanted.' She sighs. 'I couldn't talk to you there. You wouldn't listen to me, and Nonna always said, "Don't talk to your father like that." I have to come all the way here to have a proper talk with you on the phone! I didn't want to have to run away. It would have been much better to talk this out face to face but you wouldn't.' There is more agitation from the other end of the phone.

'Papà you wouldn't listen to me when I said I wanted to come here, you never even told me Mamma was coming down to see us.' Michela's voice has risen, full of indignation but not angry. There is silence for a few seconds.

'Papà you made it impossible to talk to you. I felt like I had no choice but to come here.' Michela's voice is quieter and so is the response from the other end. 'Yes, I'm here now, home safe. Mamma's okay, she's doing lots of therapy and stuff and looks happier.' She throws a grin across the room at me. 'Right you'll ring tomorrow to talk to her.' I nod. 'I know, I love you too. Give my love to Beppe when he gets back from football. Mamma sends her love to Beppe too. Good night.' Michela puts the phone down.

I walk across the room and wrap my arms around her. 'I can't believe you said all those things to him.'

'They were things I've wanted to say for a long time.' We pull out of our embrace and sit on the sofa together. 'It's weird isn't it?' she says. 'I couldn't talk to him but now I'm here, I can.'

'I think when you were in Calabria, he was afraid of you coming here, wanted to stop it from happening. Now it has happened, he's not afraid of it any more.'

'Mmmm, well that's probably true.'

'He just wanted to make sure you were safe, Michela. I guess he was afraid that you wouldn't be safe with me.'

'Well, that's daft. You're not dangerous.'

'No, but I felt very lost for a while, quite . . . disconnected from life in a way. I was scared, I hated scaring you and Beppe and Papà. I think maybe the fear was too much sometimes, so I cut myself off from it.'

'Is that why you painted?'

'When I painted I was in another world, yes and I felt . . .

sometimes I felt happy. Other times just more okay than if I didn't paint.' I chuckle. 'If you see what I mean.'

'Yeh, I do get that mum.'

'I'm still learning about what happened and slowly beginning to understand why. I think that in his way Papà wanted to keep the family together.'

'But he split it up by getting the transfer.'

'I know. For some reason it was something that he had to do.'

'It was a terrible thing to do, Mamma. He forced us all to go down there against our will and it nearly drove you . . ..'

'Mad?'

'Well, you said it,' she grinned. 'Being there, in Nonna's house, didn't help.'

'No, it didn't, but there were lots of factors and, as I said, with the help of therapy and art therapy and talking to friends, I'm beginning to understand what happened to me and to be, well . . . okay again.'

'I'm so glad.' She turns and hugs me.

'I think it's going to be quite a process, though,' I say, stroking her hair.

'Well, just as long as you are getting stronger and feeling happier, Mamma, that's what counts.' I wrap my arms round my wise daughter in a very long hug and wonder if the future will include bringing the family back together again.

Chapter 24

Anna, my new homeopath, has olive skin and long, thick, dark hair. She greets me with a warm smile and indicates a comfortable armchair for me to sit in. I felt very sad when Gaetano retired but Rina recommended that I see Anna who specialises in treating people with cancer. She asks me how Rina is, saying she hasn't seen her for a while as they're both so busy with their work and their children. Anna strikes me immediately as very likeable I think I'll feel comfortable talking to her.

'Well, Lori I'm sure you've been through all this with Rina and Gaetano but perhaps you could start by telling me about the time you discovered that you had cancer and anything else you think is relevant.'

As I tell her about the doctor giving me my diagnosis and walking away from me down the corridor, I feel really tense and tears start flowing. My heart starts beating fast and I feel shaky and scared. Anna picks up a box of tissues from her desk and hands it to me. As I apologise for crying, she tells me it's fine to cry and to cry as much as I need.

'I didn't expect to react like this,' I say. 'After nearly two years, it feels as if it's still with me.'

'What do you feel is still with you?'

'Um . . ..' It's hard to put it into words. 'Well, when I was given the diagnosis, the fear and shock, I think . . . I thought they'd gone. With Rina we did tapping for some things but maybe not for that.'

'Trauma and shock can stay with you for a very long time.' Anna smiles gently as I pull another tissue out of the box.

I cry for what seems like ages, but, as it finally subsides, I feel much better. Anna asks me questions about how I'm feeling and how I felt when I was diagnosed. Having had a good cry, I find it much easier to talk about what happened. I describe the shock of the diagnosis, having to tell the children, and the reaction to the chemo.

Colour me in

Anna asks a few more specific questions and writes everything down in her notebook.

'It's so strange,' I say. 'Just then, I really felt it all over again - shock and fear and just . . . great sadness.'

'You experienced the diagnosis as a big shock,' says Anna. 'Have you seen films - usually horror or science fiction movies . . . where someone is moving, maybe running, but then suddenly becomes frozen in position? It's a bit like that, suspended in shock.'

'Suspended in shock,' I repeat slowly. 'Wow . . . yes . . . that is . . . that's how I've been feeling. So that shock has stayed with me all this time?' Anna nods, watching me.

'It can stay with people for years,' she adds. 'Tell me a little more, if you can, about how the cancer and treatment made you feel.'

'I felt invaded,' I say. 'I felt turned inside out.' I told her about the two male nurses in the hospital that night examining my breasts on both sides. I described having to take my top off in front of male nurses every day during radiotherapy. About doctors, too, often grabbing my right breast without asking my permission. 'I felt invaded and violated,' I say.

Anna listens carefully to my words and takes notes. 'Do you realise the language you are using could be described as the language of rape?'

'I . . . suppose it is.' I find myself gripping the arms of my chair.

'Actually, it's very common. A lot of people say that cancer or its treatment make them feel raped. I've had lovely elderly ladies feeling really horrified and embarrassed when describing nightmares of being gang-raped. They feel guilty about their own nightmares having no idea that it's a very common symbol for cancer or its treatment.' My hands tighten their grip on the chair arms, as a memory comes back to me.

'Oh goodness, I had a dream once . . . ..' I tell her my

dream about Michela being raped.

Anna looks at me carefully. 'Do you think the nightmare could have been about you being raped, not Michela?' I find myself nodding as it dawns on me. Anna continues talking slowly 'I think she could be a symbol of you. Maybe you dreamt about Michela because, as she is your daughter, you see her as vulnerable and you feel protective of her or guilty about what has happened to her. But actually it is you, you who have been vulnerable and in need of protection.' Her words begin to sink in and the tears come again.

'I think that is how I feel.' We talk some more and I cry some more. Through talking and crying I feel as if I have unblocked something. By the end of the session I feel a lot calmer and lighter.

Anna prescribes me some Arnica for shock. She says it will help me get rid of the shock of the diagnosis that I've been holding inside me. It seems to me that with her help I have released a lot of it already.

Learning that on top of everything else I've been walking around still traumatised by the diagnosis is a strange feeling but when I think about it, it makes sense. It's a huge relief to feel that now I can begin to let go of that trauma. Now I know why I've often felt that I can't move on and leave the cancer behind me.

Understanding what my rape nightmare meant makes me feel a lot better. I'd thought it was about me neglecting Michela, which had made me feel even guiltier than I did already. Knowing that the nightmare was about me and not Michela was a huge relief. It was a tough session, but an incredibly revealing one. I give in to an urge to give Anna a hug as I kiss her goodbye on both cheeks.

It's strange but I feel both drained and yet energised as I make my way out of her office and head for the nearest café. I think a cappuccino with chocolate on the top, and maybe a pastry, is in order!

***

Colour me in

I fling myself down gratefully on the sofa and swing my tired feet up. I had been really scared about going back to work at the language school. Since the cancer I cannot rely on my energy levels anymore, sometimes I just don't seem to have any, and the idea of standing on my feet in a classroom for even just an hour and a half was scary. But after Michela got back I was determined to do something. I had managed to get some private lessons together since my return to Bologna but they were not going to be enough to keep us both. Alberto sends us money, but I knew that to justify staying in Bologna and keeping our home here, I had to find more stable work so I called the language school. I was lucky. Even though it's a few weeks into the new term they still had two courses that were yet to start and for which the school still needed teachers. They were pleased that I wanted to come back. I feel so much better be able to earn a regular income again so I can help support my children.

Michela comes out of her bedroom, 'Hi Mamma, how was your first day?'

'I have to say I'm shattered, but so glad I made it.' In spite of my exhaustion I feel incredibly relieved to have got through two courses of one and a half hours each plus preparation. Not a great deal in the grand scheme of things but I'm going to do that twice a week and need to know that I can cope with it. If they go well the school will gradually give me more courses over time. I really need to prove to myself, and if I'm honest to Alberto, that I can start to earn a living again.'

She laughs and comes over to give me a hug. 'Don't overdo it though, Mamma. Remember, as you said, it's a process and will take time.' I smile it's so lovely having her around.

'Don't worry, my body won't let me forget.'

Just at that moment my mobile phone buzzes. Michela pulls away and goes into the kitchen. I reach for my bag and find my phone. Leo's name is on the screen. I stare at it for a few seconds and then switch it off, feeling guilty and confused at the same time.

I join Michela in the kitchen.

'Who was on the phone?'

'Oh, Francesca, she just wanted to confirm meeting up tomorrow. Have you eaten?'

'I grabbed a salad when I got in from school but I'm pretty hungry again. I could murder a plate of pasta.'

'So could I.' I hunt around in the cupboard for the pasta while Michela starts chopping onions for the sauce. I watch her for a moment hardly believing that she is here with me. It's such a relief, I feel so much more at home now. I take some fresh tomatoes and basil from the fridge and start chopping them, standing side-by-side with my daughter.

***

'Leo called again the other day.'

'What did you say?'

'Nothing, I switched him off because Michela was there. The thing is I lied to her. She asked me who had phoned and I said "Francesca." I can't lie to my daughter like this. I felt so guilty.'

Simona and I are sitting in a café near the Montagnola market the following Saturday, enjoying being in the warm and out of the chilly, misty, autumn day. Michela and Simona's four year old daughter, Luana, are with us. They are up at the bar choosing cakes.

'Does he want to see you again?'

'He said he did as he left the other night, but it's the kind of thing he'd say. I don't know if he meant it. I must text him and tell him that Michela is back so I can't meet at the moment and not to call on the land line.'

'What do you want? Do you want to see him again?'

'I've been returning to an old fantasy, well, actually it's a new version of the "What if I were with Leo?" fantasy. I can't get it out of my head.'

Colour me in

'I guess that's not surprising is it? He's made you feel like a woman again. Oh . . . that sounds corny, I didn't mean it like that.'

I laugh, 'he did, and it is corny but it means a lot doesn't it? To feel sexy, fancied, wanted. That's what I thought when we started taking each other's clothes off "he wants me," Alberto doesn't.'

'Leo is back in your life; you've always fancied him and you once loved him. He says he wants to see you; it's very tempting especially as things are not good with Alberto right now. The fantasy looks good but what would the reality be like?'

'I really don't know. I can only imagine. Leo can be lovely and caring and understanding but . . ..'

'He's a smooth-talker and deceived you before.'

'Yes, and he would never leave Cassandra.'

'Would you want him to?'

'If I think about Cassandra and his sons, the hurt it would cause them, and then Alberto, Michela and Beppe . . . no, absolutely not, I couldn't do that to them.'

'Lori, you're in a very vulnerable position right now, recovering from cancer and the treatment, the trauma and lots of emotions around your marriage. Plus stuff from your past, your relationship with your parents, rediscovering painting . . .. There is so much going on that it's not surprising that you fantasise about being in a caring, loving relationship with someone who makes you feel looked after.'

'That's it. I would love to feel looked after.' It feels like a revelation. 'Just having Michela at home, making me tea and coffee, telling me to be careful, is fantastic. Though it's great having her here anyway for thousands of reasons.' I turn to look across the bar to where the girls are standing.

Simona smiles, 'Of course it is, and I guess . . . as you said Leo noticed you, he saw you, saw your scar . . . that's a big thing.'

Tears come to my eyes 'I wish Alberto would see me . . . me, the person I am, not just some madwoman he's saddled with.'

'Oh Lori I don't think . . ..'

I sigh, 'So the contrast between him and Leo is enormous. I dream about a relationship with a loving, caring Leo although I know he doesn't really exist . . .. I remember the look of anxiety on his face when he woke up, his worry about Cassandra finding out, watching him dress and go.'

At that moment the girls return from the bar, each carrying a plate bearing two pieces of cake. 'Wow, that looks good!' says Simona taking a piece from Luana's plate.

'That one is lemon cake, Mamma, your favourite. I chose it for you,' says Luana proudly. She scrambles onto a chair beside her mother and Michela sits on the other free chair.

We have spent a happy hour wandering round the market with our daughters and chatting as we walked. Luana adores Michela and is delighted to be with her again after the long separation.

'Mamma, when we finish our cake, can Michela and I go and look at something together, just us?' Asks Luana excitedly.

'There's a new toy stall,' explains Michela: 'We spotted it earlier and I did kind of promise we could go and look at it. We can leave you two chatting here for a few minutes, if that's okay.'

'Sure, don't let her buy up the whole stall,' laughs Simona. As the girls get up to leave she adds quietly, 'Just one small toy, if there is something she really wants. I'll give you some money.'

'No, that's fine,' says Michela. 'I've got some, thanks.'

'I'll pay you back later,' says Simona. As they leave the café, an ecstatically happy Luana holding Michela's hand, she says, 'That's happiness, isn't it? Luana is so over- the-moon to be with Michela. It's so lovely to see such natural, and open happiness.'

I laugh. 'Are we going to start getting maudlin about how we have lost the ability to do that?'

'No, but it's lovely to see.'

'It is,' I agree. 'I wasn't sure whether Luana would remember Michela. She was only just three when she left.'

'Oh, she remembered her all right. She has always loved her.'

Simona turns to me, 'Honey I know that you had a lovely time with Leo but it was a reality check wasn't it? Him worrying about Cassandra finding out, getting up and going straight after sex . . . unless he decided to leave her . . . and then . . . .'

'If I'm really honest with myself, he doesn't want to leave her.'

'What I would say, Lori, is, don't do anything now. Now is not the time for such an enormous upheaval in your life. You have so much else to deal with . . . I think this could be more about what's missing from your relationship with Alberto, than about Leo.'

I take a deep breath. 'That's the hard part; everything seems to be missing from my relationship with Alberto. He seems to have closed himself off from me. I'm not sure why and it hurts.'

***

'You promised Michela that she could live in Bologna indefinitely without consulting me. Lori, how could you?' I am expecting Alberto to be angry so I just sit holding the telephone. 'We're supposed to be bringing them up together and you go and make a decision like that, without consulting me.'

'It's the first time I've made a decision about either of the children without consulting you, but you do it all the time.'

'What? That's not true.'

I bite back the desire to bring up his move to Calabria, his decision to keep the children there and his refusal to bring them up to see me.

'This is permanent isn't it? I mean she's expecting to stay in Bologna now until she finishes school, what three more years? And you're staying there too. You really have split the family up permanently now haven't you?'

The irony of him saying this is not lost on me and I'm wondering what to say when Alberto continues, 'And without consulting me Lori I don't get it, what can we do? This means neither you or Michela are coming back to Calabria.' He sounds upset. I don't think I was expecting that.

'Did you think I was coming back?

'Well, you could have, the possibility was there . . . til now.'

'Alberto, I have wanted to sit down and talk to you about all of this for a very long time. While we weren't getting around to talking things over and sorting things out, Michela acted in the only way she felt she could. Through not communicating properly, we caused our daughter to run away from home.'

'She ran to another,' says Alberto dryly.

'She did, she took things into her own hands because no one was listening to her.'

'I wasn't listening to her you mean.'

I was glad he realised that was what I meant but didn't want to argue about it.

'Alberto, she asked me if she could stay here with me, to study here, be with her friends and be with me while I recover. She was very clear and I felt that I had to give her a sure answer. She needs the security right now of knowing that she can stay here as long as she wants at least until she finishes school. I know it would have been better if we had talked it over but do you know what? I realised when she asked me that I could not trust that we would make a decision. We haven't talked anything over properly for such a long time so I felt that I had to give her an answer on my own, otherwise we would leave her hanging in uncertainty again. She has had enough of that.'

There is a long pause and then, 'You're right, Lori, we do need to talk.' I lift my eyes to the ceiling and send up a little prayer of thanks.

Chapter 25

'Michela, have you seen my green folder?' No reply. Why do teenagers become deaf when you want something from them?

I'm on my way to a meeting about organising the exhibition and can't find my folder with the list of the exhibitors and what they're exhibiting.

The phone rings and Michela picks it up, 'Mamma, it's for you.' I walk into the living room where the phone is.

'Who is it?' She shakes her head, looking puzzled.

'Michela, can you please see if my green folder is in the desk drawer or maybe it's on the kitchen table.' I take the phone from her.

'Hello.'

'Lori,' it's Leo's voice.

'I asked you not to call on the land-line.' I'm almost whispering. Michela has gone into the kitchen but she could return at any minute.

'I've been calling your mobile and you've been ignoring me. Lori, we need to talk. I thought the other night was really special, but it's over two weeks now and I haven't been able to talk to you.'

'I'm sorry. I would have liked to talk but . . . as I told you in my text, Michela is back and I've been really busy. Things are different now.'

'Are you saying you don't want to see me again?'

'No, well, I . . . listen I don't feel comfortable talking about this right now. Michela is likely to come in any second.'

'Okay, can we meet?' I hesitate. 'Lori, we need to talk things through . . . don't you want to?'

'Yes, yes, of course.' On the one hand I didn't want to talk on the phone, on the other I'm afraid of seeing him again. What if he is prepared to leave Cassandra?

The living room door opens and Michela pops her head round, 'your green folder is on the kitchen table. I'm going

Colour me in

round to Lisa's, remember I told you?'

'Oh, right, yes, take your key as you'll probably be back before me.' She nods and her head disappears. I hear the front door open and close behind her.

'Michela was just going out.'

'Do you want to meet for lunch this week? Or can you manage an evening. Maybe I can persuade you to rent a hotel room.'

'Leo, you're kidding!'

'Nope, I'm deadly serious. I mean it Lori, I want to carry on seeing you.' He does sound serious, I think I was expecting him to be much more casual, like before.

'Would you leave Cassandra?' Silence. 'It's okay, I'm not really asking you to . . ..' I feel shaky. Why did I say that? 'I can't deal . . . with this right now. I have to go out.'

'Okay, what about lunch tomorrow? Can you manage that?' I stand still holding the phone.

'Okay, yes, okay, lunch tomorrow.'

***

'Do you think it needs more light behind her?' I ask.

'No, it's fine as it is,' says Luca. We are looking at my painted lady on her large piece of wood leaning against the wall. 'There's something in that wistful look, something of you, Lori,' he adds.

'Really, do you think so? I wasn't trying to make it look like me at all. I wouldn't dare attempt a self-portrait, I could never get that kind of likeness.'

'You are there though, in the eyes; the pain is there.'

I feel myself blush. 'Thank you.' I feel awkward; the pain visible in her eyes is my pain, there for all to see. 'It's easier to paint standing in front of an oil painting than to be the canvas yourself and behind the painting.'

'I'm sure it is. It sounds like quite a feat, but then it gave rise to this more permanent version which is wonderful and is going to be a centrepiece for our exhibition.'

'Do you really think so?' I'm astonished. Luca nods, and

then goes over to the door to greet Giovanni and a couple of others as they arrive for the meeting.

A lot of the discussion is centred on encouraging people that their work is good enough to go into the exhibition. Most of us have never done anything like this before and it's difficult to think about showing something created out of such personal experience and emotions.

We have chosen to hold the exhibition at the end of November to coincide with the local hospital cancer-awareness week. This means we have just over three weeks left to organise and we're aware that we have to make firm decisions this evening.

Giovanni is pink eyed as Luca praises his self-portrait and we all say we think it should go into the exhibition.

Six people from the art therapy class are going to exhibit. Three of them will probably put in one piece each. The other three, including Giovanni and myself, are going to show a few pieces.

Three people from the breast cancer support group have agreed to become involved. Donna is putting in a few paintings, Maria has contributed two wonderful sculptures and Carla has contributed three poems, which she has asked me to illustrate. I was really daunted by the prospect wondering how I could ever do her words justice. In the end I decided to keep the illustrations as simple as possible, her poems are about her experience of diagnosis and coping with cancer and speak volumes by themselves, so I'm doing sketchy ink drawings, trying to compliment her words. I've shown her the first one, of a woman sitting alone, and she really likes it. I'm so relieved as it almost felt like a greater responsibility than exhibiting my own work.

'You have to put that crow character in, Lori,' says Carla. 'She's so amazing.'

'Don't you think she's too bizarre?' I ask. 'I painted it to . . . to get out the feeling of imprisonment I felt, the feeling of being judged all the time . . . and,' I giggle, 'Assunta did

Colour me in

remind me of a crow as she flew across the table towards me!'

'I wish I'd been there,' laughs Giovanni.

'Me too," says Carla. I wish they'd been there too.

'You have a real talent for figure painting,' says Luca. 'Maybe you could try recreating your imaginary painting of Roberto's back with the swirls on. That could be very interesting.' Some of the people in the meeting look puzzled as they haven't heard the whole story, so Luca recounts it, as I'm too embarrassed.

'I won't have time to do it for the exhibition,' I say.

'Never mind, you can do it afterwards. There will be more exhibitions,' smiles Luca.

I'm amazed at his confidence and feel a flutter of excitement mixed with fear.

***

As I walk towards the café where I'm meeting Leo for lunch I have no idea what I'm going to say to him. I feel so unsure. The memory of that night creeps back warm and lovely and yet is it worth all the pain it could cause?

I see Leo through the window standing at the bar. I walk in. He turns, sees me and smiles a nervous smile, and my heart warms to him.

We order sandwiches and sit at a table by the window. My stomach cramps up. I don't want to eat.

Leo chats for a while about work and then asks how Michela is. I tell him how much I love having her here and he says, 'I can understand that things are different now but Alberto is there and you are here. Is that really working?'

'I don't know. We're trying. It will be easier when I see him again.'

'Lori, I know that everything is still very much up in the air for you but maybe I can be a bit of an anchor. Be there for you.'

I swallow. It sounds nice and I want him to be there for me. 'When we met again in the fog you seemed to rescue me. I was pleased to meet you again. I hoped . . . that there could be something special between us, but, maybe just friends, maybe just support.' As I say the words I don't really believe that it's possible.

'Lori, we've got something special.' He looks at me intently. 'I know this is a very difficult time for you right now but wouldn't it help to have some support? We had a good time the other night didn't we? I'd really like to do it again. Hey . . .' his voice grows softer, 'surely you would too.'

It's strange looking at him across the table. The awkward twenty one year old who fell for him is still inside me somewhere, her heart beating a little faster at his words. But then, at the same time she seems very distant. Today's Lori can sit back and look at Leo leaning forward across the table smiling his seductive smile and ask herself whether this is really what she wants. The problem is, she doesn't know.

'The other night was lovely but . . . you had to go home to Cassandra. You'll always do that, won't you?'

'Are you asking me if I would leave her?'

'I . . . no not really. I know the answer. If you would though, it would make me think . . ..'

'Really, would it?'

'Oh, I don't know. How can I know if I could really ever trust you?'

'Lori why don't we just see each other again, spend another night . . ..'

'Evening you mean.'

'I could manage a night sometime.'

'By lying to Cassandra?'

'Well, yes.'

I pick up my sandwich and put it down again, my stomach is still cramped up tight. I look down at the table. 'I really don't think I can do it. Things are complicated and weird at the moment. I'm married and yet I'm alone.' I raise

Colour me in

my eyes from the table and look at Leo. 'But I'm not doing too badly alone. I'm slowly getting stronger and I'm painting. For the first time in my life, it feels as though I'm doing what I really want to do, something I've always dreamt of doing but didn't think I could. It would be great to be really loved and supported and I have longed for you to do that . . . but you can't, you can't leave Cassandra and I can't have an affair.'

'Why don't we try just one more night?' I look at him; he looks anxious and vulnerable even. I'm tempted to say, "oh what the hell why not another night?" But something stops me.

'Leo I would need much more than that . . ..' My voice is shaking, my arms and hands are shaking, my mouth is dry. I'm glad I'm sitting down, I hold on to the chair and take a deep breath, and then another.

'Are you okay?' Leo looks anxious. I nod, continuing to breathe deeply. As I gradually calm and realise that I'm not going into a panic attack, I also realise that it was the thought of an affair with Leo that brought it on. I manage to speak.

'I have to focus on getting my energy and strength back, on my painting, my family and on solving the problems in my marriage. It's very strange to be saying this after all the years of idolising you. Even after you hurt me, I still held you up as the only man I could really love.' Leo looks shocked. 'I know - sad, isn't it?' I let out a big sigh. 'I get the impression that maybe you should be doing the same. Cassandra deserves better than this and I think that I do too.'

Chapter 26

'Ow!' Carla yells as she hammers a nail too close to her finger and catches the side of it.

'Anyone got a tissue or hanky?' calls out Donna. They are building a plinth to exhibit one of Donna's sculptures on.

Giovanni runs up to her, 'hold your hand up high that'll help stop the bleeding,' he fishes a handkerchief out of his pocket and wraps it round Carla's finger.

'I've got some plasters in my bag,' I say, picking it up off a nearby chair and rummaging around in it.

We're all feeling nervous as we've only got a couple of hours until the exhibition opens and there's a lot more setting up to do yet.

Carla's face is screwed into a pain-ridden grimace. I find the packet of plasters in the bottom of my bag. As I pass them to Donna my hand is shaking. 'I'm not sure these plasters are big enough, you may need a bandage,' I say. 'I think there's a first aid kit in the cloakroom. I'll see if there is a bandage in there, or at least something bigger than these plasters.'

I walk into the cloakroom at the back of the hall and stand there, in between the rows of coat hooks, taking deep breaths. "I'm not going to have a panic attack." I tell myself firmly. I stand, "breathe in . . . breathe out."

I hear footsteps behind me and turn round to see Giovanni standing looking bemused.

'Was I talking out loud?'

'Are you okay Lori?'

'I'm not going to have a panic attack. I'm just breathing it away.'

'Just keep on breathing, you're doing fine.'

I carry on breathing, Giovanni watches me carefully.

'I should probably join you,' he says. 'This is very nerve wracking isn't it? I could quite easily go into one myself.' For some reason the idea of this makes me laugh.

Colour me in

'We could all just have a mass panic attack, that would be good wouldn't it? Well I suppose it wouldn't as there's be no one there to say "breathe in . . . breathe out,"'

'Luca could do that.'

'Yes, he always seems to stay calm doesn't he?'

Carla comes in and plonks herself down on the bench, her hand securely plastered up. I remember the bandage.

'Oh god, I'm sorry, I forgot to find the first aid kit.'

She holds up her hand. 'Don't worry Donna put two of your plasters on it, seems to have done the trick. Are you okay?'

'Yeh just a bit shaky, doing some deep breathing, Gianni here has been breathing in sympathy.'

'Oh bless you Lori. What are we like?' She grins at me. 'I was cack-handed, I know, should have been more careful driving in that nail.'

'I wish we didn't have to do it all in such a rush. I wish we could have put everything up yesterday, but the hall had to be used last night. It just feels so frantic and people are going to come and look at our work!'

'Hey now, Lori! Deep breaths,' Giovanni reminds me. 'Everything is okay,' he reassures me, 'just a couple more things to put on the wall and we're there.'

I continue to take deep breaths, but I know I'm going to be okay.

'And it looks great,' adds Donna.

'Your sculptures look wonderful, and will look great on those lovely high plinths,' I say.

'Thanks, Lori, if we get the plinths done in time.'

'I think my hammering days are over for the moment, though,' says Carla.

'Looks like Luca has finished the hammering,' says Donna, standing by the door to the main hall. 'I'll go and see if he needs a hand.' She chuckles at her own pun and waves her hand as she goes.

'The idea of people seeing my paintings, the sense that

your personal feelings are on show . . ..' I look at Giovanni.

'It's really scary.'

'That's what started me off.'

'But you stopped it Lori, you didn't have a panic attack, you're in control.'

'Oh thank you, Giovanni, I hope that's true.'

'And I reckon we've got a good exhibition together.'

'Yeah, you're right, but I just keep thinking, "In less than two hours people are going to be walking in here, looking at our stuff!"'

'And two hours after that they will all go home and it will be over,' adds Giovanni.

'Now that's a nice thought.' I manage a grin.

***

'Five minutes till the doors open, folks!' Luca calls out. I stand looking at my painted-lady picture on the wall opposite the entrance.

'It's the first thing people will see as they come in,' I say to Luca, who just grins and says, 'Exactly.' I take a few deep breaths to stay calm

'I think you'll be okay once those doors have opened and people are inside. It's just the anticipation that gets to you.' Donna squeezes my hand reassuringly. She glances through the door into the main hall, 'Oh, here we go, Luca is opening the doors.'

Donna and I join Carla and Giovanni by the front doors as Luca opens them, I'm surprised to see that there are a few people waiting to come in.

'It seems that your article in the local paper may have worked,' says Giovanni to Carla.

'I don't know about anyone else but I need a glass in my hand.' Donna heads for the drinks table at the side of the room where the other exhibitors are clustered. Giovanni and Carla follow her example. Luca looks at me.

'Well here we are,' he smiles, 'the exhibition has started. Look,' he nods towards a couple of people standing in front of my painted lady. My stomach turns over, for the first time people I don't know are looking at my work. I'm tempted to run over to the drinks table.

Then, Francesca appears through the open doors, followed closely by Michela. Francesca hugs me while Michela stares at my painted lady.

'Wow, Mamma! That's yours, isn't it?' I nod.

'It's really good! She looks so real but kind of surreal somehow.' She lowers her voice, 'Is that how you painted yourself?' I nod. She stares at it for a moment and then wanders off to look at the other exhibits.

'Thanks for bringing her,' I say to Francesca.

'It's a pleasure, but she would have come by herself. She was determined to see your work. She's your number-one fan,' she chuckles. 'Your painted lady is amazing. Lori did you really paint those flowers onto your skin?' I nod. Francesca stands in silence in front of the painting.

Michela is waving frantically at us from across the room. 'Oh my God, Mamma, this is Nonna, isn't it?' She is standing in front of my mother-in-law crow.

'You have to remember, darling, that this is art therapy. So it's representational, a way of painting emotions out.' I'm grinning.

Michela laughs. 'Some emotions here!' she says. 'It's just as well she's not coming to see it - she'd kill you. What if you get famous and it's exhibited all over the world and printed in magazines and newspapers? Someone who knows her is bound to see it and they'll show it to her.' Francesca and I are laughing.

'What a vivid imagination,' I say.

'Rather like her mother,' laughs Francesca.

'My love,' I put my arm round Michela, 'I don't think we need to lose sleep about the consequences of me getting famous just yet. I think we can cross that bridge if we ever come to it.'

'You never know,' she says with a grin, wandering off to

continue her journey round the room, examining everything very carefully.

The hall is now filling up and I am feeling fine, actually enjoying being part of this exhibition, feeling proud of what we have all achieved. As Carla said, the anticipation is the worst thing.

'Would you like some wine?' asks Francesca.

'Yes thanks, good idea.' She goes off to get some.

Jenny, Carlo and Simona arrive, all hugging me in turn and praising the painted lady.

'This is good,' says Jenny. 'I am so proud of you being part of an exhibition.' She squeezes my arm, 'what an amazing achievement Lori. This could be the beginning, you know.'

'I think it is,' says Simona. 'I'm really proud of you too.'

'Oh, thank you guys,' tears prick my eyes. 'You're making me all emotional!'

'Now, there's a change,' laughs Jenny, looking round. 'I love those sculptures on the plinths.' She wanders off to look at them, the others following after her.

Carla comes over, eyes shining. 'See that woman over there?' She points to a tall silver haired woman in a long black coat. 'She said that she loved my poems and your illustrations, and would like to see more of them, she thinks that we should do a book.'

'Wow! Really? Wow!'

'She's involved in publishing said she'd be really interested in helping us.'

'Oh my god! Really!' I'm standing with my mouth open. I manage to close it. 'Well Carla you need to do a collection of your poems; they are so good.'

'With your illustrations,' says Carla firmly.

At that point Francesca comes over with our drinks and Carla tells her about the book.

'That's a lovely idea. Your poems are really moving, Carla, and so are Lori's paintings. Together they would make an inspiring book.'

Luca comes over to us, grinning cheerfully. 'Isn't it going well?' He gestures around the room.

'Fantastic,' says Francesca, smiling very brightly. 'You have all done such a wonderful job putting this exhibition together. It's truly amazing.'

'Well, thank you very much,' Luca smiles right back at her. Then someone calls him away. 'Do excuse me,' he says, not taking his eyes off Francesca.

'I do believe you have gone a little pink,' I say, grinning.

'Well, you didn't tell me how nice he is. I spotted him earlier and didn't have a chance to ask you who he was. I gather he is Luca.'

Carla and I both nod. 'He's very nice,' says Carla, 'a really supportive and kind guy.'

'He must be married or gay then,' says Francesca, laughing.

'Well, it could be your lucky day, he's divorced,' I say. 'He and his ex-wife split up quite a few years ago. It seems to have been quite amicable and, as far as I know, he's still on his own.'

'Mmm,' says Francesca.

'I think,' I say, noticing that Luca is standing by himself again, 'that you have lots of burning questions to ask him about art therapy and putting together exhibitions.'

'Really? You think I should just go up and talk to him?'

'Yes, I do. Go for it.'

A look of resolve comes over Francesca's face. 'Okay, wish me luck.' She moves across the room. Carla laughs, 'Well, well, new romance! How lovely, fingers crossed.'

'It would be great if it works out,' I say. 'Francesca has been single for far too long; I think they could be a great match they both deserve someone lovely. Fingers crossed.' We grin at each other and then Carla goes over to greet a friend.

I wonder over to Giovanni's paintings. They seem

different hanging up with space around them rather than propped on the floor as I've seen them before. I stand in front of his self-portrait. You can tell it's him but the face is so gaunt and tense. I think it's that "I've got to cope" face that many of us have when living through something like cancer. As I look at the painting I have a sense of what Giovanni has been through and am pleased that he looks more relaxed now.

Suddenly a pair of arms clutch me round my waist, almost knocking the breath out of me.

'Mamma!'

'Beppe!' I turn and wrap my arms around him, holding him tight, hardly believing that he is really here in the flesh. Finally he wriggles from my grasp.

'We just got here, Mamma. We've been driving all day.' As I come out of his embrace, I notice the back of a familiar head looking at my painted lady. Beppe pulls me towards him, 'Papà, Papà, I've found Mamma!' Alberto turns round. He smiles at me a little sheepishly and says, 'Well, this looks very . . . interesting.'

Beppe goes scampering off across the room to Michela. Alberto steps towards me awkwardly and kisses me very lightly on each cheek.

'I thought you couldn't come. I wasn't expecting . . ..'

'We managed it in the end.'

I don't know what to say. I'm tempted to make a comment about him having seen enough of my painting, but don't want to argue, I'm so glad he's come. Alberto stands with his hands deep in his pockets, shifting slightly from one foot to another.

'Papà!' Michela hurls her arms around his neck sending him backwards, almost into the wall. He grins happily at this show of affection and seems to relax. 'Oh, thank you, thank you, Papà. I'm so glad you made it. It's good, isn't it? Well worth coming for.' She is babbling excitedly. I look at her flushed face.

'Michela, you . . . you knew they were coming?'

'Aren't you pleased? Isn't it a lovely surprise?' I have to nod. 'It's an important day for you, Papà and Beppe had to come.' She links her arm through Alberto's. 'Come on, I'll show you all Mamma's paintings. You'll love the crow!' She flashes me a wicked grin.

'You didn't!' says Alberto.

'Come on Papà.' Michela takes his hand, and leads her father and brother across the hall.

Chapter 27

I hold the warm quilt tightly in my arms. It's the end of November and the nights can be pretty cold.

I open it out and spread it on our bed, the bed that Alberto and I haven't shared since he left nearly eighteen months ago.

In Calabria we only slept together for a few nights and then Alberto moved to the spare single bed in Beppe's room. He said my nocturnal wakefulness disturbed him. It was nice not having to worry about waking him up but I had longed to be held. It had felt lonelier sleeping in the same house as him, in different rooms than it had being alone in the flat in Bologna.

Alberto comes into the room. 'Beppe is tucked up in bed but seems too excited to sleep. He wants you to go in and read to him. He's bored with me.' He grins ruefully.

'It's so lovely having my little boy here again.' I'm conscious of trying to be light. Alberto smiles awkwardly and turns to leave the room. I follow him out and go to Beppe.

***

I stand, glass of wine in hand, looking out of the kitchen window over the balcony. Alberto is sitting at the table with a beer in front of him. Beppe is asleep and Michela is watching TV in the living room.

My stomach tightens.

I turn round. Alberto is looking at me. I sit down opposite him. I'm about to say, "It's nice for us all to be here together again," when he speaks.

'I wanted to be there for you.' His voice is very quiet.

'I'm so glad you came,' I say, 'it was important to me.'

'No, I . . . mean, I wanted to give that surgeon a piece of my mind. I wanted to come into the hospital when you were doing chemo.'

I swallow.

'I felt useless.' He takes a slug of beer and stares ahead,

Colour me in

not looking at me. 'I thought, hoped, that moving to Calabria was something I could do to help, something I could offer you but it wasn't what you needed, was it?'

I'm holding my breath, scared of blowing away this fragile moment of honesty.

'I convinced myself that it was for all of us.' Neither of us speaks for a moment.

'You're different.' Alberto looks up at me. 'In these last months you've changed so much.' I meet his eyes. 'I was so scared.'

'Scared?'

'Well at first that you would . . . not recover. But then, this summer . . ..'

'What?'

'Well, you seemed so . . . I didn't know what to think. Yeah, okay, I was scared that you . . . you know . . ..'

'Were going mad?'

'"Well I wouldn't . . .. Something like that.'

I let out a big sigh.

'Lori, I saw a counsellor.'

'What?'

'He helped me to understand that you were just trying to cope . . . in your way. I went a few times. You said you were seeing a therapist and Maria Teresa recommended someone she saw after her husband died. He's not just a bereavement counsellor he helped . . ..'

'Maria Teresa?'

He says nothing for a moment and then, 'I did see her a few times.'

'What?'

'We're friends, I could talk to her. Lori, you're being amazing, your painting is so good. I . . . should have . . ..'

'You are friends?'

'Oh. I was desperate for someone to talk . . . I missed you, I missed us . . .. From a long time ago.'

'What are you telling me, Alberto?' A cold feeling hits my

stomach. Alberto is waving his hands around; he puts them in his lap and stares down at them.

'You didn't sleep with Maria Teresa, did you?'

Alberto closes his eyes and screws up his face, still looking down. My stomach feels colder. We sit in silence.

'I'm sorry,' he whispers. 'I wish I'd come up before. You've done so much. I didn't understand . . . my counsellor helped. We only slept together a few times. I . . ..' Alberto finally raises his head and takes a deep breath. 'I wish I could undo it all and just be here with you.'

I slowly get to my feet and look around for the wine bottle; it's in the fridge. I get it out and top up my glass.

***

A double espresso to keep me awake, I reach for the little coffee cup.

'How are you feeling now?' Simona sits down in the chair at right angles to mine at the glass-topped table in Luigi's.

'I don't know.' I smile at Simona, grateful to her for meeting me. 'It's funny when you don't see someone for a long time you . . . well . . . imagine them staying still. I didn't picture Alberto seeing Maria Teresa, sleeping with Maria Teresa, having counselling. He's been having quite a life down there.' I take a sip of my coffee. 'Funny though I don't think I feel angry with her. Well, I'm not sure. I felt jealous of her years ago because Assunta wanted Alberto to marry her, but now I don't think I feel jealous. It's all very strange I have never imagined that Alberto would have an affair.'

'It's quite a shock isn't it?'

'I can't get my head round it.'

'It's good that he went to counselling though.'

'Yes I suppose so though I'm sure she suggested it, I can't see him deciding to do that all by himself.'

'Maybe she did, he could have asked her advice. You said that she had counselling after her husband died, perhaps he asked her to recommend someone.'

Colour me in

'Well, she's certainly been supportive, beyond the call of duty.' I can't keep the sarcasm out of my voice. 'Funny we've both needed support from someone else. I have to say though it pisses me off that he had a full blown affair, slept with her quite a few times, while one night with Leo made me feel too guilty to continue.'

Simona chuckles, 'you have every right to feel pissed off, that's how men are.'

'Yeah I guess it is, but I always thought Alberto was different, solid and trustworthy somehow.'

'Did you tell Alberto about Leo?'

'Yes I did.'

'How did he react?'

'I think if it wasn't for his affair with Maria Theresa he would have been angry. He did seem to be jealous; he asked me if I was still seeing him. Maria Theresa on the other hand is widowed and I bet Assunta would be overjoyed if they got to together.'

'He's not going to do that is he?'

'He says he regrets it, that he just wants to be here with me.'

'Do you believe him?'

'I think so, but I'm not sure. All this time I've wanted the family together here in Bologna. Now it seems to be possible. Alberto is talking about transferring back, there is a vacancy coming up apparently, in a different branch of the bank but in Bologna and he says he'll apply for it. I should be happy . . . but I can't feel it.' Simona squeezes my hand.

'It's a lot to take in.' She says.

'I had begun to think that we were actually apart. We were physically, and if I had known about Marie Theresa I would have felt that our marriage was over and that he had moved on.'

'Were they lovers in the past?'

'He says not. She was just someone who liked him, the

one his mother wanted him to marry, a nice girl from the village.'

'It does sound though as if she has done you a favour Lori. He's had counselling and

is able to apologise to you and to understand that his reaction to your cancer didn't help you at all. He now knows that he wants to come back and be with you.'

'You're saying that I have Maria Teresa to thank?'

'Well, partly at least.'

I'm quiet for a few seconds trying to take this in. 'It makes sense that he wouldn't have figured it all out by himself. I'm amazed that he went to counselling. Perhaps I should send her a thank you card.'

Simona chuckles, 'now there's an idea. So, is he really coming back?'

'Yes, I think so, if he gets the transfer.'

'How do you feel about that?'

I pause. 'I do want the family back together all in Bologna it will be great for the children. But apart from that . . ..' I fiddle with my coffee cup. 'I feel different now. I love my children more than anything in the world and it's fantastic having them both here. I don't ever want to be apart from them again. If my cancer came back . . . if the lump in my lungs . . .. I don't want to leave them, after everything that's happened, I appreciate them more than ever.'

'Honey, everything is looking good, the lump on your lungs looks like nothing.'

'I know but . . . what I'm saying is . . . I still love my children that obviously hasn't changed. If anything my love for them feels even stronger. But everything else . . . I feel differently. I know it couldn't work with Leo but with him I felt passion again, I felt like a woman, I felt the blood course through my veins. I'd love to feel that again, somehow.'

Simona chuckles, 'I think we'd all love that.'

Colour me in

'Is it impossible?"

'No, it's good that you felt that alive again Lori.'

'I'd like to stay alive,' I say. 'The other night I found myself saying to Luca "I just want to paint." It's not only that I have to paint for my sanity, but life makes much more sense when I paint, it's what I want to do with my life.'

'Wow, Lori that's great, it's great that you've discovered that.'

'It's weird but I have the cancer to thank for that.'

Simona nods, 'that often happens, a serious illness or crisis can do that, especially fear of death, it can bring you back to who you really are.'

'So I really am a painter?'

'Oh yes, definitely.'

'So I can spend all my spare time painting and not feel guilty.'

'That's right, your health, your children and your painting. Focus on them and everything else will fall into place.'

'Even Alberto.'

'Even him.'

***

Michela and her friend Elisa are standing at a shop window pointing at clothes and giggling. Beppe and his friend Matteo are running in front of us, dodging between people in the shopping crowd.

Every now and again Beppe runs back and gives me a quick hug. 'Can we have some chestnuts Mamma?' His arms lock round my waist. Alberto goes up to the man roasting chestnuts on a grate and buys three packets, one he gives to the boys, one to the girls and one for us to share.

He grins as he hands me the packet. I take one out: it's so hot that I have to hold it in my gloved hand while I try and peel it with the other. Sharing chestnuts with Alberto, the cosiness of it all feels odd. We're walking down via

Rizzoli facing the two towers; soon they will be festooned with Christmas lights.

'Mamma, can we go and play in piazza Maggiore?' asks Beppe.

'Let's all go across there,' says Alberto. At that moment the girls come up to us.

'Mamma, Elisa and I are going in here to have a look around.' Michela indicates the shop we're standing outside.

'Come and find us in the piazza - don't be long Michela, no going off on a shopping spree. Ten minutes or text me . . ..' I call.

'Then we'll go and get pizza,' calls out Alberto.

We walk to the centre of the piazza and stand watching the boys playing some kind of tag.

'He's happy,' I say.

'He is,' says Alberto. 'He's been looking forward to coming here for weeks.' He grins, 'that crow picture you painted, I can't get it out of my head.' I'm glad he's grinning. 'We must make sure my mother never sees it.'

'Absolutely.' I grin too.

In this moment of sharing a joke Alberto reaches out to take my hand. I find myself pulling it away automatically.

'I got used to you not being here.'

'I know.'

'You can't just walk back and expect everything to be just the same as it was before I was diagnosed.'

'I know that, I don't expect that.'

'You walked away, you decided to go.'

'I know,' his voice rises, ' I have apologised . . . I know, before you say anything, I know it isn't enough, I know all that. Can't you accept that I did my best, that I was wrong but in my way I was trying?'

'I . . . maybe, but I felt so abandoned just when I needed you.'

'Let's not go over all this again Lori. I didn't feel that you needed me.'

Colour me in

'I told you I did.'

'Yes, well, I'm sorry.'

'Do you really want to come back to Bologna?'

'Yes I do. I want to be with you. I don't mind sleeping on the sofa, just as long as . . . one day . . . .'

'I don't know Alberto.'

He looks at me, sadness in his eyes. 'I have to wait for the application to go through, work in Calabria for at least another couple of months.'

'I really wanted the family back together.' I say, 'but now . . . I have been coping on my own . . . .'

'I know I hurt you Lori. I get that, it will take time.'

There was so much I wanted to say but couldn't. There was a sore feeling rising from my chest and up to my throat.

'Would you rather I didn't come back?' His voice shakes.

'I didn't say that.'

'Would you though?'

My stomach knots. 'No . . . for the children . . . .'

Alberto digs his hands into his pockets and stares in the direction of Beppe and Matteo, but he's not looking at them.

'I could sell Zio Donato's place and buy a little flat here,' he says. 'I could live in that until . . . well . . . .'

'Would you really do that?'

He shrugs. 'It's an idea.'

'I think it's a good idea,' I say. 'It will give us time.'

I wonder if time is enough though.

***

The bougainvilleas should be brighter. I need to add more red, but also some blue, to create that cool acid pink. I want them to be tumbling over the wrought iron balcony in a cascade of colour. The foliage needs a greater variety of greens. Stepping back for a better look I wipe my pink-stained hands on my overalls.

The shiny black of the wrought iron balcony has come out really well. Just beyond it you can see the beach. As yet,

I've just put down a light yellow wash but you can make out the sand dunes and I fancy that I can almost feel the heat rising from them. On the left I have sketched out a palm tree, and, where the beach fades out I'm going to paint the sea.

'Wow, you are getting on well!' I hadn't heard Monica come in. She hands me a glass of orange juice. 'I thought you might like this.' She stands back on the other side of the room to get the full view.

'Oh Lori, it's lovely. I just want to go and lie on that beach.'

'Well, that's the effect you want to have on your customers isn't it?'

'You could argue that once people have come into our travel agency, they are already on the way, but this will clinch it, and it will be great for us to work with such a lovely scene, although it's going to get me day-dreaming of hot sunny beaches. But hey, as long as the customers do that too, we'll be okay.'

'I'm so glad you like it. I was planning to finish off the bougainvilleas on the balcony today, and maybe start on the sea.' I find myself blushing, 'I guess that's my favourite part.' Monica smiles. She has heard about my sea-painting experience.

'I'm so glad Francesca suggested you do this, Lori,' she says. 'This scene is perfect for our wall. I'm just sorry you can only work when we're not here. It would be too difficult otherwise, customers tripping over paint, and no space for our desks.'

'That's fine, Monica. As tomorrow is Monday, I'll come in when you close for lunch. You're closed from one till three thirty, aren't you?' She nods 'I can sketch some things out and maybe paint some high up bits that people can't lean against. Then I can come again when you close at seven. Whatever I manage to do in the evening will be dry by the time you all arrive in the morning.'

Colour me in

I lean against the wall next to Monica and gaze at my handiwork. I feel so lucky to be commissioned and paid to do a mural. I started painting on Saturday lunchtime when the travel agency shut for the weekend and, apart from a few hours sleep, have been painting ever since.

When Francesca told me that she had suggested to her friend Monica, the manager of a travel agency, that I do a mural on their office wall, I was horrified.

'I can't do a proper commission I'm nowhere near good enough. I have no experience, not of doing what someone else wants.'

'You can do it, Lori,' said Francesca firmly. 'I've seen your paintings and I know you can. And it looks like murals could be your thing,' she grinned. 'Go on girl, give yourself a chance. Monica is really nice. You can negotiate a fee. She will be great for your first customer.'

'My first customer? A fee? Oh my.'

So here I am, looking at the beginnings of my first commissioned mural. I still feel the thrill of painting on the brushstrokes and watching the picture grow. It's still a joy to have a sense of bringing the beauty of the outside, inside.

I've painted over one or two places where it didn't quite work, but that's bound to happen. I spent quite a while painting a scaled down version on paper which I use as my reference. It's not as ad hoc as my painting of Assunta's wall. It's different painting without the desperation I felt then, but there is still the sense of creating my own reality, of spreading some of myself on the wall, but this time I will be heard, this time people will look at it, and, I hope, take pleasure from it.

There is a banging on the front door. I can see figures hovering outside and someone trying to peer through the shop window. Monica walks to the door. 'We are closed. Come back tomorrow.'

'Monica, it's me,' it's Francesca's voice.

Monica opens the door and in troop Francesca, Jenny

and Michela. 'We've come to see the work in progress,' says Jenny. They stand in front of the wall.

'Oh, wow, Mamma, it looks great!' says Michela. 'Where's the sea? You are going to paint the sea, aren't you?'

Francesca is peering closely at the wall, 'of course she is. Look, here's the beach. I'd say the sea will be right here,' she waves her hand at the wall. 'Am I right, Lori?'

I nod, feeling quite shy all of a sudden. I'll have to get used to seeing my work under such scrutiny.

She turns and looks at me, 'It's great, really great!'

'Do you mean it?'

'Of course I do. You have certainly earned these.' She holds out a beautifully wrapped parcel of cakes from the local pastry shop. Monica makes coffee and we pull chairs over and sit round one of the desks.

'It will be impossible to come in here without booking a holiday,' says Jenny. 'I certainly don't have that kind of self-restraint.'

Michela puts her arm round me. 'Well, Mamma, you've done it! You're a mural artist now. You did right to practise on Nonna's wall!'

'I doubt she would agree,' I chuckle.

'When you're famous she'll regret having had it painted over,' laughs Francesca.

I laugh too, a warm feeling in my stomach as I sit with my daughter and my friends, aware that in a few minutes I will paint the sea.

About the Author

Nicola Sellars followed various callings, including residential social worker, graphic designer, language teacher, and translator before allowing herself to take writing seriously. The events in this novel while being largely fiction, are partly based on her own experiences while living in Italy where she was diagnosed with breast cancer. While she didn't manage to paint any murals, Lori's feelings and reactions to the diagnosis do mirror hers in many ways. Nicola is now perfectly well and feels lucky to be alive. She is currently working on her second novel, a series of plays and writes and performs poetry. She hopes one day to publish a collection of poetry.

To find out more about the author and read more examples of her work visit www.nicolasellars.com

Made in the USA
Charleston, SC
14 April 2014